New York Times and *USA TODAY* bestselling author **B.J. Daniels** lives in Montana with her husband, Parker, and three springer spaniels. When not writing, she quilts, boats and plays tennis. Contact her at bjdaniels.com, or on Facebook, or Twitter, @bjdanielsauthor.

Nicole Helm grew up with her nose in a book and the dream of one day becoming a writer. Luckily, after a few failed career choices, she gets to follow that dream—writing down-to-earth contemporary romance and romantic suspense. From farmers to cowboys, Midwest to the West, Nicole writes stories about people finding themselves and finding love in the process. She lives in Missouri with her husband and two sons and dreams of someday owning a barn.

New York Times Bestselling Author

B.J. DANIELS

SHOTGUN SURRENDER

HARLEQUIN
BESTSELLING®
AUTHOR
COLLECTION

HARLEQUIN®
BESTSELLING
AUTHOR
COLLECTION

Recycling programs
for this product may
not exist in your area.

ISBN-13: 978-1-335-00812-1

Shotgun Surrender
First published in 2005. This edition published in 2023.
Copyright © 2005 by Barbara Heinlein

Stone Cold Texas Ranger
First published in 2016. This edition published in 2023.
Copyright © 2016 by Nicole Helm

For questions and comments about the quality of this book, please contact us at CustomerService@Harlequin.com.

Harlequin Enterprises ULC
22 Adelaide St. West, 41st Floor
Toronto, Ontario M5H 4E3, Canada
www.Harlequin.com

Printed in U.S.A.

CONTENTS

Also by B.J. Daniels

Harlequin Intrigue

A Colt Brothers Investigation

Murder Gone Cold
Sticking to Her Guns
Christmas Ransom
Set Up in the City
Her Brand of Justice

Cardwell Ranch: Montana Legacy

Steel Resolve
Iron Will
Ambush Before Sunrise
Double Action Deputy
Trouble in Big Timber
Cold Case at Cardwell Ranch

HQN

Powder River

Dark Side of the River
River Strong

Buckhorn, Montana

Out of the Storm
From the Shadows
At the Crossroads
Out of the Blue
Before Memories Fade
Before Buckhorn
Under a Killer Moon
When Justice Rides

Visit her Author Profile page at Harlequin.com,
or bjdaniels.com, for more titles!

SHOTGUN SURRENDER

B.J. Daniels

This one is for Kayley Mendenhall.
A ray of sunshine for everyone who has had
the honor of knowing her. Best wishes for a bright,
fun and romantic future!

Prologue

The moment the pickup rolled to a stop, Clayton T. Brooks knew he should have put this off until morning. The night was darker than the inside of an outhouse, he was half-drunk and he couldn't see two feet in front of him.

Hell, maybe he was more than half-drunk since he was still seriously considering climbing the nearby fence and getting into a pasture with a bull that had almost killed its rider at a rodeo just a few days ago in Billings, Montana.

To make matters worse, Clayton knew he was too old for this sort of thing, not to mention physically shot from years of trying to ride the meanest, toughest bulls in the rodeo circuit.

But he'd never had the good sense to quit—until a bull messed him up so bad he was forced to. Just like now. He couldn't quit because he'd come this far and, damn, he needed to find out if he was losing his mind. Quietly he opened his pickup door and stepped out.

He'd coasted down the last hill with his headlights out, stopping far enough from Monte Edgewood's ranch house that he figured his truck wouldn't be heard when he left. There was no sign of life at the Edgewood Roughstock Company ranch at this hour of the night, but he wasn't taking any chances as he shut the pickup door as quietly as possible and headed for the pasture.

If he was right, he didn't want to get caught out here. The whole thing had been nagging him for days. Finally tonight, he'd left the bar when it closed, climbed into his pickup and headed out of Antelope Flats. It wasn't far to the ranch but he'd had to make a stop to get a six-pack of beer for the road.

Tonight he was going to prove himself wrong—or right—he thought as he awkwardly climbed the fence and eased down the other side. His eyes hadn't quite adjusted to the dark. Wisps of clouds drifted low across the black canvas stretched on the horizon. A few stars twinkled millions of miles away, and a slim silver crescent moon peeked in and out.

Clayton started across the small pasture, picking his way. Just over the rise, he froze as he made out the shape of the bull dead ahead.

Devil's Tornado was a Braford brindle-horned, one-ton bull—a breeder's Molotov cocktail of Brahma and Hereford. The mix didn't always turn out good bucking bulls, but it often did. The breed had ended more than a few cowboys' careers, his included.

He stared at the huge dark shape standing just yards from him, remembering how the bull had damn near killed the rider at the Billings rodeo a few days before.

The problem was, Clayton thought he recognized the bull, not from Billings but from a town in Texas some years before. Thought he not only recognized the bull, but knew it intimately—the way only a bull rider gets to know a bull.

Unless he was losing his mind, he'd ridden this brindle down in Texas four years ago. It had been one of his last rides.

Only back then, the bull had been called Little Joe. And Little Joe had been less than an exciting ride. No tricks. Too nice to place deep on and make any prize money on.

The other bulls in the roughstock contractor's bag hadn't had any magic, either—the kiss of death for the roughstock contractor. Last Clayton had heard the roughstock outfit had gone belly-up.

Earlier tonight, he'd finally remembered the roughstock contractor's name. Rasmussen. The same last name as the young man who'd showed up a few weeks ago with a handful of bulls he was subcontracting out to Monte Edgewood.

If Clayton was right—and that was what he was here to find out—then Little Joe and Devil's Tornado were one and the same.

Except that the bull at the Billings rodeo had been a hot-tempered son-of-a-bucker who stood on its nose, hopped, skipped and spun like a top, quickly unseating the rider and nearly killing him. Nothing like the bull he'd ridden in Texas.

But Clayton was convinced this bull was Little Joe. Only with a definite personality change.

"Hey, boy," he called softly as he advanced. "Easy, boy."

The bull didn't move, seemed almost mesmerized as Clayton drew closer and closer until he could see the whites of the bull's enormous eyes.

"Hello, Little Joe." Clayton chuckled. Damned if he hadn't been right. Same notched ears, same crook in the tail, same brindle pattern. Little Joe was Devil's Tornado.

Clayton stared at the docile bull, trying to make sense of it. How could one bull be so different, not only from years ago but also from just days ago?

A sliver of worry burrowed under Clayton's skull. He definitely didn't like what he was thinking because if he was right...

He reached back to rub his neck only an instant before he realized he was no longer alone. He hadn't heard anyone approach from behind him, didn't even sense the presence until it was too late.

The first blow to the back of his head stunned him, dropping him to his knees next to the bull.

He flopped over onto his back and looked up. All he could make out was a dark shape standing over him and something long and black in a gloved hand.

Clayton didn't even get a chance to raise an arm to ward off the second blow with the tire iron. The last thing he saw was the bull standing over him, the silver sickle moon reflected in the bull's dull eyes.

Chapter 1

As the last cowboy picked himself up from the dirt, Dusty McCall climbed the side of the bucking horse chute.

"I want to ride," she said quietly to the elderly cowboy running this morning's bucking horse clinic.

Lou Whitman lifted a brow as he glanced down at the only horse left in the chute, a huge saddle bronc called The Undertaker, then back up at her.

He looked as if he was about to mention that she wasn't signed up for this clinic. Or that The Undertaker was his rankest bucking bronc. Or that her father, Asa McCall, or one of her four brothers, would have his behind if they found out he'd let her ride. Not when she was supposed to be helping "teach" this clinic—not ride.

But he must have seen something in her expression, heard it in her tone, that changed his mind.

He smiled and, nodding slowly, handed her the chest protector and helmet. "We got one more," he called to his crew.

She smiled her thanks at Lou as she took off her western straw hat and tossed it to one of the cowboys nearby. Slipping into the vest, she snugged down the helmet as Lou readied The Undertaker.

Swallowing any second thoughts, she lowered herself onto the saddle bronc in the chute.

None of the cowboys today had gone the required eight seconds for what was considered a legal rodeo ride.

She knew there was little chance of her being the first. Especially on the biggest, buckingest horse of the day.

She just hoped she could stay on long enough so that she wouldn't embarrass herself. Even better, that she wouldn't get killed!

"What's Dusty doing in there?" one of the cowboys along the corral fence wanted to know. "Dammit, she's just trying to show us up."

She ignored the men hanging on the fence as she readied herself. Bucking horses were big, often part draft horse and raised to buck. This one was huge, and she knew she was in for the ride of her life.

Not that she hadn't ridden saddle broncs before. She'd secretly taken Lou Whitman's clinic and ridden several saddle broncs just to show her brothers. Being the youngest McCall—and a girl on top of it—she'd spent her first twenty-one years proving she could do anything her brothers could—and oftentimes ended up in the dirt.

She doubted today would be any different. While she no longer felt the need to prove anything to herself and could care less about what her four older brothers thought, she had to do this.

And for all the wrong reasons.

"Easy, boy," she said as the horse banged around in the chute. She'd seen this horse throw some darned good cowboys in the past.

But she was going to ride him. One way or another. At least for a little while.

The horse shook his big head and snorted as he looked back at her. She could see her reflection in his eyes.

She leaned down to whisper in his ear, asking him to let her ride him, telling him how she needed this, explaining how much was at stake.

She could hear the cowboys, a low hum of voices on the corral fence. She didn't look, but imagined in her mind one in particular on the fence watching her, his dark eyes intrigued, his interest piqued.

Her body quaking with anticipation—and a healthy dose of apprehension—she gave Lou a nod to open the gate.

In that split second as the gate swung out, she felt the horse lunge and knew The Undertaker didn't give a damn that she was trying to impress some cowboy. This horse had his own agenda.

He shot straight up, jumped forward and came down bucking. He was big and strong and didn't feel like being ridden—maybe especially by her. Dust churned as he bucked and twisted, kicking and lunging as he set about unseating her.

But she stayed, remembering everything she'd been taught, everything she'd been teaching this morning along with Lou. Mostly, she stuck more out of stubborn determination than anything else.

She vaguely heard the sound of cheers and jeers over the pounding of hooves—and her heart.

When she heard the eight-second horn signaling she'd completed a legal rodeo ride, she couldn't believe it.

Too late, she remembered something her father always warned her about: pride goeth before the fall.

More than pleased with herself, she'd lost her focus for just an instant at the sound of the horn and glanced toward the fence, looking for that one cowboy. The horse made one huge lunging buck, and Dusty found herself airborne.

She hit the ground hard, the air knocked out of her. Dust rose around her in a cloud. Through it, she saw a couple cowboys jump down into the corral, one going after the horse, the other running to her.

Blinking through the dust, she tried to catch her breath as she looked up hoping to see the one cowboy she'd do just about anything to see leaning over her—Boone Rasmussen.

"You all right?" asked a deep male voice.

She focused on the man leaning over her and groaned. Ty Coltrane. The *last* cowboy she wanted to see right now.

"Fine," she managed to get out, unsure of that but not about to let him know if she wasn't.

She managed to sit up, looking around for Boone but didn't see him. The disappointment hurt more than the hard landing. Just before she'd decided to ride the horse, she'd seen Boone drive up. She'd just assumed he would join the others on the corral fence, that for once and for all, he would actually take notice of her.

"That was really something," Ty Coltrane commented sarcastically as he scowled down at her. Ty had been the bane of her existence since she'd been born. He raised

Appaloosa horses on a ranch near her family's Sundown Ranch and every time she turned around, he seemed to be there, witnessing some of her most embarrassing moments—and causing more than a few.

And here he was again. It never failed.

She took off the helmet, her long blond braid falling free. Ty took the helmet and motioned to the cowboy on the fence, who tossed her western straw hat he'd been holding for her. It sailed through the air, landing short.

Ty picked it up from the dirt and slapped the dust off against his jeaned thigh. "Yep, that one could go down in the record book as one of the dumber things I've seen you do, Slim." He handed her the hat, shaking his head at her.

As a kid, she'd been a beanpole, all elbows and knees, and she'd taken a lot of teasing about it. It had made her self-conscious. Even when she began to develop and actually had curves, she'd kept them hidden under her brothers' too large hand-me-down western shirts.

"Don't call me that," she snapped, glaring at him as she shoved the hat down on her blond head, tucking the single long braid up under it as she did.

He shook his head as if she mystified him. "What possessed you to ride The Undertaker? Have you lost all sense?"

The truth was, maybe she had. She didn't know what had gotten into her lately. Not that as a kid she hadn't always tried to be one of the boys and ride animals she shouldn't have. It came with being raised on an isolated ranch with four older brothers and their dumb friends.

That, and the fact that for most of her life, she'd just wanted to fit in, be one of the boys—not have them make fun of her, but treat her like one of their own.

All that had changed a few weeks ago when she'd first

laid eyes on Boone Rasmussen. Suddenly, she didn't want to blend in anymore. She didn't want to be one of the boys. She felt things she'd only read about.

Now all she wanted was to be noticed by Boone Rasmussen.

And apparently there was no chance in hell of that ever happening.

"Here," Ty said extending a hand to help her up.

She ignored it as she got to her feet on her own and tried not to groan as she did. She'd be sore tomorrow if she could move at all. That *had* been a fool thing to do, but not for the reason Ty thought. She'd only done it to get Boone's attention. She couldn't believe she'd been so desperate, she thought as she took off the protective vest. Ty took it as well and handed both vest and helmet to one of the cowboys along the fence.

She hated feeling desperate.

Being that desperate made her mad and disgusted with herself. But the problem was, even being raised with four older brothers, she knew nothing about men. She hadn't dated much in high school, just a few dances or a movie. The boys she'd gone out with were like her, from God-fearing ranch families. None had been like Boone Rasmussen.

She realized that might be the problem. Boone was a *man*. And Boone had a reckless air about him that promised he was like no man *she'd* ever known.

"Nice ride," one of the cowboys told her as she limped out of the corral.

"Don't encourage her," Ty said beside her.

There was a time she would have been busting with pride. She'd ridden The Undertaker. She'd stayed on the eight seconds for the horn.

But today wasn't one of those days. The one cowboy she'd hoped to impress hadn't even seen her ride.

"You don't have to go telling my brothers about this," she warned Ty.

He grunted. "I have better things to do than go running to your brothers with stories about you," he said. "Anyway, the way you behave, it would be a full-time job."

She shot him a narrow-eyed look, then surreptitiously glanced around for Boone Rasmussen, spotting him over by the bull corrals talking to the big burly cowboy who worked with him, Lamar something or other.

Boone didn't even glance in her direction and obviously hadn't seen her ride or cared. Suddenly, she felt close to tears and was spitting mad at herself.

"You sure you're all right?" Ty asked as he reached to open her pickup door for her.

She could feel his gaze on her. "I told you I'm fine," she snapped, fighting tears. What was wrong with her? She normally would rather swallow tacks than cry in front of him or one of her brothers.

"You're sure you're up to driving back to the ranch by yourself?" he asked, only making her feel worse.

She fought a swell of emotion as she climbed into the pickup seat and started to close the door.

Ty stopped her by covering her hand on the door handle with his. "Okay, Slim, that was one hell of a ride. You stayed on longer than any of those cowboys. And you rode The Undertaker. Feel better?"

She looked at him, tears welling in her eyes. He thought she was mad at *him* because he'd chewed her out for riding today?

She half smiled at him, filled with a sudden stab of

affection. Funny, but since Boone, she even felt differently about Ty.

Unlike Boone though, Ty had blue eyes like her own. There was no mystery about Ty. She'd known him her whole life. Boone on the other hand, had dark eyes, mysterious eyes, and everything about him felt...dangerous.

"You wouldn't understand even if I could explain it," she said.

Ty smiled ruefully and reached out to pluck a piece of straw from a stray strand of her blond hair. "Probably not, Slim, but maybe it's time you grew up before you break your fool neck." He let go of her hand and she slammed the pickup door. So much for the stab of affection she'd felt for him.

Grow up? Without looking at him, she started the truck and fought the urge to roll down her window and tell him what she thought. But when she glanced over, Ty had already walked away.

She sat for a moment in a stew of her own emotions. The worst part was, Ty was right. It was definitely time for her to grow up. Too bad she didn't have the first clue how to do that.

She shifted the pickup into gear. Boone Rasmussen was still talking to Lamar by the chutes. He didn't look up as she pulled away.

Ty mentally kicked himself all the way to his truck. He'd only come by the rodeo grounds this morning to see if Clayton T. Brooks was around. The old bull rider hadn't shown up for work.

Everyone said Ty was a fool for hiring him. Even part-time. But Clayton was a good worker and Ty knew Clayton needed the money. Sometimes he showed up late, but he always showed for work. Until today.

"Any of you seen Clayton today?" he called to the handful of men on the corral fence. Several of the cowboys were trying to get Lou to let them ride again. Couldn't let some little gal like Dusty McCall show them up.

"Saw him at the bar *last night*," one of them called back. "He was three sheets to the wind and going on about some bull." The cowboy shook his head. "You know Clayton. Haven't seen him since, though." The rest shook their heads in agreement.

"Thanks." Ty *did* know Clayton. For most of his life, Clayton had ridden bulls. Now that he couldn't ride anymore, he "talked" bulls. Or talked "bull," as some said.

Still, Ty was worried about him. He decided to swing by Clayton's trailer on the opposite side of town before returning to the ranch.

Dusty McCall drove past as Ty climbed into his truck. He let out a sigh as he watched her leave. All he'd done was make her mad. But the fool girl could have gotten herself killed. What had been going on with her lately?

Not your business, Coltrane.

Didn't he know it.

In spite of himself, he smiled at the memory of her riding that saddle bronc. She was something, he thought with a shake of his head. Unfortunately, she saw him at best as the cowboy next door. At worst, as another older brother, as if she needed another one.

He shook off that train of thought like a dog shaking off water and considered what might have happened to Clayton as he started his pickup and drove into town.

Antelope Flats was a small western town with little

more than a café, motel, gas station and general store. The main business was coal or coal-bed methane gas. Those who worked either in the open-pit coal mine or for the gas companies lived twenty-plus miles away in Sheridan, Wyoming, where there was a movie theater, pizza parlors, clothing stores and real grocery stores.

Between Antelope Flats and Sheridan there was nothing but sagebrush-studded hills and river bottom, and with deer, antelope, geese, ducks and a few wild turkeys along the way.

Antelope Flats had grown some with the discovery of coal-bed methane gas in the land around town. There was now a drive-in burger joint on the far edge of town, a minimall coming in and talk of a real grocery store.

Ty hoped to hell the town didn't change too much in the coming years. This was home. He'd been born and raised just outside of here, and he didn't want the lifestyle to change because of progress. He knew he sounded like his father, rest his soul. But family ranches were a dying breed and Ty wanted to raise his children on the Coltrane Appaloosa Ranch just as he'd been raised.

Clayton T. Brooks had bought a piece of ground out past town and put a small travel trailer on it. The trailer had seen better days. So had the dated old pickup the bull rider drove. The truck wasn't out front, but Ty parked in front of the trailer and got out anyway.

The sun was high in a cloudless blue sky. He could smell the cottonwoods and the river and felt the early spring heat on his back as he knocked on the trailer.

No answer.

He tried the door.

It opened. "Clayton?" he called as he stepped into the cool darkness. The inside was neater than Ty had expected it would be. Clayton's bed at the back looked as if he'd made it before he left this morning. Or hadn't slept in it last night. No dishes in the sink. No sign that Clayton had been here.

As Ty left, he couldn't shake the bad feeling that had settled over him. Yesterday, Clayton had been all worked up over some bull ride he'd seen the weekend before at the Billings rodeo.

Ty hated to admit he hadn't been listening that closely. Clayton was often worked up about something and almost always it had to do with bulls or riders or rodeo.

Was it possible Clayton had taken off to Billings because of some damn bull?

Texas-born Boone Rasmussen had been cursed from birth. It was the only thing that explained why he'd been broke and down on his luck all twenty-seven years.

He left the rodeo grounds and drove the twenty miles north of town turning onto the road to the Edgewood Roughstock Company ranch. The road wound back in a good five more miles, a narrow dirt track that dropped down a series of hills and over a creek before coming to a dead end at the ranch house.

Boone could forgive those first twenty-seven years if he had some promise that the next fifty were going to be better. He was certainly due for some luck. But he'd been disappointed a few too many times to put much stock in hope. Not that his latest scheme wasn't a damned good one.

He didn't see Monte's truck as he parked in the shade of the barn and glanced toward the rambling old two-story ranch house. A curtain moved on the lower floor. She'd seen him come back, was no doubt waiting for him.

He swore and tried to ignore the quickened beat of his heart or the stirring below his belt. At least he was smart enough not to get out of the truck. He glanced over at the bulls in a nearby pasture, worry gnawing at his insides, eating away at his confidence.

So far he'd done two things right—buying back a few of his father's rodeo bulls after the old man's death and hooking up with Monte Edgewood.

But Boone worried he would screw this up, just like he did everything else. If he hadn't already.

He heard someone beside the truck and feared for a moment she had come out of the house after him.

With a start, he turned to find Monte Edgewood standing at the side window. Monte had been frowning, but now smiled. "You goin' to just sit in your pickup all day?"

Boone tried to rid himself of the bitter taste in his mouth as he gave the older man what would pass for a smile and rolled down his window. Better Monte never know why Boone had been avoiding the house in his absence.

"You all right, son?" Monte asked.

Monte Edgewood had called him son since the first time they'd met behind falling-down rodeo stands in some hot, two-bit town in Texas. Boone had been all of twelve at the time. His father was kicking the crap out of him when Monte Edgewood had come along, hauled G. O. Rasmussen off and probably saved Boone's life.

In that way, Boone supposed he owed him. But what Boone hadn't been able to stand was the pity he'd seen in Monte's eyes. He'd scrambled up from the dirt and run at Monte, fists flying, humiliation and anger like rocket fuel in his blood.

A huge man, Monte Edgewood had grabbed him in

a bear hug, pinning his skinny flailing arms as Boone struggled furiously to hurt someone the way he'd been hurt. But Monte was having none of it.

Boone fought him, but Monte refused to let go. Finally spent, Boone collapsed in the older man's arms. Monte released him, reached down and picked up Boone's straw hat from the dust and handed it to him.

Then, without a word, Monte just turned and walked away. Later Boone heard that someone jumped his old man in an alley after the rodeo and kicked the living hell out of him. Boone had always suspected it had been Monte, the most nonviolent man he'd ever met.

Unfortunately, Boone had never been able to forget the pity he'd seen in Monte's eyes that day. Nor the sour taste of humiliation. He associated both with the man because of it. Kindness was sometimes the worse cut of all, he thought.

Monte stepped back as Boone opened his door and got out. Middle age hadn't diminished Monte's size, nor had it slowed him down. His hair under his western hat was thick and peppered with gray, his face rugged. At fifty, Monte Edgewood was in his prime.

He owned some decent enough roughstock and quite a lot of land. Monte Edgewood seemed to have everything he needed or wanted. Unlike Boone.

But what made Monte unique was that he was without doubt the most trusting man Boone had ever met.

And that, he thought with little remorse, would be Monte's downfall. And Boone's good fortune.

"How's Devil's Tornado today?" Boone asked as they walked toward the ranch house where Monte had given him a room. He saw the curtain move and caught a glimpse of dyed blond hair.

"Son, you've got yourself one hell of a bull there,"
Monte said, laying a hand on Boone's shoulder as they
mounted the steps.

Didn't Boone know it.

Monte opened the screen and they stepped into the
cool dimness of the house and the heady scent of perfume.

"Is that you, Monte?" Sierra Edgewood called an instant before she appeared in the kitchen doorway, a sexy
silhouette as she leaned lazily against the jamb and smiled
at them. "Hey, Boone."

He nodded in greeting. Sierra wore a cropped top and
painted-on jeans, a healthy width of firm sun-bronzed
skin exposed between the two. She was pinup-girl pretty
and was at least twenty years younger than her husband.

"It will be interesting to see how he does in Bozeman,"
Monte continued as he slipped past his wife, planting a
kiss on her neck as he headed for the fridge. He didn't
seem to notice that Sierra was still blocking the kitchen
doorway as he took out two cold beers and offered one
to Boone.

After a moment, Sierra moved to let Boone pass, an
amused smile on her face.

"He's already getting a reputation among the cowboys," Monte said heading for the kitchen table with the
beers as if he hadn't noticed what Sierra was up to. He
never seemed to. "Everyone's looking for a high-scoring
bull and one hell of a ride."

Boone sat down at the table across from Monte and
took the cold beer, trying to ignore Sierra.

"Are you talking about that stupid bull again?" she
asked as she opened the fridge and took out a cola. She
popped the cap off noisily, pushing out her lower lip

and giving Boone the big eyes as she sat down across from him.

A moment later, he felt her bare toes run from the top of his boot up the inside seam of his jeans. He shifted, turning to stretch his legs out far enough away that she couldn't touch him as he took a deep drink of his beer. He heard Sierra sigh, a chuckle just under the surface.

He knew he didn't fool her. She seemed only too aware of what she did to him. His blood running hot, he focused on the pasture out the window and Devil's Tornado, his ticket out, telling himself all the Sierra Edgewoods in the world couldn't tempt him. There was no greater lure than success. And failure, especially this time, would land him in jail—if not six feet under.

Devil's Tornado could be the beginning of the life Boone had always dreamed of—as long as he didn't blow it, he thought, stealing a sidelong glance at Sierra.

"Everyone's talking about your bull, son," Monte said with pride in his voice but also a note of sadness.

Boone looked over at him, saw the furrowed thick brows and hoped Monte was worried about Devil's Tornado—not Boone and his wife.

There was a fine line between a bull a rider could score on and one who killed cowboys. And Devil's Tornado had stomped all over that line at the Billings rodeo. Boone couldn't let that happen again.

Sierra tucked a lock of dyed-blond hair behind her ear and slipped her lips over the top of the cola bottle, taking a long cool drink before saying, "So what's the problem?"

Monte smiled at her the way a father might at his young child. "There's no problem."

But that wasn't what his gaze said when he settled it back on Boone.

"The bull can be *too* dangerous," Boone told her, making a point he knew Monte had been trying to make. "It's one thing to throw cowboys—even hurt a few. But if he can't be ridden and he starts killing cowboys, then I'd have to take him off the circuit." He shrugged as if that would be all right. "He'd be worth some in stud fees or an artificial insemination breeding program at this point. But nothing like he would be if, say, he was selected for the National Finals Rodeo in Las Vegas. It would be too bad to put him out to pasture now, though. We'd never know just how far he might have gone."

A shot at having a bull in the National Finals in Las Vegas meant fifty thousand easy, not to mention the bulls he would sire. Everyone would want a piece of that bull. A man could make a living for years off one star bull.

That's why every roughstock producer's dream was a bull like that. Even Monte Edgewood, Boone was beginning to suspect. But only the top-scoring bulls in the country made it. Devil's Tornado seemed to have what it took to get there.

"I wouldn't pull him yet," Monte said quickly, making Boone smile to himself. Monte had needed a bull like Devil's Tornado.

And Boone needed Monte's status as one of the reputable roughstock producers.

After more rodeos, more incredible performances, everyone on the circuit would be talking about Devil's Tornado. That's when Boone would pull him and start collecting breeding fees, because it wouldn't matter if the bull could make the National Finals. Boone could never allow Devil's Tornado to go to Vegas.

But in the meantime, Devil's Tornado would continue to cause talk, his value going up with each rodeo.

If the bull didn't kill his next rider.

Or flip out again like he did in Billings, causing so much trouble in the chute that he'd almost been pulled.

Devil's Tornado was just the first. If this actually worked, Boone could make other bulls stars. He could write his own ticket after that.

But he could also crash and burn if he got too greedy, if his bulls were so dangerous that people got suspicious.

Monte finished his beer and stared at the empty bottle. "I don't have to tell you what a competitive business this is. You've got to have good bulls that a cowboy can make pay for them. But at the same time you don't want PETA coming down on you or those Buck the Rodeo people."

Boone had seen the ads—Buck the Rodeo: Nobody likes an eight-second ride!

Monte looked over at him. "When I got into this business, I promised myself that the integrity of the rodeo and the safety of the competitors would always come first. You know what I'm saying, son?"

Boone knew *exactly* what he was saying. He looked out the window to where Devil's Tornado stood in his own small pasture flicking his tail, the sun gleaming off his horns, then back across the table at Sierra Edgewood. Boone had better be careful. More careful than he had been.

Chapter 2

Sundown Ranch

Asa McCall heard the creak of a floorboard. He turned to find his wife standing in the tack room doorway. His wife. After so many years of being apart, the words sounded strange.

"What do you think you're doing?" Shelby asked, worry making her eyes dark.

"I'm saddling my horse," he said as he hefted the saddle and walked over to the horse. The motion took more effort than it had even a few weeks ago. He hoped she hadn't noticed, but then Shelby noticed everything.

"I can see that," she said, irritation in her tone as she followed him.

Shelby Ward McCall was as beautiful as the day he'd met her forty-four years ago. She was tall and slim, blond and blue-eyed, but her looks had never impressed him as much as her strength. They both knew she'd always been stronger than he was, even though he was twice her size—a large, powerfully built man with more weaknesses than she would ever have.

He wondered now if that—and the fact that they both knew it—had been one of the reasons she'd left him thirty years ago. He knew damn well it was the reason she had come back.

"I'm going for a ride," he said, his back to her as he cinched the saddle in place, already winded by the physical exertion. He was instantly angry at himself. He despised frailty, especially in himself. He'd always been strong, virile, his word the last. He'd never been physically weak before, and he found that nearly impossible to live with.

"Asa—" Her voice broke.

"Don't," he said shaking his head slightly, but even that small movement made him nauseous. "I need to do this." He hated the emotion in his voice. Hated that she'd come back to see him like this.

Shelby looked away. She knew he wouldn't want her to see how pathetic he'd become. He wished he could hide not only his weakness but his feelings from her, but that was impossible. Shelby knew him with an intimacy that had scared him. As if she could see into his black soul and still find hope for him. Still love him.

"I could come with you," she said without looking at him.

"No, thank you," he added, relieved when she didn't argue the point. He didn't need a lecture on how dangerous it was for him to go riding alone. He had hoped to die in the saddle. He should be so lucky.

He swung awkwardly up onto the horse, giving her a

final look, realizing how final it would soon be. He never tired of looking at her and just the thought of how many years he'd pushed her away from him brought tears to his eyes. He'd become a doddering sentimental old fool on top of everything else. He spurred the horse and rode past her and out of the barn, despising himself.

At the gate, something stronger than even his will forced him to turn and look back. She was slumped against the barn wall, shoulders hunched, head down.

He cursed her for coming back after all the years they'd lived apart and spurred his horse. Cursed himself. As he rode up through the foothills of the ranch his father had started from nothing more than a scrawny herd of longhorn cattle over a hundred years ago, he was stricken with a pain far greater than any he had yet endured.

His agony was about to end, but it had only begun for his family. He would have to tell them everything.

He tried not to think about what his sons and daughter would say when he told them that years ago, he'd sold his soul to the devil, and the devil was now at his door, ready to collect in more ways than one.

J.T., his oldest, would be furious; Rourke would be disappointed; Cash would try to help, as always; and Brandon possibly would be relieved to find that his father was human after all. Dusty, his precious daughter, the heart of his heart… Asa closed his eyes at the thought of what it would do to her.

He would have to tell them soon. He might be weak in body and often spirit, but he refused to be a coward. He couldn't let them find out everything after he was gone. Not when what he'd done would put an end to the Sundown Ranch as they all knew it.

Sheridan, Wyoming, Rodeo

It was full dark and the rodeo was almost over by the time Ty Coltrane made his way along the packed grandstands.

He'd timed it so he could catch the bull riding. No one he'd talked to had seen Clayton, nor had there been any word. But Ty knew that if Clayton was anywhere within a hundred-mile radius, he wouldn't miss tonight's rodeo.

Glancing around before the event started, though, he didn't see the old bull rider. He did, however, see Dusty McCall and her friend, Leticia Arnold, sitting close to the arena fence.

Dusty didn't look the worse for wear after her bucking bronc performance earlier today. He shook his head at the memory, telling himself he was tired of playing nursemaid to her. She wasn't his responsibility. He couldn't keep picking her up from the dirt. What if one day he wasn't around to save her skinny behind?

"Now in chute three, we've got a bull that's been making a stir across the country," the announcer bellowed over the sound system. "He's called Devil's Tornado and for a darned good reason. Only a few cowboys have been able to ride him, and those who have scored big. Tonight, Huck Kramer out of Cheyenne is going to give it a try."

Ty felt a start. Devil's Tornado. *That* was the bull that Clayton had been so worked up over. Ty was sure of it. He angled his way through the crowd so he could see the bull chutes as he tried to recall what exactly Clayton had said about the bull.

Devil's Tornado banged around inside the chute as Huck lowered himself onto it to the jangle of the cowbell attached to his rosin-coated bull rope. The cowbell acted as a weight, allowing the rope to safely fall off the bull when the ride was over. Riders used rosin, a sticky substance that increased the grip on their ropes, to make sure they were secured to the bull in hopes of hanging on for the eight-second horn.

Huck wrapped the end of the bull rope tightly around his gloved hand, securing himself to the one-ton bull. Around the bull was a bucking rigging, a padded strap that was designed to make the bull buck.

A hush fell over the crowd as the bull snorted and kicked at the chute, growing more agitated. Huck gave a nod of his head and the chute door flew open with a bang and Devil's Tornado came bursting out in a blur of movement.

Instantly, Ty knew this was not just any bull.

So did the crowd. A breath-stealing silence fell over the rodeo arena as Devil's Tornado slammed into the fence, then spun in a tight bucking cyclone of dust and hooves.

Devil's Tornado pounded the earth in bucking lunges, hammering Huck with each jarring slam. Ty watched, his heart in his throat as the two-thousand pound bull's frantic movements intensified in a blur of rider and bull.

The crowd found its voice as the eight-second horn sounded and bullfighters dressed like clowns rushed out.

With his hand still tethered to the monstrous bull, Huck's body suddenly began to flop from side to side, as lifeless as a dummy's, as Devil's Tornado continued bucking.

The bullfighters ran to the bull and rider, one working frantically to free the bucking rigging from around the bull and the other to free Huck's arm from the thickly braided rope that bound bull and rider.

Devil's Tornado whirled, tossing Huck from side to side, charging at the bullfighters who tried desperately to free the rider. One freed the rigging strap designed to make the bull buck. It fell to the dirt, but Huck's bull rope wouldn't come loose. The cowbell jangled at the end of the rope as Huck flopped on the bull's broad back as the bull continued to buck and spin in a nauseating whir of motion.

Other cowboys had jumped into the arena, all fighting to free Huck. It seemed to go on forever, although it had only been a matter of seconds before one of the bullfighters pulled a knife, severing Huck from Devil's Tornado.

Huck's lifeless body rose one last time into the air over the bull, suspended like a bag of rags for a heart-stopping moment before it crumpled to the dirt.

The crowd swelled to its feet in a collective gasp of horror as the rider lay motionless.

Devil's Tornado made a run for the body. A bullfighter leapt in front of the charging bull and was almost gored. He managed to distract the bull away from Huck, but only for a few moments.

The bull started to charge one of the pickup riders on horseback, but stumbled and fell. He staggered to his feet in a clear rage, tongue out, eyes rolling.

Cowboys jumped off the fence to run to where Huck lay crumpled in the dirt. A leg moved. Then an arm. Miraculously, Huck Kramer sat up, signaling he was all right.

A roar of applause erupted from the grandstands.

"That was some ride," the announcer said over the loudspeaker. "Let's give that cowboy another round of applause."

Ty sagged a little with relief. He hated to see cowboys get hurt, let alone killed. Huck had been lucky.

Ty's gaze returned to Devil's Tornado. The bull ran wild-eyed around the other end of the arena, charging at anything that moved, sending cowboys clambering up the fence. Ty had seen this many times during bull rides at rodeos.

Devil's Tornado was big and strong, fast out of the chute and one hell of a bucker, but those were attributes, nothing that would have gotten Clayton worked up.

"Whew," the announcer boomed. "Folks, you aren't going to believe this. The judges have given Huck a whopping ninety-two!"

The crowd cheered as Huck was helped out of the arena. He seemed to be limping but, other than that, okay.

Had Clayton just been impressed by Devil's Tornado? No. Ty distinctly remembered that Clayton had been upset, seemingly worried about something he'd seen at the Billings rodeo involving Devil's Tornado. But what?

The pickup riders finally cornered the bull, one getting a rope around the head and a horn and worked him toward the exit chute. Devil's Tornado pawed the earth, shaking his head, fighting them.

Ty worked his way in the direction of the exit chute, hoping to get a closer look. As Devil's Tornado was being herded out, he seemed disoriented and confused, shying away from anything that moved.

Usually, by the time a bull got to the exit chute, he recognized that it was over and became more docile. Not Devil's Tornado. He still seemed worked up, maybe a little high-strung, stopping when he saw the waiting semi-trailer, looking scared and unsure. Still, not that unusual for a bull that had just scored that high a ride.

Ty wouldn't have thought anything more about the bull if he hadn't seen Boone Rasmussen rush up to the exit chute and reach through the fence to touch the still aggravated Devil's Tornado. What the hell? Ty couldn't see what Boone had done, but whatever it was made the bull stumble back, almost falling again. Rasmussen reached again for the bull, then quickly withdrew his hand, thrusting it deep into his jacket pocket.

How strange, Ty thought. Devil's Tornado was frothing at the mouth, his head lolling. Ty saw the bull's eyes. Wide and filled with…panic? Devil's Tornado looked around crazily as if unable to focus.

Ty tried to remember where he'd seen that look on a bull before and it finally came to him. It had been years ago in a Mexican bull ring. He was just a kid at the time, but he would never forget that crazed look in the bull's eyes.

Is this what Clayton had witnessed? Is this what had him so upset? Had Clayton suspected something was wrong with Devil's Tornado, just as Ty did? But what would Clayton have done about it?

Ty wasn't even sure what he'd just witnessed. All he knew was: something was wrong with that bull. And Boone Rasmussen was at the heart of it.

"Did you see that?" Letty asked, sitting next to her friend.

Dusty stared through the arena fence toward the chutes and Boone Rasmussen, not sure what she'd seen or what she was feeling right now. "See what?"

Letty let out an impatient sigh. "Don't tell me you missed the entire bull ride because you were gawking at Boone Rasmussen."

Dusty looked over at her friend, surprised how off balance she felt. She let out a little chuckle and pretended she wasn't shaking inside. "Some ride, huh."

But it wasn't the ride that had her hugging herself to ward off a chill on such a warm spring night. She wasn't sure what she'd seen. Letty, like everyone else, had been watching Huck Kramer once the bull had gone into the chutes.

Dusty had been watching Boone. That's why she'd seen the expression on his face when he reached through the fence and hit Devil's Tornado with something. Not a cattle prod but something else. The bull had been in her line of sight, so she couldn't be sure what it had been.

Boone Rasmussen's expression had been so…cold. It all happened so fast—the movement, Boone's expression. But there was that moment when she wondered if she'd made a mistake when it came to him. Maybe he wasn't what she was looking for at all.

Ty moved along the corrals to the exit chute where Devil's Tornado now stood, head down, unmoving. Rasmussen stood next to the fence as if watching the bull, waiting. Waiting for what?

A chill ran the length of his spine as Ty stared at Devil's Tornado. This had to be what Clayton had seen. The look in that bull's eyes and Rasmussen acting just as strangely as the bull.

"Where do you think you're going?" Lamar Nichols stepped in front of him, blocking his view of the bull and Rasmussen.

Ty looked past the big burly cowboy to where Rasmussen prodded the bull and Devil's Tornado stumbled up into the trailer. Rasmussen closed the door behind it with a loud clank.

A shudder went through Ty at the sound. "That's some bull you got there."

"He don't like people." Lamar stepped in front of him, blocking his view again. "Unless you're authorized to be back here, I suggest you go back into the stands with the rest of the audience."

Ty looked past Lamar and saw Rasmussen over by the semitrailer. "Sure," Ty said to the barrel-chested cowboy blocking his way. No chance of getting a closer look now.

He knew if he tried, Lamar would call security or take a swing at him. Ty didn't want to create that much attention.

As Ty headed back toward the grandstand, he searched the crowd for Clayton T. Brooks with growing concern. Now more than ever, he wanted to talk to the old bull rider about Devil's Tornado and what had happened at the Billings rodeo that had riled Clayton.

But Ty didn't see him in the crowd or along the fence with the other cowboys. Where was Clayton anyway? He never missed a rodeo this close to home.

"Thanks for hanging around with me," Dusty McCall said as she and her best friend, Leticia Arnold, walked past the empty dark grandstands after the rodeo.

The crowd had gone home. But Dusty had waited around, coming up with lame excuses to keep her friend there because she hadn't wanted to stay alone—and yet she'd been determined not to leave until she saw Boone.

But she never got the chance. Either he'd left or she just hadn't seen him among the other cowboys loading stock.

"I'm pathetic," Dusty said with another groan.

Letty laughed. "No, you're not."

"It's just…" She waved her hand through the air unable to explain all the feelings that had bombarded her from the first time she'd laid eyes on Boone a few weeks before. He was the first man who'd ever made her feel like this, and it confused and frustrated her to no end.

"Are you limping?" Letty asked, frowning at her.

"It's nothing. Just a little accident I had earlier today," Dusty said, not wanting to admit she'd ridden a saddle bronc just to impress Boone and he hadn't even seen her ride. She hated to admit even to herself how stupidly she'd been behaving.

"Are you sure Boone's worth it?" Letty asked.

Right at that moment, no.

"He just doesn't seem like your type," her friend said.

Dusty had heard all of this before. She didn't want to hear it tonight. Especially since Letty was right. She didn't understand this attraction to Boone any more than Letty did. "He's just so different from any man I've ever met," she tried to explain.

"That could be a clue right there."

Dusty gave her friend a pointed look. "You have to admit he *is* good-looking."

"In a dark and dangerous kind of way, I suppose," Letty agreed.

Dark and dangerous. Wasn't that the great attraction, Dusty thought, glancing back over her shoulder toward the rodeo arena. She felt a small shiver as she remembered the look on his face when he'd reached through the fence toward the bull. She frowned, realizing that she'd seen something drop to the ground as Boone pulled back his hand. Something that had caught the light. Something shiny. Like metal. Right after that Monte had picked whatever it was up from the ground and pocketed it.

"You're sure he told you to meet him after the rodeo?" Letty asked, not for the first time.

Dusty had told a small fib in her zeal to see Boone to-night. On her way back from getting a soda, she'd seen Boone, heard him say, "Meet me after the rodeo." No way was he talking to her. He didn't know she existed. But when she'd related the story to Letty, she'd let on that she thought Boone had been talking to her.

"Maybe I got it wrong," Dusty said now.

Maybe she'd gotten everything wrong. But that didn't explain these feelings she'd been having lately. If she hadn't been raised in a male-dominated family out in the boonies and hadn't spent most of her twenty-one years up before the sun mending fence, riding range and slopping out horse stalls, she might know what to do with these alien yearnings. More to the point, what to do about these conflicting emotions when it came to Boone Rasmussen.

Instead, she felt inept, something she wasn't used to. She'd always been pretty good at everything she tried. She could ride and rope and round up cattle with the best of them, and she'd been helping run the ranch for the past few years since her father's heart attack.

But even with four older brothers, she knew squat about men. Well, one man in particular, Boone Rasmussen. And after tonight, she felt even more confused. She wasn't even sure that once she got his attention, talked to him, that she would even like him. Worse, she couldn't get that one instant, when he'd reached through the fence, out of her mind. What had fallen on the ground?

"Dusty?" Letty was a few yards ahead, looking back at her.

Dusty hadn't realized that she'd stopped walking.

But then again, she was a McCall. She'd been raised

to go after what she wanted. And anyway, she couldn't wait around for Boone to make the first move. Heck, she could be ninety before that happened. She was also curious about what Boone had dropped. Stubborn determination and unbridled curiosity, a deadly combination.

"Oh, shoot, I forgot something," Dusty said, already walking backward toward the arena. "I'll talk to you later, okay?"

Letty started to argue with her, but then just nodded with a look that said she knew only too well what Dusty was up to.

She thought again about the look she'd seen on Boone's face earlier and felt a shiver as she wandered back through the dark arena.

The outdoor arena looked alien with all the lights off, no crowds cheering from the empty stands, no bulls banging around in the chutes or cowboys hanging on the fences. Even the concession stands were locked up.

As Dusty headed toward the chutes, stars glittered in the dark sky overhead. The scent of dust, manure and fried grease still hung in the air. She felt a low hum in her body that seemed to grow stronger as she neared the chutes, as if the night were filled with electricity.

The same excited feeling she'd had the first time she'd seen Boone Rasmussen a few weeks before. He'd been sitting on a fence by the bull chutes, his cowboy hat pulled low over his dark eyes. He'd taken her breath away and set something off inside her. Since then, Dusty hadn't been able to think straight.

Like now. If she had a lick of sense, she'd turn around and hightail it out of here. She heard the scuffle of feet in the dirt behind the chutes, a restless whisper of movement and saw a dozen large shapes milling inside a corral. The bucking horses.

The roughstock contractor hadn't finished loading up. That meant Boone could still be here since he had been working with Monte Edgewood, who provided the stock for the rodeo. Maybe Boone had stayed behind to help load the horses.

She climbed over the gate into the chutes. It was dark, but the stars and distant lights of the city cast a faint glow over the rodeo grounds. She moved along the chutes, stopping when she heard voices.

She looked past the empty corral and the one with the bucking horses and saw what appeared to be several cowboys. All she could really see were their hats etched against the darkness. Boone? She couldn't be sure unless she got a little closer.

Climbing over the fence, she dropped into an empty corral next to the one with the bucking horses. On the cool night breeze came the low murmur of voices. She felt her stomach roil as she tried to think of what she would say to Boone if that was him back there.

Unfortunately, she found herself tongue-tied whenever she saw him. She'd never had trouble speaking her mind. Quite the opposite. What the devil was wrong with her?

She knew she couldn't keep trying to get his attention the way she would have when she was ten. She had a flash of memory of her bucking horse ride earlier and Boone completely missing it. She still hurt from the landing. And the humiliation of her desperation.

Through the milling horses, she caught sight of the dark silhouette of three cowboy hats on the far side of the corrals. She couldn't see enough of the men to tell if one of them was Boone. It was too dark, and the horses blocked all but the men's heads and shoulders.

She stepped on one rung of the fence and tried to peer over the horses, surprised to hear the men's voices rise in anger. She couldn't catch the words, but the tone made it clear they were in a dispute over something.

She recognized Boone's voice and could almost feel the anger in it. Suddenly, it stopped. Eerie silence dropped over the arena.

Hurriedly she dropped back down into the corral, hoping he hadn't seen her, but knowing he must have. She felt her face flush with embarrassment. What if he thought she was spying on him? Or even worse, stalking him?

Boone caught movement beyond the horses in the corral and held up his hand to silence the other two.

A light shone near the rodeo grounds exit, but the arena and corrals lay in darkness. He stared past the horses, wondering if his eyes had been playing tricks on him. Through a break in the horses, he saw a figure crouch down.

"Go on, get out of here," he whispered.

Lamar nodded and headed for the semitruck and trailer with Devil's Tornado inside.

Boone glanced at Waylon Dobbs. The rodeo veterinarian looked scared and ready to run, but he hadn't moved.

"Who is it?" Waylon whispered.

Boone motioned with an impatient shake of his head that he didn't know and for Waylon to leave. "I'll take care of it. Go. We're finished here anyway."

Slipping through the fence into the corral with the bucking horses, Boone used the horses to conceal himself as he worked his way to the far gate—the gate that would send the massive horses back into the corral where he'd just seen someone spying on them.

Had the person heard what they'd been saying? He couldn't take the chance. Everyone knew accidents happened all the time when nosy people got caught where they didn't belong.

The horses began to move restlessly around the corral, nervous with him among them. His jaw tightened as he thought about who was just beyond the horses. He couldn't see anyone, but he knew the person was still there.

Carefully, he unlocked the gate and stepped back in the shadows out of the way of the horses. Whoever had been spying on him was in for a surprise.

Chapter 3

Ty Coltrane cupped his hands around his eyes and tried to see into the dark semitrailer. He could smell the bull, hear him breathing, but he couldn't see anything.

Unfortunately, there didn't seem to be anything to see. Devil's Tornado was so calm now that the bull had him doubting he'd seen anything unusual earlier.

Rodeo roughstock were raised to be as rank as possible. No one—not the bull rider, nor the audience—wanted a bull that didn't buck, that didn't put on show, that let the rider score big.

Devil's Tornado had done that and more.

So why had Ty stayed until the rodeo was over to sneak back here and get another peek at that bull? Because he couldn't forget what he'd seen in that bull's eyes. Or quit wondering what Rasmussen had done to the bull as it came down the exit chute.

But he wasn't going to find out anything tonight.

Earlier, he thought he'd heard voices over by the corrals, but hadn't been close enough to recognize them. When he'd been looking into the back of the semitrailer, he'd heard what sounded like the voices escalate into an argument.

But suddenly he realized that he couldn't hear them anymore. A sliver of worry burrowed itself under his skin. He didn't want to be caught back here snooping around the trailer. If he had reason to be suspicious, he didn't want Rasmussen or his cowboy thug getting wind of it.

He moved along the side of the trailer in time to see a short, squat figure moving toward a shiny black Lincoln. Veterinarian Waylon Dobbs.

The sound of the semitruck door opening made Ty jump. He peered between trailer and cab and caught a glimpse of Lamar Nichols a moment before the springs on the cab seat groaned under the big cowboy's weight. The semi's engine roared to life. Ty realized he'd be in clear view once the truck pulled away.

He glanced toward the horses in the corral and caught a glimpse of someone over by the gate. Boone Rasmussen.

In that instant, Ty felt a wave of apprehension as he realized that the voices he'd heard raised in argument had to have been those of veterinarian Waylon Dobbs, Boone Rasmussen and his employee, Lamar Nichols.

What the hell had they been arguing about? Devil's Tornado? Had the veterinarian seen what Ty had and confronted Rasmussen?

As Ty stared through the darkness past the horses, he heard the faint squeak of a gate and realized Rasmussen had just opened the gate to let the large bucking horses back through toward the arena.

Now why would he do that?

The semitruck pulled away and Ty made a run for the corrals hoping Lamar wouldn't glance back.

Ty hadn't gone two feet when he saw Lamar's face reflected in the side mirror. The cowboy slammed on the semi's brakes as Ty slipped through the corral fence, disappearing into the dark.

Dusty listened, afraid to move. She heard the sound of the semitruck engine and what could have been another vehicle starting to leave. She waited, crouched in the darkness just inside the empty corral.

She felt like a fool. Could her timing be any worse?

The bucking horses in the next corral began to mill nervously, as if they were also aware of her presence.

She really needed to get out of here—hopefully, without being seen again. She tucked her long blond braid up under her western straw hat and tried to see through the moving horses. Dust rose around them. Her legs were starting to cramp. She leaned forward, one hand holding on to her leather-fringed shoulder bag, the other dropping to the soft earth. Her fingers felt something cold and hard in the dirt.

Dusty squinted down, shocked to see a used syringe lying in the dirt. What if one of the horses had stepped on it? Or one of the cows had eaten it? Carefully, she picked it up with two fingers and dropped it into her shoulder bag, planning to throw it away as soon as she reached the trash cans. She forgot about it almost at once as she heard a sound behind her.

She didn't dare turn and look. Straightening, she took

a breath, rose and started back across the empty corral as if she weren't dying of embarrassment. Several of the horses snorted, and suddenly the whole bunch began to lap the adjacent corral behind her.

She winced, realizing she must have spooked them. Leticia had been right. She shouldn't have come back here looking for Boone. What had happened to her common sense?

She was halfway across the corral when she heard a gate groan open behind her. She turned, foolishly thinking all might not be lost. Maybe Boone had seen her and come after her. She tried to come up with a good excuse for being there.

But what she saw was the herd of huge bucking horses pour through the now open corral gate in a stream of pounding hooves, headed right for her.

Dusty started to run for the fence, her boots sinking in the soft turned earth. But she realized she wouldn't be able to reach it in time. She swung around, knowing the only way to keep from being trampled was to stand her ground.

As the horses thundered toward her, she waved her arms wildly, stomped her feet and yelled. The giant horses swelled around her, towering over her, the ground trembling under their weight, dust billowing up around them.

She could feel hot breath on the back of her neck as the dark shadows of the horses blocked any light from the stars above her. She waved, stomped and yelled as she edged back toward the fence.

A hand suddenly grabbed the back of her jean jacket and hauled her roughly up onto the rails as the horses circled the dark corral in a dusty stew.

She turned to face the man who'd just hauled her up on the fence, expecting to see Boone Rasmussen's handsome face.

"Ty?" she croaked, unable to hide her disappointment for the second time today. Ty Coltrane. "What are you doing here?" she demanded and shot a look past the corral. There was nothing but darkness where the three men had been earlier. In the distance, she heard the sound of vehicles leaving.

"How about, 'Ty, thank you for saving my skinny butt and not for the first time,'" he whispered, dragging her down off the fence. "Come on, let's get out of here."

She didn't argue. She could hear the horses racing around the corral behind her, which meant Boone would have a hard time getting them loaded now. If there was a chance he hadn't seen her...

She hightailed it through the space between the grandstands, glad for the darkness as Ty led her toward the nearly empty parking area.

"What were you doing back there?" Ty demanded once they were a good distance from the arena. He sounded like he always did after bailing her out of one of her messes. He was worse than one of her brothers.

"None of your business. Don't you get tired of following me around?"

It was too dark to see his blue eyes under the brim of his western straw hat. And she was glad of it. He shook his head at her as if he didn't know what to do with her. How about leaving her *alone*?

"My pickup's parked over there." He motioned toward the street and his black truck. Her tan ranch pickup was parked in the rodeo lot in the opposite direction. "Think you can make it home without getting into any more trouble?"

"I do just fine by myself, thank you very much." She mugged a face at him.

"Right."

She turned and stomped off toward her truck. It appeared to be the only one left in the lot. And to think earlier today she felt some semblance of affection for him.

As she neared the ranch truck, she realized there was another rig parked on the other side, all but hidden by the size of her truck. She quickened her step. Was it possible Boone had been out here waiting for her this whole time?

Rounding the front of the truck, she saw that it was only Leticia's yellow VW Beetle. Letty leaned against the car, waiting.

Dusty felt a surge of emotion to see that her friend had waited for her.

"Did you see Boone?" Letty asked.

Dusty shook her head.

"What happened? You look like you got rolled in the dirt," Letty said, straightening in alarm.

Dusty recounted her tale of woe as Ty made a circle through the empty parking lot, slowing as if he planned to follow Dusty home. But he sped up, seemingly relieved to see Letty with her.

"Was that Ty Coltrane?" Letty asked, as surprised as Dusty had been to see him earlier.

"Yes." She brushed at the dirt on her jeans feeling foolish. "Just my luck, I run into Ty instead of Boone."

"What was Ty still doing there?" Letty asked as he left.

What *had* he been doing hanging around the rodeo grounds this late? Dusty shook her head, thinking instead about the men she'd heard arguing.

"You couldn't tell who the men were that Boone was arguing with?" Letty asked.

Dusty shook her head. "Boone's voice was the only one I recognized and I couldn't hear what he was saying." The sound of a large truck engine made them both turn to look toward the rodeo grounds again. A semi-truck left by the back way.

The night suddenly seemed darker. A quiet fell over the rodeo grounds. Only a few lights from town could be seen in the distance.

"I'd better get home." Letty started to get into her car, as if she were tired and did not want to hear any more about Boone.

Dusty couldn't blame her. She touched her sleeve. "Me, too." Things were weird enough at the ranch. Dusty didn't want her father worrying about her, and as long as she still lived in the main house… "Thanks for waiting for me."

Letty nodded and seemed to hesitate. "Sorry things didn't work out the way you'd hoped. Boone will come around."

Dusty smiled at her friend. Boone, she was beginning to realize, didn't just make her heart jump or her pulse pound. He made her crazy. No, she thought, he made her reckless, which right now seemed much worse. "Talk to you tomorrow."

Letty nodded and waited as Dusty got into the truck and started the engine. They'd brought separate vehicles because Letty had had to work late. Letty followed her all the way north as far as Antelope Flats before honking goodbye as she turned into the motel her parents had left her when they had retired.

Dusty continued north toward the ranch. Her disappointment hit her the moment she and Letty parted. She'd gone to the rodeo with such high hopes tonight.

She brushed at her tears of frustration. She hated feeling like this. Worse, acting like this.

Something flashed in her rearview mirror. She glanced back to see a set of headlights as a vehicle came roaring up the highway behind her.

The headlights grew brighter, as if whoever was driving was trying to catch her. She couldn't imagine who it could be, unless Ty had been waiting to follow her home. That would be just like him.

She shook her head and sped up. Because of the hour, there were no other vehicles on the road. The lights behind her grew brighter and brighter. She glanced back in the rearview mirror, surprised how fast the vehicle was coming up on her.

The headlights were high, the rig definitely a pickup. That might have narrowed it down in any other place except the ranching town of Antelope Flats, Montana, where trucks outnumbered cars ten to one.

The truck was right behind her now. She flipped the rearview mirror up so the lights weren't blinding her. But she was still silhouetted in the glare of them.

Ahead, through her own headlights, she could see the county road turnoff. She waited, expecting the truck behind her to pass. But instead, it stayed right behind her.

She touched her brakes, hoping the driver would back off. But he didn't and she had the horrible feeling that he planned to force her off the road.

As the turnoff came up, she took the turn onto the county dirt road a little fast, fishtailing on the ruts. Behind her a wall of dust kicked up under her tires.

Forced to slow a little on the washboard dirt road, she

looked back and saw nothing but dust. She tried to relax, thinking she'd lost him. It had probably just been somebody with a few too many beers under his belt.

But she kept her speed up anyway. She knew this road, had driven it since she was twelve and had conned her dad into letting her get her license early, with the stipulation that she was only to drive on the ranch. That wasn't uncommon for ranch and farm kids in the state of Montana. What was uncommon was Asa McCall allowing it.

She hadn't realized how fast she was going until the pickup started to fishtail again on the washboard. Having driven more dirt roads than paved highway, she quickly got the pickup back under control and allowed herself to slow down a little.

In the distance, she could see the lights of the McCall ranch house and the turnoff to the ranch. Behind her, nothing but dust. Maybe.

She knew she'd have to slow down to make the turn onto the road down to the ranch, but once she did, she was sure no one would follow her up to the house. No one who knew the McCall men, anyway—and how protective they were.

Behind her, dust roiled up into the darkness. The entrance to the ranch road loomed in her headlights, the log arch, the sign: Sundown Ranch. Home. Safety. She'd never felt afraid here, didn't want to now.

She hit her brakes and cranked the wheel—glancing back as she did. The rearview mirror filled with headlights.

She swung through the ranch arch and onto the road that led to the ranch house, her pulse a war drum in her ears. The other rig had been right behind her!

Racing down the quarter-mile-long road to the house,

she roared into the yard, shut off the engine and jumped out, ready to run as she looked back, half expecting to see the other rig coming after her. A few more stars had popped out, and there was just a sliver of moon.

As the dust settled, she felt her breath seize in her chest. A quarter mile back on the county road by the entrance to the ranch road, she could see the dark shape of a pickup, the headlights turned out. It was too far away and too dark to see who was behind the wheel. But the driver was sitting there in the darkness as if… Her heart began to pound furiously…as if watching her.

She turned and ran to the house. Racing up the steps and across the porch, she jerked open the door.

"What in the hell?" Asa McCall demanded as he came out of his den scowling at her. "I heard you come driving in. Are you drunk or just crazy, girl?"

"Someone followed me home." She pointed toward the road, shaking with fear.

Her father stepped out onto the porch and looked toward the gate. Asa was a big man with a reputation for being hard and uncompromising. Dusty knew he had a soft spot—at least where she was concerned. Soft spot or not, he would kill to protect his family.

"What are you talking about?" he demanded.

She moved to his side and followed his gaze. The dark shape of the pickup was gone, the road empty. "But he was just there."

"He?" Asa asked looking over at her.

"I just assumed it was a man," she said. "It was a pickup. Sitting up there by the gate with the headlights off. He chased me home."

Her father was still eyeing her. Dust hung like low clouds over the county road from where she'd raced home. Her father knew her, knew she didn't scare easily; he had to believe her.

"Was this some man you met at the rodeo?"

"No. I don't know who it was."

A muscle jumped in his jaw as he looked back out at the road. "I don't like you hanging around a rodeo this late at night."

"I was with Letty."

He glanced down at her as if sensing the truth. It was as if he could smell it on her.

"Ty Coltrane was there, too," she added quickly, knowing how much her father liked Ty.

He glanced back toward the road. "I'll take a look around in the morning."

She touched his arm as he turned to go back inside. "Thank you." She hadn't realized how much she'd needed him to believe her.

He smiled at her and cupped her cheek with one callused hand before he left her on the porch, the door closing behind him.

Dusty stood listening to the sound of his footfalls disappear down the hall as she stared at the ranch gate. The county road was empty, the pickup gone. Had he turned around and gone back to town? Or gone on up the road?

Someone had chased her home. But for what purpose?

She started out to the truck to get her shoulder bag, still unnerved. Had the driver planned to run her off the road or just follow her home? He'd definitely been trying to intimidate her.

She opened the pickup door and reached for her bag. Why would anyone follow her home unless… Her heart thudded in her chest. Unless he wanted to see where she lived.

Clutching the leather pouch to her, she closed the truck door, telling herself that made no sense. All the person would have to do was mention her name and anyone in the county could tell him where to find the McCalls' Sundown Ranch.

McCall had always been an impossible name to live down, thanks to her four older brothers. They were to blame for how protective her father had always been with her. And the reason her teachers had warned her the first day of school that they weren't putting up with any more shenanigans from McCall kids.

She started up the front steps of the house and stumbled as a thought hit her. What if the driver of the pickup hadn't known who she was? Or where she lived?

Well, he did now, she thought with a shudder.

Chapter 4

Outside Antelope Flats

Sheriff Cash McCall slid down the steep embankment toward the partially hidden wrecked pickup lying in the bottom of the ravine. Coroner Raymond Winters waited in the shade of a chokecherry tree.

Winters was fifty-something, a quiet, mournful man who, besides being coroner for the county, owned Winters Funeral Home, just across the border in Sheridan, Wyoming.

The pickup had obviously rolled several times before coming to rest at the base of the tree. A rancher had spotted it while out on his four-wheeler checking calves and called 911.

As Cash neared the battered truck, he could see the Montana plates. Same county as Antelope Flats. He leaned into the cab, afraid he would know the driver.

He did.

"It's Clayton," Winters said behind him, sounding regretful. "Clayton T. Brooks. I saw him ride during Cheyenne Days. He was one hell of a bull rider. Damned shame. Heard he started hitting the bottle hard after he was forced to quit. That last bull broke him up good."

Cash nodded. Clayton T. Brooks was a legend in these parts. "They don't make 'em like him anymore," he agreed. What a hell of a way to end up, though, Cash thought.

Clayton was crumpled, beaten and broken on the floorboard on the passenger side of the pickup—and he'd been there for a while.

"Takes a certain kind of man to keep climbing back up on an animal that weighs a ton and would just as soon stomp you as not, don't you think?" Winters commented.

Unlike his brothers, and even his little sister Dusty, Cash had never rodeoed. Nor had he ever really understood the attraction. But then, he'd never been that much into ranching, let alone trying to ride animals intent on stopping you.

Cash tried the pickup door on the uphill side of the cab. Jammed. He went around, yanked on the other door. A dozen empty beer cans clattered to the ground.

"I would suspect his blood alcohol level was over the legal limit when he left the road," the coroner said dryly. "No skid marks up on the pavement. He didn't even try to hit his brakes. Wasn't wearing his seat belt, either."

"How long would you say he's been here?" Cash asked.

Winters shook his head. "Hard to say. My guess is at least a day, maybe more. I'll know more once I get him out of there."

Cash heard the whine of the ambulance siren.

"This has always been a bad curve," Winters said

as the siren suddenly stilled, followed by the sound of doors opening and closing from the highway above them. "Looks pretty cut-and-dried. Alcohol-related fatality. Damned shame."

Cash agreed as he stepped back from the pickup, the smell of stale beer and death making him queasy this early in the morning. He turned to go up and help the ambulance crew with the stretcher, remembering the last time he saw Brooks.

The bull rider had been down at the Mint Bar with some of his drinking buddies. He'd been talking rodeo, all he ever talked about. It had been his life. Rodeo and the bulls he'd ridden. Clayton had been bragging about how he never forgot a bull.

As far as Cash knew, he had no family. But Clayton wouldn't be forgotten. The rodeo community would mourn his loss and he would go down in history as a cowboy who had ridden some of the most famous bulls in history during his career. Cash guessed that was more recognition than most people got after they were gone.

Still, it was a shame that Brooks couldn't have died doing what he'd loved instead of missing a curve on some dark stretch of narrow two-lane highway with too many beers under his last winning rodeo belt buckle.

Dusty McCall bit down on her lower lip, hesitating as she looked toward the cool shaded entrance to the Coltrane Appaloosa Ranch barn.

For a moment, she almost turned around and rode back to her own ranch. But she'd come this far...

The sun was hot on her back. She slipped off her horse and sidled toward the barn door, stopping to peer in. There was still time to change her mind.

She could hear the low murmur of a male voice. Ty Coltrane's. She eased into the cool darkness, aware of something in the air. An electricity like static heat, taut with tension.

"Easy, pretty girl," Ty murmured from one of the horse stalls. "You're just fine. The first time is always the toughest."

Dusty edged deeper into the barn until she could peer over the top of the stall door. Ty sat on a bed of straw, his back to her and the stall door. In front of him a mare, her belly swollen to enormous proportions, paced in the confined space, her eyes on Ty, her expression worried.

In obvious agitation, the mare turned to her side to look back at her belly as if she felt the foal inside her and was confused by it. She stopped and nickered at Ty as if needing reassurance.

"It's all right," Ty murmured as he watched her. "That's it. Take your time. Nothing to be afraid of."

From experience, Dusty knew that most mares foal between midnight and 3:00 a.m. for some unknown reason. The fact that this mare was running late didn't bode well.

Dusty wasn't sure how long she stood there listening to Ty's soothing murmur and watching the pregnant mare, worrying that something was wrong.

Suddenly, the mare awkwardly lay down, her legs under her. With a groan, she went to her side.

Ty stroked the mare as he moved into position. From where Dusty stood she could see the foal start to appear. She stared at the purplish white bag covering the foal, trying to see the new life inside it.

After a few minutes, she could make out the front hooves and then the head. The foal started out feet first, nose between its front legs as if diving. Then stopped.

Dusty stood transfixed, anxious now for the rest of the foal's body to be expelled. It was taking too long. She could feel Ty's nervousness as well as her own. She bit down on her lower lip, gripping the top of the stall door.

Ty rolled up his sleeves, still quietly encouraging, his hands and voice working to soothe the mare.

Nothing happened.

Dusty chewed at her lip, afraid as she watched him pull gently on the foal each time the mare pushed. It took everything in her not to go into the stall to help, but Ty was doing all that could be done and she didn't want to upset the mare.

Without warning the foal popped out—right into Ty's lap. He let out a surprised relieved laugh as he held the bundle.

Dusty felt her chest swell, tears burned her eyes as she watched Ty carefully brush back the white covering of the sack to let the gawky little thing breathe.

The foal had dark curly wet hair that looked like crushed velvet. As a ranchwoman, she'd seen dozens and dozens of births, but this one felt as if it were the most amazing. She gazed awestruck as Ty toweled the little colt dry, rubbing it gently, clearing away the protective cover, all the time murmuring to both. Talking softly, he rubbed the foal's ears, handled the hooves, flipped him over.

The mare watched. Dusty could feel the trust between the horse and Ty. He drew the foal over so the mare could tenderly nose it, smell it and as Dusty stared into the stall, the foal awkwardly got up on stick-like legs and stumbled to its feet, all legs and big eyes.

Dusty choked back a laugh. The foal nuzzled around the mare until Ty helped him get his first sips from one of the mare's two teats. The mare looked surprised for a moment, then seemed strangely content.

Dusty stared at the two horses standing next to each other, sensing the instinctive mother-child bond between them. She swallowed back the lump in her throat.

Ty turned, surprised to see Dusty McCall standing at the stall door, watching, her eyes wide and shiny as she stared down at the new foal.

As always, he felt that little flutter in his chest whenever he saw Dusty. He stepped out of the stall, closing the door as the mare began to clean up her new offspring.

"Hi."

Dusty didn't respond, seeming at a loss for words over the birth. He smiled at that. She never ceased to amaze him. After as many livestock as she'd seen birthed, she still got teary-eyed. He knew the feeling.

"It's just so incredible, isn't it?" she said after a moment.

He nodded. He'd seen more foals born than he could count, but he never got over the wonder of it.

He watched her peer into the stall, the expression on her face tender. He couldn't remember the last time she'd just dropped by like this. He had to wonder what she was doing here. Not that he was complaining. He liked her. He'd always liked her. Sometimes, he almost thought they were friends.

"It's just so…cool," she said, peeking over the stall door at the new foal again.

"It is that." He studied her, realizing she must have ridden over here. That's why he hadn't heard her drive up.

She was dressed in her usual: jeans, boots and one of her brother's cast-off western shirts under one of her brother's large cast-off canvas jackets, no makeup, her long blond hair plaited in a single braid down her back, her western straw hat pulled down low.

He had a sudden memory of her standing in the middle of the rodeo corral last night with wild bucking horses pounding around her. What the hell had she been doing there? After watching her ride one of the bucking broncs yesterday morning at the clinic, he wouldn't put anything past her.

"What are you going to name the foal?" she asked, finally looking over at him. She had the palest blue eyes he'd ever seen, peering out of gold dusted lashes.

He wondered what she saw when she looked at him. She usually treated him like one of her brothers——her least favorite, he thought with a wry smile.

"Haven't given a name any thought," he said. "What do you suggest?"

"Miracle," she said without hesitation. "What's his mother's name?"

"Rosie."

"Rosie's Little Miracle."

He laughed. "Great name for a roping horse." He pretended he was a rodeo announcer. "And our next contestant is Big Jim Brady on his horse Rosie's Little Miracle…" He laughed again.

Dusty mugged a face at him.

He headed deeper into the barn, needing to check several other mares that were due to foal. Unlike Rosie, though, those mares were old hands at this and wouldn't need any help. He'd been worried about Rosie. The first time was always the hardest.

Dusty followed him like one of the ranch dogs.

He stopped in front of a stall and she practically plowed into him. She hadn't just dropped by. The girl had something on her mind. He was dying to know what it was. "There something I can do for you, Slim?"

"Last night, did you go straight home from the rodeo?"

He raised a brow, amused. "You asking if I have myself a girlfriend in town?"

She rolled her eyes. "I just wondered, since you left before I did."

"Sorry to disappoint you, but I came straight here." He frowned. His horse ranch was down the county road from the McCalls' Sundown Ranch. "You rode all the way over here this early in the morning to ask me that? What's going on?"

She looked down as she dug the toe of her boot into the dirt and shook her head. "Nothin'."

He'd learned that *nothin'* with Dusty McCall was always *somethin'.* He leaned against the stall and crossed his arms. "Come on, what gives, Slim?"

She made another face at him. "I wish you'd quit calling me that."

He studied her. "Why do you care when I got home?"

She looked away, worrying her lower lip with her teeth the way she did when something was bothering her. "Someone followed me last night from town."

He felt his insides go cold. "What do you mean *someone*?" Last night, he'd seen Boone move through the bucking horses, heard him open the gate. At the time, Ty hadn't understood why Boone had sent the horses back through the empty corral—until Ty had hauled Dusty out a few moments later.

Had Boone known Dusty was in there? Or had he just heard someone and been afraid they'd overheard his argument with Dobbs and Lamar? Maybe Boone thought it was Ty in the corral spying on him. But that didn't explain what Dusty had been doing in there, did it?

"All I know is that whoever followed me was in a dark-colored pickup." She met his gaze. "Whoever was behind the wheel pretty much *chased* me home though."

"You mean like tried to run you off the road?" he asked, his mouth dry as straw.

"I never let him get that close."

Ty sighed, thankful Dusty was one kick-butt girl. "You couldn't tell the make or color of the pickup?"

"It was too dark." She cocked her head at him. "I just thought it might have been you because you're always turning up where I am. Like last night after the rodeo." Her big blue eyes narrowed. "What were you doing there anyway?"

"Well, I wasn't following you, Slim," he said, shoving off the stall door. "I need to get to work, even if you don't." He didn't like hearing that someone had followed her home. Any more than he liked hearing her complain about him always turning up around her.

"Well, you don't have to get mad."

He ground his teeth. Sometimes he wanted to ring Dusty McCall's slim neck. Other times…

It was the other times that had him walking away from her. She was just a kid. Just an annoying, pain-in-the-neck kid.

Dusty trailed after him until he stopped and spun on her. "I told you it wasn't me who followed you home."

"I believe you," she said, looking indignant.

"I could ask you what you were doing there," he said.

"I already told you. Nothing."

"Right. Well, now that we got that cleared up, is there something else I could help you with?"

"If you have to know, I left my bag and went back for it," she said.

He cut his eyes to her. "You left your bag in the horse corrals."

"I found it in the grandstand where I left it and then I wandered down to the horse corral."

He didn't believe a word of it. "Just to see the horses."

"No," she snapped. "I heard arguing. I was curious."

That, he believed. But something was bothering her. "Okay, Slim, spill it. Whatever it is, let's hear it."

She gulped air. "I need to ask your opinion on something." She swallowed and seemed to be having trouble finding her voice. A rare occurrence, considering how many times she'd told him what she thought in no uncertain terms. "It's kind of…personal."

Today he'd seen her wordless *and* choked up, all in the same morning. And now she wanted to ask him something…personal?

She opened her mouth to speak, but closed it as a truck came up the road.

Ty swore under his breath when he recognized the rig. This didn't bode well, he thought, as the dark brown pickup pulled up in the yard and Boone Rasmussen climbed out.

"Stay here," Ty said to Dusty.

She didn't answer. Nor did she move.

As he stepped out of the barn, he glanced back. She was standing right where he'd left her, still as a statue. What the heck was going on with that girl, anyway? She never did what he told her. Hell, she did just the opposite to show him she didn't have to listen to him.

Except for just now.

Rasmussen got out of his truck and sauntered toward

him, his face expressionless. Ty fought the bad feeling in the pit of his stomach.

Rasmussen had never been out to the Coltrane Appaloosa Ranch before. For that matter, he'd never acknowledged Ty, even though they'd met numerous times at rodeos. Every time they'd been introduced, Boone acted as if it had been the first, saying, "Coltrane? You raise... horses?"

Roping horses. Some of the best known in the world, including horses now being ridden by the top ropers in professional rodeo. But Boone Rasmussen knew that. Ty wondered why the man seemed to purposely rub him the wrong way. Or maybe that was just Boone Rasmussen's way. Whatever, Ty hadn't liked him. Didn't trust him. Especially after last night.

"Mornin'," Rasmussen said, glancing toward the barn, his gaze skimming over Dusty who stood silhouetted in the doorway, head down, her straw hat hiding her face. He shifted his dark eyes to Ty again without giving her another glance.

Ty waited, afraid he already knew what was on the cowboy's mind.

"I heard you raise horses," Rasmussen said, shoving back his hat.

"You know damned well I raise Appaloosa ropers."

Rasmussen's brow shot up. He pushed back his hat and smiled. "A little testy this morning, ain't we."

If he thought his good ol' Texas boy routine was going to work, he was sadly mistaken. "What is it you want, Rasmussen?"

"I was looking for a horse." He glanced toward the green pasture dotted with Coltrane Appaloosas.

Ty knew Rasmussen had no need of a roping horse.

"You just missed our production sale. You might want to check it out next spring if you're still around. We'll have some yearlings and two-year-olds. The competition is pretty stiff, though."

Buyers came from all over the country. A Coltrane Appaloosa often went for thousands of dollars, especially progeny of one of his more famous roping horses with potential as breeding stock.

"But you're probably looking for a trained horse," Ty added. "Those go even higher and faster at the sale."

"I can train my own horse. And I will be around next spring." Rasmussen's jaw tightened. "You seem to have a burr under your saddle when it comes to me."

"You didn't come out here for a horse. What is it you're really after?"

"I could ask you the same thing." He glanced toward the barn again. Dusty was still standing in the same spot, hat down over her blue eyes, probably straining to hear their conversation. Ty doubted she could from this distance, but he knew she was damned sure watching them from under the brim of her hat. Slim was nothing if not nosy.

Rasmussen pulled off his straw hat and burrowed his fingers through his thick black hair. "What's your interest in my bulls?" he demanded, flicking a look at him.

"Who told you I was interested?" Ty asked, although he knew it was that rough-looking cowboy Rasmussen used in his chutes, Lamar Nichols.

"Doesn't matter. I just wondered why a man who raises roping horses would care about roughstock," Boone said. "You thinking of raising bulls?"

Ty wanted to laugh. Boone Rasmussen knew damned well that wasn't the case. "There a problem with me checking out your bulls?"

Boone shifted on his feet, looked down at his boots, then back up, the dark gaze boring into him. "Nope. But if you're that interested I'd suggest you come out to the ranch in the daytime. Easier to see when it isn't pitch-dark."

"I just might take you up on that," Ty said. "The last time I saw a show like the one your bull put on last night was in Mexico."

Something dark and threatening flickered in Rasmussen's eyes before he looked away toward the barn. Ty followed his gaze. Dusty was gone.

For no reason he could put his finger on, Ty was relieved. She'd been near the corrals last night after the rodeo and had almost been trampled by the bucking horses, thanks to Rasmussen. Had she been snooping, too? More to the point, had Rasmussen seen her? Someone had followed her home. No, *chased* her home, she'd said.

Ty wanted to confront Rasmussen about opening that corral gate last night, but then that would mean involving Dusty and that was the last thing Ty wanted to do.

When Rasmussen looked at him again, Ty could feel rage coming off him in waves. They were about the same age, Rasmussen a few years older. Ty was a little taller and a little lighter, but he figured he could take Rasmussen in a fair fight. Except he doubted Boone Rasmussen had ever been in a fair fight in his life.

"You got quite the spread here," Rasmussen said, his voice sounding strange as if he were fighting to get some control over that rage. "Must be tough for someone your age. Have to keep your eye on things all the time. Probably don't have time to do much else."

Like snoop around rodeo arenas after dark? Ty heard the jealousy in Boone's tone and what sounded like a threat. He'd been running the Coltrane Appaloosa Ranch since his father's death two years ago. Rasmussen was right about one thing: it didn't leave much time for anything else.

"There a point you're trying to make?" Ty asked as he crossed his arms over his chest.

"Just making conversation."

"Well, if that's all, I've got some mares about to foal and don't really have time for conversation this morning."

Rasmussen flashed a smile that had no chance of reaching his dark eyes and tipped his hat. "I'm sure we'll be seeing each other again."

Count on it, Ty thought as he watched the cowboy get into his pickup and drive off.

Why had he driven all the way up here to begin with? Not for a horse, that was for sure. No, he wanted Ty to know that he knew about last night—knew Ty had been snooping around Devil's Tornado. And he'd come out here to warn him off.

This morning, Ty had half convinced himself that he'd been wrong about Devil's Tornado last night. That there wasn't anything to find out. Hell, hadn't Rasmussen invited him out to see the bulls in the daylight?

If there was something about Devil's Tornado that Rasmussen didn't want him to see, then why make that offer?

It didn't make any sense.

So why was Ty even more convinced that Rasmussen had something to hide? Because he'd seen the cowboy's rage and something more. Boone Rasmussen had a mean streak that made him dangerous to anyone who got in his way.

And Ty had gotten in his way.

As he looked back toward the barn, Ty wondered if Dusty had also gotten in Boone Rasmussen's way.

Chapter 5

Shelby McCall was waiting for him when Asa came down to breakfast. They hadn't talked yesterday after his ride. He got the feeling she'd been afraid to ask him anything for fear he might tell her.

That wasn't like Shelby.

But one look at her face this morning told him everything he needed to know—even before she pulled the envelope from her apron pocket.

How ironic that his first thought was that he'd rather die than face her right now.

"When were you going to tell me?" Her voice quavered, eyes filling with tears but not falling, as if by her strength of will she could hold back the torrent.

He started to muddy the waters by demanding to know what she thought she was doing going through his things, but she would have seen right through that.

That day he'd gotten the letter, he'd been the one to

go down to the mailbox at the end of the road. He'd seen her watching him from the window. He'd had to stuff the letter into his pocket to keep her from seeing it when he entered the house.

He smiled ruefully now. Of course she would have noticed. He couldn't get anything past her. Never could.

"Where did you find the letter?" he asked, stalling.

She gave him an exasperated look. "In your jacket pocket where you put it. Not that it matters where I found it. *Asa*." The pain in her voice was heart-wrenching, but he could tell she was trying to be strong for him. For the children. "You have to tell them."

He nodded as he pulled out a chair at the kitchen table and lowered himself into it. He couldn't remember ever feeling so bone-weary.

"There's more," he said, his voice sounding hoarse even to his own ears. He looked up at her.

She straightened to her full height, head going up, that stubborn determined look in her beautiful face as she took the chair across from him. "Tell me."

"It's rather a long story."

"I have time," she said, then seemed to bite her tongue. One errant tear spilled over her cheek. She hurriedly wiped it away and met his gaze, still refusing to acknowledge something they'd both known for a long time.

He was dying.

The letter only confirmed what he'd suspected. For him, time had run out.

Ty found Dusty by Rosie's stall. She stood on tiptoe, peering in at the new foal she wanted to name Miracle. Her expression was so tender he felt his heart do a slow painful somersault in his chest.

It surprised him she hadn't come out of the barn when Rasmussen was here. It wasn't like her. Normally, she would have been right in the middle of the conversation. Strange, she had almost seemed...shy.

He shook his head at such a thought. This was Dusty McCall, he reminded himself. Dusty and shy didn't go together.

But was it possible she was scared of Rasmussen?

"What did Boone want?" Dusty asked as she glanced toward the barn door. Dust still hung in the air from the trail his pickup had left behind.

"Nothin'," Ty said. She looked pale to him. He watched her burrow down into her jacket. "You all right?"

"I'm fine."

"Any reason you didn't want to see Rasmussen just now?" he asked.

She gave him a surprised, wide-eyed look. "I've never even met him, just know who he is. Anyway, you told me to stay here."

Ty studied her. *She never does what I tell her.* He sighed. "What was it you were going to ask me before he showed up?"

She looked away. "It wasn't important."

"Fine. Whatever." Turning, he headed down between the stalls. He'd never understand that girl. He checked the mares again, mentally noting that he might have to call in a couple of his hands if the mares decided to foal at the same time, just to keep an eye on them in case anything went wrong.

Still no word from Clayton. He was torn between worry and annoyance. Mostly worry. No one seemed to have heard from him for several days.

Ty turned, surprised to find Dusty had followed him.

"I thought you left." He didn't know what was bothering her, but she was starting to irritate him. He knew Dusty too well. Something was on her mind and he was getting tired of waiting to hear what it was.

He thought of Rasmussen and was reminded again that Dusty had almost been trampled by the bucking horses last night. Just the thought made his stomach churn. He told himself that Dusty had just been in the wrong place at the wrong time last night. But if he was right about Boone Rasmussen, then he didn't want Dusty anywhere near the man. Or his roughstock.

"Last night after the rodeo, you didn't happen to hear what Boone and his buddies were arguing about, did you?" he asked, thinking that might be the problem.

She shot him a surprised look. "No. Why?"

"Just curious," he said and wished he hadn't said anything. She was giving him that fish-eye look of hers and he could almost see the wheels turning in her head.

"Is that what you were doing there? Trying to hear what they were saying?"

"I stayed around to see one of the bulls." He turned to walk away from her, hoping she dropped it.

But then that wouldn't have been like her.

"Why would you want to see one of Boone's bulls?" she demanded, trailing after him. "The two of you didn't seem all that friendly a few minutes ago."

He spun on her. "Was there some reason you came up here today other than to give me a hard time?"

She seemed to deflate before his eyes. She let out a sigh. "There's something I need to know." She sighed again. "You're a man."

He let out a laugh. "Last time I checked."

She rolled her eyes. "You know what I mean."

He didn't really, but she'd definitely gotten his interest. Where in the world was she headed with this, though? He gave her his full attention as he waited to see.

"Do you think I'm…*cute*?" She practically choked on the word.

"Cute as a button," he said meaning it, relieved beyond words that this was all she wanted to know.

She swallowed and bit her lower lip, lowering her eyes. "I mean do I turn you on?"

"I beg your pardon?"

"Oh, I knew you were the wrong one to ask." She spun around and stalked toward the barn door.

He went after her, grabbing her arm and spinning her around so he could see her face. Damned if she wasn't crying. He let go of her in surprise. "Talk to me, Slim."

She made an angry swipe at her tears. "Do you have any idea what it's like being raised on a ranch far from anything in an all-male family? I've spent my whole life trying not to be different. I just wanted to fit in, and that meant trying to be just like my brothers."

He raised a brow. "I don't think being a tomboy is a bad thing, Slim. Hell, you can ride better than most men and before your brothers Rourke and Brandon started helping, you and J.T. were running the Sundown spread."

She windmilled her arms and let out an exasperated breath. "I'm not saying I don't love ranching. And I never wanted to be one of those prissy girls like you've dated." She made a face. "It isn't about that."

He waited, trying not to comment on her jab about the prissy girls he'd dated.

"It's about *sex*," she said on a breath and looked down at her boots.

Ty reared back. "Wow. Slim, if this is about the birds and bees, then you should be talking to your mama."

She mugged a face at him. "I've known about sex since I was old enough to peer through the fence at the cattle."

"Then you've lost me," he said just wanting this conversation to be over.

"Lately, I've been having these...*feelings*," she said, her head down again.

Ty let out a nervous laugh. Oh, brother.

"I should have known you wouldn't help me."

As she started to stomp off, he reluctantly grabbed her arm again. "Look, I'd help you if I could. It's just that this is the kind of thing you discuss with your mother or a friend."

"I can't talk to Shelby about anything."

He knew that Dusty was still having trouble accepting her mother. Shelby McCall had only recently returned after being gone most of her children's lives—all of Dusty's.

"And I thought you *were* my friend," she accused, eyes narrowing.

He took off his hat and shot a hand through his hair. "I was thinking more of a *girl*-type friend."

"Letty?" she cried.

Letty, who was even more of a tomboy than Dusty, probably had less experience with this type of thing than Slim. "You have a point. What about your sisters-in-law?"

"I hardly know them and they're...old."

He smiled at that. Her sisters-in-law were all in their thirties. "Okay," he said before she could take off again. He was five years her senior. Did she see him as "old" too?

He groaned at the thought. The problem was: he'd never seen her like this. Sure, he'd seen her upset. Usu-

ally after she'd been bucked from a horse. Or tossed into a
mud puddle by one of her brothers when she was younger.
But this was different, and he knew he couldn't just let
her leave thinking he wasn't taking her seriously.

"Come over here," he said, and pulled down a straw
bale for her to sit on. He dragged up one for himself and
sat facing her. "What brought this on, anyway?"

She bit down on her lower lip, eyes down, then slowly
raised her lashes, those blue eyes huge in the cool darkness of the barn and swimming with tears. "I'm *twenty-
one*. I'm tired of being treated like a kid."

Twenty-one. He stared at her, realizing it was true.
He hadn't even thought about how old she was, even
though he'd known her since they were kids. She'd always
just been the girl next door—well, the tomboy down the
road at the next ranch, anyway. He'd pretty much always
thought of her as a kid.

On top of that, she still *looked* like a kid. For starters,
she was only about five-five, lean and youthful-looking.
But he knew it was more than that. She was the kid sister of the very protective McCall boys. That alone made
any man with any sense shy away from her. Just as that
alone should have made him nervous about having this
conversation with her.

"Have you mentioned this to your brothers?" he asked.

She rolled her eyes and shot to her feet. "Just forget it."

"Hold on," he said, pulling her back down to the straw
bale. "I'm not sure I'm the right person," he said, add-
ing quickly before she tried to hightail it again, "but I'll
help you if I can."

"You do know *something* about women, don't you?"

He smiled. "Something."

Her blue eyes pleaded with him. "Well, then help me. I want people to see me as a…woman."

Oh, man, Slim. He told himself that she wouldn't be here asking him—of all people—unless she was desperate. "Okay," he said uncomfortably. "Don't take this wrong, but it could be the way you dress."

She looked down at her clothes. "What's wrong with the way I dress?"

"Well, for starters, you look like a boy. You have any of your own clothes? Or is everything you own handed down from your brothers."

Her jaw tightened. "I like roomy shirts."

He nodded. Either she was wearing a tight-fitting sports bra under one of her brother's western shirts and canvas jacket or she had no boobs and didn't even need a bra. "Don't you ever look at magazines? Or try makeup and fixing your hair different?"

"*Of course.* I looked like a streetwalker!" She let out a half sob, half laugh. A couple of big tears shimmered in her blue eyes. She ducked her head again, obviously embarrassed as she made a swipe at them. "I need one of those makeovers like on TV."

He shook his head. "You don't need a makeover. You just need a little help. Look, if you're serious about this—"

"I am."

"—then I'll help you," he said with a groan.

The relief in her face made him smile. Then realization hit him. What did he know about girl stuff? Clearly more than Dusty, which wasn't much. Fortunately, he knew someone he could get to help them, a young woman he'd dated a few times who owned a boutique in Sheridan.

"We'll go down to Sheridan."

She stood as if ready to go right now.

He wondered what the hurry was. "Can you go this afternoon?"

She nodded, looking determined and a little worried.

"I'll pick you up after lunch."

She launched herself at him. He hugged her back in surprise and then she was racing toward the barn door. He smiled, thinking he didn't see any reason for her to change. Personally, he liked her just fine as a tomboy.

Over her shoulder, she called back, "If you tell a soul about this—"

"It will be our little secret," he said, getting up to follow her to the barn door. No chance he was going to tell anyone.

She swung up onto her horse outside the barn and cut her eyes at him. "It had better be our secret, Ty Coltrane, or you will regret the day you ever met me."

No chance of that, he thought as he watched her ride away. He'd never met anyone like Slim. She was one hell of a horsewoman. And she had spunk and something he couldn't put his finger on. Something that had always drawn him to her. Yep, as far as he was concerned, there was nothing about Dusty McCall that needed to be made over.

As she disappeared over the horizon, he turned back to the barn. A bad feeling settled over him as he thought again of Rasmussen's visit and Dusty's.

What *had* Dusty been doing in the corral last night after the rodeo?

Asa had known the day would come when he would have to tell his family. Telling them he was dying seemed easy compared to the really bad news. Telling Shelby took ever ounce of strength he had left in him.

"Remember Charley Rankin?" he asked.

She frowned. "The two of you owned that land together to the north."

Asa nodded. "Charley helped me buy up some other prime acreage that is now part of the main ranch. I bought the land from him when we dissolved our partnership."

"That must have been when Charley married and moved back east."

Asa nodded, realizing not for the first time that Shelby had kept close track of his life and the kids all the years he'd forced her out of their lives. It added to the weight of his guilt to know that she'd been watching them all from the sidelines, staying involved in their lives as much as she could. As much as he'd allowed her.

He met her eyes, wanting desperately to tell her how sorry he was but never able to find words to encompass the extent of that sorrow—of that regret.

Ashamed, he looked away.

"I heard Charley and his wife were both killed when his private plane crashed," she said when he didn't go on.

He nodded and plunged in, needing to get the words out before he didn't have the courage. "When our partnership was dissolved, I didn't have enough cash to buy him out, so I signed an agreement giving him the mineral rights to the ranch."

She let out a small gasp, her eyes widening with alarm as the enormity of what he'd done hit her.

"It was collateral, nothing more," he continued, not wanting to drag it out. "Just before he was killed, I mailed the last of the land payments. Charley had never cashed the checks. He didn't need the money, so I guess it was his way of helping me out. With the last check, I also sent him a legal form to sign that would void the mineral rights agreement."

He looked at Shelby. He could tell by her expression that she knew what was coming.

"Charley and his wife had a son," she said. "Reese. He must be about twenty-five by now."

Asa nodded, figuring Shelby also knew that Reese had never gotten along with his father and been in trouble since he was young. "He found all the paperwork on the deal after his father's death, including all the uncashed checks and the unsigned document that would have voided the agreement."

"Oh, Asa," she breathed.

He nodded. "Thanks to the discovery of coal-bed methane, the mineral rights on the ranch are worth fifty times what I paid Charley for the land."

"He plans to drill wells on the ranch." Shelby covered her mouth with her hand, eyes welling with tears. She knew better than anyone how much this ranch meant to him.

She pushed herself up from the table and went to the window, her back to him. "There has to be some way to stop him."

"Even if I mortgaged the entire ranch, there wouldn't be enough capital to buy him off. He always resented Charley. Charley's dead. But Charley's best friend is still alive. At least for a while."

She turned from the sink and sat down at the table again. Reaching across the table, she covered his weathered old hand with her still pale pretty one. "Have you told J.T.?"

J.T. was their oldest, the one who had been running

the ranch along with Dusty the past few years. Asa shook his head. "Other than my lawyer, you're the only one who knows."

"You have to tell them."

He turned his hand so hers was enclosed in his rough weathered one. He squeezed it gently as he looked at her. He'd been so angry at her for coming back from the dead the way she had. Breaking their agreement without notice. Just showing up at the door. Giving him no choice but to let her stay because she'd learned about the cancer.

Then when it had gone into remission, she'd stayed, refusing to leave him again. He'd been angry at her, not wanting her pity. Not wanting her to come home only to watch him waste away and die.

Now he wondered what he would have done if she hadn't come back. How he and the children would have gotten through this without her here. How could he ever tell her how much it meant to him? How much she meant to him?

"You have to tell the children," she said again.

He nodded. The cancer was no longer in remission. The letter had only confirmed what he'd already known.

He drew his hand back and stood. His eyes burned at just the thought of leaving her and the children with the mess he'd made. "I need a little more time."

It was so like Shelby not to say that he might not have more time. "Take all you need."

He smiled ruefully at that. He would need another lifetime and even then, he doubted it would be enough time to undo all the mistakes he'd made in this one.

Instead, he had a few weeks. If he was lucky.

Chapter 6

Letty Arnold stared at the caller ID as the phone rang again. She'd been waiting for this call all her life. She just hadn't known it.

Her hand shook as she picked up. She crossed her fingers and closed her eyes. "Hello?"

"Ms. Arnold?"

She held her breath, squeezing her eyes tighter.

"This is Hal Branson with Branson Investigations."

She recognized his voice from the day she'd hired him. The same day she'd found out from the sheriff that she'd been illegally adopted.

The truth about her adoption had only come out because of an investigation involving a local doctor. It seemed he'd taken babies from what he considered unworthy parents, telling them that their infant had died. Then he had given the babies to couples desperately wanting a child, couples he considered more worthy.

The doctor had handled everything, including birth certificates that made it appear the new mother had given birth to the baby. If he hadn't told the sheriff about her in a deathbed confession, she might never have known the truth. "Did you find my birth mother?"

"Maybe," Hal Branson said.

Letty opened her eyes. *"Maybe?"*

"I found a woman who gave birth to a baby at the clinic where the doctor worked on the day you were supposedly born." He seemed to hesitate. "She was an unwed mother." Just the kind of woman the doctor would have considered unworthy. "I don't want to get your hopes up. The only way to be certain of your maternity will be DNA tests."

He'd already told her all of this. Why was he telling her this again?

"Keep in mind that the date of your birth could be incorrect," he continued. "You could have been a home birth. There are just too many factors. And with the doctor not keeping any records of the adoptions—"

"Mr. Branson—"

"Hal." He sounded young and she wondered how old he was. For all she knew, she'd hired a kid. That's what she got for not taking care of this in person. Not that she hadn't checked out Branson Investigations on the Internet to make sure it was licensed, bonded and reputable.

She hadn't wanted anyone in Antelope Flats to know that she was one of the crazy doctor's "babies." And she hadn't had the patience that day to drive clear to Billings to find a P.I. It was also easier to talk about this over the phone rather than in person.

She knew she shouldn't feel this way, but it was embarrassing not knowing who her parents were. Not knowing who *she* was.

And she had to know. She'd always suspected that she didn't really belong to the Arnolds. It wasn't only their advanced ages and the fact that they were more like grandparents. She'd never looked like either of them or acted like them or even really understood them. The Arnolds were quiet, solitary, stable and bland. Both were short and round.

Letty was thin as a stick, with a wide toothy smile, and had been all cowgirl from the time she could walk. Neither of her parents had ever ridden a horse in their lives and didn't like rodeos. And while both of the Arnolds had light brown hair, Letty had a wild mane of hair red as a flame, a face full of freckles and emerald green eyes. Both Arnolds had brown eyes.

The truth? She'd been relieved when they'd retired and left her the motel so they could move to Arizona. Not that they hadn't been good to her. She *loved* them.

That's why she felt guilty about her feelings. They were the only parents she'd known and she felt as if she were disrespecting them by even looking for her birth mother.

"Are you still there?" Hal asked.

"Tell me how I can find this woman you think might be my birth mother." Letty unconsciously glanced toward her reflection in the mirror on the wall. She had to know who she was. No matter the outcome.

"Her name is Florence Hubbard. She goes by Flo."

Letty heard the slight catch in his voice and braced herself.

"She…plays in a rock 'n' roll band," Hal said. "It's called Triple-X-Files. I understand they play some rock, but mostly heavy metal music."

She could hear his distaste and smiled. "What kind of music do you like?"

"What?" He sounded more than surprised, maybe even embarrassed. "Country," he said almost sheepishly.

Her smile widened. "Me, too. So where does this X band play?"

"Well...there's a three-day rock concert next weekend during a fair in Bozeman. Triple-X-Files will be there. If you like, I could e-mail you all the information. You can camp near the concert or stay in one of the local motels."

"Thanks, you've been very thorough."

"It's what you're paying me to do." Again, he sounded embarrassed.

"You'll send me a bill?" she said, thinking this might be the last time they talked if Flo Hubbard really was her mother.

"Ms. Arnold—"

"Letty."

"Letty, if I were you, I wouldn't go to meet this woman alone. Do you have a friend or relative who could go with you?"

She smiled ruefully at the relative part. None who lived nearby, none she was all that close to even before she found out they weren't blood-related. She had no one who could go with her. Except Dusty McCall, her best friend.

But she wasn't ready to tell even Dusty about this yet. Dusty knew something had been bothering her. Letty wished she could confide in her friend. She wasn't even sure what was holding her back. Maybe the need to find out who she was before she told the world that she was one of the babies the doctor had stolen.

"If you would like, I could meet you there," Hal said

guardedly. "I mean, I wouldn't mind. In fact, I think it might be good to have someone who isn't involved in the situation there with you."

To her surprise, she heard herself say, "Would you?"

"Of course." He sounded relieved, almost excited, as if he wanted to see this through to the end. "Just tell me when and where to meet you."

They worked out a plan and she found herself torn between her anxiety at the thought of meeting her possible birth mother and her curiosity about Hal Branson as she hung up.

For a moment, she thought about calling Dusty, telling her the news. She hesitated, feeling guilty. But the truth was, Dusty hadn't been interested in much of anything lately except Boone Rasmussen.

Letty told herself that wasn't fair. She knew Dusty would just think she was jealous. But it was something else that bothered her about Dusty's obsession with Boone. A fear that she might lose her best friend. But not to love.

Boone Rasmussen stormed into Monte Edgewood's ranch house, letting the door slam behind him. Hadn't he known Coltrane was going to be a problem? The Coltranes of the world were always a problem.

The ten-mile drive from Coltrane's ranch hadn't calmed him in the least. He'd driven too fast on the way to Monte's, reckless from his anger. How dare Coltrane butt into his business?

Coltrane had everything Boone had ever wanted—one hell of a ranch, money, standing in the community—and all of it handed to him on a silver platter when his old man died.

Boone hadn't been so lucky. His father hadn't left him a thing. In fact, he'd had to pay out of his own pocket to have the old son of a bitch cremated. He smiled bitterly at the memory. He should have let the state deal with G.O. Rasmussen's sorry remains.

But Boone had gotten the last laugh. He'd spread that bastard's ashes over the local cow lot. Ashes to ashes, so to speak. It was little consolation for the years his old man had worked him, paying him with biting criticism and the back of his hand, but it was something.

The difference in their lives alone made Boone hate Coltrane. But now the horse rancher was snooping into the wrong cowboy's life. No way was he going to let Coltrane ruin everything he'd worked so hard for.

Monte looked up from the kitchen table. Boone saw the older man's expression and felt his stomach clench. Something *else* had happened. Something to do with Devil's Tornado? Or did this have something to do with Coltrane?

Monte lowered his big head as if in prayer. "I guess you heard about Clayton," he said with a wag of his head.

Boone tried not to let Monte see his relief. So this was only about that ranting old drunk bull rider. He thought for a moment of pretending he hadn't heard, but everyone in town was talking about Clayton's death.

"I heard," Boone said, drawing up a chair at the table and sitting down, trying to mirror Monte's sorrowful expression. "Did you hear what happened?" Monte had more reliable sources than Boone did.

"His body was found in a ravine south of here. Guess he missed a curve," Monte said.

"Probably blind drunk."

Monte gave him a hard look, disappointment shining

in his light eyes. "Shouldn't speak ill of the dead, son. Clayton had his share of demons like all of us, but he was a good man." He reached across the table to drop a big palm on Boone's shoulder and gave it a squeeze as he smiled sadly. It was clear to both of them that Boone would never be the man Monte had hoped.

But Monte refused to give up on him.

And that was what Boone was counting on.

With each passing day, though, the stakes got higher and higher. So did the danger of being caught.

Sierra sashayed into the room. "What's going on? You look like you lost your best friend."

Monte gave her an indulgent smile and motioned for her. She stepped into his open arms, stroking his hair as she looked across at Boone.

"A bull rider I admired died in a car accident," Monte told her. "Clayton T. Brooks. He was quite the rodeo star in his day."

"That's too bad," Sierra said, her gaze heating up as her eyes locked with Boone's.

Boone pushed to his feet. "Need anything from town?"

Monte shook his head, dropping his gaze again to the table as Sierra stepped away from him. He looked old and tired, and more upset over Clayton than Boone would have expected. It made Boone wonder how well the two had known each other. And if that was a problem he should be worrying about.

He shoved that worry aside and concentrated on a more immediate one. Judging from her size, it had been a cowgirl he'd seen in the empty corral next to the bucking horses last night after the rodeo. A lucky cowgirl who'd somehow escaped being trampled by the bucking horses.

Coltrane had fished her out of the corral. Boone had

seen the two head for the parking lot. Then he'd lost sight of them. At first, Boone had been worried that she'd over-heard him and Lamar arguing with Waylon Dobbs. That alone would have been a loose end he couldn't afford.

But he'd seen the cowgirl reach down in the horse cor-ral and pick up something from the ground. His hand had gone to his jacket pocket. The syringe was gone! It must have fallen out of his pocket when he'd climbed over the corral fence earlier.

He'd seen her put it in her purse! It made no sense. Why had she been there in the first place? Why put a used sy-ringe into her purse?

"Pick me up some ice cream if you're going to town," Sierra said.

"I'll buy you some ice cream, sugar," Monte spoke up.

Boone glanced back at Monte, trying to read his ex-pression. Monte met his gaze and for an instant, Boone thought he saw something he didn't like flicker in the older man's gaze. Just his imagination?

Well, there would be plenty of time to deal with Monte later—if it came to that.

And Sierra too, he thought stealing a look at her as he left.

Dusty paced on the porch, mentally kicking herself for asking for Ty's help. What had she been thinking? Surely she wasn't *that* desperate.

At first, all she saw was the dust on the county road. Her heart lodged in her throat as Ty turned onto the road to the ranch. She would tell him she'd changed her mind. Didn't women do that all the time?

She groaned, reminding herself why she *was* so desperate for a makeover to begin with. But desperate enough to see this through with Ty, of all people?

He pulled up in the yard and she ran out, jerked open the passenger side door of his pickup and jumped in before she could change her mind—or he could get out.

He looked over at her and slammed his partially opened door.

"What?" she asked seeing his annoyed expression.

"You might have given me a chance to open your door for you," he said.

She rolled her eyes. "You have to be kidding. Does anyone do that anymore?"

"I do when I come by to pick up a woman," he said, sounding indignant.

She cut her eyes at him. "Why?"

"Because it's polite."

"I can open my own door."

"That isn't the point," he said as he shifted the pickup into gear and started out the gate. "Look, think of dating as a game between men and women with certain rituals involved. There are steps a man and woman go through in the relationship. Certain roles each sex plays."

She groaned. "Why does it have to be so complicated? Why can't we just cut to the chase? Be honest? Tell the person how we feel? Have them tell us how they feel? And if we both feel the same…"

Ty laughed and shook his head. "Sorry, Slim, but it doesn't work that way. It's the anticipation, not knowing what's going to happen, that adds to the excitement."

She thought about Boone. She wanted to know what was going to happen. She couldn't stand the suspense.

"It's all part of the mating ritual. You just need to get into your role."

Dusty scoffed. "This role you're talking about. Tell me it doesn't mean I have to act helpless because I'm never going to be one of *those* women," she informed him haughtily. "So if that's what I have to do, forget it." She could feel him studying her out of the corner of his eye as he drove.

He laughed. "No, you're never going to be one of those. Lucky for you, there are men who actually like strong independent women. But no man may be ready for *you*."

She punched his arm but laughed with him, then turned to gaze out at the countryside. Was Boone ready for her? White billowing clouds scudded through the summer-blue sky overhead, casting pale shadows over the red rock cliffs, the silken ponderosa pines and tall, dark-green grasses. The land stretched to the horizon. McCall land.

Dusty welled with pride, never tiring of the landscape. This was her home. Her mother and father hadn't understood why nothing could dislodge her from the isolated ranch.

A few months ago, Shelby had cornered her, questioning her about her future. "You need to go to college," her mother had insisted. "You need a good education."

"I have a good education," Dusty had snapped. "Not that you would know, but I graduated from high school early and have been taking college courses for years online. I'll have at least two degrees, one in business and another in agriculture by this time next year."

"I'm aware of that," Shelby said tightly. "But it's not the same as actually attending a university, meeting other people your age, broadening your horizons."

Dusty had laughed. "Look at my horizons," she'd said

widening her arms to encompass the ranch. "They're plenty broad."

"What do you have to say?" Shelby had asked turning to her husband.

Asa had studied Dusty for a long moment. "Dusty's always known her own mind. Much like her mother," he'd added, his gaze shifting to Shelby. "I've never been able to change either of your minds. And God knows, I've tried."

Dusty had seen the look that passed between her parents. There was little doubt they had a secret, one she and her brothers obviously weren't privy to.

She'd never regretted her decision to stay on the ranch. Her father had given her some acreage to the south and told her she could build a house on it someday if she wanted to—now, or when she got married. Unless the man she married wanted to live elsewhere.

She had laughed. "I wouldn't marry anyone who wanted to leave here. Don't you know me better than that?"

Her father had frowned. "You haven't been in love yet. Love changes everything."

She had scoffed at the idea. But now as she watched the land blur by, she thought of Boone Rasmussen. Was this love? She felt all jittery inside. Her heart beat out of control half the time. And it made her unsure about everything. Especially herself. Was that love?

Ty turned onto the highway. Dusty's shoulder bag rolled off the seat, hitting the floor with a loud thump.

"What have you got in there? Bricks?"

"Stuff. A bridle I need to get repaired. Books," Dusty said scooping the heavy bag up from the floor. "Sometimes I want to read when I have to go into town on errands for the ranch. There's nothing wrong with reading."

He laughed. "I didn't say there was." They passed through Antelope Flats, the small Montana town quickly disappearing behind them.

Dusty reached over and turned on the radio, not surprised to find it tuned to a country-western station. Leaning back, she watched the willow-choked Tongue River twist its way through the valley as she and Ty wound south toward Wyoming, not wanting to talk. She had a lot on her mind.

"Did you find out who that was who followed you home last night?" Ty said reaching over to turn down the radio.

She shook her head, the memory still making her uneasy. "Just a dark-colored pickup. The driver stopped at the ranch gate and sat there with his headlights out for a while. The next time I looked, he was gone. It was probably nothing." She wished she could believe that.

She saw Ty's concerned expression. The last thing she wanted was Ty Coltrane keeping an eye on her. He'd done that her whole life.

"Any chance it could have been Boone Rasmussen?" he asked.

The question took her by surprise. "Why would *he* follow me?"

Ty looked over at her. "Good question. Maybe because you were spying on him last night in the horse corral. I heard him open that gate. It was no accident that you were almost trampled by those bucking horses."

She stared at him in shock, remembering the sound of the gate latch being pulled back, the gate swinging open.

"That's crazy. Why would Boone want to hurt *me*? He doesn't even know who I am."

Ty lifted a brow. "Maybe. Or maybe he thought you overhead something you shouldn't have last night."

The thought chilled her. "I didn't hear *anything*."

"But maybe Boone doesn't know that. Just be careful, okay?" His tone was relaxed enough, but she could tell he was anything but. "Stay away from Boone Rasmussen."

She cut her eyes at Ty. Did he know the real reason she was in that corral last night? Was he just trying to keep her away from Boone? A thought struck her. Was it possible Ty was…jealous? She rejected that explanation instantly. No, Ty was just playing big brother like he always had.

"You never told me why *you* were there last night," she said. Did it have something to do with Boone and why Boone had stopped by Ty's ranch this morning?

From the barn, she hadn't been able to hear what the two had been saying to each other, but she could darn well tell by reading their body language that they'd been at odds over something. Could it have been about *her*?

"Well?" she demanded when Ty didn't answer her.

"Settle down, Slim. What do you want me to say? That I saw your truck was still in the lot and figured you were in some kind of trouble, as usual? That when I heard arguing, I just assumed you were at the center of it?"

She angled a look at him. He didn't take his eyes off the road making her suspect there was more to it.

Didn't he realize that trying to keep a secret from her was like throwing a rodeo bullfighter at a bull? Especially since whatever Ty was hiding had something to do with Boone Rasmussen.

Boone wouldn't have purposely opened the corral gate. But she had a flash of memory: the expression on Boone's face when he'd reached through the chute toward

Devil's Tornado. She shivered, hugging herself. Ty turned on the heat in the pickup, but this chill went bone-deep.

If Boone had opened that corral gate, then it had been to scare her away. But then she had to wonder what he'd been arguing about with the two other men that he'd feared she'd overheard.

Just north of Antelope Flats, Boone Rasmussen turned onto a dirt road that wound down to the Tongue River Reservoir. The beat-up, older model truck and camper were parked next to the water near the dam.

As Boone got out, he saw no sign of life, but a pile of crushed beer cans glinted in the sun outside the camper. He swore under his breath as he pounded on the door and waited. Inside, he could hear rustling. "It's me," he said.

The door opened. Lamar Nichols squinted down at him. He held a Colt .45 at his side. Lamar was almost as wide as he was tall, a burly cowboy with a smoker's gravelly voice, dull brown eyes that could bore a hole through hardwood and hands large and strong enough to throttle a grown man.

"What the hell time is it?" Lamar demanded with a scowl. He wore nothing but a pair of worn jeans, his furry barrel chest bare like his feet.

"Almost two in the damned afternoon," Boone snapped. An odor wafted out of the camper. The damp small space smelled of mold, stale beer and B.O. The last thing Boone wanted was to go inside the camper with Lamar. He motioned to the weathered wooden picnic table outside next to the camper.

"Give me a minute," Lamar said and stepped back inside, closing the door.

Boone took a seat at the table facing the lake. A breeze

rippled the silken green surface of the water. A few fishing boats bobbed along the edge of the red bluffs on the other side.

"So what's up?" Lamar said behind him.

Boone turned at once, never comfortable with Lamar behind him. "Clayton T. Brooks' body was found in a ravine."

"Where else would you expect a drunk has-been bull rider to end up?" Lamar said, making the picnic table groan under this weight as he sat down across from Boone. He'd put on a flannel shirt and wet down his dark hair—hair the same color as Boone's. Other than hair color, Boone had little else in common with his older half brother.

"That it?" Lamar asked rubbing a hand over his grizzly unshaven jaw, his eyes never leaving Boone's face.

"Monte's taking Devil's Tornado to the Bozeman rodeo."

Lamar nodded. "No big surprise there. He needs that bull. You've got him right where you want him." His beady eyes narrowed to slits. "What about last night?"

"I told you I'd take care of it." He didn't want Lamar going off half-cocked and ruining everything.

"You talk to Coltrane? He tell you what the hell he was doing back by Devil's Tornado's trailer?" Lamar asked.

"Said he was just curious about the bull. But he doesn't know anything." At least Boone hoped to hell that was true.

"You sure about that?" Lamar challenged. "What was he doing nosing around, then?"

Boone looked past him to the lake, his jaw tightening. "Coltrane isn't the only one interested in the bull. Everyone's curious. We just have to be careful."

Lamar cut his eyes at him. "There was someone else there last night. Someone over by the horse corrals."

Boone had hoped that Lamar hadn't seen the cowgirl.

"Coltrane tell you who the cowboy was with him?" Lamar asked.

Lamar thought it was a cowboy in the corral? Obviously he hadn't gotten a good look. Boone tried not to show his relief. Nor did he mention that asking Coltrane about the cowgirl would have been stupid. Lamar had been told too many times in his life he was stupid. He didn't take it well anymore.

Nor was Boone going to tell his half brother that he'd tracked down the drivers of both vehicles that had been in the lot last night after Coltrane left. One led him to the Lariat Motel in Antelope Flats. The other to Asa Mc-Call's Sundown Ranch.

"You don't think it was Monte, do you?" Lamar asked.

Boone sighed. "Trust me, it wasn't Monte."

"Yeah, well, he might think you're the greatest thing since sliced bread, but I wouldn't trust him," Lamar said picking at his ear with a thick finger. Lamar didn't trust anyone.

Boone pushed himself to his feet. "Don't worry about last night. You just take care of your end. We're going to Bozeman. Three-day rodeo. I'm thinking we might throw in a couple more bulls. See how they do."

Lamar gave him a lopsided crooked-tooth grin.

"I just want them to look promising," Boone said. "Nothing like Devil's Tornado. He's our star. But last night in Sheridan… Let's try not to let him be quite that wild, okay?"

Lamar's expression made it clear he thought Boone was making a mistake. "You're the boss."

Boone studied his half brother, hoping he didn't forget that. He didn't need to worry about keeping Lamar in line. He had other worries. Ty Coltrane. And the cowgirl who had something that belonged to him. A syringe he had to get back.

Chapter 7

Ty Coltrane looked over at Dusty as he slowed the pickup on the outskirts of Sheridan, Wyoming.

He couldn't help worrying about her, even though he figured she was probably right. Rasmussen hadn't even seemed to notice her this morning at the ranch. He couldn't have known she was in the horse corral last night. Maybe it *had* been an accident. And maybe it hadn't been Rasmussen who'd followed her home last night.

But warning Dusty about Boone Rasmussen was still a good idea. Ty's instincts told him that Rasmussen was dangerous. And up to *something*. He just hoped to hell that it really didn't have anything to do with Dusty.

Ty parked in front of the Sheridan Boutique. Dusty shot a look at the front window and the mannequin outfitted in a skimpy cocktail dress. He could see her already digging in her heels.

"Here's the first rule," he said quickly. "You do as I say, or I take you back to the ranch right now."

She shot him a look. He could see her struggling with the need to tell him what she thought while being forced to bite her tongue.

He grinned at her. "Sit," he ordered and got out to open her door.

She scowled at him, but let him open her door. "Oh, I get it. Guys want to open your door just so they can look at your butt, huh?"

He laughed as she swayed her hips as she walked away from him. "Now you're starting to get the idea," he called as he slammed the pickup door and turned to find her waiting for him outside the shop.

Her head was tilted back, the western hat on her head no longer shading her lightly freckled face. In that instant, with the sun shining down on her, she looked like a goddess, capable of ruling the world. Certainly capable of stealing a cowboy's heart.

"Okay, let's get this over with," he said shaking off the image. "Go into that dressing room. I'll have clothes brought to you." She gave him a narrowed look. "This was your idea. You wanted my help," he reminded her as they entered the shop.

She clutched at his arm. "Promise you won't make me look silly?" she whispered. Her eyes were big and blue, as clear and sparkling as a Montana summer day.

He would have promised her anything right then. He nodded. "I promise. Now get in there."

The moment she disappeared behind the dressing room curtain, Ty looked around for Angela. She came out of the back, smiling as she recognized him.

"Ty," she said, surprise and what sounded like pleasure in her voice. She was an attractive twenty-five-year-old, tall, slim, with big brown eyes and hair the color of an autumn leaf.

"Hi." He felt a stab of guilt. He liked Angela. They'd dated a few times. He hadn't seen much of her since then, though. He'd been busy at the ranch, but he wished now that he'd called her.

Angela was waiting, no doubt wondering what he was doing in a women's clothing shop if not there to see her.

"How long do I have to wait in here?" came Dusty's plaintive voice from the dressing room.

"Hold your horses," he called back.

Angela glanced toward the closed curtain of the dressing room, then at Ty. Her expression altered, as if it were all suddenly clear. "Your girlfriend?"

Ty hoped to hell Dusty hadn't heard that. He took Angela's arm and led her out of earshot of the dressing room. "I'm just helping out a friend. She needs everything from the ground up. Feminine stuff."

Angela nodded as Dusty stuck her head out and Ty shooed her back into the dressing room.

"It isn't what you think," he said to Angela.

She chuckled. "When a man says that, it's exactly what a woman thinks."

"Not in this case. Dusty's just a neighbor girl."

Angela nodded, clearly not buying a word of it.

"She asked me to help her. She needs some girl clothes and I haven't a clue—"

"Let's have a look at this...*girl*," Angela said, heading for the dressing room. Ty followed her as she drew back the curtain a little and stared at the fully clothed Dusty McCall and smiled, as if relieved. "Hi. I'm Angela. Let me see what I can find for you."

Dusty looked from Angela to Ty, a smug knowing glance that said she knew at once what his relationship was with the saleswoman. He closed the curtain on her look and wandered over to a rack of blouses. He found one the color of Dusty's eyes.

"What do you think about this one?" he asked Angela.

She cocked her head at him. "You have good taste. It matches her eyes." She pulled out a pair of slacks to go with the blouse. "Dresses?"

He nodded. "Nothing too…" He made a motion with his hand. "She's just a kid."

"Right," Angela said with a note of sarcasm and headed for the dress rack.

"Also, I promised her I'd help with her hair and makeup," Ty said quietly as he followed Angela to the back of the store.

She shot up an eyebrow.

"Exactly. I know nothing about either. Any suggestions?"

"Maxie next door at the beauty shop." Angela pulled down a half-dozen dresses and looked over at him. "I suppose she will need lingerie as well."

Angela moved to the lingerie and held up a black lacy bra and panties. He nodded wondering if he looked as ill at ease as he felt. Dusty in black lace? He didn't want to think about it any more than he did the red silk teddy Angela held up. This was Slim, the girl he'd teased and tormented, trailed after and picked up from the dirt. Recently.

"Why don't you go down to the Mint Bar and have a beer," Angela suggested, seeing his discomfort. "I'll send her down when she's done." His instant relief made Angela laugh. "How did you get roped into this, anyway?"

"Like I said. She's a friend and I guess there wasn't anyone else."

Angela smiled, looking unconvinced.

"I really appreciate this," he said. "Maybe you and I could have lunch one of these days," he suggested.

"Maybe," she said, but something in her tone said there was little chance that was going to happen.

Sheepishly, he sneaked out the door as Angela headed for the dressing room and Dusty. He couldn't get out of the place fast enough and he did have some chores he could do before getting the beer.

He was too antsy to sit still, anyway. The way he figured it, if Dusty didn't kill him when she saw the clothes Angela had picked out, then Asa McCall or one of the McCall boys would for sure when they heard about this.

The good news was that Dusty wouldn't ever ask for his help again. That thought stopped him cold. He couldn't imagine not having Slim around.

He told himself that was because he'd always been around to protect her. Like a fifth older brother. And Dusty needed him around. Maybe especially now, he thought, frowning, wondering why she'd suddenly decided she needed a makeover.

Letty was surprised when she heard someone ring the bell in the motel office and realized she hadn't locked the door.

The No Vacancy sign was still up outside. She hadn't had time to take it down yet. The housekeepers were busy cleaning the rooms and since it was pretty early for anyone to be checking in...

If it was anyone she knew, they would have called out

to her and then come on back through the narrow hallway that attached the motel office to the house.

She frowned as she stopped what she was doing—packing. Excited and anxious about the coming weekend, she'd already started packing, thinking she might camp out, as Hal Branson had suggested. In case she stayed. Sleeping bag, tent, cooler. She really needed to trade off the VW Beetle her parents had bought her for high school graduation and get herself a pickup truck.

The idea appealed to her, even though she knew it would shock her parents—that is, the Arnolds, she amended, who felt a young woman shouldn't drive a truck.

As she passed the hall mirror, she glanced at her image again. Her bright red, long, curly, unruly hair was pulled back into a ponytail, her pale skin sprayed with reddish freckles, her eyes green, her mouth too large and filled with too many teeth.

She wondered what kind of car her birth mother drove. Would the woman look like her? Or was this the first of a long line of wild goose chases?

"There is a possibility that you were stolen from your birth mother and might never know the truth," Sheriff Cash McCall had told her when the doctor who'd done the illegal adoptions had confessed that she was one of the babies involved.

Stolen. Or maybe her mother hadn't wanted her. She couldn't help but think about Dusty's mother giving her up to Asa McCall when Dusty was a baby. Letty sighed. Maybe she and Dusty had more in common than either had known.

Letty told herself that she would tell her friend *everything* as soon as Letty herself knew the truth. But first she had to know who her birth parents were, what blood ran through her veins, what relatives she might have out there somewhere. She'd always envied Dusty her four brothers. A brother, or even a sister, would be cool.

Maybe even a mother named Flo who played in a heavy metal band. She cringed at the thought, glad Hal would be going with her to meet the woman.

The bell in the office rang again. She'd been hoping whoever it was would just go away. No such luck.

As she headed for the office, she knew part of her problem was that she'd resented the fact that her "adoptive" parents had lied to her. She'd argued with them on the phone about it recently, which only made her feel more guilty. But how had her shy, couldn't-tell-a-lie-if-her-life-depended-on-it mother managed to keep such a secret? Or, for that matter, covered up the fact that she was never really pregnant?

By isolating herself from everyone, Letty thought as the bell in the office dinged again. Her adoptive parents had been standoffish, not mixing with the community at large. Now she knew why. All to hide the biggest lie of all—Leticia herself.

As Letty came down the hallway toward the motel office, she saw the broad shoulders of a man standing with his back to the counter. He wore a gray Stetson on his dark head. Even before she saw his face, she felt a premonition quake through, just a flash of danger, fear and ultimately pain.

Boone Rasmussen turned, his dark eyes fixing on her. "Leticia Arnold?"

Dusty stared at the tiny red silk bra in her hand. "You have got to be kidding." She felt like she did the first time she and Letty tried on bras. How humiliating. She'd gotten all wrapped up in the stupid thing and Letty had had to help her out of it.

Angela handed in more clothing. Dusty took it, thanked her and made sure the curtain was closed all the way before she slipped the sports bra over her head and looped the cool red silk around her, fastening it, then drawing it up over her breasts and slipping the straps over her shoulders.

The effect shocked her. She'd never owned anything but sports bras. They worked better for horseback riding.

She pulled off her boots and jeans and the same style of cotton underwear she'd worn since she was six and drew on the skimpy red silk panties. She was glad Letty wasn't here. She would have been rolling on the floor with laughter.

But the truth was, the cool red silk felt…good. Maybe too good. And she looked…okay. Better than okay. She crossed her arms over her chest, a little embarrassed. The bra made her look stacked! And the thin silk was so *revealing*!

She reached for one of the dresses and slipped it on over her head. The lightweight material dropped over her like a whisper, making her suck in her breath as she looked in the mirror.

She let out a laugh of surprise, quickly covering her mouth. That was *not* her in the mirror. No way. Well, the head was still hers, the face, the hair—but the rest…

Angela slid a couple pairs of high heels under the door and some strappy sandals.

Dusty snatched up the sandals in a pale blue that matched the color of the dress. She slipped them onto her feet—feet that hadn't seen anything but cowboy boots since she was three. Flipping her long braid up and brushing her bangs out of her eyes, she stared at herself in the mirror. The partial transformation left her speechless.

In the mirror, she saw Angela peek through the curtain behind her. "How are you doing?"

Dusty could only nod, filled with a strange mixture of having a lump in the throat and being embarrassed.

"Stunning," Angela said and gave her a smile and thumbs up.

Dusty blushed.

"Maxie next door said to send you over and she'd show you how to do your makeup and your hair," Angela said. "This for a party?"

Dusty shook her head. "I just need a change."

Angela nodded. "Who's the guy? Never mind, I think I already know. Ty Coltrane is a lucky man." She ducked back out before Dusty could set her straight.

Dusty stood in the front of the mirror, hating to take the dress off. She tried on the others, picked three, and put the blue dress back on. "Is it all right if I wear this now?" she asked Angela when the clerk returned. She handed her the extra lingerie, the blue blouse and black slacks and two other dresses. "I'll take these, too, and the sandals. And could you box up my boots and clothing I wore in?"

Dusty took another look in the mirror, hating to admit that Ty might have been right. Maybe it *was* the clothes. She couldn't wait to get the rest of her makeover.

It surprised her, but she was anxious to see Ty's reaction. As soon as she got her makeup and hair done and figured out how to walk in these sandals. If the new her passed the Ty Coltrane test, then she would be ready for Boone. But even as she thought about it, she wondered

if she would ever be ready for Boone Rasmussen. Or if
she wanted to be. Something about Boone still drew her
and at the same time repelled her. If he really had opened
that gate last night...

Well, she would find out for herself soon enough.

Letty stopped short of the motel counter as her gaze
met Boone Rasmussen's dark one. She didn't like or trust
him, and she feared it showed in her expression because
his eyes darkened at the mere sight of her.

"Leticia Arnold?" he repeated staring at her as if trying to recognize her.

"Letty," she said out of habit and wished one of the
motel housekeepers would come into the office. Both
housekeepers were only local high school students, but
Letty didn't like being alone with Boone. It was silly.
She could see a housekeeper cart just two doors down.
If she had to scream—

The thought shocked her. What did she think Boone
would do that she would have to scream?

"Have we ever met?" he said looking around the motel
office, down the hallway toward her house, then over his
shoulder to the empty parking lot. Empty except for his
dark green pickup.

She shook her head. "But I know who you are."

He raised a brow. "Really?"

She flushed. "If you're looking to rent a room, check-in
isn't until one."

He let out a deep chuckle. "I don't want a motel room."
He glanced around again, making her nervous. "I wanted
to talk to you about last night. After the rodeo." He looked
down the hallway again, toward her house. "Is there some
place we could sit down?"

Why would Boone want to talk to *her* about last night? No way was she going to ask him into her house. "I was just going out to get some lunch." She was a terrible liar and it showed in his expression.

He flashed her a cool smile. "This late? Okay, I could use some lunch."

The last person she wanted to have lunch with was Boone Rasmussen. She'd only said that in hopes that she could cut short whatever he wanted. But clearly, he was determined to talk to her. Better at the café than here.

"We can take my truck," he said, pushing open the motel door and waiting for her. "Don't you need to get your purse?"

She hesitated, then nodded.

"Don't get me wrong," Boone said with that same slick voice. "I'm buying. But most women I know don't go anywhere without their purses."

"I'm not like most women you know," she said without moving.

He chuckled at that. "I'll be in the truck."

This had to be about Dusty. She was doing this for her best friend.

She waited until Boone was behind the wheel of his truck before she went down the hall to her house and grabbed her small leather clutch. As she left, she locked both the house and the office. No one locked their doors in Antelope Flats. But today she was feeling strangely vulnerable.

Boone leaned across the seat as she approached the pickup and shoved open her door. With a sigh, she climbed in and closed the pickup door. *Dusty, you owe me.*

Boone looked over at her, his gaze going to her purse, his lips turning up fractionally before he started the engine.

The older model pickup was covered in mud and manure on the outside, which wasn't that out of the ordinary in a ranch town. But the inside was dirty as well, with dust, a stack of papers on the bench seat between them and empty fast-food containers on the floorboard. The cab interior smelled vaguely of onions and manure. Great combination.

"Sorry about the truck," he said as he glanced over at her again. "The hired help's been using it."

She nodded as he pulled onto the highway and drove through Antelope Flats. She'd expected him to stop at the Longhorn Café, but he drove right past it. She felt her apprehension spike before she realized where he was going. That new In and Out Drive-In outside the city limits, near the soon-to-be completed strip mall.

"Mind if we eat in the truck?" he asked as he pulled into the drive-through. "Sorry, but I don't have a lot of time. Cheeseburger, fries, cola?"

She nodded and he ordered for them both.

The radio was on low. He turned it up. "This is one of my favorites," he said of the country-and-western song playing.

She watched him tap his boot on the floor mat, the palm of his hand keeping time on the steering wheel. He's nervous, she thought. The realization made her even more apprehensive.

They were the only car in line this late. She just wished he'd get to the reason he wanted to talk to her. It certainly hadn't been for her sparkling conversational skills.

Boone took the food shoved through the window and handed her a cola, putting the sack of burgers and fries between them on the stack of papers as he paid, then drove around to the back and parked under a lone tree.

They were hidden from the main road, she noted. No one would see them. Was that the idea?

He turned toward her, reached into the sack and handed her a burger and a package of fries. Her fingers trembled as she unwrapped her burger. Not that he seemed to notice. He wolfed down his burger and fries, tapping his boot to the music as if oblivious of her.

She tried to eat, but every bite seemed to grow in her mouth and didn't want to go down.

Boone finished eating and balled up his wrappers. He rolled down his window and took a three-point shot at a fifty-five-gallon barrel garbage can nearby. He missed. Letty tried to hide her smile as he swore and swung open his door, climbing out to pick it up. She bet he would have left it if she hadn't been with him.

She looked down at her food, took another tentative bite and almost jumped out of her skin when her side door suddenly swung open. She recoiled instinctively.

But Boone only moved her purse aside on the dash where she'd put it to grab some junk mail. The purse fell to the floor, spilling what little was in it. "Sorry," he said, and scooped up the contents and handed it to her before gathering up the garbage on the floorboard and taking it over to the barrel. When he slid behind the wheel again, he seemed almost too quiet.

"So what is it you want to talk to me about?" she asked. "If this is about Dusty—"

"Dusty?" he asked.

"Dusty McCall. My best friend."

He raised a brow and seemed more interested. "She was with you the other night at the rodeo?"

Finally. She knew this had to be about Dusty. She

nodded. "She's the blonde with the big blue eyes. The cute one."

He nodded and rubbed the side of his jaw. "She was the one driving the pickup?" He sounded surprised by that.

"She's a ranch girl. Rides better than half the men around here. Practically ran the ranch after her dad's heart attack."

Boone smiled over at her. "Your best friend, huh?"

Letty blushed. She hadn't meant to go on so.

"So let me guess," he said glancing at her small leather clutch on the dashboard. "Dusty was the one I saw down by the corrals after the rodeo?"

She wasn't going to admit that her very smart, very capable best friend had been chasing after him. She wasn't even sure she should hint that Dusty had a crush on him. But didn't she owe her friend to at least let him know that Dusty was interested?

"She has four brothers, you know," Letty blurted out. "And they are very protective of their sister."

"I've heard of the McCall boys." Boone smiled a slow unnerving smile. "You're a little protective of her as well, it seems." His gaze shifted to her lap. "You've hardly touched your food. You seemed so anxious to have lunch when we were back at the motel."

Letty blushed again. She looked down at her lap and took a bite of her burger, knowing she'd never be able to swallow it. This had been a terrible mistake.

"I'm curious," Boone said. She could feel his eyes on her. "What exactly was your friend doing wandering around the rodeo grounds so late after the rodeo was over?"

Letty practically choked on her burger. "She was looking for you! You told her to meet you there!"

He drew back in surprise, one eyebrow going up. "Where would she get an idea like that? I don't even know her."

Letty stared at him, all kinds of smart retorts galloping through her brain. She reminded herself that her best friend had a crush on this guy. "I guess there was a misunderstanding," she said feebly. But then Letty added, "She was almost trampled by the bucking horses!"

"That corral gate has a bad latch. She was lucky," he said, the words *this time* seeming to hang in the air.

Letty felt a chill and told herself she was overreacting. What if Boone hadn't been talking to Dusty, hadn't told her to meet him, hadn't had anything to do with the latch on the gate? What if she was dead wrong about him?

"She risked her life to meet you," Letty said.

His brow shot up again and he smiled, this time the humor reaching his eyes. "I'm flattered."

Letty felt her face flame again.

He started the pickup.

She hadn't finished her burger, but he didn't seem to care as he drove her back to the motel.

"Hey," he said when she started to get out. "Why don't you give me Dusty McCall's number? If there was a misunderstanding last night, I'd like to apologize to her."

He took a pencil and a scrap of paper from the glove box and scribbled down the number Letty hesitantly gave him. "Thanks."

"Thank you for lunch," she said, good manners taking over.

As he drove off, Letty stared after him wondering what that had been about. One thing was clear. Boone Rasmussen hadn't even known Dusty McCall existed.

Well, he did now, thanks to her. Dusty was going to get her wish—a call from Boone Rasmussen.

But Letty wasn't sure she'd done her best friend a favor.

Chapter 8

Ty was sitting in the Mint Bar drinking a cold beer, worrying about Dusty when he heard the news.

Clayton T. Brooks had been found—dead.

He took the news hard. He'd liked Clayton. "What happened?"

The bartender, a short stocky man named Eddie, told him that he'd heard that Clayton had been killed when his pickup went off the highway north of town. "He was in here Thursday night. Closed down the place, as usual."

"Do you remember him mentioning anything in particular?" Ty asked.

The bartender laughed. "Kept talking about someone named Little Joe." He shrugged. "Have no idea."

Ty nodded, remembering how Clayton had been that day at work. Now that he thought about it, he did remember Clayton mentioning Little Joe and Devil's Tornado.

If only he could remember what exactly had Clayton so worked up.

"Anything specific he said about this Little Joe?" Ty asked.

The bartender shook his head. "You know Clayton. Never shut up." He smiled sheepishly. "You just tuned him out after a while. Sorry."

Ty knew exactly what the man meant. "Any idea what he was doing north of town?" There was little north of Antelope Flats, and Clayton lived in the opposite direction.

Eddie shrugged and shook his head. "No clue. Not much up that way."

Except for the Edgewood Roughstock Company ranch, Ty thought. And Devil's Tornado. Was it possible the damned fool had been going to see the bull? But who was Little Joe?

The door opened and Ty caught a whiff of perfume, something light, like a spring day, that made him turn toward the entrance for a moment.

Couldn't be Slim. She wouldn't be caught dead wearing perfume. He turned his attention back to his beer. Maybe he shouldn't have deserted her. As if his staying in the boutique would have helped matters. But he hated the thought that she might be mad at him. Might never trust him again.

He caught movement out of the corner of his eye and looked up to see a young woman moving through the series of arches along the bar's entryway. All he caught was a glimpse of her. A flash of blue and short, soft blond curls, but they were enough to hold his attention as she moved in and out of the archways. Flash. Flash. Flash. She was slim and leggy, the blue dress fluttering just above her knees as she moved. The dress the same color as the blouse he'd picked out for Dusty. The same color as Dusty's eyes.

Even when she came around the corner toward the bar, he didn't recognize her at first. True to his gender, he was looking at her curves, not her face. That is, until she stopped just feet from him.

His gaze flicked up to her face and all the breath rushed from him. "Slim?" He tried to get to his feet, practically knocking over his stool. She looked so…different. So not like the tomboy he'd known his whole life.

All he could say was, "You cut your hair!"

Her long braid was gone, her hair now chin-length, the pale blond a cap of loose curls that framed her incredible face. But that wasn't the half of the transformation. Slim had curves! He stared at her, dumbstruck.

She smiled tentatively. "So what do you think?"

When had she grown up? Sometime over the past few years and he hadn't noticed. Probably because she'd hidden it so well under those huge shirts and jackets.

He dropped back on his stool, simply flummoxed. This was Slim. The tomboy from the next ranch, the cowgirl he'd teased and tormented for years. "You're…you're gorgeous."

She cut her eyes at him as she slid onto the stool next to him. Did she think he was kidding? She let out a long sigh, as if she'd been holding her breath. Her eyes shone. She blinked, and he realized she'd been close to tears. Did it matter that much to her what he thought?

"You aren't just saying that, are you?"

He shook his head, unable to quit staring at her. He'd wanted to help her find her girl side. He hadn't expected this kind of transformation. Asa was going to kill him. If Dusty's brothers didn't get to him first.

Eddie gave her an appreciative look, took her order and poured her a cola.

"You're okay with this new look?" Ty asked, watching her pluck up the maraschino cherry Eddie had put on top.

She leaned back her head, holding the cherry over her mouth. She was even wearing lipstick! With perfect white teeth, she nipped the cherry from its stem and took a sip of her drink, dropping the stem on her napkin.

"I feel so...different," she said and shot him a grin, the same grin that had always captivated him.

He couldn't believe this *woman* had been hidden under all that loose western clothing and that tomboy attitude. Worse, he couldn't believe she was his Slim. He felt bowled over—stunned by this change in her, of course, but even more shocked at how it made him feel.

He'd always liked her. But she'd just been a kid. The daughter of Asa McCall. The kid sister to J.T., Rourke, Cash and Brandon McCall. In other words, someone he thought of more as a buddy. A safe thought.

The thoughts he was having now weren't safe.

"Thank you for helping me," she said and took another sip of her cola.

"I think we should keep my part in this our little secret."

He caught her checking out her image in the mirror across the room. As far as he knew, the old Dusty had avoided mirrors, never seeming to care what she looked like. In a way, he missed that. He frowned, suddenly afraid he'd created a monster as she licked her lips and gave him a slow smile, as if she knew exactly the effect she was having on him.

"I can't wait to see—" she ran her finger along the top of her glass "—everyone's reaction."

Everyone? Letty, her brothers, her parents or someone else? He hated to think what effect she was going to have on young, impressionable ranch hands. He was still trying to get over the effect she was having on him.

He cut his eyes at her as a thought struck him. Was it possible she'd done this for some boy she had a crush on? He caught a gleam in her eye that he'd seen too many times before—usually when she was about to do something either dangerous or crazy, or both.

"What are you up to?" he asked, more than a little worried as he caught a whiff of the perfume he'd smelled earlier. The scent was definitely coming from Slim.

"You're scaring me," he said and meant it.

She laughed and downed the rest of her cola. The look she shot him making it clear she wasn't going to tell him, she said, "Ready?"

He frowned at her. He wasn't ready for this new Dusty, that was for sure.

"Would you drop me off at Letty's?"

"Sure." He was relieved it was Letty she wanted to try her new look on first. That would give him time to high-tail it back to his ranch before Asa McCall came looking for him with a shotgun. "Don't forget. My part in this is our little secret."

She nodded distractedly. It seemed she had already forgotten about him. The story of his life.

Sheriff Cash McCall was sitting in a booth at his sister-in-law's Longhorn Café when he saw the coroner come through the door. Cash had just finished a late lunch—bacon cheeseburger, extra homemade fries and a piece of her field berry pie—when Raymond Winters slid into the booth across from him.

Cash took one look at Winters' face and said, "Whatever it is, I don't think I want to hear it."

The coroner dropped his voice and glanced around the nearly empty café. "You're going to think I'm nuts."

"I've never thought you were nuts." Raymond Winters was the most sane man Cash knew, especially considering what he did for a living.

He dropped his voice even lower. "Clayton was murdered."

Cash groaned, knowing Winters wouldn't be saying this unless he had good reason. Cash pushed his plate away. "Okay, let's hear it."

"Well, this is where it gets crazy," Winters said. "I was examining the body and I found abrasions that could only have been made *after* Clayton was dead."

Cash frowned, trying to understand.

"There appeared to be several blows to the head that caused his death," Winters continued. "One bled profusely, but when I checked the pickup, there wasn't the type of blood splatter I would have expected to find, given that he was contained inside the pickup as it rolled. Should have been blood all over the place. Also, the head wounds aren't consistent with those from a car accident."

"You're saying he didn't die in the pickup."

Winters nodded. "But that isn't all." He looked even more upset. "I found something on the knees of his jeans and on one hand."

"What?" Cash asked, fear heavy as stones in his belly.

"Fresh bovine dung."

"I beg your pardon? Why in the hell would he have dung on him?"

Winters shook his head. "Good question. But I think you might want to order an autopsy because I'd wager my right arm that Clayton T. Brooks was murdered in some cow pasture and put in that pickup to make it look like an accident."

Dusty couldn't wait to see Letty's face. She walked into the motel office and rang the bell rather than go right on in to her friend's attached house as she normally did.

"May I help you?" Letty asked coming out from the back.

"I'd like a room."

Letty looked up at the sound of the familiar voice, her eyes widening in shock. "Dusty?"

Dusty laughed a little embarrassed, practically crossing her fingers in the hopes that Letty wouldn't hate her new look. "What do you think?"

Letty seemed speechless. "What happened to your hair?"

"I cut it. This is the latest style. I had no idea I had naturally curly hair. What about the dress?" She turned in a slow circle and waited for Letty's reaction, a little disappointed in it so far.

"I've never seen you in a dress before."

"Because I've never had one before," she said, wishing she wasn't feeling a little annoyed by Letty's lack of enthusiasm at the change. She'd thought Letty would be as excited as she was.

"Did you do this for Boone?" Letty asked, not sounding pleased about the prospect.

"No," Dusty snapped, although she had and they both knew it. "I just decided it was time I stopped dressing like a boy."

Letty glanced down at her own clothing: jeans, boots, western shirt. The two of them had always dressed the same.

"Not that I won't still wear my jeans and boots most of the time," Dusty added.

"You look nice," Letty said.

Nice? Dusty looked away, not wanting Letty to see how hurt she was. Part of her wanted to just turn and leave in a huff. The other wanted to say something to fix the distance she felt between them. It seemed to be widening lately, and she didn't know how to change that. "So what are you up to?"

"Nothing much."

Past her, Dusty saw what looked like a suitcase by the wall. Beside it was a cooler. A sleeping bag was rolled up on top of it. "Are you going camping?"

Letty glanced back at the suitcase. "Just putting some things away."

"Wanna grab something to eat?" Dusty asked, feeling as if she were clutching at straws.

"Already ate." Letty turned back and met her gaze. "Boone Rasmussen stopped by and took me to lunch."

Dusty couldn't hide her shock. Or avoid that sinking feeling in the pit of her stomach. "He asked you to lunch?"

"He just wanted to talk about you," Letty said quickly.

From sinking, the feeling shot to dizzying. Her stomach came alive with butterflies, her head spinning. Wasn't this what she'd wanted? "What did you tell him?"

"It was a quick lunch. He just asked your name. He saw you back by the corrals after the rodeo."

Dusty groaned. "Did he say anything else about me?"

"I'm sure you'll be hearing from him. He asked for your number. Is that lipstick you're wearing?"

Dusty nodded and fluttered her lashes. "Mascara, too."

Letty let out a long breath. "You look so…different."

"Different good, though, right?"

Her friend nodded, her smile wavering a little.

"Letty, I haven't changed."

Letty's look said she wasn't so sure about that.

Asa found Shelby in the kitchen. She hadn't heard him come in. Her back was to him, ramrod straight, shoulders squared, her head up as she stood at the sink, staring out the window as if lost in thought.

She must have sensed him because she tensed, as if braced for a blow.

He stepped up behind her and, on impulse, wrapped his arms around her, burying his face into the soft sweet spot between her neck and shoulder.

She leaned back against him, a small sound escaping her throat.

He gripped her tighter, wishing he never had to let her go, needing her as he'd never needed her before and hating that even more. She deserved better. She always had.

"I love you," he whispered against her warm skin, words he had uttered too few times to her.

"Oh, Asa," she said, her voice breaking. Her body began to shake. She turned and he drew her close, cradling her head in his hands as she buried her face in his chest.

He stroked her hair, closing his eyes as he filed away the memory of its feel beneath his fingers, just as he had filed away every touch they'd shared so he would never forget.

Past her through the window he could see the warm gold cast of the sun flowing over the land. The land he'd loved so much. More than he'd loved his own wife. Fool's gold, he thought. He would give anything to turn back the clock. To undo his two most unforgivable sins. He'd chosen the ranch over Shelby, sending her away from not only him, but also from her own children.

And then he'd turned around and ransomed the ranch. Betraying his children. In the end, he'd lost what he loved most.

He smiled at the irony. His entire life had been about the ranch. Hadn't he promised his father on his deathbed that he'd make the Sundown Ranch the biggest and best? That he would do whatever it took? Sacrifice everything? Sell his very soul?

If only he could renegotiate his deal with the devil. It wouldn't be to save the ranch. It would be for those wasted years he'd spent apart from this woman in his arms. How could she ever forgive him? He'd taken her home, her life, her children. And still she loved him.

His throat closed at the thought, his chest swelling with an unbearable pain. It wasn't cancer that was eating away at his insides—it was regret.

She pulled back to look up at him, hastily wiping at her tears, as if ashamed to have broken down in front of him. Her eyes met his. He felt her stiffen, as if bracing herself. She had always known him too well.

"I'd hoped this could wait until after Cash and Molly's wedding…" He swallowed, trying not to let her hear the anguish he was feeling, failing miserably.

Her eyes filled with tears. "When do you want me to tell them all to be here?"

"Tonight," Asa said. "It's time."

Chapter 9

By the time Dusty got home, her feet were killing her. The new bra was pinching her and the cool evening breeze had chilled her bare legs.

Letty dropped her off, declining to come in. "It's been a long day."

Her friend had told her a little more about her lunch with Boone. The important thing was that he'd not only asked about her, he'd also taken down her phone number.

Maybe he had already called, she thought as she entered the house, having forgotten about her new look—except for an unconscious eagerness to get into something more comfortable.

"What in the world?" said a familiar deep male voice from the direction of one of the chairs near the fireplace.

Dusty froze as she spotted her oldest brother, J.T., sitting in a chair by the fireplace, a stack of papers in front of him. While J.T. had married and lived on another part of the ranch with his wife, Reggie, he still did most of the actual running of the ranch and spent a lot of time at the main house. She'd hoped to just sneak in without being noticed. No such luck.

"I cut my hair," she said defensively.

J.T. grimaced. "I can see that. *Why?*"

"Why not? Anyway, I like it and that's all that matters."

"That's good, because it will take a long time to grow back out."

"Who says I'm going to grow it back out?" She groaned, knowing that she'd have to go through this with all four of her brothers. J.T. was the oldest and married to Reggie. Cash, was the sheriff, and marrying Molly in a few weeks. Rourke worked the ranch with J.T. since getting out of prison and marrying Cassidy. Rourke and Cassidy had one boy and another on the way. Brandon had eloped with Anna, the daughter of the family's worst enemy.

Asa was still fit to be tied over that, since the McCalls and VanHorns had been feuding for years.

"I hope you haven't forgotten that we're taking the herd up to summer pasture tomorrow morning starting at daybreak," J.T. said.

Dusty groaned under her breath. She *had* forgotten. "Of course I hadn't forgotten." No getting out of it, either. "I'll be saddled up and waiting for the rest of you before the sun comes up." She didn't give J.T. a chance to say anything else smart to her and would have stormed up the stairs to her room, but her feet were killing her. She slipped off her high-heeled sandals and, carrying them, limped toward the stairs.

Behind her, she heard her brother chuckle. "Women."

Dusty smiled to herself as she topped the stairs. All

her life she'd been called kid or girl. Her oldest brother had just called her a woman. That meant that this make-over had worked. Maybe Ty knew more about women than she'd thought.

Dusty tossed the sandals aside with a sigh of relief and got out of the dress and the silk underthings. With a kind of welcome-home feeling, she pulled on her cotton pants, sports bra, worn jeans and her favorite faded soft flannel shirt, one that had belonged to her brother Brandon.

Glancing in the mirror, she told herself that Letty was wrong. She hadn't changed. But when she saw her image in the glass, she knew better. Haircut aside, she now saw herself differently. She kind of missed her long hair. But there was no going back now. She had changed—and more than just her hair.

She hugged herself, remembering how she'd felt with Ty at the Mint Bar. All tingly and warm. And that was with *Ty.*

What would she feel with Boone? The thought scared her. Boone was the unknown. He was danger. Excitement. Was that why she was attracted to him? Because he was like nothing she'd never known? And only he could fulfill this desire that burned in her?

She jumped at the soft tap on her bedroom door. *"Yes?"* It had better not be J.T. to give her more grief.

Shelby opened the door and peeked in, her eyes widening at the sight of her daughter's short hair. She opened her mouth, closed it, opened it again. "We're all waiting downstairs."

Dusty blinked. "Why?"

Shelby pushed the door all the way open. "I thought one of your brothers had told you. Everyone is here for dinner. At your father's request."

Family dinners were never good news. Her brothers all had their own houses and only came to dinner at the ranch when summoned. They were all expected to attend without question.

It still irked Dusty that Shelby had come back after all those years and thought she could just step into being the mother. A mother didn't abandon her children.

"I really don't want—"

"Your father has something he wants to tell all of you," Shelby cut in, an edge to her words that brooked no argument.

"Fine. I'll be right down."

Shelby studied her for a moment, reminding Dusty of her makeover, but, to Dusty's relief, said nothing as she closed the door and left.

Dusty turned to look in the mirror. On impulse, she took off Brandon's old shirt and slipped into the blue blouse that Angela had told her Ty picked out. Amazing. As Dusty stared at herself in the mirror, she realized the blue was the same color as her eyes. Not that Ty would have realized that.

She considered putting on the slacks. Even the sandals again, but stuck with the jeans and boots. Fluffing up her short curls, she took one last look at herself in the mirror. Why tonight, of all nights, did she have to face the entire family?

But she knew that wasn't what was bothering her. The moment Shelby told her about the family dinner, worry had begun to gnaw at the pit of her stomach. For months, she'd known something was going on between her parents, ever since during one of these "family dinners" Shelby had come back from the dead.

Dusty feared that whatever her father had to tell them tonight would be even worse.

Just off the highway, not a mile down the road toward the Edgewood Roughstock Company ranch road, Boone Rasmussen saw the big black car pulled to the side, motor running, and knew the driver had been waiting for him.

He swore as he slowed, telling himself he shouldn't have been surprised. Waylon Dobbs. He'd wondered how soon he would be hearing from the veterinarian.

Pulling his pickup behind the big shiny Lincoln, he cut the engine, leaned back and waited. If Waylon thought he was going to make this easy, he was a bigger fool than Boone had suspected.

From behind the wheel of the Lincoln, Dobbs peered into his rearview mirror. Then, seeming to realize that Boone wasn't going to come to him, he finally opened the car door and got out.

Dobbs looked nervous as hell as he walked toward Boone's pickup. Boone rolled down the window as the rodeo veterinarian came alongside and smiled as if glad to see Dobbs when he was anything but.

Waylon Dobbs was a local veterinarian who volunteered at rodeos to make sure the animals were fit. For volunteering, Dobbs got his name on one of the large signs that ringed the rodeo arena. Nothing like free publicity.

In return, Dobbs—a short, squat, bald fifty-something urban cowboy—did basically nothing, which seemed to suit him just fine—and worked well for Boone. What Dobbs didn't see didn't get him into trouble.

That was until last night's rodeo. Unfortunately, Dobbs had seen something he shouldn't have.

"I wanted to continue our discussion from last night," Dobbs said looking around nervously. He had a high, almost squeaky voice that made Boone want to strangle the life out of him. "I didn't want to take the chance that we might be overheard again."

There wasn't another soul for miles, the land spreading out in rolling hills of grass and silver sage. No one could possibly hear what they had to say, if that was what Dobbs was worried about.

"I thought we'd pretty much settled things last night," Boone said, resenting the hell out of the fact that he'd had to cut Dobbs in.

Dobbs licked at his thin lips. "It's just that I've been thinking."

Boone smiled and slowly shook his head back and forth. "That could be a mistake, Waylon." His gaze cut straight to the older man's gaze, as stark and deadly as a bullet.

Dobbs swallowed and straightened his just-out-of-the-box black Stetson. Boone wondered if the vet was already spending his take. Now that would *really* be a mistake.

"I'm risking a lot going along with this," Dobbs said, shifting from one foot to the other, his gaze traveling up and down the road for a moment before he looked at Boone again. "I have a reputation to worry about."

Boone laughed and moved so fast Dobbs never saw it coming. He swung open his pickup door, catching the vet in the chest. The force sent Dobbs windmilling backward, off balance, seemingly destined to land hard on his backside. The man's eyes were huge, his open mouth gasping like a fish thrown up on the bank.

But before Dobbs could hit the ground, Boone was out of the pickup. He grabbed the lapels of Dobbs's western-cut suit jacket and swung him around, slamming him hard against the side of the pickup.

"Reputation?" Boone ground out. "Let's not b.s. each other here, Dobbs. I know why you ended up in Antelope Flats. You got run out of your practice back east. Something to do with gambling and prostitutes?"

"It was never proved," Dobbs cried. "They didn't have any evidence to—"

Boone twisted the fabric of his jacket, strangling any further denials as he leaned into Dobbs's face. "Don't underestimate my generosity," Boone said quietly. "Or my patience. That would be a mistake." He shoved Dobbs away so he could open his pickup door.

"Are you *threatening* me?" Dobbs said behind him, voice breaking.

Boone looked down at the toes of his boots and closed his eyes for a moment, then turned slowly to face him again. "Let me make this easy for you. You tell anyone what you know and I'll kill you, Waylon."

Dobbs let out a nervous laugh. "You aren't *serious.*"

"Want to stake your life on that, Waylon?" Boone asked in a louder voice as he advanced on the man again.

Dobbs stumbled back, his Adam's apple bobbing up and down as he shook his head.

"So we understand each other?"

"No reason to start making threats," Dobbs said in a meek voice. "I just thought we could talk some business, that's all."

"We've talked all the business we're ever going to talk, Waylon," Boone said, feeling unusually tired.

"I understand."

"Do you, Waylon? I'd hate like hell for this to be a problem between us."

"No problem, Boone. No problem at all."

Boone studied him, afraid there was indeed a problem. One he'd have to deal with. "And you wouldn't be stupid enough to take this any further than between the two of us, would you, Waylon?"

"Just forget I even mentioned it."

"I'll try," Boone said.

Dobbs turned and practically ran back to the Lincoln.

Boone leaned against his pickup as Dobbs revved the engine and swung the car around, driving down into the shallow ditch and back up onto the road, leaving deep tracks in the dirt as he hightailed it back toward Antelope Flats.

Dust boiled up behind the Lincoln. Boone closed his eyes, fighting the dull ache behind his eyes. He couldn't trust Dobbs. Hell, the man was a walking time bomb.

With a curse, he turned and started to get into his truck when he saw something that stopped him. A second set of tracks in the ditch on the other side of the road, opposite the ones Dobbs had just made.

Boone felt something give inside him.

Waylon had turned around twice. Just now to leave. And earlier, when he'd parked to wait for yours truly.

Which meant… Boone looked up the road toward the Edgewood Roughstock Company ranch. The stupid son of a— No, Boone told himself, Waylon wasn't stupid enough to go to Monte with this. Or was he?

Just as Dusty had feared, all eyes were on her as she walked into the dining room. "I cut my hair," she announced before anyone could say anything. "And I like it!" She took her chair next to her brother Rourke and looked around the table, daring any of them to give her a hard time.

"I like it, too," Shelby said.

Dusty didn't look at her mother. She didn't care if Shelby liked it or not. She took a drink from her water glass, hating that she couldn't forgive Shelby for giving her up all those years ago. It was bad enough that a mother would just turn her four young sons over to their father and leave. But to also give up her only daughter...

The rest of the women, all her brothers' wives, chimed in with complimentary things to say.

Dusty shifted her gaze to the head of the table where her father sat. She was still angry with him for the lie he and Shelby had cooked up. Not just about Shelby's alleged death. Almost twenty-two years ago, the two had met supposedly to discuss matters. The one-night "meeting" had resulted in Dusty's conception.

Later, Asa had brought Dusty back to the ranch, telling everyone he had adopted the infant after her parents had been killed.

She looked so much like her father and brothers that Dusty doubted anyone had believed that story. In fact, her brothers recently told her that they thought she was the result of an affair their father had had. They'd just never dreamed it was with their mother—not when they were putting flowers on her grave at the cemetery.

What a twisted pact her parents had made. All, according to them, because they couldn't live together and refused to get divorced. Dusty still couldn't believe the lies they'd told. Still couldn't forgive either of them. But because she'd always been her father's favorite, it was harder to continue being angry with him.

As she waited for him to comment on her new look,

she realized she was holding her breath, desperately wanting his approval.

He reached for his wineglass and raised it in a salute.
"You look even more like your mother."

Oh, great. As if she needed a reminder of how much
she looked like Shelby.

Her father met her gaze, holding it with a tender one of
his own, then looked over at Shelby in the chair to his left.

"Both the most beautiful women I have ever known,"
he said.

The room fell silent for a long uncomfortable moment
at the intimacy of his words.

Fortunately, Martha came in to serve dinner and everyone started in at once, the men talking ranching, the
women discussing drapery and wall colors since all of
them except Cash and Molly had new houses. Eventually, the women began to talk about Cash's and Molly's
wedding.

Dusty's new look was quickly forgotten. She breathed
a sigh of relief and listened for the phone, hoping that
Letty was right, that Boone would call. And that this was
just a family dinner, like normal families had. Not a Mc-
Call family dinner that bode anything but well.

"So what is *this* dinner about?" her brother J.T. asked,
making Dusty want to hit him. "Going to reveal another
big secret?"

Silence dropped like a bucket of cold water over the
room. Dusty stole a glance at her brothers. They all
looked as worried as she felt, their wives just as uncomfortable and concerned.

"Getting everyone together doesn't have to be about
anything," Shelby said, a little too sharply. "We're *fam-*

ily." Her voice cracked. "Can't we just eat our dinner in peace?"

No one said anything, but there were sideways glances and Dusty noticed that Shelby seemed to purposely avoid looking at Asa.

But the rest of them were looking at him. Waiting.

He cleared his throat, reached over and covered his wife's hand with his own. "J.T.'s right." She seemed to wince at his touch. Or maybe his words. Slowly she lifted her head, her lips quivering for a moment, eyes shiny.

The phone rang.

Dusty's pulse jumped. Not Boone. Not now. Not when maybe they would finally find out what was going on between her parents. The two had been acting more than weird ever since Shelby's return.

Martha appeared in the doorway. "I'm sorry to interrupt," she said quickly. "But it's the fire chief for Cash. He says it's urgent."

Cash excused himself to take the call on the phone in the hall, returning almost at once to say he had to leave. "There's been a fire at Waylon Dobbs's place tonight. He's dead. He was trapped inside. I'm sorry, but I have to go."

Shelby made a small sound, her hand going to her throat. "Cash, can't it wait for just a few—"

"Cash has to do his job," Asa said patting Shelby's hand. "It's all right. We'll do this another night. Soon."

Shelby's shoulders slumped. She dropped her head. Clearly she had hoped to finish whatever she and Asa had planned tonight.

Dusty was relieved. She'd been on an emotional roller coaster for weeks now. While she would worry and wonder, she could wait. She'd been worrying and wondering ever since Shelby had returned.

"Martha, would you serve dessert," Shelby said, surprising Dusty at how quickly her mother could compose herself.

The conversation around the table resumed with talk of Waylon Dobbs. He hadn't lived in Antelope Flats for long and Dusty hadn't known him. She shuddered at the thought of the man being burned up in his house, though.

Her mind had gone back to niggling her about what her father had been about to announce when something her brother Rourke said caught her attention.

"He had this high-pitched and kind of squeaky voice," Rourke was saying. "Odd-looking little man. Drove a black Lincoln."

Dusty felt herself start. She'd heard that voice last night at the rodeo. That was one of the men Boone Rasmussen had been with by the horse corrals. She frowned, wondering now what they'd been arguing about.

The conversation finally came back to cattle, decorating and wedding plans, but the life felt drained out of it. Everyone seemed to be trying to act normal. As if this family could ever be normal, Dusty thought.

She picked at her dessert. Her parents had both grown exceptionally quiet, especially Shelby. What had their father been about to tell them? Dusty stared down the table at her father, hoping he would look up and that she might see the answer in his eyes. He didn't. He seemed engrossed in the chocolate tart Martha had baked—and nothing else.

But she knew better. Her heart felt heavy. She opened her mouth, desperately needing to get his attention.

He looked up, surprising her. Their eyes locked. And

she saw a pleading in his look, as if asking for her forgiveness. Her heart dropped like a stone down a bottomless well as he dragged his gaze away, the set of his jaw making it clear she would learn nothing tonight no matter how hard she pushed him.

She took a bite of her tart. Waiting for the next family dinner would be like waiting for that stone to hit bottom.

Dinner over, the women got up to help clear the dishes. Dusty hesitated, but her father didn't give her a second glance as he excused himself saying he had some business he had to attend to.

Her brothers all wandered into the living room in front of the fireplace.

The phone rang again. Shelby took it in the hall on the way to the kitchen. Dusty watched her mother's expression as she took the call.

She heard Shelby say, "Yes, Dusty is here. May I say who's calling?"

Dusty felt her pulse jump. Was it Boone?

Shelby turned to look back toward the dining room, her grave expression softening. "Oh, I'm sorry, Ty, I didn't recognize your voice. Dusty's right here. No, you didn't interrupt dinner. We'd just finished." She signaled with the phone.

Ty? Disappointment made her body heavy as Dusty put her dishes in the sink and went to take the call. She waited until her mother had returned to the kitchen before saying, *"Yes?"*

"Nice to hear your voice, too, Slim," Ty said. "Why so grumpy?"

"I'm not grumpy. There is probably a good reason you called me?"

Ty sighed on the other end of the line. "I was worried about you, okay? How did the new look go over?"

"Fine. My brothers hate it, my dad said I looked just like Shelby, then he got all teary-eyed and my mother said she loved it."

"That bad, huh?" He chuckled. "I just wanted to make sure you were okay."

"I'm okay." She glanced in the hall mirror, still surprised by what she saw, and ran a hand through her short blond curls. "Thank you for today."

"No problem."

Suddenly, she felt like crying. She told herself it was because she was worried about her father and disappointed that the call hadn't been Boone. She felt awful for being short with Ty. He'd been so good to her today. "What did you name the foal?"

"What do you think? Miracle."

She smiled. "I'm glad you called."

He chuckled, sounding almost shy. "Sure you are. You take care of yourself, okay, Slim?" He sounded worried about her, as if there was reason to be.

"Thanks," she said and hung up. Up in her room, she threw herself on the bed, feeling so overwhelmed she felt as if she were drowning. What was wrong with her?

Her private line rang. She sat up and reached for it, quickly wiping her tears. As bad as she was feeling, she hoped it would be Letty. She really needed to talk. She snatched up the phone.

"Dusty McCall?" a male voice asked.

Her pulse roared in her ears. She swallowed the lump in her dust-dry throat. "Yes?" she managed to get out.

"It's Boone. Boone Rasmussen."

Chapter 10

Boone sat on the edge of his bed in the bedroom Monte Edgewood had given him on the second floor at the back of the house.

Now that he had her on the line, he wasn't sure what to say. If her friend Letty was telling the truth, Dusty McCall was the one who'd been in the horse corral after the Sheridan rodeo. The one who might have overheard his argument with Waylon Dobbs. The one whom he'd seen pick up something gingerly from the dirt and put it in her bag.

The syringe he'd dropped.

He rubbed a hand over his face. "I got your number from your friend Letty?" he said tentatively. "I hope I have the right person. You were at the rodeo with your friend last night in Sheridan? I think I saw you afterward?" He thought he heard a choking sound.

"I'm Dusty McCall," a young-sounding female voice said. "I was at the rodeo last night."

Boone smiled. "Good. Then you're the one I'm looking for."

Silence.

This was going to be harder than he'd thought. What had he hoped? That she'd blurt out what she'd heard. More important, what she'd not only seen, but also now had in her possession? All day, he'd kept telling himself that maybe she didn't know what the syringe had been used for.

But it came down to only one thing: then why had she picked it up?

"Letty told me that you were almost trampled by the bucking horses when they broke through the corral gate last night," he said, trying a different approach. "I wanted to be sure you were all right."

She let out an audible sigh followed by what could have been a little laugh. "I'm fine." She sounded nervous. Or maybe she was scared. He'd tracked her down. He knew who she was.

"I'm glad to hear you're all right. I would hate for you to get hurt because of me." He waited, hoping she would say something. She didn't and he realized he was going to have to get her alone. He couldn't tell anything over the damned phone. "Letty told me you thought you were supposed to meet me after the rodeo."

A strangled sound.

"I don't think we've ever met, have we?" he asked.

"No." Definitely nervous. What did she know?

He felt his skin crawl with worry. "I apologize if there was a misunderstanding last night. Let me make it up to you. What are you doing tonight?"

"Tonight?"

He glanced at the clock on the bedside table and swore under his breath. "Sorry, I didn't realize how late it was." His disappointment was real. "How about tomorrow night?"

A groan. "I'm going to be on a cattle drive with my brothers the rest of the week."

How lucky for her. And unlucky for him. Breaking into the ranch was out of the question. Far too risky. Hell, she might not even have the syringe anymore. Or it could have fallen to the bottom of her bag and she'd completely forgotten about it.

The one thing he was sure of—she hadn't given it to Ty Coltrane, or the sheriff would already be at Boone's door. "What day will you be back?"

"Friday."

Damn. "Oh, that's too bad, I'll be in Bozeman Friday night at the rodeo." A thought. "You wouldn't be planning to go to the Bozeman rodeo, would you?" Better than seeing her in Antelope Flats. If he could get her away from town, away from her family, away from Ty Coltrane.

"The Bozeman rodeo?" she echoed.

He held his breath.

"Yes, that is, I was thinking about going," she said.

Boone began to relax a little. This might work out better than he'd hoped. "Great, then it's a date."

"Great." She sounded strange.

He thought of Dobbs and hoped he didn't have another blackmailer that he would have to deal with on his hands.

"There's just one thing," he said. "I thought I saw you with Ty Coltrane last night. If the two of you are... involved..."

He heard a gasp on the other end of the line. "No! We've just known each other since we were kids."

"You're not...seeing him then?"

"No."

"My mistake. I thought I saw you together last night."

Another strangled sound. "We ran into each other after the rodeo."

With a silent groan, Boone lay back against the headboard and closed his eyes. There was no way he'd told this Dusty McCall chick to meet him after the rodeo. Then on top of that, Ty Coltrane had been sneaking around Devil's Tornado and then he and Dusty had just happened to hook up.

At least Coltrane had been honest about the fact that he'd been there prying into Boone's business.

What did Dusty McCall want? If she'd given the syringe to anyone, wouldn't they have taken it to the rodeo veterinarian? And Waylon Dobbs would have told Boone today on the road. Dobbs would have used it as leverage for more money to keep his mouth shut.

Boone had feared that Waylon had driven down to the Edgewood Ranch house today, maybe told Monte what he knew, hoping to get even more money.

But fortunately Monte had been the same old Monte, clasping him on the shoulder, calling him son, offering him a cold beer, which meant his only loose end now was Dusty McCall. She either still had the syringe. Or, if he had any luck at all, would have discarded it by now, not realizing what she had in her hot little hands.

Either way, Boone would find out in Bozeman. It was the being patient part that was hard. He couldn't chance the syringe getting into the wrong hands.

"So I guess I'll see you Friday night," he said, trying to

keep the frustration out of his voice. "Look me up when you get to the rodeo and we can make plans for later."

"Okay."

"Good. I'm really looking forward to this." He hung up and swore. Dusty McCall was the last thing he needed.

Dusty hung up and mentally smacked herself for being so tongue-tied on the phone with Boone. She sat for a moment, too stunned to move. Boone had asked her out. Wasn't that what she'd been hoping for?

She picked up the phone and called her best friend.

"Boone called. He asked me out," she blurted, surprised that she was half hoping Letty would try to talk her out of it.

"I figured he would." Letty didn't sound all that happy about it, but didn't put up an argument.

"We're going out Friday after the rodeo in Bozeman. Go with me. Please."

"I can't," Letty said.

"Go. I promise I'll make it up to you. I need you with me," Dusty pleaded.

"I can't. Really. There's something I have to do next weekend."

"Oh."

"I'll tell you about it as soon as I can," Letty said.

Dusty rolled her eyes, pretending it didn't hurt. But it did. "If there is something I've done—"

"No. It's not like that. It's just something I have to take care of."

Sure. Dusty couldn't believe this. "Okay." She bit back a snotty reply, telling herself that Letty was obviously going through something, something big, something she didn't want to share. Dusty wondered if it could have anything to do with part of an argument she'd overheard between Letty and her elderly parents who lived in Arizona.

Whatever it was, Letty hadn't confided in her and that hurt more than she could bear. Letty had been her best friend since grade school and they'd never kept secrets from each other. Until now.

"Well, I guess I'll talk to you when I get back then." She hung up, feeling even more apprehensive about her date with Boone and sick inside over Letty. She was losing her best friend.

Smoke drifted up from the blackened shell of what was left of Waylon Dobbs's house. A few firemen moved around in the debris, putting out spot fires.

Cash parked his patrol car behind the coroner's van and got out. The acrid air burned his throat and eyes as he walked toward where Coroner Raymond Winters stood leaning against a fire truck.

Winters took a drink from a can of root beer, tipping the can at Cash in greeting. "We have to quit meeting like this. You know Waylon?"

"Just to say hello. How about you?"

The coroner shook his head. "This used to be the old Hamilton place. I always liked this house. No other houses close by."

"Morgan know what happened?" Cash asked.

Winters peered at him over the top of his root beer can, but said nothing as he took a drink. Cash was beginning to know the look only too well. Past Winters, Cash saw Fire Chief Jimmy Morgan head his way, face covered in soot, expression grim.

The Antelope Flats Fire Department, like those in a lot

of rural towns in Montana, was made up of volunteers, except for the chief and assistant chief.

Morgan pulled off a glove and mopped a hand over his face. "Started at the back of the house. Some kind of accelerant was used. Place went up like a torch."

Cash frowned. "Arson?"

"Won't have a definite on that until the investigators get here from Billings," Morgan said. "For my money? Arson."

"Fire started at the back of the house?" Cash asked, not liking what he was thinking. "It was too early for Waylon to be sleeping. He would have had time to get out."

"Don't see why not," Morgan said. "There would have been a rush of noise when this baby was set and lots of smoke. No way he could have missed it unless he was passed out."

"Or already dead," Winters said.

Cash shot him a look.

Winters shrugged. "Just a thought."

"Is it possible Waylon started the fire?" Cash asked Morgan.

The fire chief looked doubtful. "Suicide?" He pulled his glove back on slowly, studying it as if thinking about that possibility before he spoke. "I suppose it's possible. Found the body in the first-floor bedroom. On the bed."

"That's not suicide, that's just plain crazy," Winters said. "Start the fire, take off to the bedroom and wait to burn to death?"

"He probably would have died of smoke inhalation before the fire reached him," Morgan said.

It sounded as implausible as hell. But otherwise, why wouldn't Waylon get out? Unless Winters was right and Waylon had already been dead.

"The neighbor up the road there called it in." Morgan pointed a few blocks away. "Remember Miss Rose?" Now retired, she'd taught first grade to most of them. "I'll send you a copy of my report, along with the state fire inspector's. He's on his way from Billings."

One of Morgan's men called to him. He excused himself and went back toward the house.

"We'll need an autopsy," Cash told Winters.

Winters nodded. "I know you're hoping for accidental death here. Or if not, suicide. But if the fire really was arson, then we gotta wonder if we don't have another suspicious death on our hands."

Cash was thinking the same thing. "I'm going to talk to Miss Rose and see if she saw anything, since hers and Waylon's were the only two houses on this road. Go ahead and move the body. Morgan will have photographed everything for his report." First Clayton. Now Waylon.

He walked the few blocks to Miss Rose's house and knocked. Rose Zimmer answered immediately. Clearly she'd been expecting him.

"Hello, Cash," she said in that tone he remembered too well from first grade. Instantly, he felt like her student again.

"I just need to ask you a few questions about the fire."

She had to be eighty if she was a day, but she didn't look it. She motioned him in with an impatient flick of her wrist.

He wiped his feet on the mat and stepped in. Before he could even ask, she succinctly told him what she had witnessed, explaining that she had smelled smoke, gone to the window, seen flames coming from the roof of Waylon Dobbs's house and dialed 911.

Cash jotted it all down in his notebook, taking care not to let her see his penmanship. "Did you see anyone near the house?"

"Not at the time," Rose said. "But after the call, I looked out and saw a dark-colored pickup go by. I'm sorry I didn't get a license plate number for you. It was too muddy. Didn't recognize it or the driver. Too much glare off the windshield with the sunset."

Cash thanked her, not surprised by her thoroughness. The problem was that ninety-percent of the county drove dark-colored pickups.

"He was inside, wasn't he," she said.

"I'm afraid so."

"I saw him come home earlier." She gave a small shake of her head, lips pursed. "He was driving so fast, kicking up way too much dust. I wondered what his big hurry was."

Cash wondered, too. "And he didn't leave again?"

She shook her head.

"Did you know him very well?"

"No one did," she said without having to think about it. "Stayed to himself. I'd see his light on late at night and the flicker of the television screen. I don't think he was much of a reader." Disapproval tainted her tone.

Cash closed his notebook and put it back into his pocket. "Well, thanks again. If you think of anything else, would you please call me?"

She clucked her tongue. "I think you know me well enough, Cash McCall, that you don't have to ask me that."

He smiled. "Good night, Miss Rose."

"Good night, Cash."

As Cash started back toward his patrol car, he saw Ty Coltrane pull in and get out of his pickup.

* * *

Ty had been in town when he'd heard the fire trucks and seen the smoke. But it was a disturbing rumor that brought him to Waylon Dobbs's place to look for the sheriff.

"Ty," Cash said as he approached.

"Got a minute, Cash?"

"Sure." He motioned toward his patrol car. Ty climbed in as Cash slid behind the wheel. "What's up?" the sheriff asked.

"I just heard that Clayton was murdered. Is that true?"

"I should have known the moment I started asking questions around town, it would hit the grapevine," Cash said with a shake of his head. "Let's just say his death is under investigation."

Ty pulled off his straw hat and raked his fingers through his hair. "I don't know if this has anything to do with anything."

"If you know something Ty, I'd like to hear it."

He shoved the hat back on his head and looked at Cash again. "The day he died, Clayton was all worked up over a bull. I know," Ty hurried on, "Clayton was always worked up over some bull or another, but this bull was Devil's Tornado. I'm wondering if Clayton didn't go out to the Edgewood Roughstock Company ranch the night he died to have another look at the bull."

"This bull, it's one of Monte's?" Cash asked.

Ty shook his head. "No, it's Boone Rasmussen's. I saw the bull perform at the Sheridan, Wyoming, rodeo and I got to tell you, it was acting pretty strange."

"Strange how?" Cash asked.

"Like maybe it had been drugged," Ty said, the words finally out.

"*Drugged?* I don't know anything about rodeo, but is that possible?"

"I've never *heard* of anyone drugging roughstock," Ty agreed. "But I think it's possible. This bull seemed disoriented, confused, I don't know, high on something, something that made it buck like a son of a gun."

"Let's say you're right. Wouldn't the rodeo veterinarian have noticed?"

"Not necessarily. Rodeo vets are volunteers and usually only concerned if an animal appears sick or hurt, or falls down three times in the arena," Ty said.

"So you don't know if the volunteer veterinarian noticed anything unusual about Devil's Tornado at the Sheridan rodeo," Cash said.

"No."

Cash pulled out his notebook. "Well, there is one way to find out. Do you know who the veterinarian was?"

"Waylon Dobbs."

Ty looked toward what was left of Waylon's house. "Is he...?"

"Dead," Cash said.

Ty sighed and shook his head. "Maybe it's nothing, but last night after the rodeo in Sheridan, I heard Waylon arguing with Boone Rasmussen and that cowboy who works for him, Lamar."

"Did you happen to hear what they were arguing over?" Cash asked.

"No. But I'm wondering if Waylon hadn't noticed the same thing I did about the way Devil's Tornado was acting and confronted Boone about it," Ty said.

Cash was wondering the same thing.

* * *

Boone had just hung up the phone when he heard the soft click of his bedroom door opening. He looked up from where he sat on the bed. The room Monte had given him was in a small addition off the back on the second floor—fortunately not within hearing distance of the master bedroom Monte shared with his young bride downstairs at the front of the house.

Sierra slipped in, closing the door behind her. She wore a thin white gown that seemed to shimmer in the pale light from the lamp beside Boone's bed. She'd come straight from the shower. Her blond hair was wet and dark against her skin. She smelled of the French soap she liked. Her feet were bare.

He swung his boots up on the bed, stretching out, hands behind his head on the pillow as he watched her, pretending that this didn't scare the hell out of him.

She hadn't moved from just inside the door. Nor had she said a word. She just stood there, looking at him.

It wouldn't take much to send her away. A word. Even a look. He hated that he wanted her. And she knew it.

With a curse, he reached over and turned out the lamp. He could still see her in the faint light that bled through the thin curtains as she walked over to the side of the bed.

He closed his eyes. The bed squeaked softly as she curled up next to him. He felt her fingers in his hair, then her lips at his temple, her breath skittering over his skin.

It wasn't too late to send her away.

"Your shirt smells like smoke," she whispered, pulling back a little.

"Lamar's been smoking in my pickup again." He grabbed her shoulders, shoving her down on the bed as he rolled over on top of her, jerking the flimsy gown up as he unzipped his jeans and took her, driving himself into her again and again. The only sound was the squeak of the bedsprings and his own ragged breath until he finally found release.

Spent, he rolled off and sat on the side of the bed, his back to her. But not before he'd seen her smile up at him. A knowing smile that said she owned him.

He heard the bedsprings squeak once more as she got up and left, closing the door quietly behind her, leaving behind not only her scent on his skin, but also the memory of her still in his blood. He rushed into the bathroom, dropped to his knees and threw up in the toilet, just as he'd done all the other times she'd come to him.

Chapter 11

Boone woke up hung over. He opened one eye a crack. Daylight bled through the thin curtains, the sky outside a pale pink.

Monte was sending him to Texas for a few days to look at some bulls. Boone couldn't shake the feeling that he just wanted to get him out of town. Otherwise why trust him with something this important?

According to Monte, everyone in town was in an uproar because the sheriff was asking a lot of questions about Clayton T. Brooks's death. Rumor had it that Clayton had been murdered.

Boone tried to sit up, but fell back sick to his stomach. He had to catch a late morning flight out of Billings, which meant he had a three-hour drive ahead of him, so he had to get up.

He started to close his eyes, desperately needing more sleep. But he couldn't chance missing the flight.

Lifting his left arm, he squinted at his wristwatch. Maybe he could get in a few more minutes.

Both eyes flew open. Only a white strip shone on his wrist where the watch had been. He sat up, head reeling from the sudden movement. Swiveling around, he looked to the small table beside the bed, trying not to panic.

Monte had bought him the watch after Devil's Tornado's first rodeo. He couldn't have lost it.

But the watch wasn't on the table—just the empty bourbon bottle. He had hit the bourbon hard after Sierra left last night and must have passed out.

Getting up, he searched the small room, finally dropping to his knees to look under the bed.

No watch.

Awkwardly, he got to his feet, his heart beating abnormally fast, his pulse a deafening drum. He gripped his head in both hands, telling himself it was just a watch. Hell, would he really want to keep it when this was over? He could buy his own watch one day. An even more expensive one.

But he knew that wasn't the problem.

He plopped down on the foot of the bed and scrubbed at his face with his hands as he tried to remember the last time he'd seen it. Did he have it on yesterday when he'd stopped to talk to Waylon? He couldn't remember.

It was one thing to lose the watch. It was another to worry about where it would turn up.

Monte had had Boone's damn initials engraved on it.

Sheriff Cash McCall was disappointed when he called Monte Edgewood to find that Boone Rasmussen had flown to Texas and wouldn't be back until Thursday.

But he told Monte he still would drive out; he had a

few questions for him. Monte had seemed surprised, but said he would be there.

True to his word, Monte was waiting on the porch. He walked toward the patrol car as Cash parked.

"Howdy, Sheriff." He extended his hand.

Cash had known Monte his whole life. After years of riding saddle broncs, Monte had started the Edgewood Roughstock Company. Cash did a little research and found out that while Monte wasn't one of the top roughstock producers in the country, he was definitely getting a name for himself. Especially in the past six months, when he'd hooked up with Boone Rasmussen and his bulls. The name Cash kept hearing was: Devil's Tornado.

"What can I do for you?" Monte asked. "I get the impression this isn't a social call."

"I need to ask you some questions about Clayton T. Brooks's murder."

Monte drew back in surprise. "Clayton's *murder*? I thought he was killed in an automobile accident."

"It appears his killer just wanted us to believe that," Cash said.

Monte frowned as he rubbed a hand over his jaw. "Clayton murdered. I can't believe it."

"The day Clayton died, all he'd been talking about that day was one of your bulls, Devil's Tornado," Cash said. "It seems Clayton saw the bull at the Billings rodeo."

"Yeah, Devil's Tornado was in rare form that night in Billings, that's for sure," Monte said. "But what does that have to do with Clayton's...death?"

"Maybe nothing. It sounds like your bull is causing quite a *lot* of talk," Cash said. "I understand the more talk, the more money's he's worth."

Monte smiled and nodded. "But you know he's not my

bull. He's Boone's. I'm helping him out by using some of his bulls. As it turns out, Devil's Tornado is helping us both."

"What is Boone doing in Texas?" Cash asked.

"Checking out some more bulls for us. He has a good eye. His father was in the roughstock business, you know."

Cash knew. He'd been learning more about rodeo and roughstock than he'd ever wanted to. "When will Boone be back?"

"He's flying in to Billings Friday morning but going straight to Bozeman for a three-day rodeo we're putting on there." Monte seemed to hesitate. "Boone didn't have anything to do with Clayton's death. I've known Boone since he was a boy. He's had his share of troubles, but he's trying to turn his life around."

Cash wanted to warn Monte about Boone. He'd learned a lot about rodeo roughstock—and Boone Rasmussen. Boone had been in trouble since he was fifteen. Nothing that had him behind bars for more than a few months, but the pattern was there.

"As for Devil's Tornado…" Monte pointed toward a bull standing alone in a small pasture. "That's him *right* there."

Cash shaded his eyes, squinting as he walked to the pasture fence, surprised at how ordinary the bull looked. "He's not what I expected."

"Doesn't look like much, does he?" Monte chuckled as he joined him. "But put him in a chute and look out. I've never seen a bull like him. He just keeps coming up with new tricks to throw riders."

"Is there any chance Clayton came out to the ranch

the night he died?" Cash asked. "That would have been Thursday, probably after the bars closed."

Monte looked surprised. "Why would Clayton come out here?"

"I don't know. Maybe to see Devil's Tornado."

"We had the bull in the pasture down there." Monte pointed up the road. "But I would have heard a vehicle drive in. Even if it was late. I'm a light sleeper."

"Monte, I'm going to need a sample of Devil's Tornado blood."

Monte drew back. "His blood? You're serious."

Cash studied the docile bull in the pasture. "If I have to, I can get a warrant."

Monte shook his head and gave him a smile weighted with sadness. "That won't be necessary, Cash. I have a contract with Boone to use the bull for rodeos. I can okay any tests you need to run. Especially if it will help you find Clayton's killer. It just upsets me to think that your investigation has led you here."

All Boone wanted was a good night's sleep. But when he parked his pickup in front of the Edgewood house after the long flight from Texas and then the three-hour drive home, he saw that a light was on in the kitchen.

He'd changed his flight at Monte's request so he could come back early rather than meet Monte in Bozeman. Boone was worried about his damned watch, worried about leaving Lamar alone for too long, worried about Dusty McCall and the syringe, just plain worried and anxious.

"Boone, son, could you come in here?" Monte said, the moment Boone stepped inside the house.

Something in Monte's tone warned him. Boone tried to keep his cool as he stepped into the kitchen.

Monte sat at the table alone, a bottle of beer in front of him, several empties off to the side. He'd been there for a while.

The older man looked up and Boone saw at once that whatever had kept Monte up so late wasn't good.

"The trip went really well," Boone said filling in the silence. "I found a couple of bulls that would be great additions to your herd. I'll tell you all about them in the morning. I'm really beat."

"Have a seat, son," Monte said as if he hadn't heard.

Boone stood for a moment, then pulled out a chair. He wondered where Sierra was and how worried he should be.

"The sheriff stopped out while you were gone," Monte said and took a drink of his beer.

Boone held his breath and waited.

"He seems to think Clayton was murdered and that he came out here the night he was killed to look at Devil's Tornado."

Boone tried to show the right amount of surprise and sorrow. He'd never gotten it right. "Why would Clayton be interested in our bull?"

Monte smiled slowly at *our bull*, but the smile fell short of his eyes. "There anything you want to tell me, son?"

Boone gave that some thought, pretty sure Monte was asking about a lot more than just Clayton. What would Monte do if he told him the truth? "I don't know what you want me to say."

Monte seemed disappointed by that answer. Or was it relief? "Cash is going to want to talk to you."

Boone nodded, pretending that didn't worry him. He hated the law and unfortunately had had more than his share of run-ins with police in the past.

"It troubles me that the sheriff's investigation led him to my door," Monte said and took another drink.

Boone could only nod, his mind racing. "I guess you won't want to use Devil's Tornado at the Bozeman rodeo, then."

"Cash had the lab come out and take some blood from the bull," Monte said picking at the label on his almost empty beer bottle. "The sheriff had it in his head that the bull might have been drugged."

Boone couldn't breathe, even if he had dared to take a breath.

"But when I talked to him yesterday, he said he didn't find any drugs." Monte looked up. "Where would he get a fool idea that we were drugging Devil's Tornado?"

Boone forced himself to take a breath. "I'm just glad the sheriff knows there was no truth to it."

Monte nodded, even smiled a little. "You ought to get to bed. You look like you've been rode hard and put to bed wet. We're taking Devil's Tornado to the Bozeman rodeo tomorrow. We'd be fools to pull the bull now, don't you think? He's a star in the making."

Boone got to his feet. Every instinct in him told him to hit the road and not look back. With the sheriff sniffing around asking questions about that damned dead bull rider and Ty Coltrane snooping around Devil's Tornado, the safest thing he could do was sell his bulls to Monte, cut his losses and move on. There would always be other bulls. Unfortunately, there were few marks as easy as Monte Edgewood.

"I suppose you heard the other news," Monte said as

Boone started toward the door. "Someone set a fire at Waylon Dobbs's place the night before you left for Texas. Burned to the ground. Poor Dobbs. I guess he couldn't get out."

"That's too bad," Boone managed to say as he glanced back at Monte.

Without getting up, Monte reached into the fridge and snared another bottle of beer from the door. "'Night, son," Monte said and snapped open the twist-off with his huge paw of a hand.

Boone went upstairs to his bedroom. That night, after everyone was asleep, he told himself he could get up and leave. But he knew he wouldn't. He'd come this far, risked so much; he'd be a fool not to see this through.

If he had to, he'd sell Devil's Tornado and the other bulls after the Bozeman rodeo and leave town.

By then, he would have taken care of the only other loose end he had to worry about now—Dusty McCall. He could only hope that she'd discarded the syringe days ago. But if there was a chance she'd held on to it for any reason...

Tonight, he locked his bedroom door. He thought he heard the soft rattle of the knob sometime during the night, but maybe he'd just imagined it.

Bozeman Rodeo Grounds

Ty Coltrane told himself he had no business in Bozeman. He had a horse ranch to run. But the talk around Antelope Flats was that Clayton T. Brooks had been murdered—and possibly Waylon Dobbs as well.

First, an old bull rider who had been upset about Devil's Tornado had been found dead on the highway north of town, just miles from the Edgewood Rough-stock Company ranch. Then Waylon Dobbs, the veterinarian that Ty had seen arguing with Boone Rasmussen after the rodeo not a week ago had been killed in a fire.

Both tied to Rasmussen.

Cash had called yesterday to say that the blood sample on Devil's Tornado showed no sign of drugs and while he was still investigating both Clayton's and Waylon's deaths, he had nothing that tied either to Rasmussen.

Ty had been so sure Devil's Tornado had been drugged the night of the rodeo in Sheridan. He'd been around livestock his whole life. He knew when an animal was acting strangely. How could he have been that wrong?

He shook his head.

But Ty knew he hadn't driven five hours because of Boone Rasmussen—or Devil's Tornado. No, he thought, as he parked at the back of the rodeo lot and got out. He wasn't here because of some bull or some roughstock producer. He was here because of Dusty.

And he was late. The rodeo was almost over.

But the truth was: he hadn't been able to get her off his mind. Not the cowgirl who'd peeked over the stall door to watch the birth of the foal, nor the one who'd come into the Mint in that blue dress.

This afternoon when he'd called the McCall ranch and found out that Dusty had gone to Bozeman to the rodeo, he'd had the craziest feeling that she needed him.

Yeah, right.

But hey, look what had happened to her at the last rodeo. She'd almost been trampled by a herd of bucking horses. Then someone had followed her home. There was true cause for concern when it came to her.

And now she'd driven five hours to go to a rodeo in

Bozeman? And without Letty, according to Shelby. What was up with that? Dusty and Letty had been attached at the hip since grade school.

As he started toward the rodeo arena, he spotted the Sundown Ranch pickup that Dusty drove. He'd never believed in premonitions, but he couldn't shake the feeling that she was in trouble.

Or maybe that was just an excuse to see her.

Either way, once inside, he scanned the grandstands for Dusty's adorable face, warning himself that she wasn't going to be happy to see him.

Letty knew the moment she saw the man standing in the shade at the entrance to the rock concert that he was Hal Branson. She smiled to herself as she watched him try to smooth down the cowlick in his carrot-orange hair.

Her heart did a little flip inside her chest. She knew it was silly, but the fact that he had red hair struck her as fortuitous.

He wore new jeans and a button-down blue checked shirt. She couldn't help smiling as she neared him, betting with herself whether his eyes would be blue or brown. Blue, she decided.

He spotted her and straightened, his smile tentative. "Leticia?" His gaze went to her hair and she saw his expression almost relax.

She touched her wild mane of red hair, a shade darker than his own. "It seems we have something in common," she said and gave him a shy smile, even though she'd always been self-conscious about her teeth.

His smile broadened, lighting up his blue eyes. Up close she could see a sprinkling of freckles across his nose and cheeks. She knew without having to ask that he'd hated them since kindergarten, just as she had hated hers.

He seemed to study her, his jaw dropping slightly, his eyes wide and intent. He was about her age, maybe a few years older. Her heart beat a little faster and her face flushed warm under his perusal.

He cleared his throat. "Sorry. I didn't mean to stare. It's just…"

She'd only talked to him a couple of times on the phone, but both times she'd liked his voice. It was soft and re-assuring.

He was still staring. "We could be twins. We're not," he added quickly. "Related, that is."

She laughed nervously. "I'm glad to hear that."

His eyes locked with hers. He swallowed, as if he had a lump in his throat. "You're probably going to think I'm crazy but do you believe in…fate?"

She smiled, forgetting that she'd always felt her teeth were too big for her mouth. "I'm beginning to."

Ty wondered if he would ever find Dusty. The grand-stands were full. A truck circled the dirt oval dragging a rake as a team prepared the arena for the next event. Loud country music played over the outdoor speakers and a clown told jokes to the crowd.

He caught sight of Lamar by one of Monte Edgewood's semitrucks and trailers. A few cowboys hung around the empty chutes talking. He wondered if he'd get to see Devil's Tornado tonight. No sign of Rasmussen.

And no Dusty.

At least, not in the stands. Maybe she was at one of the concession stands.

He turned. His heart did a two-step at the sight of her

coming toward him. She smiled and waved, and all he could do was stare.

She was dressed in jeans, ones that fit like a glove, and a sleeveless halter top that hugged her curves.

All these years, he'd liked her. But at that moment, he finally admitted it had been a whole lot more than that. He couldn't keep kidding himself. He was wild about her, and always had been.

He stopped walking, frozen in midstep, his breath seizing in his chest as the simple truth of it staggered him.

She was still coming toward him, her grin turning into a dazzling smile as she got closer. She looked a little shy, a little unsure. He knew *that* feeling! He couldn't move. Couldn't speak.

He wasn't sure when he realized that she wasn't looking at *him*, but at someone over his right shoulder.

He glanced back and in that instant, saw whom she was headed for—Boone Rasmussen.

It came to him in a blinding flash. The smile. The wave. The gleam in her blue eyes. The *new* look.

It had all been about *Boone Rasmussen*!

No! Anyone but Rasmussen.

Dusty didn't even seem to notice Ty as she walked right past. Her eyes were only on Rasmussen. And from the way he was looking back at her...

Ty let out a curse. He had to be mistaken. But even before he turned to watch her with Boone, he knew he wasn't.

Dusty shifted one hip and cocked her head, the soft blond curls swaying a little as she leaned toward Rasmussen grinning that devilish grin of hers, blue eyes wide. No mistake. She was flirting! And to make matters worse, Rasmussen was responding. But then, what man wouldn't?

Ty let out another curse. When had this all happened? He frowned as he remembered the morning at his ranch. Rasmussen hadn't even noticed the old Dusty. So why the interest now?

Could it simply be because that Dusty had looked like a cow*boy*? Because this one looked like what she really was: a very desirable woman? Mentally he kicked himself. Slim had been transformed. And what fool had helped with this makeover?

Ty groaned. Or could there be more to Rasmussen's interest in Dusty? Did this go back to the night after the Sheridan rodeo?

He swore. He'd tried to warn Dusty off Rasmussen, but in retrospect he realized that would only have made her more curious about the cowboy. Ty could only blame himself that Dusty was now a Scud Missile—and headed right for Boone Rasmussen. Right for a man that Ty believed capable of anything. Even murder.

Chapter 12

It took every ounce of Ty's restraint to keep him from going after Dusty.

All he could do was stand back and watch as Rasmussen ran a finger down Dusty's arm to her hand clutching the top of her leather shoulder bag. Dusty was nervous, something Ty noticed because he knew her so well. What the hell did she think she was doing?

The rodeo announcer called for the last event: bull riding. Rasmussen leaned toward Dusty, whispered something in her ear. Ty swore, desperately wanting to slug the guy.

As she swung around, Ty saw her face. It was flushed. She headed right for him but he could tell she hadn't seen him yet.

He swore under his breath and tried to go back to thinking of her as just the kid next door.

No chance of that.

"Slim," he said as she approached. It didn't matter that the nickname no longer fit her. She was still his Slim. Past her, he saw that Rasmussen had stopped to look back.

"Ty? What are you doing here?" She looked more than surprised. She looked worried. "You're going to mess up everything." She started to walk past him.

"Oh, no you don't," he said grabbing her arm before she could get away. "You and I need to talk."

The Triple-X-Files were just coming on stage when Letty and Hal reached the bandstand.

Letty quickly scanned the band members. They were all at least in their fifties, all hippies with long hair, a lot of it gray, wearing ragged shirts and worn jeans. But they appeared to be the real thing, and she found something about that endearing.

There was no sign of Flo Hubbard.

The band broke into a rock introduction and a tall woman with flaming red hair streaked with gray came bounding onto the stage, strumming a guitar. She wore a cutoff western shirt and worn jeans that hugged her slim body. She was barefoot, her toenails painted a rainbow of colors.

Her head was down so all Letty saw at first were her hands—hands that were so much like her own she felt tears burn her eyes. Her heart began to pound louder than the music.

The woman raised her head.

Letty's chest swelled, filling as if with helium. Her joy spilled out in tears. She felt Hal take her hand and squeeze it. She squeezed back, choking on the sobs that rose in her throat.

All those years of desperately needing someone who

looked like her. Letty stared at the woman on stage, the face and green eyes so like her own, and felt as if she'd finally come home.

She'd found her birth mother.

Boone watched Coltrane draw Dusty McCall around the corner of the grandstands, their heads together conspiratorially. Something definitely going on between them. Dusty had lied about how close she and Coltrane were. He could see that just looking at the two of them together.

Why did that surprise him? Just moments ago, she'd been flirting with him. Teasing him. She had the syringe. Of course she did. He recalled now the way she'd had her hand over the top of her shoulder bag.

Women, they were all alike. Hadn't he learned that from his mother, who'd run off and left him with that low-life father of his?

He swore and turned to go back to find out what was going on with little Miss Dusty McCall. Sierra Edgewood stepped in front of him.

"Going somewhere?" she asked as she caressed the collar on his shirt.

He stepped back just out of her reach. Speaking of women... "I don't have time for this right now," he said impatiently. Was the woman crazy? Monte was over by the chutes. He could be watching them at this very moment.

She lifted one finely sculpted brow. "Maybe you'd better *make* time."

Something in her tone brought his attention away from the spot where Coltrane and Dusty had disappeared.

Sierra smiled, but something was different about her. "Now you're listening. That's more like it." She was look-

ing at him as if she knew something. No, as if she had
something on him. Even more leverage than just his in-
ability to turn her away from his bed?

"Is this about my watch?"

She frowned. "Your watch?"

"Never mind," he said seeing her confusion. "What
is it you want?" He hated being cornered.

"I missed you last night," she said with a nervous
laugh.

So she *had* tried his door. He glanced toward the
chutes, saw Monte watching them. Monte motioned to
him. "I've got to get to work."

"Tonight after the rodeo. And Boone, don't disappoint
me." She turned and walked off before he could answer.

Boone looked toward the chutes and saw Monte's eyes
following Sierra, the look on his face twisting Boone's
insides. Monte loved his wife, trusted her. Trusted everyone. Even Boone Rasmussen. Maybe especially him.

When Boone glanced back toward the grandstands
where Coltrane and Dusty had gone, he swore. He should
be helping Monte and Lamar with the bull riding. But
he had to find out what Coltrane and little Miss McCall
were up to first.

Cash and his soon-to-be wife Molly had just finished
dinner when State Fire Inspector Jim Ross called.

"Sheriff? I've got the final report on the Waylon
Dobbs fire. There's something you need to see."

Cash drove over to what was left of the Dobbs place.
Ross was waiting for him in his Chevy Suburban and
motioned Cash inside.

"You already know that the fire was intentionally set
at the back of the house. It appears the arsonist entered

through a window and made his exit through the same window. We found this caught on a nail of the window frame." Ross lifted an evidence bag.

Cash's pulse jumped at the sight of a watch inside. The leather band, now partially burned, appeared to have broken prior to the fire.

Ross nodded. "It gets even better. The back of the watch is engraved with three initials. B. A. R."

Cash took the bag. B.A.R.

"Will that help narrow down your suspect list?" Ross asked.

Cash nodded. When Boone Rasmussen had been arrested in Texas, his full name had been on the paperwork. Boone *Andrew* Rasmussen. B. A. R.

Ty drew Dusty under the grandstands, where it was dark and cool and somewhat quieter. People wandered past to the concessions or the restrooms, but with the rodeo in full swing, no one paid them any mind.

"All right," Dusty said the moment he let go of her. "What?"

"You should have told me that all this—" he waved a hand over her, taking in her new look "—was about *Boone Rasmussen.*"

She frowned. "Excuse me?"

"*Rasmussen?* Dusty, have you lost your mind?"

"Look Ty, I know you don't like Boone—"

"He's up to his neck in something. Have you forgotten that he almost killed you in the horse corral?"

"He said the gate latch was faulty."

"And you believe that?" Ty let out an exasperated sigh. "Slim, I think Boone had something to do with Clayton's murder and Waylon Dobbs's fire and his death."

"That's crazy," she snapped. "Why would Boone want to kill anyone?"

"It's all tied in somehow with Devil's Tornado," Ty said.

She stared at him. "You just don't want me going out with Boone. You're…" Her eyes widened. "You're… j*ealous*!"

"Jealous?" He practically choked on the word. "This has nothing to do with how I feel about you."

"*Feel* about me?" she echoed.

She was close enough he could smell the light scent of her perfume. Slim, wearing perfume! Her lashes were dark with mascara, making the blue of her eyes seem bottomless.

This was Slim, he reminded himself. The girl next door whom he'd grown up with, looked out for, teased, tormented, adored. Slim. The pouty red lips, the palest blue eyes he'd ever seen, that adorable face. That body. He groaned. *His* Slim.

And all he wanted to do was throw her over his shoulder and haul her butt back to Antelope Flats. Either that or…kiss her.

He went with the kiss, drawing her to him. She was soft and lush-feeling in his arms. Her eyes lit with surprise in that instant before he dropped his mouth to hers.

He half expected her to pull away. Maybe even cuff him up side the head. That would be like the Dusty he knew and loved. Once he had her in his arms, once his mouth was on hers, he deepened the kiss.

Her reaction was nothing like he'd expected. No kick to the shin. No slugging him. She responded to his kiss. Not at first. But within a split second, her lips parted. Her body melted against his. All with stunning effect.

She let out a soft, almost pleased moan, then slowly, she drew back, eyes wide, her breath coming in short gasps.

He opened his mouth to speak. Nothing came out. He was breathing hard, surprised and delighted and confused by what had just happened. He watched Dusty slowly run her tongue along her upper lip. She was still breathing hard, just like him, her face flushed with heat.

"Ty?" she whispered, staring at him as if she'd never seen him before.

He could only look at her, words lost on him.

"Why did you—" She broke off suddenly, her eyes narrowing. "Was *that*—" she waved an arm through the air "—about *Boone*?"

He scowled at her. "Hell, no. Listen to me, I know it sounds crazy, but I think Boone's drugging Devil's Tornado to make him perform better and I think Clayton and Waylon figured it out and that's why they're dead. Look, I know Cash didn't find any drugs when he tested Devil's Tornado, but don't you see the drug must be one that doesn't stay in the system long. He drugs the bull to work it up for the ride, then must give it something to bring it back down once the ride is over."

"What?" She looked shocked as she stepped back, her hand dropping to her shoulder bag.

Behind her, Boone came around the end of the grandstands. Had he been there the whole time listening, watching them?

Following Ty's surprised gaze, Dusty turned to look behind her. "Boone," she said, the name coming out on a surprised gasp.

"Dusty and I are having a private conversation," Ty said starting to step past Dusty to confront Boone, but Dusty grabbed his arm to stop him.

Rasmussen smiled at Dusty, completely ignoring him. "I have a surprise for you." He motioned for her to come with him.

Ty cursed. "Dusty—"

She gave him a warning look and slipped something into his hand. "I'll talk to you later, Ty," she said without looking back at him.

At the end of the first song, Flo Hubbard spotted Letty. Letty saw it happen—saw the instant of recognition, then the confusion.

Had her mother known she existed? Or had she been told, as some of the doctor's victims had been, that her baby was stillborn?

Flo turned to the bass guitarist and said something to him. He seemed a little surprised, but swung into another song. Flo looked at Letty, motioned for her to come around to the side of the stage. Leaning her guitar against one of the speakers, she disappeared from view.

Hal let go of Letty's hand.

"Come with me?" she pleaded.

His eyes met hers and locked for a long moment. He took her hand again, and they worked their way through the crowd to the side of the bandstand.

Flo shifted on her bare feet, her hands fluttering in front of her as if she didn't know what to do with them. The band was playing something slow and melodious. Without discussing it, the three stepped away toward the concessionaires until the noise level was such that they would be able to hear each other.

Flo stopped, turning to look at Letty. "You're going to think I'm totally out of my mind..."

Letty shook her head. "I think you're my birth mother."

Flo seemed to slump, as if her bones had suddenly dissolved. She stumbled into a chair under the covered sitting area at a taco concession and sat down heavily, her gaze never leaving Letty's face. "It's not possible," she whispered.

Letty pulled up a chair next to her. Hal took one across from them. "It is possible." She glanced at Hal for help.

"Didn't you give birth twenty years ago on March 9 in Antelope Flats, Montana, at the clinic?"

Flo's green eyes filled with tears as she nodded. "Was that the name of the town? My van ran out of gas just outside of it. I was hitching into town when I went into labor. Just when I thought my luck had really run out, I was picked up by a doctor who worked at the clinic."

"That might not have been so lucky," Hal said.

Flo didn't seem to hear him. She appeared lost in the past as she said, "I was so young and scared, and it wasn't time yet for the baby to be born." She looked up at them. "But the baby was a boy, the doctor said. He was stillborn."

"Did you see your baby?" Hal asked.

She seemed to think for a moment, then shook her head. "The doctor put me out right before the baby was born. He told me something was wrong and wanted to spare me."

As Letty stared at her mother, Hal filled Flo in about the do-gooder doctor. "Let me guess. The doctor took care of everything, right?"

She nodded.

"I'm willing to bet, unless my eyes deceive me, that the doctor stole your baby and gave it to an older couple in town who couldn't have children," Hal continued. "Of course, DNA tests will be required to be absolutely sure..."

Flo let out a sudden laugh. "This is so freaky. I knew.
I knew the moment I looked out into the crowd and saw
you. I said, 'That's my kid.' I mean, how could I know
something like that when I thought there was no way?"

"History has proven that a mother often knows her
child on some level that we will never understand," Hal
said quietly.

Flo nodded, studying her daughter's face. "You look
exactly like I did at your age," she said with a laugh.
"Sorry about that, kid."

Almost shyly, she reached out and placed her hand
over her daughter's. Letty intertwined her fingers with
her mother's, and the two began to laugh and cry at the
same time.

Dusty felt Boone slip his arm around her waist and
pull her to him, his hand going to her shoulder bag.

Her head was spinning. Ty's kiss had left her weight-
less, trembling, excited and a little scared. She'd never
felt anything like that. Still couldn't believe it. Ty?

She couldn't think. Everything was happening too
fast. Ty thought Boone had been drugging Devil's Tornado? Was it possible the syringe she'd found and had
just given to Ty had been used on the bull?

She didn't want to believe it of Boone, but she was reminded of his odd behavior at the Sheridan rodeo. She'd
seen him jab the bull with something. A syringe? The
one that she'd had in her purse all this time?

Boone suddenly stopped and turned her toward him.
"You all right?" he asked, eyes narrowing.

"Fine." She forced a smile and added, "Great." Just
great. For weeks, all she'd thought about was getting

Boone to notice her. In her wildest dreams, he would ask her out and, if she got lucky, kiss her.

As he drew her toward him, she felt his hand part the top of her shoulder bag and his fingers dig inside. He was looking for the syringe! He must have seen her pick it up that night after the rodeo. All he'd ever wanted was the syringe!

He dropped his mouth to hers, his kiss hard and punishing as she felt him dig deeper in her bag.

Ty fought to breathe, the weight on his chest crushing his heart, his lungs, making him sick inside as he watched Boone kiss Dusty. She was right. He *was* jealous. Jealous as hell. But it was fear and anger that simmered inside him, making him want to do something stupid like bust this up right now. He could see that Boone had his hand in her purse as if looking for something.

Frowning, Ty looked down in his own hand and saw what Dusty had put there. A used syringe. He quickly stuck it into his jacket pocket, his hand shaking. That's what Boone was looking for. But what would Boone do when he didn't find it?

Boone drew back from the kiss, his dark eyes boring into hers for a long moment, before he shot Ty a look filled both with contempt and a warning as he drew Dusty toward the arena.

"You can watch the bull rides from the chutes with me," Boone said to Dusty, gripping her arm.

Ty saw Dusty wince and started to go after her but at that moment she glanced over her shoulder at him and mouthed, "Call Cash." Her look warned him. "Call Cash," she mouthed again. As she disappeared around the corner of the grandstands, Ty saw her shake off Boone's grip.

Boone looked angry but didn't reach for her again as she went with him willingly.

Oh, hell, what was she up to? Knowing her, she was going to try to get more proof. Where had she gotten the syringe? *When* had she gotten it? Had to have been that night at the Sheridan rodeo.

That look of shock on her face when Ty had told her his suspicions about Boone—it hadn't been because she didn't believe him, but because she *did*!

He took a breath, trying to think. Dusty was safe as long as she was at the rodeo around other people, right? He had the syringe in his pocket. If a lab could determine the drug inside, it might explain Devil's Tornado's behavior.

Unfortunately, it wouldn't be enough to put Boone Rasmussen behind bars. Not unless Boone drugged the bull again tonight and Ty could get a sample of the bull's blood right after the ride.

But if Boone had overheard Ty's conversation with Dusty, he wouldn't drug Devil's Tornado tonight. Unless it was already too late...

Over the loudspeaker, the final bull ride was being announced. Devil's Tornado in chute three. Ty didn't catch the bull rider's name as he hurried to the arena. Pulling his cell phone from his pocket, he dialed Sheriff Cash McCall's number.

Her legs still quivering, Dusty climbed up onto the fence, oblivious to the noise, the dust, the action in the arena in front of her.

"You're sure nothing's wrong?" Boone asked. His dark

eyes drilled into her as if he could read her thoughts. She tried to smile, tried to act normal, whatever normal had been before today.

"I heard Coltrane warn you to stay clear of me. What is it he thinks he has against me?"

If he had heard Ty warn her about him, then Boone knew exactly what Ty thought he had against him. *"Nothing."*

Boone narrowed his dark eyes, a mocking smile curling his lips.

"It doesn't matter what Ty thinks," she said.

Boone didn't look convinced. "Stay here. I'll be right back."

It wasn't her nature to stay. Especially when ordered. But she wanted Boone to believe that everything was all right. Ty would have called Cash. The police would come. This would be over soon. She just had to keep pretending that she liked Boone Rasmussen.

That was going to be the hard part.

She watched him rush over to the chute, saw his intense conversation with Lamar. Clearly, they were arguing. Boone looked furious. And…scared.

She stared at him, wandering what had ever attracted her to him. She touched a finger to her lips, remembering Ty's kiss. The feeling still burned inside. Ty. She smiled, still too surprised to believe it.

Now she knew what Ty had been doing that night after the Sheridan rodeo. She looked across the arena, hoping to see him. By now, he would have called Cash. If her brother could get the local cops down here fast enough…

She didn't see Ty anywhere. Devil's Tornado was kicking up a ruckus inside the chute. Boone and Lamar were hanging over the chute now, the rider trying to get his rope wrapped around his hand.

All these weeks of dreaming about Boone and then Ty Coltrane kissed her and—

Her heart kicked up a beat just at the thought of Ty. She felt her face warm. She smiled and caught her lower lip in her teeth, feeling a little lightheaded. Ty Coltrane. Who would have known?

Suddenly, the chute banged open. Devil's Tornado lunged out, twisting and turning, a blur of movement. The rider tried to stay with him, but was quickly unseated. The pickup riders rode in an attempt to corner the bull. One of the horseback riders managed to get the bucking rope off, but it had little effect on Devil's Tornado.

Dusty stared at the bull as he stopped just feet from the fence where she sat. She could see now what Ty had seen. And Clayton and Waylon, had they seen it too?

Her pulse thundered in her ears. Had Boone killed to keep his secret? He didn't have that much to lose if he got caught drugging the bull, did he? He could just pack up and go somewhere else. Start over again. But murder…

The riders cornered Devil's Tornado, got a rope on him and dragged him out the exit chute.

She looked around for Boone, finally spotting him by Devil's Tornado. Past him, she saw Monte Edgewood climb into his pickup. He seemed to glance around as if looking for someone. His wife, Sierra?

Dusty knew Monte Edgewood to say hello to on the street. He'd always seemed nice. She'd heard that he'd married a woman not much older than she was a while back. She'd only seen Sierra Edgewood a few times and felt sorry for her since Dusty knew only too well what it was like to have the whole county talking about you. He glanced at Boone, then slammed the door and drove off.

Because it was a three-day rodeo, the animals would be staying on the rodeo grounds. She could see the bucking horses in an adjacent pasture. The semitrucks and trailers were parked in a line along the back road.

Dusty saw Boone moving Devil's Tornado toward one of the corrals. She thought about when he'd kissed her and how she'd felt him digging in her purse. Looking for the syringe. Did he think she'd discarded it? Did he feel safe, even though he'd overheard Ty voicing his suspicions?

The lights went out, pitching the arena into darkness. In the distance, she thought she heard the wail of sirens but it was quickly lost in the boom of fireworks as the show got underway and some of the crowd began to wind their way out to their cars to beat the rush.

Dusty rubbed her arms, suddenly chilled at the memory of the anger she'd seen in Boone's eyes. Was it possible this man she'd thought so intriguing was a murderer? She rubbed her arm where he'd grabbed it.

Fireworks burst in bright colors over her head. She looked toward the corral where Boone had been headed just moments ago. He and Devil's Tornado were gone!

Her gaze leaped to the semis parked out back. All three were there. He couldn't have gotten away. He must just have moved the bull to another corral. Or maybe the pasture out back.

She shivered in spite of herself as another volley of fireworks exploded, showering the night sky in blinding white.

Suddenly, she sensed someone behind her. The next instant, two strong hands grabbed her shoulders and hauled her off the fence and back into the shadows.

Chapter 13

"You're coming with me and don't even try to argue," Ty whispered as he dragged Dusty off the fence and back into the dark shadows of the rodeo grounds as fireworks exploded all around them.

The moment he released her, Dusty swung around to face him. To his shock, she planted a quick kiss on his lips before he could speak again and hugged him fiercely.

Fireworks set the night sky ablaze. The boom reverberated in his chest.

"Why haven't you ever done that before?" she demanded drawing back to look at him.

"Done what?"

"Kissed me."

He quirked a smile at her. "What? And get my head knocked off? No way was I going to chance that."

As fireworks detonated overhead, she smiled at him

in the brightly colored light. What he saw in her eyes bowled him over. He never dreamed that he and Slim—

"Who would have known?" they both said in unison, then laughed, instantly sobering at the distinct sound of sirens between bursts of fireworks.

"The police are on their way," he said, and drew her closer. He had the syringe in his pocket. Once the police got blood from Devil's Tornado, they'd at least have a motive for Clayton and Waylon's murders.

The fireworks finale began, with one rocket blast of color and noise after another, ending in a thunderous boom.

Sparks drifted down, blinking out in the odd quiet that settled over the arena. Ty heard the distinct sound of a semitrailer door slam shut.

He and Dusty both turned in the direction of the trucks in time to see someone climb into the cab of the last one in line. Ty could make out the large shape of a bull in the back.

"Boone!" Dusty cried. "He's taking off with Devil's Tornado."

As the lights came on in the arena and people began to leave, the truck engine revved.

"We can't let Boone leave with that bull!" Dusty cried and took off running toward the semitruck before Ty could stop her.

He swore as she slipped through the chute fence, running ahead of him. He had to leap the fence, coming down hard in the soft earth.

Ty tried to keep his eye on the semi as Dusty closed the distance on it. On the other side of the truck, he saw boots as a second person moved along the back side of the trailer. The boots stopped at the driver's side door.

Dusty was almost to the semi, Ty right behind her. The motor suddenly revved even louder, but the truck didn't move as Dusty jumped up onto the running board and grabbed for the passenger side door handle.

Ty only got a glimpse of the boots on the other side of the truck before they disappeared as Dusty flung open the door and screamed.

Letty had parked in the rodeo grounds parking lot as everyone else was leaving. Dusty had said she was meeting Boone near the concession stands after the rodeo was over, so Letty headed there. She was surprised to hear sirens. They sounded as if they were headed this way.

What kind of trouble had Dusty gotten herself into? Letty joked to herself. With an affectionate smile, she thought of her friend. She couldn't wait to tell Dusty the news. Not just about her birth mother, but about Hal, whom she was meeting later tonight.

The concessions were all boarded up and dark. With a wave of disappointment, Letty looked around but didn't see Dusty. Maybe she'd missed her. Letty chastised herself for not confiding in her friend sooner. But then, Letty hadn't known things would turn out so right.

Hugging herself, she glanced toward the back of the rodeo grounds and spotted a semitruck and trailer parked behind two others. She could hear the truck's motor running. Starting toward the line of semis, she heard the crunch of a boot sole on gravel and saw someone moving along the other side of the trucks.

"Boone?" she called softly. The figure behind the semitruck froze. Her heart kicked up a beat. She licked her lips and took a breath. "Boone?"

Behind her, two police cars came tearing into the parking lot. Several officers jumped out and ran toward a dark-colored pickup parked in the lot. Boone's truck?

At a sound behind her, Letty swung back around. The figure behind the semitruck was gone!

Run! She barely got the thought out before he came out of the dark, his arm locking around her neck so quickly she didn't have time to react. She opened her mouth to scream but his free hand clamped over it.

She struggled, kicking and clawing as he dragged her deeper into the darkness.

"Keep fighting and I'll have to hurt you," a male voice whispered hoarsely in her ear, his breath hot, his arm tightened on her neck, cutting off her air.

She stopped struggling.

Dusty's scream was lost in the sound of the sirens.

"Wait!" Ty yelled after her. But that, too, was lost in her scream.

Ty was right behind her, leaping up to grab the edge of the door, afraid the truck would take off and kill them both.

Dusty shoved back against him, her mouth a perfect *O*, her eyes filled with horror in the dash lights of the truck cab.

Ty caught her and held her with one arm as he ducked down to look inside. Lamar's huge shape was behind the wheel, his head lolling back against the seat as if resting, his eyes wide with terror, his throat cut from ear to ear, his shirt crimson with his blood.

"Son of a bitch," Ty said and pulled Dusty from the running board to the ground. She was shaking hard. He wrapped his arms around her, burying his face into the hollow of her neck, his mind racing. He'd seen the killer's boots moving along the back side of the truck.

"I saw Boone arguing with Lamar before Devil's Tornado's ride," Dusty said glancing back at the semi. Boone. Where the hell was he?

"We have to find the cops," Ty said, turning to look back toward the arena. The grandstands were empty now, smoke from the fireworks show hanging heavy in the air.

"Boone is long gone," Ty said trying to still Dusty's trembling.

She shook her head and stepped from his arms to move along the side of the steel semitrailer. "He wouldn't leave without Devil's Tornado."

Through the narrow slit openings, Ty could see a bull standing inside the trailer.

But Boone and Devil's Tornado were gone.

Dusty couldn't quit shaking. She stared at the bull in the stock trailer. Boone had fooled them! He'd put a different bull in the trailer. He'd made them think he was the one in the semitruck trying to get away with Devil's Tornado, get away with what he'd done. Instead, he'd disappeared with the bull—after he killed Lamar.

She shuddered at the memory of Lamar, his throat cut.

Ty put an arm around her. "Come on, Slim. Let's find the cops."

She snuggled into him. Ty had always been there for her. What about that had she equated with a lack of mystery, no surprises? She'd known him since she was a child, and yet she didn't know him. Not the man who'd kissed her. Not the man who made her quake in his arms. Nor the strong, capable man who held her now.

"How did Boone get the bull out of here without us

seeing him?" Dusty asked, turning to stare at the line of semis.

Ty shook his head. She could tell he was wondering the same thing she was. Boone might be a lot of things, but he was no magician. So didn't that mean that he and the bull had to still be here somewhere?

Or maybe he'd left with the crowd, disappearing among the other cowboy hats. And Devil's Tornado? Where was the bull?

She shivered, chilled to the bone at the thought of what Boone was capable of. Instinctively, she'd known he was dangerous. That had been the attraction. The unknown. Letty had tried to warn her, but Dusty hadn't listened.

They hadn't gone more than a few yards from the trucks when Dusty sensed someone behind them. She saw Ty tense and spin around, pushing her to one side to protect her with his body.

Before Ty could get an arm up, Boone raised a gun and brought the butt end down on the side of Ty's head.

"No!" she cried as Ty crumpled to her feet and Boone Rasmussen grabbed her arm and jerked her to him.

"Where is the syringe?" Boone demanded, grabbing her shoulder bag and dumping it on the ground while keeping a firm grip on Dusty's arm.

"Ty," Dusty cried. He didn't answer, didn't move. She could hear the sirens again, only this time they seemed to be going away from the rodeo grounds.

Boone kicked away the larger objects that had fallen from the bag, then jerked Dusty to him hard. "*Where* is the syringe?"

"I threw it away," she said.

"You're a worse liar than your boyfriend."

He dragged her over to Ty and pulled her down next to him as he quickly went through Ty's pockets.

Questions ran through her mind: Why would Boone stay around here after killing Lamar to get the syringe? Was he crazy?

But Dusty quickly forgot Boone as she touched Ty's face. He felt ice-cold. "You bastard, you killed him!"

Boone let out an oath as he found the syringe in Ty's pocket. Clutching it in one hand, he dragged her up with the other. As he tried to stuff the syringe into his own pocket, Dusty launched herself at him. The last thing she remembered was seeing his fist, feeling it connect with her temple just before the earth came up to meet her.

Boone knew he shouldn't have been surprised that things were going so badly. Hell, hadn't he blown every chance he'd ever gotten? Why should this time be any different?

He stared down at Ty Coltrane. Dusty lay beside him, out like a light.

What the hell should he do now? He looked to the road past the rodeo grounds and blinked as he saw his pickup go racing by. Two cop cars were in hot pursuit. What the hell? *Someone had stolen his pickup?*

He felt in his pocket. How was that possible? He had his keys. Who in his right mind would go to the trouble to hot-wire and steal an old pickup?

The sound of the sirens grew fainter and fainter, the flashing lights disappearing in the distance.

How was he supposed to get out of here now?

The arena lights were still on. From this corner of darkness, he couldn't see anyone left around the rodeo grounds. Monte had left earlier. Apparently none of the cops had stayed behind—both police cars were chasing a car thief instead. Lucky for him, except now he had no vehicle to get the hell out of here.

What had the cops been doing here in the first place? All he could assume was that Coltrane had called them, planning to hand over the syringe—and Boone. That would explain why they were hot after his pickup.

Coltrane moaned. He wasn't dead. Boone was surprised at his relief. He couldn't stand the sight of Coltrane. What did he care if he was dead? But his body would be a complication Boone didn't need right now. He had enough complications.

He touched the syringe in his pocket. He had taken Devil's Tornado out to a field a quarter mile from the rodeo grounds. The bull wouldn't be found for a while and by then, there would be nothing *to* find. Hell, what did the cops have on him, anyway?

Nothing. He had the syringe. There was no evidence he'd been drugging the bull. Coltrane might have him jailed for assault, but other than that the cops couldn't prove anything.

Dusty was starting to come around. He knew she would start screaming her head off the moment she did. He didn't want to be around when that happened, he thought, glancing back at the semitruck and trailer.

He wished there was another way as he moved to the hulking shadow of the semi and swung open the driver's side door.

At first, his mind refused to accept what he was seeing. Blood. Lamar. So much blood. His stomach did a slow sickening roll. He stumbled back, fighting to keep from throwing up. His head was reeling. Someone had killed Lamar? Who—

He never saw the tire iron. Or the hand that wielded it. A blinding pain ripped through this skull an instant before the darkness as Boone pitched forward.

Dusty opened her eyes and was instantly assaulted by the smell, the noise and the jarring movement. She blinked, her head aching. Her hands and ankles were bound with duct tape. Another strip had been put across her mouth, forcing her to breathe through her nose.

The darkness stank of manure and hay, and she couldn't be sure which she was lying in.

Only a little light bled in through the slits along the side of the semitrailer as it rattled down the highway through the dark. At the front of the trailer where she lay was blackness. No headlights from other vehicles on the highway illuminated the interior.

She tried to sit up, but fell over as the semi took a curve. Pushing with her feet, she managed to work her way into the corner and get her back against the walls of the trailer, her eyes finally adjusting to the dizzying darkness.

At the far end of the trailer by the door, she saw a shape. She stared until her eyes burned. The dark shape moved and Dusty let out a muffled cry as she realized it was a bull. Devil's Tornado?

Fear paralyzed her. She could feel the bull looking at her. She'd seen what Devil's Tornado had tried to do to the cowboys in the arena after the bucking rigging had been removed. The bull was a killer. He'd stomp her to death or gore her or—

Devil's Tornado seemed to sway before her eyes, then dropped to his knees, going all the way to the floor of the trailer as he lay down as docile as an old cow.

Closer, Dusty heard another sound. Movement and a low moan. She looked to her left, to the adjacent dark corner of the trailer. Ty?

Her eyes widened in horror!

Letty—her hands bound, her mouth taped, her eyes wide and terrified stared back at her from the darkness!

What was Letty doing here? And where was Ty? She searched the darkness, but quickly realized that she and Letty were alone with a bull in the back of the semitrailer headed for God only knew where with a killer at the wheel. Where was Boone taking them?

Frantically, Dusty began to work at the tape on her mouth, pushing it with her tongue as she rubbed at the corner with her shoulder along the rough edge of her jacket. She could feel the edge start to peel back. Her skin chafed from the effort, but she had to be able to talk to Letty. To reassure her. To reassure herself that somehow they were going to get out of this.

Blinded by the bright light, Ty Coltrane closed his eyes and tried to sit up. "Where's Dusty?"

"Easy," one of the policemen standing over him warned. "You've got quite the knot on your head. We've called for an ambulance. Can you tell us who hit you?"

"Boone Rasmussen. I have to find Dusty," Ty said, pushing to his feet. His gaze went to the spot where the semitrucks and trailers had been. One was missing. "He's got her. He's taken the truck." Ty turned to head for his pickup, but one of the cops grabbed his arm.

"Hold on," the officer said. "You're not going anywhere. We need to ask you some questions."

Ty jerked free and probably would have ended up in jail if he hadn't stopped to watch a helicopter set down

in the middle of the arena—and see Sheriff Cash Mc-
Call climb out of it.

"Cash!" he called as the sheriff ran toward him. "Rasmussen has Dusty. I think he took her in one of the
Edgewood semitrucks. Lamar is dead."

Cash began barking orders, starting with getting an
APB out on the semitruck, then turned to the police officers in confusion. "Did you just get here? I called you
hours ago."

One of the officers, Sgt. Mike Johnson, stepped forward. "After your call, we came to the rodeo grounds,
spotted Boone Rasmussen's pickup, based on the description and plate number you gave us, and pursued the
pickup as the driver gave chase."

Ty stared at the cop. "But Rasmussen was here with
me and Dusty."

The cop nodded. "We finally forced the driver of the
pickup off the road about twelve miles out of town and
took her into custody. It wasn't Boone Rasmussen, but a
woman by the name of Sierra Edgewood."

"Sierra was driving Rasmussen's pickup?" Ty asked
in surprise.

"She'd been drinking," the cop said. "Told us that she
thought her husband, Monte Edgewood, had set us on her
and that she had kept going out of fear of what her husband would do to her if she was caught and turned over
to him." The cop looked to Cash. "Is there any basis for
her concerns about her husband?"

"Not that I know of," Cash said. "She had a key to
Rasmussen's pickup?"

The cop nodded. "A single key. She said she'd had it
made one day when she'd borrowed the pickup. Planned
to use it to get away from her abusive husband."

"No way," Ty spoke up. "She was a diversion so Boone could get away." His head ached. He rubbed a hand over his face. "But why would Sierra Edgewood help Boone Rasmussen?"

"Good question," Cash said.

From over by the other two semis, one of the police officers yelled, "I've got a body over here."

"His name is Lamar Nichols," Cash said after taking a look. "If you have any more questions for Mr. Coltrane, they will have to wait. It appears the killer might have my sister. Don't try to apprehend him if you find him. Wait for me." He looked to Ty. "Let's find Dusty."

The two ran to the highway patrol helicopter and buckled up as the chopper took off.

"Boone could be headed in any direction," Cash said. "He's originally from Texas. I'd think he would head south on 191 along the Gallatin River."

Ty tried to calm the panic rising in him as Cash told the pilot to head south toward West Yellowstone and the Idaho border. Had Boone taken Dusty? What would he do to her? Was she even still alive?

Ty stared down at the dark ribbon of highway and river below them. Who knew where Rasmussen would go. Or what he would do. Ty tried to concentrate and not panic.

Would he go back to Texas? Or hide somewhere? "He'll have to get rid of the semi for something less conspicuous," Ty said out loud. But why take Dusty? "She has to be a hostage in case he's cornered and has to bargain his way out."

"We can only hope that's the case," Cash said. "That means he will want to keep her alive."

Cash checked in with the highway patrol and sheriff's

departments on the ground. Ty could tell from this side of the conversation that there was still no sign of the semi.

Ty thought about what Cash had told the Bozeman police. It was believed that Rasmussen had killed three people to keep his secret—Clayton T. Brooks, Waylon Dobbs and Lamar Nichols. He was desperate. He could do anything.

Cash took another call on the radio. Ty saw him frown and held his breath, terrified it was news of Dusty. Bad news.

"Is it…?" he asked.

Cash shook his head. "No word on Rasmussen or Dusty."

Cash got another call and took it as Ty watched the highway below them for the semi.

Cash clicked off and Ty could tell from his expression that this call hadn't been good news. "It was one of the roughstock producers in Texas I'd contacted about Rasmussen." Cash frowned. "Did you know that Lamar was Rasmussen's half brother?"

Ty shook his head.

"If Rasmussen had one allegiance, it would be to his own blood, wouldn't you think? And given that he'd brought Lamar up here with him from Texas, given him a job…"

"Unless he killed him to keep him from talking," Ty said.

Cash shook his head as if struggling with the same thing Ty was. If Rasmussen hadn't killed Lamar, then who did that leave?

Cash let out an oath. "You aren't thinking what I'm thinking?"

"That Sierra was a diversion, but not for Boone Rasmussen?" Ty said.

Cash swore again and leaned toward the pilot. "Take us to Antelope Flats as fast as you can get this thing to go."

Chapter 14

Dusty managed to peel back the edge of the tape on her mouth. She used her tongue to free all but one corner.

"Letty!" she cried as she scooted toward the opposite corner to her friend. Tears shone in Letty's eyes. "Turn around and I'll try to free your hands."

Dusty squirmed around until she had her back to Letty's. She began to work at the tape around Letty's wrists. It was slow going. As she worked, she told Letty everything, about Ty and the kiss, about Boone, about the syringe she'd picked up in the corral that night in Sheridan and had forgotten about. She left out the part about Lamar, not wanting to scare Letty even worse.

She almost had Letty's hands free when the truck slowed, throwing them both off balance. The semi turned onto a bumpy dirt road. Dusty worked her way close to Letty again and tugged faster at the duct tape holding Letty's wrists together.

Dusty could feel time slipping away. The semi moved slowly along the dirt road, giving her the feeling that it wasn't going far. She had to get Letty free and quickly.

As the truck began to slow down even more, the last of the tape pulled free.

Letty reached up and jerked the tape from her mouth with a cry of pain then hurriedly began tugging at the tape on Dusty's wrists. She talked ninety miles an hour, telling Dusty about having been stolen from her birth mother, about meeting Hal Branson, finding her birth mother and coming to the rodeo to tell her best friend.

As Letty freed Dusty's wrists, the two hugged fiercely, both crying in relief and fear, before quickly working to free their ankles.

As the truck rolled to a stop, Devil's Tornado stirred at the rear of the trailer.

A yard light came on. Light cut through the slits in the side of the trailer.

Dusty blinked, seeing something she hadn't been able to earlier. There was something lying on the other side of Devil's Tornado. Ty?

She scrambled to her feet and rushed toward the bull, forgetting about her safety in her fear that she would find Ty lying dead at the back of the semitrailer.

But Devil's Tornado didn't move. Just watched her with a disinterested, almost too calm look. *He's drugged*, Dusty thought, an instant before she saw the cowboy stretched out on the floor next to the bull.

It wasn't Ty, she saw at once. Behind Dusty, Letty let out a small cry. "Boone? If Boone's in here with us, then who—"

Letty didn't get to finish as the door of the trailer

clanged open and the two stood staring down at Monte Edgewood—and the gun he held in his hand, the barrel pointed in their direction.

"Well, aren't you two clever getting loose," Monte said congenially. "Come on down from there."

"I don't understand what's going on," Dusty said as she looked from Monte's big open face to the gun in his hand. Everyone in the county liked Monte Edgewood. Some had wondered if he'd lost his mind when he married a woman half his age. No one had ever really liked Sierra. But if anything, they were kinder to Monte because of their dislike for his young wife.

"Come on down, girls," Monte said and motioned with the gun for Dusty to step down first. Letty followed, hanging on to the back of Dusty's jacket.

He herded them toward a small old barn. Dusty could see the moon peeking in and out of the clouds overhead and tried to estimate how long they'd been in the back of the semitrailer. She didn't recognize the barn. It was old and crumbling and could have been located anywhere in Montana, or for that matter, in Idaho or Wyoming.

But she got the feeling that it was on Monte's property as he swung open the door and ushered them both inside. Straw bales were stacked along one wall. An old lantern sat on a bench nearby, the flickering flame lighting the small interior.

Dusty stumbled in with Letty at her side as Monte forced them back against the straw bales. There was little else in the barn. She tried to see past the lantern light to dark corners, looking for something she could use as a weapon. There was no doubt in her mind that Monte Edgewood intended to kill them.

"Where is Ty?" she asked, afraid of the answer. But she had to know.

"At the rodeo, where we left him." Monte patted her shoulder. "Don't worry. He's fine. By now, the police have found him. He'll live."

Dusty felt Letty shudder next to her, the words, *he'll live* hanging in the air as if to say Ty would live, unlike her and Letty.

"Mr. Edgewood—" Letty began.

"Call me Monte," he said. "You're the Arnolds' girl, right?"

Letty didn't answer. "What are you going to do with us?"

"Not me. Boone." He made a disappointed face. "He was like a son to me. I trusted him. I took him into my home. I taught him about the roughstock business. I would have given him anything." Monte let out a laugh that chilled Dusty to the bone. "Hell, I *did* give him everything." His eyes narrowed, darkened; the hand holding the gun seemed to quiver. "Including my wife."

Dusty took Letty's hand and squeezed it, trying to reassure her when Dusty herself was scared speechless.

Monte looked up at them as if he'd been gone for a moment. He blinked, seemed to refocus. "Boone was such a fool. If he'd just come to me with his plan. Hell, I would have helped him. But he didn't trust me." He shook his head. "Trust. It all comes down to trust, doesn't it?"

Dusty thought about making a run for it with Letty, but she knew Monte would chase them down even if they split up, which Dusty wasn't about to do.

She listened, thought she heard something, a faint hum in the distance. A vehicle? Ty had called her brother.

Cash would be looking for her. Only both Ty and Cash would think that Boone had her—not Monte Edgewood.

"It's funny," Monte said more to himself than Dusty and Letty. "You never know what you will do. You think you know yourself. You have this image of the kind of person you are. Then something happens. You have everything you've ever wanted and more, and someone comes along and offers you a chance to be famous. And even though you know it's a false kind of rise to fame, you latch on to the dream because you want so desperately to be a part of it."

Dusty let her gaze scan the barn for a weapon. She had no idea what Monte was talking about. He sounded half-crazy. That scared her as much as the gun. The hum in the air she'd heard earlier seemed to be getting louder. Not a vehicle. More like a plane. Or a helicopter!

She spotted a pitchfork by the door and an old ax handle on the floor in the corner, nothing else. Neither was close enough to get to them before Monte fired the gun.

But the lantern was only a few yards away on the other side of Letty.

Dusty realized that Monte had stopped talking. "What was the dream?" she asked hurriedly, latching on to the only word she could recall.

He frowned. "A bull that would make everyone in the country remember the name Edgewood Roughstock Company. Devil's Tornado."

Everyone will remember that name now, Dusty thought.

Monte had stopped talking again and was listening now, his expression making it clear that he, too, heard the sound of what could have been a helicopter outside, coming closer.

"I'm sorry it has to end like this," he said. "Boone was

a bad seed. It was my fault for letting him infect me and my wife. Once he is gone… I'm just sorry that he killed so many people before he was stopped." Monte raised the gun, pointing it at Letty.

Dusty still had hold of her friend's hand. "No!" Dusty cried, stepping in front of Letty to lunge for the lantern Monte had left on a small bench nearby. She flung the lantern in Monte's direction as she dragged Letty to the barn floor with her.

The deafening sound of a gunshot boomed in the empty barn, sending a flock of pigeons flapping down from the rafters overhead. Dust filled the air an instant after the lantern ricocheted off Monte's arm. Glass exploded as the lantern hit the floor. Fuel and flames skittered up the dry wood wall, setting the straw bales on fire.

Dusty and Letty scrambled to their feet. But Monte was blocking the door, the gun raised as he tried to take aim at them. They dove for the back of the barn, realizing too late there was no way out as flames lapped at the dried wood of the old barn, thick smoke quickly filling the small space.

Dusty's eyes burned as she pulled the corner of her jacket up to cover her mouth and nose. Letty did the same. They were trapped. There was no place to run. No place to hide. Monte raised the gun.

Something moved behind Monte. Dusty felt her heart jump, praying it would be help. Boone Rasmussen materialized in the doorway.

"Monte!" He picked up the pitchfork and called again. "Monte!"

Monte turned slowly, seeming surprised to see Boone, even more surprised to see the pitchfork in his hand. The older man shook his head, as if he knew Boone wouldn't use it. He raised the gun and fired.

Boone stumbled back a step and looked down at the blood pouring out of the bullet hole in his chest. Then he raised the pitchfork and lunged at Monte.

Monte fired again. Through the smoke, Dusty saw Boone fall to his knees. Behind him, Ty appeared like a mirage from out of the darkness in the barn doorway.

The fire crackled all around them, sweeping up the walls, setting the roof on fire.

Dusty called to Ty to watch out as Monte raised the gun to fire at him. She rushed Monte, Letty beside her. They hit him hard from behind. He stumbled and went down.

Ty grabbed Dusty and Letty and dragged them out of the inferno. Dusty caught sight of her brother as Cash pulled Boone's body out as charred timbers began to fall from overhead.

Cash started to go back for Monte, But it was too late. The roof collapsed in a shower of sparks and smoke. Dusty buried her face in Ty's chest as flames engulfed what was left of the barn—and Monte Edgewood.

Chapter 15

Dusty felt as if she were in a fog as they left the Edgewood ranch and headed for the clinic in town.

Boone had already been pronounced dead at the scene. Parts of the barn still burning. The fire department and coroner had been called.

Cash had the helicopter take Dusty and Letty to the clinic, sending Ty along with them. Although everyone involved in the case seemed to be dead or, in Sierra's case, in jail, Cash wasn't taking any chances.

Cash stopped by the hospital with questions for Dusty and Ty. Dusty told her brother about the night after the rodeo when someone had followed her home.

"It was Boone," Dusty said. "I didn't know it at the time, but he must have seen me pick up the syringe. I stuck it in my purse and forgot all about it."

"I've seen all the stuff you have in that purse, so I can believe that," Cash said. "But why pick it up at all?"

Dusty shot him a duh look. "One of the horses could have stepped on it. Any rancher would pick it up and pocket it."

"Probably why I became a sheriff," he said.

"Sierra is singing like a canary from her jail cell in Bozeman," Cash said. "She said she'd awakened the night Clayton T. Brooks was murdered to see her husband coming in from the far pasture, his shirt and jeans covered in blood. She'd pretended to be asleep as he put the clothes into the washer and showered before returning to bed."

"So she knew," Ty said shaking his head.

"When she'd heard Clayton had been murdered and that Cash thought Clayton had come out to the Edgewood Roughstock Ranch the night he died, Sierra still couldn't believe Monte had killed him," Cash said. "At least that's her story. She said she thought Monte was covering for Boone."

"What about Waylon's murder?" Ty asked.

"Sierra says Waylon had been by the ranch the day he died," Cash said. "She'd seen Waylon and Monte out in the yard arguing."

"So you think Waylon tried to blackmail Monte?"

"Appears that way," Cash said. "According to Sierra, Monte had come into the house upset. Later he left and when he came back, she smelled smoke on him. But she also smelled smoke on Boone later that night when she went to his bed. Boone said it was from Lamar smoking in his truck. We still don't know how Boone's watch ended up in the ashes at Waylon's house if Monte set the fire."

Dusty frowned. "I might. You know that night at the rodeo in Sheridan, the night Boone chased me home? I saw Boone drop something on the ground. At the time I just saw something glitter. It must have been his watch because Monte picked it up and pocketed it."

"Then used the watch to try to frame Boone for Waylon's murder and the fire," Cash said.

"So Sierra really did take Boone's truck to get away from Monte?" Ty asked.

Cash nodded. "She says she realized he knew about her and Boone and that she feared he planned to kill her, too."

"Why?" Letty asked. "Why would someone like Monte Edgewood do this?"

"Greed, pride, the need to be somebody," Cash said. "He saw that Devil's Tornado could make him famous. Once he found out that Boone was drugging the bull, he chose to kill to cover the deception."

"By killing?" Ty asked. "He couldn't possibly think he could get away with it."

"Once he found out about Sierra and Boone, he planned to frame Boone for all the murders," Dusty said, remembering what Monte had said in the barn last night.

"According to Sierra, under the contract Monte had with Boone, if something happened to Boone, Monte would get Devil's Tornado," Cash said. "Except it turns out that Devil's Tornado is really a docile bull named Little Joe."

"What happens to the Edgewood Roughstock Ranch and Little Joe?" Dusty asked.

"Sierra inherits it all," Cash said. "She already has a lawyer looking into selling everything, lock, stock and barrel. I would imagine that will be the last we see of her."

"So it's over," Ty said.

"Seems that way," Cash agreed.

Dr. Taylor Ivers came back into the room to give Letty and Dusty some salve for the slight blistering they'd suffered on their faces. She'd already treated them for smoke inhalation and said they could go.

Dusty thanked the doctor. Taylor was part of the Mc-Call family in an extended way. Everyone had thought Taylor would leave town after everything that had happened, but she seemed determined to stay on at the clinic.

Taylor seemed to be lightening up a little. Dusty had heard that Taylor and her sister Anna Austin VanHorn McCall even had lunch once a week now.

"You need a ride home?" Cash asked Dusty.

"I borrowed a pickup from a friend," Ty said quickly. "I'll take her and Letty home."

Cash smiled and nodded, giving his sister a hug before he left.

When Ty pulled up in front of Letty's motel, Hal Branson was waiting for her.

Hal had been out of his mind when she hadn't shown up for their date and, after talking to the police, had driven clear to Antelope Flats in the middle of the night because he'd been so worried about her. The last time he'd talked to Letty, she was headed for the rodeo to meet Dusty—and Hal had feared she'd met up with more than Dusty.

Dusty couldn't have handpicked a man more perfect for Letty, she thought, when she met Hal. She could just imagine their children. And seeing the joy in both of their faces, Dusty had a feeling marriage and children wouldn't be that far off.

Hal offered to make coffee since the sun would be coming up soon. He and Letty went into the house behind the motel office.

"I'll give you a ride home," Ty offered. "Unless you want to stay here and have coffee."

Dusty shook her head. "Three's a crowd." She reached over and took one of the keys off the board behind the motel desk. "Looks like No. 9 is empty," she said and tossed the key to him.

Ty stared down at the key, then up at Slim. He'd never been so thrown off balance by any woman in his life. His gaze met hers.

"Well?" she asked.

"Slim—"

"I know. It's been one hell of a night. I have no intention of going home and having to tell this story again." Her eyes locked with his. "Nor do I plan to spend what's left of this night alone in my bed." She smiled. "I already told Cash I wouldn't be coming home tonight. You going to try to make a liar out of me?"

"You sure about this, Slim?"

"More sure than I have ever been about anything in my life," she said leaning into him to kiss him. "And you know me."

He chuckled. "Oh, yeah, I know you, Slim." And he was about to get to know her better. "But I have to tell you that I always pictured us married first, me carrying you over the threshold of our new house."

"Really?" She smiled. "How long would it take to build this house?"

"Six months, at least."

"Great," she said, taking the motel room key from his hand. "That will give us plenty of time to get to know each other better. Starting tonight."

She started to walk past him, but he reached out and pulled her to him, kissing her as he took the motel room key.

"It's not the same as our own home, mind you," he said as he swung her up in his arms and shoved open the door. "But for tonight, it will have to do."

Dusty was trembling when he set her down in motel room No. 9. Nine for luck, she thought as she looked up at him. A chill rippled across her skin, an ache in her belly. This was Ty, a boy she'd known all her life.

Only as she looked at him, she realized he wasn't a boy anymore. She was staring into the eyes of a man. A man whom she suspected would continue to surprise her until the day she died.

A shudder quaked through her as he took her in his arms and kissed her, deepening the kiss as he molded his body to hers.

"Ty," she moaned against his wonderful mouth.

His large hands took her shoulders and backed her up until she was pressed against the wall. His mouth dropped to hers again. The sensation was like fireworks exploding through her body.

He rested his hand on the curve of her hip. Snaked his fingers up her rib cage and slipped it under the edge of her bra. A soft sigh escaped her lips as his warm hand cupped her breast. He bent to press his mouth against her throat, sending a shiver of kisses along the rim of her ear. His tongue licked across her warm skin as his hands skimmed over her body, as if he were memorizing every inch, tasting every inch.

Her fingers dug into his muscled back as he carried her over to the bed. "Slim," he whispered, then drew back. "Would you rather I call you Dusty?" he asked, so serious it made her laugh.

She shook her head. She was his Slim and they both knew it.

She didn't remember him taking off her clothes. Or her taking off his. But suddenly they were naked, their bodies melding together as they rolled around on the bed, laughing and kissing, his blue eyes a flame burning over her bare skin, hotter than the fire in the barn.

His mouth dropped to her breast and she thought she would die from the sheer pleasure of it. She buried her hands in his thick hair, moaning as he gently bit down on her hard nipple, arching against him, loving the feel of flesh to flesh. Loving Ty.

He made love to her slowly, gently, with a kind of awe, as if amazed that she had given herself to him so completely. She found even the pain of her first time was pleasurable. They made love again as the sun rose on another day, all the horror of what they'd been through slipping away like clouds after a rainstorm.

In Ty's arms, she found everything she'd dreamed of and more. He fulfilled her every fantasy as if he knew exactly what she wanted. What she needed. Later, she propped herself up on one elbow and looked down at him, surprised that she felt no embarrassment.

"Your father is going to think we're too young to get married," Ty said, running his thumb along her lower lip.

She kissed the rough pad of his thumb and shook her head. "My father will be delighted."

Ty didn't look so sure about that.

"You'll see. I know my father." She fell silent for a moment, thinking about Asa. "Can I tell you something?"

"You can tell me anything, Slim."

"I think he's dying."

Ty sat up in surprise. "Oh, honey."

She nodded and brushed at the tears that blurred her eyes. "I saw something in his expression at the last family dinner. I think he planned to tell us all, but then Cash had to leave." She bit down on her lower lip as Ty pulled her to him, holding her tightly in his arms.

They made love again, slow and sweet. She fell into a deep sleep in Ty's arms, only to be awakened by the phone late the next day.

Ty answered it, listened, then handed it to her, his face set in a grim line that frightened her.

"Dusty?" It was Shelby. What was her mother doing calling her? The only way she would have known where to find her was from Cash—and there was no way he would have told Shelby about what had happened last night.

"What's wrong?" Dusty asked, sitting up, thinking it might be about her father.

"You have to come home," Shelby said.

Dusty was ready to launch into a speech about how she was twenty-one and she didn't have to explain herself when Shelby said, "I wouldn't have called you, Dusty, but it's your father."

Dusty gripped the phone tighter.

"He wants everyone to come out to the ranch," Shelby said. "Rourke, Brandon and J.T. are already here with their wives. Cash and Molly are on their way. You're welcome to bring Ty with you. This concerns everyone who your father—" her voice broke "—loves."

Dusty could hear her mother crying softly.

"We'll be right there."

Once everyone was seated around the large dining room table, Asa McCall stood. It took all the strength he had, but he wanted to do this standing. He didn't want them to see how weak he was. Soon enough, they would know.

"I appreciate you all coming on such short notice," he said, looking around the table at each of them, his sons and their wives or soon-to-be-wives, Dusty and Ty. He'd always hoped his headstrong daughter would realize that the man of her dreams lived just up the road.

There was so much he wanted to say to them.

To think he'd almost lost Dusty last night. Cash had filled him in, no doubt leaving out many of the more frightening details. The thought that Dusty might not be here with them practically dropped him to his knees.

Shelby reached over and took his hand, squeezed it and smiled reassuringly at him. The love of his life. Strong, just like her daughter. He thanked God for that.

He cleared his throat and began the story about his friend Charley and the land deal, telling the story quickly, simply.

He knew his children would understand the consequences at once. They were too smart not to.

When he'd finished, J.T. had his head in his hands. Everyone looked stricken.

"I don't see how you could have let something like this happen," J.T. said, then shook his head.

"It happened," Rourke cut in. "The question is, what can we do?"

Asa shook his head and suddenly had to sit down. "We haven't enough money or capital to buy him out. The mineral rights are worth more than the land."

"There must be some way to stop this," Cash said. "Have you talked to a lawyer?"

"The contract cannot be broken," Asa said. "I've already tried to buy back the mineral rights. He wouldn't sell to me even if I could raise that much money."

"But we're at the north end of the coal fields," Rourke said. "There might not even be any coalbed methane gas at this end of the valley. That mineral rights contract might not be worth the paper it's written on."

"It seems Charley's son is willing to take that chance," Asa said.

"It will change the ranch, but we will still own the land," Dusty spoke up, as if waiting for worse news. He'd seen the look in her eyes when she'd come into the room. She knew he was dying. Like her mother, she probably could also see how weak he was and that this was taking every ounce of his strength.

He smiled down the table at her, grateful to have such a daughter.

"There will be roads all over to the gas well heads," Rourke was saying. "Even if they don't find gas, they will drill for months. Maybe even years, putting in roads, ruining the land."

"Yesterday, I received a letter in the mail that Charley's son has sold the mineral rights lease," Asa said and looked down the table at his youngest son. "It was bought up by Mason VanHorn."

He watched Brandon look over at his wife, Anna Van-Horn McCall, in surprise. Asa had been trying to come to terms with the fact that Brandon had gone against his wishes and married Anna. He'd feared that the long-standing feud between the McCalls and the VanHorns would end up destroying his son's life. When he'd seen the letter and found out that Mason VanHorn had bought up the mineral rights lease for McCall land, Asa knew his worst fear had come true.

Only Mason VanHorn had the kind of money to buy up the lease. Asa was thankful he wouldn't live long enough to see a VanHorn drilling on McCall land.

"Is that true?" Brandon asked Anna.

She rose slowly from her seat at the table. She was a beautiful woman, just as her mother had been. Reaching into her pocket, she pulled out a thick envelope of papers and handed them to her husband. "These are for Asa."

Brandon took them and, without looking at them, passed them down the table to Asa.

"It's true, my father purchased the mineral rights lease," Anna said. "It was his wedding present to me and Brandon." She met Asa's gaze. "And a peace offering, so that the children and grandchildren of the McCalls and the VanHorns can finally live in peace."

Asa felt his hands begin to shake as he read the papers, his eyes filling with tears of gratitude as he looked down the table at his daughter-in-law. He could only shake his head in disbelief, his sworn enemy coming to his rescue.

The irony wasn't lost on him. VanHorn had made a fortune in gas wells—something Asa had sworn would never be found on his ranch. And in the end? VanHorn had used that fortune to buy back Asa's soul from the devil. In return, Mason VanHorn asked for nothing. Nothing, after all the years of the bad blood between them.

"Thank you," Asa said. "I look forward to the day when I can thank your father in person."

"But there's more, isn't there?" Cash said. "More you need to tell us."

Asa nodded and looked to Dusty. "But first, I think there is something you'd like to say?"

Dusty got to her feet, all eyes on her. "I'm in love with Ty Coltrane."

Everyone looked at her as if waiting for more.

"Of course you are," Shelby said, smiling, as if she'd known it all along.

"He's asked me to marry him," Dusty continued, her gaze shifting to her father. "It's going to be a small wedding. Just family. Tomorrow."

There were sounds of surprise around the table, but Dusty saw her father nod and Shelby start to cry quietly.

"You sure about this?" J.T. asked, looking around the table in confusion. "This is so sudden. You haven't even *dated.*"

Dusty smiled. "Someone once told me that when you found your true love, you just knew. You didn't have to kiss a lot of frogs. Or a lot of princes. You just had to know in your heart that this was the right person for you. Ty's my true love." Tears rushed to her eyes as she looked at her father, saw him squeeze the hand of his true love. "I want you to give me away," she said to her father.

His jaw tensed, as if he were fighting to keep his face from showing the emotion she saw in his eyes. "It would be my pleasure," he said, voice cracking.

J.T. let out an expletive. The rest of the family had fallen silent. He looked down the table at his father. "How long do you have?"

"Not long enough."

Epilogue

Rain fell in a light drizzle on the day of Asa McCall's funeral. Dusty stood on the hillside, her husband Ty beside her, his arm around her as she huddled against the cold and wetness and grief.

Across from her stood her brothers Rourke, Cash and Brandon, next to them their wives, their expressions somber as they stared down at their father's casket.

Brandon's eyes filled with tears. Dusty saw Anna clutch his hand tighter. Mason VanHorn held his daughter's hand as he, too, stood in the rain over his once worst enemy's grave. The two had found peace only at the end of Asa's life, a horrible waste that Dusty knew would haunt Mason to his own grave.

Shelby stood between Dusty and her eldest son, J.T., his wife, Reggie, next to him.

The pastor cleared this throat. "As anyone standing here knows, Asa McCall wasn't much of a churchgoer."

There was a slight nervous titter from the crowd. "In fact, he didn't hold much patience with a man of the collar." Pastor Grayson smiled. "I remember the first time I met Asa McCall. We got into a discussion about God." He chuckled. "Asa said he had a fine arrangement with God. God tried his patience every day—and Asa tried the Lord's. He said they'd been getting along just fine with that arrangement for years, and he saw no reason to confuse God by acting any different."

A smattering of laughter, then sniffles.

"That strong, sometimes impossible, man is who we are putting to rest here today," the pastor said. "Asa lived life on his terms and took full responsibility for the whole of it. He was a God-fearing man who, like the rest of us, made his share of mistakes." Pastor Grayson looked over at Shelby. "I had the good fortune to speak with Asa before he passed away. He told me of his regrets— the greatest one being not living long enough to see all of his grandchildren."

Dusty blinked back tears. Ty pulled her closer.

"But Asa died knowing that his children and their children would continue the legacy his father had begun so many years ago when he brought the first herd of longhorns to Montana and settled in this valley. That, he told me, was more than he ever could have wanted— to see his lifework continued by his own children and their children."

Pastor Grayson opened the small black Bible in his hands and looked down. "Asa asked me to read this today. It's something he wrote just before he died."

The pastor cleared his voice and began to read, "By the time you hear this, I will be gone from you. Don't mourn my passing. I had a long and fruitful life. Bury me on the hillside with the rest of the McCalls and then get on with your lives. You have a ranch to run and children to make and raise. Don't try to make me into a saint. I was a stubborn jackass. I want my grandchildren to know the man I really was. Maybe it will keep them from making the mistakes I did.

"I ask only one other thing. Take care of your mother. Don't blame her for my asinine behavior so many years ago. Pushing her from my life is my greatest regret, second only to never telling all of you how much I love you, admire you, respect you. You have all made an old man proud."

Tears streamed down Dusty's face as she looked over at her mother and saw the naked grief in her face. Dusty reached out and took her mother's hand. Her mother seemed surprised, then smiled through her tears and squeezed her daughter's hand.

Slowly, Asa McCall's casket was lowered into the ground on the ranch he'd loved. Dusty looked past the old family cemetery to the view of the Big Horn Mountains and McCall land stretching as far as the eye could see. Her father's view for eternity, she thought as she turned her face into Ty's strong shoulder, felt his arms come around her as she said goodbye to her father.

* * * * *

Also by Nicole Helm

HQN

Witchlore

Small Town, Big Magic
Big Little Spells

Harlequin Intrigue

A Badlands Cops Novel

South Dakota Showdown
Covert Complication
Backcountry Escape
Isolated Threat
Badlands Beware
Close Range Christmas

Carsons & Delaneys

Wyoming Cowboy Justice
Wyoming Cowboy Protection
Wyoming Christmas Ransom
Stone Cold Texas Ranger
Stone Cold Undercover Agent
Stone Cold Christmas Ranger

Visit her Author Profile page at Harlequin.com,
or nicolehelm.com, for more titles!

STONE COLD TEXAS RANGER

Nicole Helm

To all the episodes of *20/20* and *Dateline*
I watched with my grandma.
They might have given me nightmares,
but they also gave me a ton of great book ideas.

Chapter 1

Vaughn Cooper was not an easy man to like. There was a time when he'd been quicker with a smile or a joke, but twelve years in law enforcement and three years in the Unsolved Crimes Investigation Unit of the Texas Rangers had worn off any charm he'd been born with.

He was not a man who believed in the necessity of small talk, politeness or pretending a situation was anything other than what it was.

He was most definitely not a man who believed in *hypnotism*, even if the woman currently putting their witness under acted both confident and capable.

He didn't trust it, her or what she did, and he was more than marginally irritated that the witness seemed to immediately react. No more fidgeting, no more yelling that he didn't know anything. After Natalie Torres's ministrations, the man was still and pleasant.

Vaughn didn't believe it for a second.

"I told you," Bennet Stevens said, giving him a nudge. Bennet had been his partner for the past two years, and Vaughn liked him. Some days. This was not one of those days.

"It's not real. He's acting." Vaughn made no effort to lower his voice. It was purposeful, and he watched carefully for any sign of reaction from the supposedly hypnotized witness.

He didn't catch any, but he could all but feel Ms. Torres's angry gaze on him. He didn't care if she was angry. All he cared about was getting to the bottom of this case before another woman disappeared.

He wasn't sure his weary conscience could take another thing piled on top of the overflowing heap.

"How are you today, Mr. Herman?" Ms. Torres asked in that light, airy voice she'd hypnotized the man with. Vaughn rolled his eyes. That anyone would fall for this was beyond him. They were police officers. They dealt in evidence and reality, not *hypnotism*.

"Been better," the witness grumbled.

"I see," she continued, that easy, calming tone to her voice never changing. "Can you tell us a little bit about your problems?"

"Nah."

"You know, you're safe here, Mr. Herman. You can speak freely. This is a safe place where you can unburden yourself."

Vaughn tried to tamp down his edgy impatience. He couldn't get over them wasting their time doing this, but it hadn't been his call. This had come from above him, and he had no choice but to follow through.

"Yeah?"

The hypnotist inclined her head toward Vaughn and

Bennet. It was the agreed upon sign that they would now take over the questioning.

"It's not a bad gig," Herman said, his hands linked together on the table in front of him. No questions needed.

Yeah, Vaughn didn't believe a second of this.

"Don't have to get my hands too dirty. Paid cash. My old lady's got cancer. Goes a long way, you know?"

"Rough," Bennet said, doing a far better job than Vaughn of infusing some sympathy into his tone. "What kind of jobs you running?"

"Mostly just messages, you know. I don't even gotta be the muscle. Just deliver the information. It's a sweet deal. But…"

"But what?"

Vaughn could feel the hypnotist's eyes on him. Something about her. Something about *this*. It was all off. He wasn't even being paranoid like Bennet too often accused him of. The witness was too easy, and the woman was too jumpy.

"But… Man, I don't like this, though. I got a daughter of my own. I never wanted to get involved with this part."

"What part's that?"

"The girls. He keeps the girls."

Vaughn tensed, and he noticed the hypnotist did, as well.

"Who keeps them?"

Vaughn and Bennet whirled to face Ms. Torres. She wasn't supposed to ask questions. Not after she gave them the signal. Not about the case.

"What the hell do you think—"

"The Stallion," Herman muttered. "But I can't cross The Stallion."

Vaughn immediately looked at Bennet. He gave his

partner an imperceptible nod, then Bennet slipped out of the room.

The Stallion. An idiotic name for the head of an organized crime group that had been stealthily wreaking havoc across Texas for ten years. Vaughn had no less than four cases he knew connected to the bastard or his drug-running cronies, but this one…

"What do you know about The Stallion?" Vaughn asked evenly, though frustration pounded in his bloodstream. Still, hypnotism or no hypnotism, he wasn't the type of ranger who let that show.

"You don't cross him. You don't cross him and live."

Vaughn opened his mouth to ask the next question, but the damn hypnotist beat him to it.

"What about the girls?" she demanded, leaning closer. "What do you know about the girls? Where are they?"

Vaughn was so taken aback by her complete disregard for the rules, by her fervent demand, he couldn't say anything at first. But it was only a split second of shock, then he edged his way between Ms. Torres and her line of sight to the witness.

"Get him out," he ordered.

Big brown eyes blinked up at him. "What?"

"If this is hypnotism, unhypnotize him." Vaughn bent over and leaned his mouth close enough to her ear so he could whisper without the witness overhearing. "You are putting my case at risk, and I will not have it. Take him out now, or I'll kick you out."

She didn't waver, and she certainly didn't turn to Herman and take him out. "I'm getting answers," she replied through gritted teeth. Her eyes blazed with righteous fury.

It was no match for his own. Vaughn inclined his head

toward Herman, who was shaking his head back and forth. Not offering *any* answers to her too direct line of questioning.

"Mr. Herman—"

Vaughn nudged her chair back with his knee. "Take him out, or I'll arrest you for interfering in a criminal investigation."

Her eyes glittered with that fury, her hands clenched into fists, but when he rested his hand on the handcuffs latched to his utility belt, she closed her eyes.

"Fine, but you need to move."

When she opened her eyes, he saw a weary resignation in her slumped posture, a kind of sorrow in her expression Vaughn didn't understand—didn't want to. Any more than he wanted to figure out what scent she was wearing, because when he was this close to her, it was almost distracting.

Almost.

"If you say one word to him that isn't pulling him out of the hypnotism, you will be arrested. Do you understand?"

"I thought you didn't believe in it?" she snapped.

"I don't, but I'm not going to have you claiming I didn't let you do your job. Take him out. Then you will be talking to my supervisor. Got it?"

She sneered at him, like many a criminal he'd arrested or threatened in his career. He wasn't sure she was a criminal, but he wasn't affected at all by her anger.

She'd ruined the lead. The Stallion wasn't nearly enough to go on, and she'd stepped in with her own reckless, desperate questions, invalidating the whole interrogation.

She was going to pay for this.

* * *

Natalie sat in the waiting area of the Unsolved Crimes office. She wanted to fume and rage and pace, but she didn't have time to indulge in pointless anger. Not when she had information to find.

Who was The Stallion? Could this all possibly be related to her sister? She'd waited three years for this. Three years of dealing with sneering Texas Rangers hating that their higher-ups involved her in their investigations. Three years of hoping against hope that the next case she'd be brought in on would be Gabby's.

Just because the witness had talked about missing girls didn't mean it was her sister's case. As a hypnotist, she was never given any case details, legally bound to secrecy regarding anything she did hear simply by being in the room.

She'd lost her cool. She knew she wasn't supposed to jump in like that, but the interrogators had been asking the wrong questions. They'd been taking too much time. She needed to know. She needed…

She needed not to cry. So, she took a deep breath in, and slowly let it out. She focused on the little window with the blinds closed. Inside, three officers were talking. Probably about her. One definitely complaining about her.

She was angry with herself for breaking rules she knew Texas Rangers weren't going to bend, but she'd rather channel that anger onto Ranger Jerk.

Immature, yes, but the immature nicknames she gave each ranger who gave her a hard time entertained her when she wanted to tell them off.

The problem with Ranger Jerk was she could nearly forget what a jerk he was when he looked like…*that*. He was so tall and broad shouldered, and when he was always crossing his arms over his chest in a threatening manner, it was obvious he had *muscles* underneath the crisp white dress shirt he wore.

Like, the kind of muscles that could probably bench-press *her*. Not that she'd imagined that in those first few minutes of meeting him. Those were flights of fancy she did *not* allow herself. Not on the job.

Then there was his face, which wasn't at all fair. She'd nearly been tongue-tied when he'd greeted her. His dark-ish blond hair was buzzed short, and his blue eyes were downright mesmerizing. Some light shade that was nearly gray, and she'd spent seconds trying to decide what to call that color.

Until he'd insulted her without a qualm. Because his good looks were only *one* problem with him. Only the tip of the iceberg of problems.

The door opened, and she forced herself to look calm and placid. She was a calm, still lake. No breeze rippled her waters. She reflected nothing but a peaceful and reflective surface.

But maybe a sea monster lurked deep and would leap out of the water and eat all of them in one giant gulp.

Yeah, her imagination had always gotten her into trouble.

"Ms. Torres. Come inside, please."

She held no ill will against Captain Dean. He was one of the few rangers who respected and believed in what she did. He was, more often than not, the one who called her in to help with a case.

But she *had* crossed a line she knew she wasn't supposed to cross, and she was going to have to deal with the consequences—which would gall. For one, because it meant Ranger Jerk got what he wanted. But more important, because she might have finally had some insight into her sister's case, and been too impetuous to make the most of it.

"Have a seat."

She slid into the chair opposite Captain Dean's desk. The two rangers she'd been in the interrogation room with stood on either side.

They were impressive, the three of them. Strong, in control, looking perfectly pressed in what constituted as the Texas Ranger uniform: khakis, a dress shirt and a tie, Ranger badge and belt buckle, topped off with cowboy boots. The only thing the men weren't wearing inside the office were the white cowboy hats.

She wanted to sneer at Ranger Cooper's smug blue eyes, but she didn't. She smiled sweetly instead.

"You breached our contract, Ms. Torres. You know that."

"Yes, sir."

"Your job is not to question witnesses. It's only to put them under hypnosis, should they agree, to calm them and allow us to ask questions."

"I know, sir. I'm sorry for…stepping out of line." She offered both the men who'd been in the room with her the best apologetic smile she could muster. "I got a little carried away. I can promise you, it won't happen again."

"I'm afraid we can't risk second chances at this juncture. Not in this department, not in the Texas Rangers. I'm sorry, Natalie. You've been an asset. But this was unconscionable, and you will not be asked back."

She sat frozen, completely ice from the inside out. *Not be asked back*. But she'd helped solve cases. For years. She'd received a commendation even! And he was…

"Cooper, see her out?"

Ranger Jerk nodded toward the door. "After you."

She swallowed over the lump in her throat. All her chances. All the times she'd been so close to seeing something of Gabby's case. All the *possibility*, and she'd ruined it.

No, *he'd* ruined it for her. *He* had. She stood on shaky legs, clutching her phone and her purse.

"I am sorry."

She didn't look back at Captain Dean, or Ranger Stevens. She didn't want to see the pitying, apologetic looks on their faces. Just like all those other policemen who'd come up with nothing—*nothing* when it came to Gabby's disappearance.

Apologies didn't mean a thing when her sister was gone. Eight years. And Natalie was the only one who held out any hope, and now her hope was...

Well, it had just gotten kicked in the teeth.

She managed to walk stiffly to the door and stepped out, the Jerk of the Manor still behind her. Too close behind her and crowding her out and away.

"I'll see you all the way out of the building, Ms. Torres," he said, sounding so smug and superior.

She walked down the hall, still a little shaken. But shaken had no hold on her anger. She glared at the man striding next to her. "You got me fired, you lousy son of a—"

"I'd reconsider your line of thought and blame, Ms. Torres." He continued to look ahead, not an ounce of emotion showing on his face. "You got yourself fired. Now, stay out of this case. If I catch a whiff of you being involved in it anywhere, I will not hesitate to find out every last thing about you and connect you to whatever dirty deeds you're hiding."

"I am not hiding any dirty deeds." Which was the God's honest truth. She hadn't stepped out of line in eight years. Or ever, really, but especially since Gabby had disappeared.

His eyes met hers, a cold, cold stormy blue. "We'll see."

She shivered involuntarily, because that look made her feel like she *had* done something wrong, which was so absurd.

Even more absurd was the idea of her staying out of the case. She'd take what little information she'd gathered and follow it to the ends of the earth.

Because she refused to believe her sister was dead. A body had never been found, and that Herman man had said...he'd said *he keeps the girls*. Not kept. Not got rid of. *Keeps*.

Maybe Gabby wasn't one of those girls, but it was possible. More than that, she thought. The Texas Rangers might be a mostly good bunch, but they had rules and regulations to follow. Natalie Torres did not.

God help the man who tried to stop her.

Chapter 2

The phone ringing and vibrating on his nightstand jerked Vaughn out of a deep sleep. He cursed and answered it blearily. Phone calls in the middle of the night were never good, but they always had to be answered.

Much to his ex-wife's constant complaints throughout the duration of their marriage.

"Cooper," he grumbled into the speaker.

"You're going to need to get out here."

He recognized his captain's voice immediately. "Text the address."

"Yup."

Vaughn rubbed his hands over his face, then went straight to his closet where a row of work clothes hung, always a few pressed and ready to go. He never liked to be caught without clean and ironed clothes on the ready, even in the middle of the night. He looked at the clock as he dressed. Three fifteen.

He strode through his house, gave the coffeemaker a wistful glance. Even though he always kept it ready to go, he didn't have time to sit around waiting for it to brew. Not at three fifteen.

With a stretch and a groan, he strapped on his gun and tried not to wonder if he was getting too old for this. Thirty-four was hardly too old. He had a lot of years to go before he could take a pension, but more…

He had a lot of cases to solve before his conscience would let him leave. So, he needed to get at it.

He got in his car, and when his phone chimed, he clicked the address Captain Dean had texted and started the GPS directions. It took about fifteen minutes to arrive at his destination, a small neighborhood a little outside the city that he knew was mainly rental houses. Single-storied brick buildings, a few split-levels. Modest homes at best, flat out run-down at worst.

Fire trucks and police vehicles were parked around a burned-out and drowned shell of a house. Though it still smoked, the house had obviously been ravaged by the fire hours earlier.

Vaughn stopped at the barricade, flashed his badge to the officer guarding the perimeter and then went in search of Captain Dean. When he found him, he was with Bennet. Vaughn's uneasy dread grew.

"What've we got?"

"This is the hypnotist's house," Bennet said gravely.

The dread in Vaughn's gut hardened to a rock. The house was completely destroyed, which meant—

"She's fine. She wasn't home, which is lucky for her, because someone was. Herman."

"Dead?"

Captain Dean nodded. "He didn't start and botch the

fire, either, at least from what information I've been able to gather. We'll have to wait to go over everything with the fire investigator once she's done, but I think it got back to somebody Herman squealed. Body was dumped."

"The hypnotist? Where was she?"

"With her mom," Bennet offered, "who works at a gas station down on Clark. We've got guys going over surveillance, but so far she's on the tape almost the entire night. She came home just after some neighbors called 9-1-1. She's innocent."

Innocent? Maybe of this, but Natalie Torres was hardly innocent. The day was full of far too much weirdness for her to be *innocent*. "You sure about that?"

"Cooper," the captain intoned, censure in that one word. "Do you know the kinds of background checks we did on her when she got a contract with us? I know you don't agree with it, but using a hypnotist to aid in witness questioning isn't some random or careless decision. We have to jump through a lot of hoops to make it legal. She's clean. Now she's in danger."

Vaughn wasn't certain he believed the first, but he knew the latter was fact.

"Ideas, gentlemen?"

"Well, she'll need protection." Bennet rubbed a hand over his jaw. "I'd say that's on us, and it'll make certain nothing dirty's going down."

"This is escalating." Captain Dean shook his head gravely. "If it goes much further, it becomes less our business and more current crime's business. We should be working with Homicide now. Cooper? What are you thinking?"

Vaughn didn't answer right away. He caught a glimpse of Ms. Torres standing next to a fireman. She had a blanket wrapped around her, and she was looking at her burned-to-ash house with tears streaming down her cheeks.

He looked away. "We've got to get her out of here." He didn't particularly like the idea that came to him, but he didn't have to like it. Bottom line, everyone else trusted this woman way too much, so if she was going to come under their protection, it needed to be *his* protection, so he could keep an eye on her.

It couldn't be anywhere near here. "My suggestion? Stevens works with Homicide, then maybe you put Griffen on it too. I take the woman up to the cabin in Guadalupe. I go over things there, keep her safe and make sure she's got nothing to do with it."

"That's gonna necessitate a lot of paperwork," Captain Dean grumbled.

"She can't stay in Austin. We've got to get her out of here. We all know it."

The captain sighed. "I'll call the necessary people. I can't argue with this being the best option. But, you know who *is* going to argue?" He pointed at Ms. Torres.

Vaughn looked at her again. She wasn't crying anymore. No, that angry expression that she'd leveled at him earlier today had taken over her face. He didn't have to be close to remember what it looked like.

Big dark eyes as shiny as the dark curls she'd pulled back from her face. The snarly curve to those sensuous lips and—

No, there was no *and*. Not when it came to this woman.

"She'll agree," Vaughn reassured the captain. He'd make sure of it.

When Ranger Jerk stepped next to her, Natalie didn't bother to hide her utter disgust. "Well, thanks for getting to my house after it burned down. Add that to me losing my favorite job—also your fault. Would you like to, oh, I don't know…" She wanted to say something scathing about what else he could do to ruin her life, but…

Everything she had was gone. Her house, every belonging, every memento. Worst of all, years' worth of research and information she'd gathered on Gabby's case. All gone. Everything she owned and loved gone except for her car and what she'd had in it.

She tried to breathe through a sob, but she choked on it. The tears and the emotion and the enormity of it all caught in her throat, and she had to cover her mouth with her hand to keep from crying out.

She'd been here for hours, and she couldn't wrap her head around it. She hadn't even been able to text her mom the full details because she just…

How had this happened? Why had this happened?

She sensed him move, and she hoped against hope he was walking away. That he wouldn't say a word and make this whole nightmare worse. All of this was terrible, and she didn't want Ranger Jerk rubbing it in or—worse—feeling sorry for her.

But he didn't disappear. She didn't hear retreating footsteps as tears clouded her vision. No, he moved closer. She hadn't thought much about this guy having any sort of conscience or empathy in him, but he put a big hand on her back, warm and steady.

She swallowed, wiping at the tears. It wasn't an overly familiar touch. Just his palm and fingers lightly flush with her upper back, but it was strong. It had a remarkable effect. A strange thread of calm wound through her pain.

"This is shocking and painful," he said in a low, reassuring voice. "There's no point in trying to be hard. No one should have to go through this."

She sniffled, blinking the last of the tears out of her eyes. Oh, there'd be more to come, but for now she could swallow them down, blink them back. She stared at him, trying to work through the fact he'd spoken so nicely to her. He *touched* her. "Are you comforting me?"

He grimaced. "Is that considered comfort? That's terrible comfort."

She laughed through another sob. "Oh, God, and now you're being funny." Obviously she was a little delirious, because she was starting to wonder if Ranger Jerk wasn't so terrible after all.

Then she looked back at her house. Gone. All of it *gone*. There were rangers and police and firemen and all number of official-looking people striding about, talking in low voices. Around her house. Gone. All of it gone.

Ranger Jerk could be reassuring, he could even be funny, but he couldn't deny what was in front of them. "This was on purpose," she said, her voice sounding flat and hopeless even in her own ears.

He didn't respond, but when she finally glanced at him, he nodded. His gaze was on the house too, that square jaw tensed tight enough to probably crack metal between his teeth. He made an impressive profile in the flashing lights and dark night. All angles and shadows, but there was a determination in his glare at the ruins of her house—something she'd never seen in all those other officers she'd talked to today, or eight years ago.

Confidence. Certainty. A blazing determination to right this wrong—something she recognized because it matched her own.

It bolstered her somehow. "That's why *you're* here.

It's about this morning." She watched him, and finally those cool gray-blue eyes turned to her.

"Yes, that's why I'm here," he replied, his voice still low, still matter-of-fact.

Natalie had spent the past eight years learning how to deal with fear. The constancy of it, the lack of rationale behind it. But this was a new kind, and she didn't know how to suppress the shudder that went through her body.

"We're going to protect you, Ms. Torres. This is directly related to the case we brought you in on, and as long as you agree to a few things, we can keep you safe. I promise you that."

It was an odd thing to feel some ounce of comfort from those words. Because she didn't know him, and she really didn't trust him. But somehow, she did trust *that*. He was a jerk, yes, but he was a by-the-book jerk.

"What things do I need to agree to?" she asked. How much longer would her legs keep her up? She was exhausted. She'd come home after dropping her mom off at her apartment to find the neighbors in the streets and fire trucks blocking her driveway, and her house covered in either arcs of water or licks of flame.

Then, she'd been whisked behind one of the big police SUVs, made not to look at her house burning to ash in front of her, while officer after officer asked her question after question.

Oh, how she wanted to sleep. To curl up right on the ground and wake up and find this was all some kind of nightmare.

But she'd wanted that and never got it too often to even indulge in the fantasy anymore. "Ranger J—" Oh, right, she shouldn't be calling him that out loud. "Ranger Cooper, what do I need to agree to?"

He raised an eyebrow at her misstep, but he couldn't possibly guess what she'd meant to call him just from a misplaced *j*-sound.

He pushed his hands into the pockets of his pants, looking so pressed and polished she wondered if he might be part robot.

It wasn't a particularly angry movement, sliding his hands easily into the folds of the fabric, and yet she thought the fact he would move or fidget in any way spoke to something. Something unpleasant.

"You're going to have to come with me," he finally said, his tone flat and his face expressionless.

"Go with you where?"

He let out a sigh, and she got the sinking suspicion he didn't like what was coming next any more than she was going to.

"You need to get out of Austin. There isn't time to mess around. Herman is dead. You're in *imminent* danger. You agree to come with me, the fewer questions asked the better, and trust that I will keep you safe."

"Herman is… How? When? Wh—"

"It isn't important," he said tonelessly, all that compassion she thought she'd caught a glimpse of clearly dead. "What's important is your safety."

"But I… I didn't do anything."

"You were there when Herman talked. That's enough."

She tried to process all this. "Doesn't that put you in danger too? And Ranger Stevens?"

He shrugged. "That's part and parcel with the job. We're trained to deal with danger. You, ma'am, are not."

She wanted to bristle at that. Oh, she knew plenty about danger, but no, she wasn't a ranger, or even a police officer. She didn't carry a weapon, and as much as she'd lived with all the possibilities of the horrors of human nature haunting her for eight years, she didn't know how to fight it.

She only knew how to dissect it. How to want to find the truth in it. She needed…help. She needed to take it if only because losing her would likely kill her grandmother and mother like losing Gabby had likely killed Dad.

Natalie swallowed at the panic in her throat. "My family? Are they safe? It's only my mother and my grandmother, but…"

"We'll talk with different agencies to keep them protected, as well. For the time being, it doesn't look like they'd be in any danger, but we'll keep our eye on the situation."

She nodded, trying to breathe. Mom would hate that, just as she hated all police. She'd hate it as much as she hated Natalie working for the Texas Rangers, but Natalie couldn't quite agree with Mom's hate.

Oh, she'd hated any and all law enforcement for a while, but she'd tirelessly tried to find her own answers, and she knew how frustrating it could be. She also knew men like Ranger Cooper, as off-putting and as much of a jerk as he was, took their jobs seriously. They tried, and when they failed, it affected them.

She'd seen sorrow and guilt in too many officers' eyes to count.

"I'll go with you," she said, her voice a ragged, abused thing.

His eyes widened, and he turned fully to her. "You will?" He didn't bother to hide his surprise.

She was a little surprised herself, but it would get her the thing she wanted more than anything else in the world. Information. "I will come with you and follow whatever your office suggests in order to keep me safe. On one condition."

The surprise easily morphed into his normal scowl of disdain. "You're being protected, Ms. Torres. You don't get to have conditions."

"I want to know about the case. I want to know what I'm running from."

"That's confidential."

"You're taking me 'away from Austin' to protect me. I don't even know you."

He gave her a once-over, and she at once knew he didn't trust her. While she was sure he was the kind of man who would protect her anyway, his distrust grated. So, she held her ground, emotionally wrung out and exhausted. She stood there and accepted his distrustful perusal.

"I'll see what information I'm allowed to divulge to you, but you're going to have to come down to the office right now to get everything squared away. We'll be leaving the minute we have it all figured out with legal."

"Will we?"

"You don't have to do it my way, Ms. Torres, but I can guarantee you no one's way is better than mine."

She wouldn't take that guarantee for a million dollars, but she'd take a chance. A chance for information. If she was going to lose everything, she was darn well going to get closer to finding Gabby out of it.

"All right, Ranger Cooper. We'll do it your way." For now.

Chapter 3

Vaughn was exhausted, but he swallowed the yawn and focused on the long, winding road ahead of him.

Natalie dozed in the passenger seat, making only the random soft sleeping noise. Vaughn didn't look—not once—he focused.

The midday sun reflected against the road, creating the illusion of a sparkling ribbon of moving water. They still had another three hours to go to get to the mountains and his little cabin. Which meant he'd spent the past *four* hours talking himself out of all his second thoughts.

It was the only way to keep *her* safe and *him* certain she was innocent. She'd agreed to everything without so much as a peep. He didn't know if he distrusted that or if she was just too devastated and exhausted to mount any kind of argument.

She stirred, and he checked his rearview mirror again. The white sedan was still following them. There was enough space between their cars; he'd thought he was simply being paranoid for noticing.

That had been two hours ago. Two hours of that car following him at the same exact distance.

He cursed.

"What?" Natalie mumbled, straightening in the seat. "You're not going to run out of gas, are you?" She rubbed her eyes, back arching as she stretched and moved her neck from side to side.

With more force than he cared to admit, he looked away from her and directly at the road. "No. Listen to me. Do not look back. Do not move. We're being tailed."

"What?"

She started to whip her head toward the back—obnoxious woman—but he reached over with one hand and squeezed her thigh.

She screeched and slapped his hand. "Don't touch me."

He removed his hand, gripped the wheel with both now. Tried to erase any…reaction from touching her like that. It had only been a diversionary tactic. "Then do as you're told and don't look back."

Her shoulders went rigid and she stared straight ahead, eyes wide, breathing uneven. "You really think…"

"I could be wrong. I'd rather be safe and wrong than wrong and sorry." He looked at the mile marker, tried to focus on what was around them, where they could lose the tail. What it would mean if they couldn't.

Natalie grasped her knees, obviously panicking. As much as he knew he could figure this out, he understood that she was lost. Fire burning all of her possessions and sleepless nights on the road with a near stranger weren't exactly calming events.

"It'll be fine," he said, mustering all of his compassion—

what little of that was left. "I've dodged better tails than this."

"Have you?"

"Do you know a Texas Ranger has to have eight years of police work with a major crimes division before they're even qualified to apply?"

Natalie huffed out an obviously unimpressed breath. "So you had to write speeding tickets for eight years? Didn't mean you had to dodge people following you."

Vaughn didn't bother responding. Speeding tickets? Not for a long, long time. But he wasn't going to tell her about the undercover operations he'd worked, the homicides he'd solved. He wasn't going to waste precious brain space proving to her that he was the best man to keep her safe.

Maybe when they got to the cabin he could just give her Jenny's number and his ex-wife could fill Ms. Torres in on all the ways he'd put himself in danger during his years as a police officer.

Frustrated with *that* line of thought, he jerked the wheel to get off the highway and onto an out-of-the-way exit at the last second.

Unfortunately, the white sedan did the same.

"We're going to stop at the first gas station we find. We're both going to get out, go inside and pretend to look for snacks. I'm going to talk to the attendant. You will stand in the candy aisle and wait for my sign."

"What's your sign?" she said after a gulp.

"You'll know it when you see it."

"But…"

"No buts. We have to play some things by ear." Like what the purpose of an hours-long tail was. If it was to take them out, Vaughn had to believe they would have already attempted something. The hanging back and just following pointed more to an information-grabbing tail.

It took a few miles, but a little town with a gas station finally appeared on the horizon. Vaughn kept his speed steady as he drove toward it, worked to keep himself calm as he pulled into a parking spot.

"We get out. We act normal. You watch me, and you follow absolutely any and all orders I give you. Got it?"

Natalie blinked at the gas station in front of them, and he could tell she wanted to argue, but the woman apparently had *some* sense because she finally nodded.

Vaughn got out of the car first, and Natalie followed. She didn't exactly look *calm*, but she didn't bolt or run. She met him at the front of the car.

Vaughn didn't like it, but they had to look at least a little casual. Maybe these guys knew exactly who they were, but playing a part gave him a better shot of putting doubts in their heads.

So, he linked fingers with Ms. Torres and walked like any two involved people might into the building. Her hand was clammy, and he gave it a little reassuring squeeze. He leaned close to her ear, hoping the two men outside were paying attention to the intimate move.

"Go along with anything I do or say," he said, low enough so that the cashier couldn't hear.

She didn't say anything or nod, but she didn't argue with him, either. In fact, she held tightly on to his hand.

When he took a deep breath, all he could smell was the smoke that must still be in her hair from early this morning, but underneath there was some hint of something sweet.

Lack of sleep was making him delirious. "Go find a snack, honey," he said, doing his best to infect some ease into his exaggerated drawl. With only a little wobble, she let go of his hand and walked toward the candy aisle.

Casually Vaughn sauntered to the counter. He glanced at the scratch-off tickets displayed, then glanced out the doors where the white sedan was parked, one of the men filling it up.

Vaughn flicked his glance to the bored-looking cashier. "Ma'am," he said with a nod. He slid his badge across the counter to where the cashier could see it. She didn't flinch or even act impressed or moved. She popped her gum at him.

He wouldn't be deterred. "I need you to call the local police department. I need you to give them the following license plate number, description and my DSN."

She didn't make a move to get a pen or paper. Vaughn glanced out of the corner of his eye to where the white sedan and two men in big coats and big hats stood. One eyeing his truck, the other eyeing the store and Natalie.

Vaughn flicked his jacket out of the way so the cashier could also see his gun. "This is official police business. Call the local police department and give them the following information." He inclined his head to the pen that was settled on top of the cash register keyboard. "Now."

The woman swallowed this time, and she grabbed the pen.

Vaughn looked back at Natalie who was shaking in the candy aisle. He rattled off the information to the cashier.

He kept tabs on the men outside who were obviously keeping tabs on him. "Make the call now. Whatever you do, don't tell those men out there. Got it?"

The now-nervous cashier gave a little nod and picked up the phone on the counter next to the cash register.

As he moved away from the counter, one of the men

started walking toward the door. Still, Vaughn didn't panic. He'd been in a lot stickier situations than this, no matter what Ms. Hypnotist thought of his past experience.

He approached Natalie, watching to make sure the cashier got the information to the local police before the man entered the door.

It was a close call, but the cashier had some survival instincts herself and she hung up just as the man walked inside.

Vaughn took Natalie's arm. "Let's go to the bathroom."

She arched a brow, all holier-than-thou, even though terror was clearly lurking in the depths of those big dark eyes. "Together?"

"Yes, ma'am." He nodded toward the back of the store where the bathroom sign was. "Move. And whatever you do, don't look behind us."

She started to walk toward the bathroom, still shaking, still braving it out. He'd give her credit for that.

Later.

"You know, every time you tell me not to do something, I only want to do it more?"

"Okay, don't look straight ahead. Don't step into the women's bathroom, and certainly don't let me follow you inside."

Surprisingly, she did exactly what he wanted her to do.

Natalie couldn't stop shaking. She knew it showed weakness, and she tried to be stronger than that. For Gabby. For the hope that Gabby was still alive to be found.

But, she was so scared she wanted to cry. Someone was following them. Ranger Cooper seemed more than capable, but that didn't make it any less scary. It didn't erase her house being gone, and it most certainly didn't erase the fact someone was apparently *following* them.

Ranger Cooper immediately locked the door behind them as they stepped into the women's restroom. He was a blur, moving about the small room and the even smaller stalls, and she had no idea what he was looking for.

So, she simply stood in the center trying to find her own center. Trying to focus on what she was doing this for. On who she was doing this for. She'd pursued details of Gabby's case with a dogged tenacity that had alienated every friend, significant other and her own grandmother. Even Mom was close to losing any and all patience with her.

But how could they give up? How could *she* give up? Maybe she'd never anticipated this kind of danger, but that didn't mean she was going to shake apart and hide away. Gabby was somewhere out there.

She had to be. *He keeps the girls.* Maybe it wasn't Gabby's case, but maybe it *was*. She needed information, which meant she needed Ranger Cooper.

After a full sweep of the bathroom, he pulled his phone out of his pocket and typed something into it. Natalie simply watched him because she didn't know what else to do. She counted each time his blunt, long finger touched the screen to keep herself from panicking.

When he glanced up from his phone, those steely blue eyes meeting hers with a blank kind of certainty, she thought she might panic anyway.

"We can't waste much more time," he said, his voice as low and gravelly as she'd ever heard it. Surely he was exhausted. Even Texas Rangers got tired. Even Texas Rangers were human and mortal.

She'd really prefer to think of him as superhuman, and

he made it almost seem possible when he flipped back his coat and pulled the weapon at his hip from its holster.

"If it gets back to whoever sent them they're being detained, we'll just get another tail."

Natalie subdued the shaking, jittering fear in her limbs and focused on what had gotten her here. Questions. Information. "But how can we get past them? Won't they just report back to... Do you know who it is? Is this about The Stallion? I couldn't find any information on what exactly that is. A man? A gang?"

Ranger Cooper took a menacing step toward her, reminding her of that moment in the interrogation room when he'd stepped between her and Mr. Herman.

Dead Mr. Herman.

She closed her eyes and tried to focus on how much she'd hated him then. Hated him for getting in her way.

"Do not ask questions, Ms. Torres. The less you know, the better. For your own good. Now..." He curled those long fingers around the grips of his gun. "Listen to me carefully. Do everything I say to the letter. For your own good. Let me repeat that," he said, as if talking to a small child.

"For your own good, you will do as I say. Stay behind me. Listen to me and only me. Whatever you do, don't make a sound. If we can get a little bit of a head start, we're golden. Got it?"

She couldn't speak. Every muscle in her body was seized too tightly to allow her to speak, or nod.

"Torres." It was whispered, but it was a harsh bark. "Got it?"

She managed a squeaky yes, and as he unlocked the door, she stayed behind him. As much as she didn't like him, in this moment, she would have pressed herself to his back if he'd asked her to.

He might be a jerk, but he seemed to know what he was doing. Right now, with two bulky men speaking to two decidedly not bulky local police officers in front of the cash register, she pretty much *had* to trust Ranger Cooper would get them out of this.

She met gazes with one of the bulky men, and though he had his hat low on his head, she could feel the cold, black gaze.

"Behind me, Torres," Ranger Cooper whispered with enough authority to have her feet moving faster.

One of the bulky men tried to sidestep one of the local officers, but the local officer didn't back off.

"Move again, sir, and I will pull my weapon on you."

"We ain't done anything wrong, boy."

Ranger Cooper grabbed her arm. "Move," he instructed, and she realized belatedly she'd all but stopped. But she was being propelled out the door, a skirmish breaking out behind them. "Get in the car. Now. Fast."

On shaky legs, she did as she was told, but managed to glance back in time to see Ranger Cooper shoving a broom through the handles of the door. Which caused the men inside to push against the police officers even harder, even getting past one to get to the door.

Natalie got into the truck's passenger seat, her breath coming in little puffs. That broom handle wouldn't hold them in for very long. If only because there had to be another exit, and it already looked as though the officers inside were losing the battle.

But Ranger Cooper wasn't getting in the truck. She tried to breathe deeply, but a little whimpering sound came out instead.

"Get it together. Get it together," she whispered to herself, craning her neck to see where Ranger Cooper had gone.

She watched as he casually walked over to a white sedan, weapon held to his side where only someone really paying attention could see. Then he held the muzzle of the gun to the front tire and pulled the trigger.

Even knowing it was coming, Natalie jumped when the shot rang out. Ranger Cooper was back in the truck in the blink of an eye, and Natalie glanced at the store where the two men had disappeared from the windowed doors. No doubt looking for another exit.

"That'll buy us some time," Ranger Cooper muttered, zooming out of the parking lot without so much as buckling his seat belt.

"What about those police officers? The cashier?"

He merely nodded into the distance. "Hear that?"

She didn't at first, but after a few seconds she could make out sirens.

"Backup," he said, his eyes focused on the road, his hands tight on the wheel. "Since the guys fought back, they can arrest them. But that doesn't mean there aren't more tails on us. We have to be vigilant. I want you to keep your eyes peeled. Anything seems suspicious, you mention it. I don't care how silly it sounds. We can't be too careful now."

Natalie gripped the handle of the door with one hand, pressed the other, in a fist, to her stomach.

She was in so far over her head she almost laughed. She knew Ranger Cooper wouldn't appreciate that, and she was a little afraid if she started laughing, it'd turn into crying soon enough.

She was too tough for that. Too determined. No more

crying. No more shaking. No more panic. If they had bad guys to face down, she was at least going to pull her weight.

Because if she did, if they could get through all this, Gabby might be on the other side. Everything she'd been working for over the past eight years.

Yeah, no more panic. She had a sister to save.

Chapter 4

Vaughn didn't know if he trusted how relatively easy it had been to fool the tail. Or the fact another hadn't taken its place. All in all, he didn't understand what that tail had been trying to accomplish, and without knowing...

Frustrated, he scanned the road again. The Guadalupe Mountains loomed in the distance of an arid landscape. The hardscrabble desert stretched out for miles, the craggy, spindly peaks of the Guadalupes offering the only respite to endless flat.

The cabin was still forty-five minutes away, and they were the only car on this old desert highway. If he had a tail, it was a much better one.

He flicked a glance at Torres. Thinking about her as a last name helped things. He could think of her as a partner, as just a *person* he had to work with. Not a complicated mystery of a woman.

The only problem was, he didn't trust her as far as he could throw her, and that was the key to any partnership.

She sat in the passenger seat, her eyes still too big, her hands still clenched too tight. Her olive skin tone had paled considerably, but she'd gotten control of her shaking.

"You did good," he found himself saying, out of nowhere. She *had* done good for a civilian, but he had no idea why he was praising her. What the hell was the point of that?

"I just did what you told me to do."

"Exactly."

She rolled her eyes and shook her head. "You really are a piece of work, Ranger Cooper."

"Not everyone could have gotten through that, Ms. Torres. Some people freeze, some people cry, some people…" Why was he explaining this to her? If she didn't want to believe she'd done a good thing, what did he care? But his mouth just kept *going*. "There's a lot of pressure when you're under a threat, and the smartest thing you can do is listen to the person who has the coolest head. You did that. You made good choices and had good instincts."

"Well, thank you." She blew out a breath, and he noted that the hands she'd had in fists loosened incrementally.

"I wish I didn't know just *how* much I can stand up in the face of a threat," she muttered.

"Unfortunately, that was only the beginning."

"You're a constant comfort, Ranger Cooper."

She fell silent for a few moments, and he thought maybe they could make it all the way to the cabin without having any more of the discussion, certainly not any more of him telling her she'd done well. But she began to fidget. The kind of fidgeting that would lead to questioning.

It appeared that whatever nerves or fear that had kept Ms. Torres from interrogating him about what was going on had been eradicated or managed.

"Who's after us? And why? What do I have to do with any of this?" she asked, thankfully sounding more exasperated than scared.

Scared tended to pull at that do-gooder center of him. He tried to focus on *cases* rather than people. But he could get irritated with exasperation. Why couldn't she just trust him to keep her safe and leave it at that?

But he knew that she wouldn't, and he had been given permission to share certain details with her.

Considering he still didn't trust this woman, he wasn't about to give her really important details.

He focused on the road, the flat, unending desert ahead of him. "You were in the interrogation room when Herman talked."

"He didn't even say anything that was any kind of incrimination. Certainly nothing that I would understand to be able to tell anyone. And I *ruined* your interrogation. They should be sending me flowers, not…fire."

The corner of his lip twitched as if…as if he wanted to smile. Which was very…strange. But the fact she owned up to ruining the interrogation, while also making a little bit of a joke in what had to be a very scary situation for her, he appreciated that. He almost admired it. God knew he didn't make light of much of anything.

"In all likelihood, they don't know what exactly was said," Vaughn told her. *Nothing* about his tone was self-deprecating or light, which he never would have noticed if not for her. "All it took was the knowledge that he was interrogated, and that we started looking into the name he mentioned. When you're mixed up in organized crime, that's enough to get you killed."

She pressed her lips together as if a wave of emotion had swept over her. Her eyes even looked a little shiny. When she spoke, there was a slight tremor to her voice. "I just keep thinking about how he said he had a daughter, and his wife had cancer, and he's just…dead."

"He worked for a man who has likely killed more people than we'll ever know about. Herman knew what he was getting himself into and the risks he was taking. Even if he wasn't the muscle, and even if he had a family, he made bad choices that he knew very well had chances of getting him killed."

"So you're saying he deserved to die?" Natalie asked in that same tremulous voice.

It had been a long time since someone had made him feel bad about the callousness he had to employ, *had* to build to endure a career in law enforcement, and especially unsolved crimes. He didn't care for the way she did it so easily. Just a question and a tremor.

But this was *reality*, and clearly Torres didn't have a clue about that. "It's not my place to determine whether he deserved anything. I'm putting forth the reality of the situation."

"I don't understand why they burned down my house, why they *killed* a man, just because he mentioned a name and you started asking questions. How is that worth following us across Texas? I mean, if they were going to kill us, wouldn't they have already done it?"

"Yes."

She waited, and he could feel her gaze on him, but he didn't have anything else to say to that.

"Yes? That's it? You're just going to agree with me, and that's it?"

"Well, honestly, they probably did try to kill you with that fire. You were lucky you weren't home. What more of an explanation would you like?"

"One that makes sense!"

He could tell by the way she quieted after her little outburst that she hadn't meant to let that emotion show. Especially when the next words she spoke were lower, calmer.

"I want to know why this is happening. I want to understand why I'm in more danger than you or Ranger Stevens. Why my house was burned down, not yours."

"I can't speculate on why they burned your house down. The reason that Stevens and I aren't in as much danger is because we're police officers. We're trained to look for danger, and quite frankly going after us is a lot worse for them than going after you. Anyone hurts a member of law enforcement, the police aren't going to rest until they find him."

"But if you go after a civilian, it's fine?" she demanded incredulously.

She gave him *such* a headache. He took a deep breath, because he wasn't going to snap at her for deliberately misinterpreting his words. He wasn't going to yell at her for not getting it. She wasn't an officer; she couldn't understand.

"We're family, Ms. Torres," he said evenly and calmly, never taking his eyes off the road. "It's like if a stranger is gunned down in the street or your sister is gunned down in the street, which one are you going to avenge a little bit harder?"

Something in what he'd said seemed to impact her

a little more than it should have. She paled further and looked down at her lap. He wasn't sure if she was more scared now, or if she was upset by something.

"I'm going to keep you safe, Ms. Torres," he assured her, because as much as he avoided those soft, comforting feelings almost all of the time, that was his duty. He would do it, no matter what.

"Why?" she asked in a small voice. "I'm not law enforcement. I'm not your family. Why should I feel like you're going to keep me safe?"

"Because you came under my protection, and I don't take that lightly."

"I can't understand what they think I can do," she said, her voice going quieter with each sentence, her face turning toward the window as if she wanted to hide from him.

He was fine with that. He'd be even finer if he could stop answering her questions. "The thing about crime and criminals is that they don't often follow rational trains of thought like we do. Their motivations and morals are skewed."

"That almost sounds philosophical, Ranger Cooper."

"It's just the truth. It's easier to accept the truth and figure out what you can do about it than to wish it was different or understandable."

"But…what am I supposed to do? How am I supposed to… I have other jobs, and a family, and… It's all hitting me how much I'm los—"

"You're saving your life. Period. You won't have a job or a family to go back to if you're dead."

"Again, such a comfort."

"At this point, it's more important that we are honest than it is that I comfort you. Right now you're safe because you're with me. That's the only reason. I need you to not forget that."

"I don't expect you to allow me to forget it," she returned, reminding him of that hallway when she'd blamed him for getting her removed from the Rangers. Though it was frustrating that it was geared at *him*, her anger would serve them well. It would keep her moving, it would keep her brave.

"It's best if you don't. For the both of us. You're not the only one in danger here, you're just the only one who doesn't know what to do about it."

"What about Ranger Stevens?"

"Ranger Stevens can keep himself out of danger. All I need you to do is worry about listening to me. If you do that, everything will be fine."

"How do you know?"

"Because I give everything to my job. There is nothing about what I do that I take lightly."

So everyone had always told him. Too serious. Too dedicated. Too wrapped up in a career that didn't give him time for much of anything else.

But people didn't understand that it gave him everything. A sense of usefulness, a sense of order in a chaotic world. It gave him the ability to face any challenge that was laid before him.

Maybe it gives you a way to keep everyone at a safe distance. It irritated him that those words came into his head, even more irritating that they were in his ex-wife's voice. He hadn't thought about Jenny in over a year. Why had the past two days brought back some of that old bitterness?

But he didn't have time to figure it out. He had to get to the cabin, and he had to solve this case.

Personal problems always came after the job, and if the job never ended… Well, so be it.

No matter how exhausted she was, all Natalie could do was watch as the desert gave way to mountain. They began to drive up…and up. There were signs for Guadalupe Mountains National Park, but they didn't drive into it. Instead, Ranger Cooper took winding roads that seemed to weave around the mountains and the park markers.

There weren't houses or other cars on the road. There was nothing. Nothing except rock and the low-lying green brush that was only broken up by the random cactus.

He turned onto a very bumpy dirt road that curved and twisted up a rolling swell of land covered in green brush. After she didn't know how long, a building finally came into view.

Nestled into that sloping green swell of land, with the impressive almost square jut of the mountains behind it, was a little postage stamp of a cabin made almost entirely of stone. It looked ancient, almost part of the landscape.

And it was very, very small. She was going to stay here in this isolated, tiny cabin with this man who rubbed her all kinds of the wrong way.

"What is this place?" she asked, the nerves making her almost as shaky as she'd been earlier.

"It's my private family cabin."

"You have a family?" She couldn't picture him with loved ones, a wife and kids. It bothered her on some odd level.

He slid her a glance as he pulled the truck around to the back of the cabin and parked. "I did come from a mother and a father, not just sprung from the ground fully made."

"The second scenario seems much more plausible," she retorted, realizing too late that she needed to rein in all her snark.

She thought for one tiny glimmer of a second his mouth might have curved into some approximation of a smile.

Apparently she was becoming delusional. *But he doesn't have a wife or kids.* Really, really delusional.

"My sister stays here quite frequently as well, so hopefully you should be able to find some things of hers you can use."

"Oh, I wouldn't feel right about—"

"You don't have a choice, Ms. Torres. You don't have *anything.* And before you repeat it for a third time, yes, I realize I am of literally no comfort to you."

"Well, at least I don't have to say it for a third time."

He let out a hefty sigh and then got out of his truck. She followed suit, stepping into the warm afternoon sun. The air had a certain…she couldn't put her finger on a word for it. It didn't feel as heavy as the air in Austin. There was a clarity to it. A purity. She couldn't see another living soul, possibly another living thing. All that existed around her was this vast, arid landscape.

And a very unfortunately sexy Texas Ranger who appeared to be exploring the perimeter of his family cabin.

Even after being up since whatever time he had got up to go to her burned-out house, after all the time getting everything squared away to secret her out of Austin, after the incident at the gas station and driving across Texas, he was unwrinkled and fresh. All she felt was dirty and grimy and disgusting. She *smelled,* and she was afraid to even glance at what the desert air had done to her hair.

She stood next to the truck, waiting for her orders. Because God knew Ranger Cooper would have orders for her.

He disappeared around the corner of the cabin, and Natalie leaned against the truck and looked up at the hazy blue sky. She let the sun soak into her skin.

For the first time since before the fire, she had a moment to breathe and really think. All of this open space made her think about Gabby. How long she'd been gone, where she was... Did she still get to see things like this?

Natalie tried to fight the thoughts and tears, but she was exhausted. They trickled over her eyelashes and down her cheeks. She tried to wipe them away, but they kept falling.

She'd worked relentlessly and tirelessly for eight years to try to find Gabby, and she thought she'd been close. A hint. *He keeps the girls*. But now she was far away from Austin, and she was with this man who couldn't pull a punch to save his life.

The hope she had doggedly held on to for eight years was seriously and utterly shaken.

What could she do here? What could she do when her whole life right now was just staying alive? People were after her, and she didn't even know why.

Why was she crying now, though? She was finally safe. She knew Ranger Cooper would do his duty. He didn't seem like the type of man who could do anything but.

Why was it now that she felt like she was falling apart?

"Everything looks good out here. I'm going to check the inside, but I need you to follow me."

No please, no warmth, just an order. She kept her face turned to the sky, trying to wipe away all traces of the tears before she faced him. She took a deep breath and let it out.

She'd had a little breakdown, and now it was over. She'd let some air out of the pressure in her chest, and now she could move forward. She just needed a goal.

She glanced at Ranger Cooper, who was standing at the door, all stiff, gruff policeman.

She needed more information. That was the goal. Information was the goal. She couldn't lose sight of that even though he was so bad at giving it.

She began to walk toward him, wondering what made anyone in his family think this was a good place for a little getaway cabin. It was rocky and sharp and dry. If you looked closely at all, everything seemed so ugly.

But when you looked away from the ground, and took in the home and the full extent of the landscape, there was something truly awe inspiring about it. It was big and vast, this world they lived in. She never had that feeling in the middle of Austin.

She walked over to the porch. It was hard to follow orders and listen to what someone else told her to do. She wasn't used to that. She had been such a strong force in her life for the past few years. She had made all the choices, asked all the questions, sought all the answers. She'd even alienated her grandmother in her quest to find Gabby, so sitting back and doing what someone else told her to do was…hard. It went against everything she had put her whole life into.

But she knew that knee-jerk reaction didn't have a place here. Not when she was with a Texas Ranger who obviously knew way more than she did about safety and criminals.

She was going to have to bury the instinct to argue

with him, and it was going to be as big of a challenge as trusting him would be.

"The chances of anyone having breached the cabin are extremely low," he said, opening the door and analyzing the frame as though it might grow weapons and attack them. "But when you're dealing with criminals of this magnitude, you can't be too careful. Which means I can't leave you outside. I can't let you out of my sight. So, I'm going to go inside and make sure there's nothing off. I need you to follow right behind me, carefully mirroring my every step. Can you do that?"

"Can I walk behind you and do what you do?"

"Yes, that is the question."

She gritted her teeth. He didn't think she could walk? He didn't think she could do anything, did he? He thought she was some flighty, foolish *hypnotist* who couldn't follow easy orders.

Arrogant jerk of a man. "Yes, I can do that," she said through those gritted teeth.

"Excellent. Let's go."

He stepped over the threshold, immediately turning toward the left. She followed him, and since her job was to follow exactly in his footsteps, she watched him. That ease of movement he had about him, the surety in the way he strode into the cabin looking for whatever he was looking for.

He was all packed muscle, but there was something like grace in his movements. It was mesmerizing, and she had no problem following him around the inside of the stone cabin.

They did an entire tour of the kitchen and living area, which were both open, and then down a very narrow hallway that led to two bedrooms and a bathroom. All the rooms were small, and the stone that composed the outside of the cabin were used for the inside walls and floor as well.

It wasn't cozy exactly. It was beautiful, but it wasn't the sort of log mountain cabin she had in her head. There weren't warm colorful blankets or cute artwork on the walls. It was all very gray and minimalist.

"You have something against color?" she asked, forgetting to keep her thoughts to herself.

He glanced over his shoulder at her, and the question was kind of funny in light of the way his blue eyes looked even grayer here. It was like even the color of his body didn't dare shine in this space.

"If you're looking for color..." He opened the door to the last bedroom and stepped inside, doing his little police thing where he looked at every corner and around every lamp and out every window.

But Natalie didn't follow him this time. Where the rest of the cabin was stone and stark and sort of reflective of the outside landscape, this room was a riot and explosion of color. It was glitter and fringe.

"What on earth is all this?"

"This is my sister's room. Which means that, right now, it is your room, and you can feel free to use anything that's in here." He opened the closet and rifled through it. She still had no idea what exactly he was looking for, but she knew if she asked he would only give her some irritating half answer.

"I feel really strange about using your sister's things."

"Trust me, my sister has nothing but things, and when I explain to her why someone used them, she will be more than fine with it. As I reminded you earlier, you don't have a choice."

"Because I have nothing. Yes, let's keep talking about that."

He gave her a cursory once-over, just like he'd given the cabin. She wouldn't be surprised if he checked her pulse and teeth or frisked her for a wire.

She tried not to think too hard about the little shiver that ran through her at the thought of his hands on her. Those big hands that had covered so much space on her back when he'd placed them there in comfort after her house had been decimated.

She swallowed and looked away.

"Sleep." He barked the order, then walked right past her without a second glance or word. The door closed with a soft click, and she could only gape at the rough-hewn wood.

He was ordering her to *sleep*? The absolute gall of the man. How dare he tell her what she needed? She had half a mind to march right out of the room and tell him she was *fine*.

But, God, she was tired. So, for today, he'd get his way. *And probably for tomorrow and the next day and the next, because he is in charge here, remember?*

She sighed at that depressing thought and crawled into bed, hopeful to sleep all the tears away.

Chapter 5

Vaughn stared at his laptop screen and tried not to doze off. He would need to wake up Torres soon, if only so he could sleep. The tail had left him jumpy, and he didn't want both of them asleep at the same time at any point.

Unfortunately he was tired enough that the words of his files were simply jumbled letters. It was beyond frustrating he couldn't concentrate. Had he gone soft? He hadn't had a stakeout or any sort of challenging hard-on-the-body thing in a while. Had he lost his touch?

He scrubbed his hands over his face. This was ridiculous. He was fine. There was only so much the human body could handle and still be expected to concentrate on complex facts. Complex facts that had been hard enough to work out when he was well rested and well fed.

At the thought of food, his stomach grumbled. If he couldn't sleep, then he could at least eat. If he made something, then Natalie could eat when she woke up.

There wouldn't be anything fresh in the pantry, but they always kept a few extras on hand just in case. The nearest store was over an hour away, and while that was pretty damn inconvenient a lot of the time, between Vaughn's desire for complete off-the-grid privacy when he wasn't working and his sister's need for a secret spot, it worked.

He and Lucy had handled their father's fame in completely opposite ways. Lucy had embraced it. She'd followed it, becoming almost as famous a country singer as their father had been. She used the cabin only when she needed a quick, quiet, away-from-publicity break, which was rare.

Vaughn had hated the spotlight. Always. Like his mother, he hadn't been able to stand the fishbowl existence.

So he'd found a way to have almost no recognition whatsoever. He'd gotten a strange enjoyment out of going undercover back in the day, knowing no one knew who he was related to.

"You are one screwy piece of work, Cooper," he muttered, grabbing two cans of soup out of the pantry and digging up the can opener.

"Do you always talk to yourself?"

His hand flew to the butt of his weapon before he even thought about it. Before he recognized the voice, before he had a chance to smooth out the movement so Natalie wouldn't know what he had meant to do.

Quickly he put his hands back to work opening the soup, and he purposefully didn't look at her because he didn't want to see that familiar look on her face. Jenny would cry for days after he had moments like that one, wondering why he couldn't ever shut it off, that natural reaction.

Why the hell couldn't he keep his mind off his past? Dad, Jenny. Why was it in his head, mucking things up when he had to be completely clearheaded and one hundred percent in the game right now?

"I'm heating some soup if you'd like some," he offered, ignoring her previous question.

"Have you been awake this whole time?"

"Someone needs to remain vigilant."

"You can't stay awake forever."

"No, I can't. Which means at some point, I'll have to trust you enough to take over the lookout position."

He finally happened to glance at her, and she had her lips pressed together in a disapproving line. As though she was surprised to hear that he didn't trust her. He'd been nothing but clear on that front. She shouldn't be surprised.

"The only option for beverage is water, and you're going to have to learn to live on the nonperishable staples in the pantry. I don't think it's safe to go to town, and certainly not worth it unless we absolutely have to."

She finally walked from the little opening of the hallway toward the table that acted as the eating area.

She had visible bags under her dark eyes, and her hair was a tangled, curly mass. The smell of smoke drifted toward him even when they were yards apart.

"The soup will keep if you want to take a shower."

"I don't suppose there's a washer and dryer around here, is there?"

"Actually, there is in the hall closet. As isolated as this cabin is, my sister isn't one to do without the modern conveniences of life. We've got a good generator and plenty of appliances."

She glanced at him then, some unreadable expression on her face. She scratched a fingernail across the corner of the old wooden table that had belonged to his grandparents decades ago. Lucy might be all up in the modern conveniences, but she had a sentimental streak that ran much deeper than his.

"Are you close with your sister?"

There was something in the way that she asked the question... Something that gave him the feeling he got when things on a case weren't fitting together the way he thought they should.

There was something this woman was hiding. Even if she had nothing to do with The Stallion or Herman, there was something going on here. He needed to figure it out.

"Well, our careers make it pretty hard for us to spend time together, but we like each other well enough. Do you have a sister?"

Her downturned gaze flicked to his and then quickly back to the table again. There was something there. Definitely.

"We were very close growing up. But..."

"But what?"

"She's..." Natalie swallowed. "Gone."

And he was an ass. Her sister had died, and he was suspicious of this woman, who probably still had painful feelings over it. "I'm sorry," he offered, surprised at how genuine it sounded coming out of him.

She glanced at him again, this time those dark eyes stayed on his a little longer. That full mouth nearly curved. "Thank you," she said. "You know, not many people just say I'm sorry. They always have to add on and make it worse."

"It may shock you to know that I'm not much of a 'add more to it' kinda guy."

This time, she didn't just smile, she laughed. The smile did something to her face, seemed to lighten that heavy sadness that had waved off her. She was pretty; it couldn't be ignored.

She's more than pretty.

But that would *have* to be ignored. He had no business thinking of her as anything other than a civilian under his protection. He shouldn't notice that she was pretty, or the curve of her hips, or the way her smile changed the light in her eyes. He shouldn't and couldn't notice these things. Not and do what he needed to do.

"So, Ranger Cooper, tell me about your cooking skills," she said, moving toward the kitchen.

"Well, first let's not set any expectations here. I have reheating skills, and that's about it. Lucky for you, there is no chance of doing anything other than reheating for the next couple days."

"Well, whatever it is, it smells delicious. I'm starving. But I do want to take a shower."

"Everything should be in the bathroom. If you don't find it in the shower, there should be a container under the sink with things like soap. As for towels, I packed a few. I'll grab you one from my bag."

She nodded without a word, and he left the soup on low heat so he could fetch her towel.

It was strange to have another presence in the cabin with him. He only ever came here alone, unless it was Christmas, and then sometimes he and Lucy would come up here with Mom.

He'd always felt like there was plenty of room when they were here. It was a small place, but Lucy had her room and he had his. If Mom came, he never minded sleeping on the couch.

Ms. Torres seemed to take up a lot of space.

Something about the way she moved, the way she smelled underneath that smoke. There was… Something there. He couldn't put a finger on it.

Perhaps that was the thing that made her feel like such a larger presence. Because he couldn't get a handle on her, he couldn't figure out what made her tick.

But he would.

He strode into his room and grabbed the duffel bag he had packed in haste. He jerked the zipper and then stopped as she stepped into the room with him.

He had meant for her to wait in the living room, or at least out in the hall, but here she was—in his space. There was something about it that set him on edge. There was something about *her* that set him on edge.

"How come the only color is in your sister's room?"

"I don't know," he returned with a grunt.

"You seem like the kind of guy who knows everything."

"I know important things. However, I don't give a damn about interior design."

She leaned against the door frame. "Well, it's a lovely place."

"It's something."

"Do you ever get lonely out here?"

The last thing he needed to think about right now was how lonely he was and for how long. He jerked the first towel his hand touched out of the bag and tossed it at her. She caught it, albeit clumsily.

She cocked her head at him. She seemed to be forever doing that, and he couldn't help but wonder if this was some sort of hypnotist trick. Cock her head, look as though she knew exactly what was going on in his mind even though there was no way that she possibly could.

"Thanks. I'll go take a shower, and then you can get some sleep. That is, if you trust me enough?"

She said it sarcastically, because she probably knew he didn't have a choice. At this point, if he didn't purposefully and decisively take a nap, he was going to keel over and fall asleep against his will. "Trust is a two-way street, Ms. Torres."

"Natalie. Please call me Natalie. I am so tired of hearing you drawl *Ms.* in that condescending Texas Ranger tone."

"Fine. Natalie." Something about saying her full name aloud with her big dark eyes on him shimmered through him. He was tired of this weird feeling. Tired of not knowing what it was that she did to him. There was some gut *itch* there, but he couldn't figure out what it was. And that, on top of all the other things he didn't know right now, was just about enough to make him snap.

A weaker man would. But he was not a weaker man.

"I'll trust you when I absolutely have to."

"So, not at all."

"Trust is a commodity not easily imparted. If you're looking for a friend to build trust with, you shouldn't have gotten messed up in the Unsolved Crimes Investigation Unit."

"Ah, you're back to your charming self. I'll take that as my cue to go."

"Don't use all of the hot water," he called after her,

not sure why he let her get to him. She was goading him. He *knew* she was, and yet he couldn't seem to let it go.

Natalie stood in the warm pulse of the shower that was shockingly luxurious. This cabin got stranger and stranger. Parts of it were stunning in their understated elegance. This, what appeared to be, all glass and marble shower, the fancy pristinely white sink and floor. It was gorgeous.

But then other parts of the home were rough-hewn and distressed. She kind of liked that, actually. It was the strangest thing. It appealed to her, those disparate parts.

But it hardly mattered if the decor interested her. All that really mattered was that she stop sniping at Ranger Cooper and start getting to the bottom of this mystery.

He just made it so easy to snipe.

She turned off the water and toweled herself dry. She had picked out a pair of sweatpants and a T-shirt from the closet in "her" room. It felt so completely wrong to wear someone else's clothes, somehow especially since they were his sister's clothes, when all of this…hiding out was due to *her* sister. The sister Ranger Cooper didn't know might be connected to this case. She didn't think.

Maybe he'd figured it out and was pretending like he hadn't, and she was an idiot for thinking otherwise. Or maybe the "girls" Herman said The Stallion kept didn't have anything to do with her sister.

She let out a gusty sigh. Right now she was too hungry to think about anything other than the fragrant soup that had been warming on the stove when she'd left the kitchen. It wasn't gourmet or anything, but she hadn't eaten since… She actually wasn't sure when she'd last eaten. Between the fire and the paperwork and the nervousness and fear during the drive, she probably hadn't eaten more than a few bites of food.

She hurriedly got dressed and pulled her hair back with a band she'd found in a little plastic bin under the sink. It would be a curly mess later, but she was sure this was the place where what little vanity she had left had come to die.

She had none of her normal hair products. No makeup. None of the clothes that fit her properly. While she had lost her job as a hypnotist with the Texas Rangers, thank you Ranger Jerk, it still felt like Cooper was more of a colleague than anything else. She wanted to dress professionally and be taken seriously and...

And she had to put her hair back into a crazy ponytail, and wear someone else's very nearly gaudy and way-too-tight sweats.

"Just what you should be concerned about, Natalie, how you look," she muttered to herself. She was hopeless. That was all there was to it.

She stepped out into the hall, her feet propelling her forward only because she could smell that soup in the distance.

Ranger Cooper was sitting at the table, spooning soup into his mouth as he stared moodily at a laptop screen.

He flicked a glance at her and then pointed toward the stove. "Help yourself." She gave him a little nod, and then did just that. He'd set out a bowl for her, and she ladled soup into it.

She heard a choking sound and looked back to find him nearly red and coughing.

"Are you okay?"

"Fine," he said, his voice nothing more than a scrape. He wasn't the type of man to errantly choke on his soup. "What happened? Did you find something?" He had been staring at the laptop screen, but then there were windows in the kitchen too. "Did you see someone out a window?" She whipped her head around, looking for some clue as to what he'd choked over.

"No. No, none of that."

"Then what?"

"It was nothing," he replied, his voice returning to normal, his attention returning to his computer.

"Ranger Cooper, honestly, don't be—"

"It's the back of your...pants," he ground out.

"Well, they're not *my* pants," she muttered in return. She tried to look over her shoulder, searching for what he saw, but she didn't see anything except pink on the backs of her legs.

"It, uh, says something."

"It says what?" she demanded, flinging her arms in the air. "Do you have to be so infuriatingly vague?"

"Trust me, you don't want to know."

"Ranger Cooper, I swear to all that is—"

"It says Ride..." He cleared his throat. "Ride Me, Cowboy."

She blinked at him. "Ride..." She blinked again, a hot flush infusing her face. "I... I'm going to go change." She hurried out of the room and inspected every piece of clothing in the closet before choosing plain green sweatpants. She didn't quite love the too-tight fit, but that was far less...embarrassing than Ride Me, Cowboy being printed on any part of her clothing. Most especially her butt.

Wait. Why had Ranger Cooper been looking at her butt? He was probably just inspecting her for signs of weapons

or something. There was no way that man checked out
anyone in the course of his oh-so-important duty.

Only the desperate hunger situation coaxed her to return to the kitchen, otherwise she might have happily
holed up in the strange little color burst of a room and
never forced herself to have to look Ranger Cooper in
the eye again.

Ride Me, Cowboy.

She shuddered, then took a deep breath before she
stepped foot into the hallway again. She was just going
to have to accept that her face was probably going to be
beet red for the next…eight million hours.

*There are more important things to think about than
a little silly embarrassment over pants that aren't even
yours.*

Which was a very sensible thought all in all, but it
changed absolutely nothing. She was embarrassed. She
was… Well, trying very, very hard not to think about
riding of any kind.

She placed her palm to her burning cheek and in-
wardly scolded herself as she haltingly forced herself
back to the kitchen.

Ranger Cooper's gaze remained steady on the laptop, but unlike the first time she'd stepped into the open
front area, he was aware she was there. He didn't move,
he didn't look at her, but she *knew* he was aware of her.
So much different than that moment she'd caught him
lost in his thoughts.

And wondered a little too hard what those thoughts
might be.

"What do you know about The Stallion?" Ranger Cooper asked in that maddeningly professional tone. As if
nothing had happened a short while ago, as if this was

some sort of interrogation, not him protecting her. Or whatever it was he was really up to.

"I don't know what that is. A person?" Based on what Herman said, she assumed it was, but she really didn't know. It was imperative Ranger Cooper give her a hint, but she had to play that carefully. No jumping into an interrogation mode of her own.

"Yes, a person."

She finished ladling her soup and grabbed the spoon that Cooper had left out for her. She could stand here and eat it over the kitchen counter, and she'd probably be more comfortable doing that, but she didn't want to give him that kind of power over her. She wouldn't stand to eat just because she didn't want to face him.

She walked over to the table, set down her food and then slid into the seat directly across from him. His eyes remained on the laptop.

She didn't say anything because that was the technique he always used. Give her absolutely no information, even when she asked a direct question. Say only what he wanted to, and when.

So, she ate, saying nothing else, and it about killed her. She hated the silence that settled over them like an oppressive weight. She hated not peppering him with constant questions, she hated not being able to just dive in and figure out what the heck was going on.

But she didn't trust herself not to reach across the table and pummel him if he gave her another nonanswer.

"Why did you question Herman?" Ranger Cooper said at last. "According to Captain Dean you always follow the rules. Never once stepped out of line. What was going on in the interrogation room that caused you to ask questions?"

Natalie didn't tense. She'd spent enough time around cops to know how to keep herself immobile and unreadable. She kept her gaze level, and when his gray-blue eyes met hers, she tried not to shudder. She tried not to feel the guilt that was washing through her. She tried to ignore all of the emotions threatening to take over, and most of all, she tried to lie.

"As a woman, I find cases about kidnappings very disconcerting." She never once looked away, because she knew that would give her away more than anything else. She stared straight into his eyes and willed him to believe her words.

"That wasn't your first kidnapping case," he said, all calm, emotionless delivery.

She swallowed before she could will away the nervous response. She had worked a kidnapping case before, but just one. It had been the abduction of a little boy in the middle of a custody battle. It had been nothing like her sister's case, and she'd known that from the beginning. "He was a small boy. I couldn't see myself as a victim."

"Herman said he keeps *girls*. Last time I checked, you were a woman."

Natalie's pulse started thundering in her wrist and in her neck, panic fluttering through her. "Obviously you've never been a young woman in a rough part of town," she returned, proud of how steady her voice sounded.

He held her gaze, but he didn't say anything. He simply looked at her as though if he looked long enough, he could unravel all her secrets.

She almost believed he could.

"What do you know about The Stallion, Ms. Torres? I won't ask again."

"Good. Because I don't know anything about him.

I don't even know *what* he is. So, please, don't ask me again, because this is the truth. I have no clue." She managed to swallow down the "trust me, I wish I knew more." But only just.

"Lies could get us killed at this point. Remember that."

It struck her hard, because he was right. Some lies could get them killed in this situation, but not her lies. All she was doing was not explaining why she'd been superinterested in this case.

Her interest in the girls had nothing to do with why her house had been burned down, and had nothing to do with why she was stuck in this little place in the middle of nowhere with this Texas Ranger.

Her lie was personal, but it was…incidental almost. She didn't know anything about The Stallion or what he might be into that would make him the kind of man to kill people and burn down houses.

She reached across the table, not sure why it seemed necessary to touch him, but she thought she could get her truth across if there was some sort of connection. She touched her fingertips to the back of his hand and looked him in the eye.

"I have no intention of getting us killed. I have no intention of lying to you. All I want is to be able to go back to my life." She slid her fingers off his hand, and something shimmered to life inside of her. She didn't understand that odd feeling, and why she felt off-kilter and short of breath. Why the warmth of his hand seemed to stay in her fingertips.

So, she looked down at her soup as she said, "And if we're going to discuss honesty, why don't you tell me what you know about why we're being chased? Because

I think it's a whole heck of a lot more complicated than you're letting on."

She brought a spoonful of soup to her mouth and then slid a glance at him. He had narrowed his eyes, and he was still studying her, that intensity never leaving his face.

And Natalie wondered just how long she could keep her secret…

Chapter 6

Vaughn still didn't trust Ms. Torres. There was something she was hiding, he was sure of it. Despite his absolute certainty though, he found himself inclined to believe she didn't know anything about The Stallion. She wasn't scared enough. If she knew what that man was capable of, she'd be petrified.

"There's nothing about this case that seems to directly apply to you. The Stallion is the head of an organized crime ring that deals mostly in drugs. Human and sex trafficking is also a possibility."

He noted the way she paled. It could be that fear he thought she needed, but he tended to think that the mention of trafficking didn't make people pale unless they had some sort of personal stake in the matter.

He could question her again. He could keep interrogating her until she finally gave in and told him her secret.

And he would. Yes, he would, but first he needed to

finish his soup and get a few hours of sleep. That was just common sense, not caring about her feelings. He certainly didn't care about those.

"We have at least four unsolved cases we think might be connected to The Stallion and his cronies. Not to even begin to mention the current cases. Getting Herman on the leash and willing to talk was a huge breakthrough in our cases. And then you ruined my interrogation."

"You were asking the wrong questions."

"I know what the right questions are. I've been doing this for too long to ask the wrong questions. You were taking too direct an approach, and it wasn't even your job to approach anything." He gritted his teeth to stop from talking. He wasn't going to let her rile him up with her ridiculous accusations.

He finished his soup and then closed out all the files he didn't want her to have access to. He set his computer up so he'd be able to track whatever she did try to look up while he was asleep.

He didn't consider it underhanded, he considered it necessary.

"I'm going to sleep. Obviously you can make yourself comfortable, but keep all doors locked, all windows covered. You hear a noise, see anything suspicious, *anything*, you come get me immediately."

"What if someone blasts through the window and I have nothing to protect myself with?"

She made a good point, but it wasn't a particularly comfortable one. Did he trust her enough to *arm* her while he slept? "What are your qualifications?"

Her eyebrows drew together. "My…what?"

"Do you have a permit? Training?"

"Well, no."

"Have you ever used a gun before?"

"Well…" She sighed at his raised eyebrow. "No."

Vaughn resisted rolling his eyes. Barely. "We'll see about training you, but in the meantime, don't touch a firearm. If someone comes blasting in here, they'll have you disarmed before you even figure out how to aim and pull the trigger."

She scowled, but she didn't argue. He'd count that as a win.

"If you see something suspicious, come get me. Otherwise, stay out of trouble."

Her full lips remained pressed together. The lips were distracting, but not as distracting as how…formfitting his sister's clothes were on this woman. And thank goodness they were his *sister's* clothes and he could keep any wayward thoughts at bay with that reminder.

He turned abruptly and headed for his room. It didn't make sense to sit here sniping with her when he needed to catch a few hours' sleep. He didn't bother with a shower; he'd deal with that later. For now, he went straight to his bed and slid under the covers.

He was exhausted enough that his eyelids immediately closed, but he didn't drift off right away. No matter how exhausted he was, there was too much on his mind.

Unfortunately, a large portion of that was Natalie Torres. He still hadn't had a chance to dig deeper into her background beyond the file the department had kept on her while she'd been employed with them.

No criminal record. Hell, not even a speeding ticket. She'd lived at the same address for the entirety of her employment, and none of her other jobs struck him as peculiar or suspicious.

It was simply *her* that was both peculiar and suspicious. The way she'd jumped in and questioned Herman after years of following the rules. The way she'd paled when he mentioned trafficking.

The way she chewed on her bottom lip when she was thinking, leaving it wet and…

He groaned and rolled face-first into his pillow. He'd never been… He punched at the pillow, irritated with the truth. No matter how suspicious he found Ms. Torres, he was *physically* attracted to her.

Which didn't matter, of course, it was just increasingly obnoxious that the woman he didn't want to be attracted to was the one he was stuck in an isolated cabin with. For who knew how long.

But, he couldn't think like that. He had to focus on one thing at a time. If he got too worked up about what *could* happen, he'd miss something about what *was* happening, and that could get somebody killed.

He hadn't let it happen yet. He wasn't about to let it happen now. That was how he had to think. He had to be certain that he could solve this case before any more people got hurt. But he needed to get in a couple hours' sleep so he could focus on the files and find the connection he was missing.

He needed to figure out what Ms. Torres's connection was. Because she had to have one. Maybe it wasn't with The Stallion, but she was involved with *something*. He was sure of it.

And when Vaughn Cooper was sure of something, God help the person on the other side.

Natalie glanced at the hallway Ranger Cooper had disappeared down at least twenty minutes ago. Surely he was asleep. She'd been afraid to move the entire time he'd been gone, afraid that he would somehow read her thoughts and her plan and come rushing back out and take the computer with him.

But he'd left it. Ranger Cooper wasn't a stupid man. She didn't think he'd actually have anything on that computer she could access that would give her answers, but if he had the internet, or even a basic case write-up of something, she might be able to find the information she needed to make the connection. A connection between her sister and this Stallion person.

A clue. A hint. Something, something to help her figure out how to proceed.

Natalie stood, and her heart was nearly beating out of her chest. She had to get a handle on her nerves at being caught. What did it matter? He knew what she was doing. He *had* to know this was what she was going to do. Getting caught was the least of her worries.

Her heartbeat didn't seem to listen. It continued to beat guiltily in her chest, but she had do something. She took her bowl to the kitchen and rinsed it out. She waited after each movement to see if she could hear Ranger Cooper moving around or coming back out to the hallway. But the cabin was eerily silent.

Now her heart was overbeating for a completely different reason. The fact someone could be out there. Someone could be out there and watching her and just…

She squeezed her eyes shut and shook her head. She couldn't think like that. She could only think about survival. Thinking about who or what was after her and why…

She had to push it away, just like the knowledge her house was gone, that her sister could be dead, that her family could be in danger. She had to push it all aside and focus on what she could do.

She walked out of the kitchen and headed for the table and the open computer. She put her hand on the touchpad, and the computer sprang to life. No password to enter. No apparent security practices in place. Just an open, easily accessible computer. She glanced back down the hallway with narrowed eyes.

There was no way he would leave his computer completely unattended. Even if nothing was on here. There was something to this. Some kind of setup. Or maybe he was simply trying to prove she was underhanded.

It was insulting. He thought she was *this* dumb. For some reason that made her want to do it all the more. To do everything he thought she would do. Because it didn't seem to matter what she did, he was going to think she was hiding something. She might as well get something out of it.

It was possible her sister had been taken by The Stallion. But it was also possible her sister was taken by some other lunatic, and Natalie would never find her. But Natalie was never going to know if she didn't take this chance—regardless of what Ranger Cooper thought.

So, she pulled up the web browser and tested the availability of the internet. She cursed when she couldn't find anything. No wireless, and he didn't appear to have any kind of hot spot. So what had he been reading so intently all through lunch?

She skimmed the names of the folders on his desktop. The one on the very top was named CASE FILES.

"Oh, you really think I am just such an idiot, don't you?" she muttered, more and more insulted.

She opened the folder anyway. Maybe this was all information he didn't mind her having, but that didn't mean it wasn't worth having. It would still be more than she knew. She would take this opportunity, no matter how he used it against her in the future.

When the folder opened, there were a variety of documents inside. They didn't appear to be official police documents. They weren't reports or labeled in the way she knew cases and information at the precinct was labeled. These had to be his personal notes.

Even better.

Each file name included the words "The Stallion" plus a number code of some sort. Either his own or one outside of police work.

She began to read them in order, getting lost in the twists and turns of all the possible cases they thought The Stallion might be involved in.

It was a lot of drugs. Things she didn't know anything about. She couldn't imagine her sister had been wrapped up in drugs. Surely Natalie would've noticed that. They had been too close for Natalie to have not known or suspected that.

When Natalie got to the suspected instances of human trafficking, her blood ran cold. A lot of it was mixed up with immigration issues, but the thing that hit her hard and left her reeling was a mention of the Corlico Plant.

Her father had worked there for twenty years. He'd only stopped when Gabby had disappeared from the parking lot, waiting for him to get off his shift.

He'd never been able to go back.

And here it was, in the cases tied to The Stallion. Natalie shivered, reading quicker through the notes.

Apparently the Rangers suspected the factory of being some sort of drop-off point, or transfer station based on one raid they'd conducted, but the two women who had been freed hadn't been able to give any information that gave the Rangers further leads.

Between Herman saying he kept the girls, and this connection, Natalie was more and more convinced The Stallion was keeping Gabby. That he *had* her.

She was alive.

It was strange that the rush of tears overtook her, considering how often and how much she'd cried over Gabby. How many moments of hope she'd had that had been dashed time and time again over the course of eight years. Yet this new little tiny trickle of a lead felt like a revelation.

She'd always been certain Gabby was still alive. Her certainty had been something of a crutch, really. But there'd always been that little question in the back of her mind. What if Mom and Grandma were right? What if Gabby was dead, and Natalie had wasted her life chasing nothing?

But it wasn't nothing. This was the biggest lead she'd ever had. It wasn't proof, and maybe it was even grasping at straws, but it was something. Something had to mean everything right now. On the run, in this tiny cabin with a man she didn't understand—and was afraid she was a little too interested in understanding—she finally had a sliver of hope.

She would hold on to that for all she was worth.

She kept scanning the documents, eager to find a connection between the Corlico Plant and The Stallion.

An eerie sound pierced the air. Natalie froze. She didn't know how to describe the sound, and she had even less of a clue where it might have come from. She didn't move a muscle and strained to hear something else. Something that might identify it as harmless.

What on earth would be harmless in the middle of nowhere? Again her heart pounded so loudly she could barely hear anything, and knowing she needed to hear made it even worse. She breathed slowly and evenly, trying desperately to listen carefully. She didn't want to wake up Ranger Cooper for something stupid.

A noise in the middle of nowhere isn't stupid. It was actually probably pretty damn important. Looking a little stupid was better than being dead.

Carefully, she stood. Her legs were shaky, but she tried to walk as quietly as possible, still straining to hear something, anything, to give her a clue as to what the sound might have been.

She inched her way toward the hallway, eyes trained on the door and the windows. She didn't know whether she was expecting someone to burst through one, or one of those red dots from a laser sight to show up on her chest.

The sound didn't repeat, and she slowly moved down the hallway. Just as she reached Ranger Cooper's door, she heard it again.

It was oddly high-pitched, but not quite mechanical. Where she had originally planned to be very careful and quiet, gently waking up Ranger Cooper, the sound repeating caused Natalie to move forward clumsily and jerkily, swinging open his door with no finesse it all.

He was bolting up in the bed before the door even banged against the wall. His hand immediately closed over his weapon, which had been placed on a nightstand next to his bed.

It was the second time he'd almost pulled his weapon

on her in the course of not very many hours, but she was glad he had such quick reflexes. It was oddly comforting to know he would immediately grab for his gun and try to protect them both. Considering he had never actually done anything with the gun, just placed his hand on it both times, she still felt safe in his presence.

He flung off the covers, getting out of the bed in one quick, graceful movement. He was wearing athletic shorts and a T-shirt, and perhaps a little bit later she'd have more time to appreciate just how sculpted his muscles were, but for right now she had her life to save.

"What's happening?" he asked, his hands clutching the gun at his side, looking like a man ready to fight.

"I...heard a noise," Natalie said, feeling foolish and scared and just damn lost.

He didn't balk, he didn't question her. He simply nodded.

Chapter 7

Vaughn tried to loosen his grip on the gun. Natalie had shocked him the hell out of sleep, and the adrenaline was still pounding through him.

He glanced at Natalie's pale face. "Tell me what you heard," he ordered gruffly, shoving his feet into his boots.

"I… I don't even know. It was kind of high-pitched, but… It didn't sound like anything I'd ever heard before."

He gave a sharp nod, not bothering to pull the laces tight. "Where did it come from?" He stepped out into the hall and motioned her to follow.

"I'm not sure. It was so sudden and out of nowhere. But, it'd had to have come from closer to the front of the cabin, I think, or it would have been more muffled."

Again, he nodded. He listened for any noise aside from the sounds of their feet on the stone floor. Nothing. "I want you to stay in the hallway while I check the windows and doors." He stopped his progress and turned to face her. "You will stay right here no matter what. Understand?"

She scrunched her nose, but she didn't argue with him. She nodded, lips clamped together as though she didn't trust herself to speak.

She was smart, he'd give her that. He entered the living area, starting at the window closest to him. As stealthily as possible, he raised the curtain, surveyed what he could and then moved to the next window—each time all he saw was rocks and dusk.

He made it to the kitchen window and still nothing. They'd have to go outside. He debated making her stay inside while he searched, but it would be more dangerous to separate. Especially separating the unarmed civilian from the man trained to handle a weapon.

"I'm not seeing anything," he said gruffly, turning to find her exactly where he'd left her in the hall.

"I swear I heard something," she said, her eyes still round, her fingers clenched into fists.

"I believe you," he returned, barely paying attention as he tried to formulate a plan on how to investigate the perimeter without getting either one of them killed.

"You *do*?"

He glanced back at the note of incredulousness in her voice, focusing more on her than his plans for the first time. "Is there a reason I shouldn't?"

"No, I just…" She shook her head, looking completely baffled. "I'm…not used to people believing me. Especially *you*."

Those last two words shouldn't have an impact on him. What did it matter if he hadn't believed her all this time? They were here, weren't they? He was keeping her safe. Yet he felt that *especially you* like a sharp pain.

But he didn't have time to dwell on that or figure it out. Quite frankly he wouldn't want to even if he did.

"We're going to have to search the perimeter together. We're going to do the same thing we did when we got here. You're going to follow me closely. Listen to whatever I say. And hopefully we'll find the source of the noise and it's nothing."

"And if it's something?"

"There are too many possibilities for us to sit here and go over all of them. You're just going to have to follow my lead, and everything will be fine."

"Is the unwavering confidence real, or do you say those sorts of things so I'll go along with whatever you say?"

Oddly, he wanted to smile. Because it was a good question—a fair one, and the dry way she delivered it. Because he appreciated her backbone. Unfortunately, now was not the time for good or fair questions. So he simply said, "Both" and then started walking toward the door.

She followed him as she had when they'd first arrived. Though her antagonism and questioning tended to grate on his nerves, he would have to give her credit for following directions when it was required.

She wanted to fight him, it was obvious, but she didn't. He admired both. Someone who didn't get a little bent out of shape about being told what to do was too much of a pushover to be of any real help. But someone who could make the choice to listen even if they didn't want to, that was a person with sense.

You're seriously having these thoughts about that woman?

He opened the door, forcing himself to focus on the task ahead and nothing else. He used the door as a shield and scanned the front yard. Since the house was nestled into one of the swells of land that wasn't rocky mountain, the land in front of the house stretched far and wide. There'd be no place to hide within shooting range, and as he scanned the land around them, he didn't see anything that might be people or the evidence of them.

The problem was going to be the back of the house. There was a small yard between the desert and the building, and walking back there would prove even trickier without having any kind of cover.

A piercing howl of a coyote echoed in the quickly cooling desert air. He always liked listening to them, but his sister had said they were as creepy as hell.

Apparently Ms. Torres agreed with his sister because her hand clamped around his arm. "That's it. That's the sound," she said, her voice little more than a squeaky whisper.

Vaughn immediately relaxed. Dropping his gun to his side, he turned to face her. Her long and slender fingers still curled around his forearm. He glanced at her hand momentarily, not sure why such a simple touch was dancing over him like…like anticipation.

There was nothing to anticipate here. So that feeling needed to go.

"Why'd you put your gun down? What is it?" She looked at him with those wide, scared eyes, and he couldn't help but smile. She blinked, clearly confused.

"It's coyotes. We have them here, and they occasionally get close to the house and do the howling. But it's just an animal. Nothing to be afraid of."

She looked horrified, and for a second he thought he was going to have to give a lecture about how coyotes weren't dangerous and there were far bigger things to worry about, but her hand dropped and she closed her eyes. Not fear etching over her face, but a pink-tinged embarrassment.

"I feel like such an idiot. Coyotes. That's it?"

"You've never heard a coyote before?"

She heaved a sigh. "I've only ever lived in Houston and Austin. In the city. Animal noises are not my expertise. It didn't sound…howly." She shook her head, disgusted. With herself, he imagined.

"Sometimes they'll sound like a big group howl, sometimes it's not quite so delineated, but it's definitely coyote."

"I'm so sorry," she said, all too sincerely, all too… worked up for an honest mistake. It made him itchy and uncomfortable, and irritably needing to soothe it away.

"There's nothing to be sorry about. It was an honest mistake. Unless you're apologizing for something else?"

Her mouth firmed. "No, I'm not apologizing for anything else. I… You…" Her eyebrows drew together, and those dark eyes studied him, some emotion he couldn't recognize in their depths. "But it was an animal, and nothing, and… You aren't mad that I woke you up and got you into police mode when it was nothing?"

"Of course not. You heard an unknown noise and you reacted exactly as you should have. Exactly as I *told* you to. Why on earth would I be mad?"

"I don't understand you at all, Ranger Cooper. All the things I expect you to be hard on me about, you're not, but the things I don't expect you to be hard on me about, you are."

"Then maybe you shouldn't expect either."

She laughed at that. A bright, loud laugh, and it was a shock how much the sound of someone else's laughter surprised him. When was the last time he'd heard anyone laugh? Sarcastic laughter, sure. All the time at work. But he had been so focused on getting somewhere in the cases connected to The Stallion there hadn't been any banter at work, he hadn't had any kind of social life and he hadn't relaxed at all.

It was only now, here, in the middle of the desert and mountains, with this strange woman's laughter ringing in his ears that he realized any of that. A very uncomfortable and unsettling realization prompted by a very uncomfortable and unsettling woman.

Maybe that was appropriate, all in all.

"You should call me Vaughn." He had no idea where that instruction came from. Why on earth would she call him Vaughn? He should be nothing to her but Ranger Cooper.

And yet something about that smile and laugh made him... Well, stupid apparently. "Let's head back inside."

"Your name is Vaughn?"

"No, I'm lying," he grumbled.

She laughed again as they stepped inside, and he found himself smiling. The last thing he should be feeling now was any kind of lightness, and yet that little exchange had done exactly that—lightened him. It had to be the sleep exhaustion.

"That's a very unconventional name for a very conventional man."

"How do you know I'm conventional?"

"Oh, please. You can't possibly *not* be conventional. You showed up at that fire at three thirty in the morning all neat and unwrinkled. You don't believe in hypnotism. You were nothing but..." She pulled her shoulders up to her ears and pretended to tense all over. "Like a tight ball of contained, by-the-book energy. Everything about you is conventional."

"Ms. Torres, trust me when I say that you do not know everything about me."

Her eyes met his, and he recognized that little weird energy that passed between them. He wished he didn't, but there was no denying the flirtatious undertone to all of this. He should stop it immediately.

But she held his gaze and she smiled. "Natalie. You should call me Natalie, remember?"

That uncomfortable and unwelcome attraction dug deeper into his gut. The kind of deeper that led a man to make foolish mistakes and stupid decisions. The kind he knew better than to indulge in.

But it was also the kind that tended to override that knowledge.

Natalie's breathing became shallow for a whole different reason than it had the past few days. Looking at Vaughn, because he said she should call him Vaughn, and knowing they were doing a very weird, and very nearly flirting thing, yeah, it made her body respond in unwelcome ways.

She was too warm, and a little shaky. Not the kind Vaughn could see, but the kind that was internal. The kind that messed with her equilibrium.

She should really look away from that ice-blue gaze, but she simply stared. She really should stop. Any minute now.

"You know, not believing in hypnotism isn't exactly unconventional. It's just common sense."

Well, the man sure knew how to kill a moment. She walked farther into the living room and decided to take a seat on the comfy-looking couch. Men like him never could accept there might be a softer way about getting information than torture or the like.

"What exactly do you think hypnotism is, fun? Magic?"

"That's the point. It's not magic. It's not real."

"That's because you have the wrong perception of what hypnotism is. It's not about magic. It's not about getting someone to do something against their will. It's about giving the person being hypnotized a safe place to express something that's hard for them to express. It's about finding a center, finding calm. It's not tricks. It's not getting someone to bark like a dog on stage. It's showing someone who has every reason to be afraid of talking a calmness inside themselves that can allow them to give information they, deep down, *want* to give."

She knew she was lecturing, but he was always ordering her about, so maybe turnaround was fair play. "You can't make someone do something under hypnotism that they don't want to do. The thing is, they *want* to do this. They just have a mental block. Calming their breathing and giving them that safe place gives them the tools to get over that block. It's not magic. It's not supposed to be magic. It's a tool."

He was silent for a few moments, and she thought maybe she'd surprised him with her answer. When people actually sat down to listen to how she explained hypnotism and why it worked in terms of witnesses, they tended to understand. Even if they didn't necessarily believe in it, they at least understood that no one thought this was some magical cure. *Most* people sneered at it a lot less once she explained. She had a sneaking suspicion that Vaughn was not one of those "most people."

"If they want to give us the answers, then what's the

point of you? Why don't they just, you know, give us the answers?"

"Let's use Herman as an example," she replied, relaxing into the couch, crossing her arms over her chest, refusing to back down to his disdain. "He knew that he was going to die. He knew that talking to you was going to get him killed. But let's start at the beginning? How did you get Herman to come in?"

Vaughn narrowed his eyes at her and stood there for a few minutes of ticking silence. As though he wasn't quite sure that she was worthy of the information. It made her want to smack him.

"He was pulled over. Since he had warrants, he was brought in."

"And then you and Ranger Stevens decided to question him because…?"

"Because he was connected to a case that we believe has to do with The Stallion."

"So, here is this man who has a family, daughters and a sick wife. He's scared of his boss, but he also knows that his boss is doing something incredibly wrong. So his conscience is telling him to talk to the police, his common sense and survival instinct are telling him not to talk to you. When you're in that kind of moral dilemma—where you want to save yourself, but you want to save others too—it's hard to make a choice. It's especially hard to make a choice that you know will put you in even more danger than you're already in. Having something to blame your answers on is freeing. It takes the personal responsibility off you, and then you can unburden yourself the way you really want to. I would bet money that if you somehow got The Stallion into one of your interrogation rooms and I tried to hypnotize him, it wouldn't work. It only works on people who are conflicted. A part of themselves actually *does* want to talk, or they don't."

"Did it ever occur to you to tell people this before you walk into an interrogation room?"

"Did it ever occur to you to trust the order of your superior who clearly did trust me and believed that what I was doing was useful?"

"The minute I start believing someone just because he's my superior is the minute I become a subpar police officer."

"Conventional."

She thought for a second that he was going to smile. His surprisingly full, nearly carnal lips almost curved before he stopped them and pressed them into a line.

"Have you changed your mind about hypnotism?"

"No."

"Do you want me to hypnotize you?"

"No." Again that little quirk like he might smile, or even laugh.

"I bet you have some juicy secrets you're just dying to tell me."

"There will be no secret sharing, Ms. Torres."

"What else are we going to entertain ourselves with for the next few days?"

"We could discuss whatever it was that you looked up on my computer." This time he did smile, but it wasn't a particularly nice one. It was sharp edges and a little bit of smug self-satisfaction.

Ugh. Why did he still have to be hot even when he was being smugly self-satisfied?

None of that. None. Of. That. "I just checked to see if you had Wi-Fi," she returned, smiling as saccharine as she could manage.

"All the way out here you thought I might have Wi-Fi?"

"You never know."

"Why don't you be straight with me, Natalie."

"How about I start when you start." Some of that flirtatious ease from earlier was cooling considerably degree by degree.

"I've been nothing but straight with you."

"No, you've been vague at best. Considering I'm mixed up in all of this, I really think that I deserve to know what all of this is."

"I can't put my investigation at risk," he returned, back to the implacable Texas Ranger.

"You have me in the middle of nowhere under lock and key. What risk is being posed?"

"I still don't know you. I don't know who you're connected to. I don't know what happens when you're cleared to go home. If you want to take that personally, that's your prerogative, but that's certainly not how it's meant. I don't know you, and until I do, until I know what you're after and what your connection is, there is nothing I can do to trust you. Not and do my job."

She shifted on the couch and looked away from him, because as true as it was, it was somehow still irritating. She totally understood what he was saying. It made nothing but sense, and that she was oddly hurt he couldn't trust her was ridiculous.

"I may have found a connection..." She swallowed. If she told him, he might trust her. For some strange reason, she really did want him to, but if she told him, was she putting herself at risk of never being able to touch one of these cases again? If he knew she was connected to this one little case, would he keep everything from her because her sister was involved? Or would he maybe have some compassion because he had a sister of his own?

Would it be worth suffering through having no answers to get a little bit of the possibility of a new answer? She didn't know, and she found the more she sat there and he stood there—an unmoving mountain of a man—the less she knew.

She stared into those gray-blue eyes, searching for some hint that there might be warmth or that compassion might be a word in his dictionary. There was absolutely nothing in his face to give her the inclination, and yet she so desperately wanted it to be so.

Later she would blame it on exhaustion, not just of the day, or the week, but over the past eight years. But for right now, she opened her mouth, and the truth tumbled out.

Chapter 8

"A connection?" Everything inside Vaughn tensed as he glared at her. She might've found a connection? A connection to what? How could she have possibly found something in cases he'd pored over for years and found next to nothing except gut feelings and hunches?

"There was a case in your files…" She cleared her throat, and she most assuredly did not look at him, but she also showed no remorse for going through his files. It was hard to blame her. He would have done the same thing in her situation. That's why he'd bothered to set her up; he knew she'd do it.

What he hadn't known was that she might actually offer some information. He thought he would have to drag that out of her.

She fidgeted on the couch and chewed on her all too distracting bottom lip. He could jump all over her and demand answers, which would stop the mouth distraction, but it wouldn't be the most effective route to take.

The most effective route to take with Natalie was, unfortunately, patience. To listen to what she said, to understand it. She was a hypnotist, but her fervor over the importance of hypnotism and what it offered pointed to the fact that she was conflicted herself—a moral dilemma, just as she'd said about Herman.

So, he stood, his hands clenched into fists, his muscles held tight. And he waited.

"There was a file on human trafficking. It mentioned that there was some sort of possibility of a drop-off point being at the Corlico Plant?" She looked up at him questioningly.

He hesitated for a second, but she'd already read the file, one he'd left available to her. Might as well give her the information. "Yes, we intercepted a group of people there. Based on all the information we could collect, it wasn't the first time that the trafficking went through there. But they immediately stopped since we intercepted, and we had no one to arrest, nothing to go on. We've never been able to find anything after it."

"Three years ago, right? That's when you intercepted?"

"Yes." Three years and eight months. He didn't even have to look it up. When it came to cases he thought had to do with The Stallion, he had most of the prominent details memorized.

She took a deep breath, clasped her hands together and then straightened her shoulders. She fixed him with a certain gaze, and he knew this was going to be whatever she'd been hiding.

"Eight years ago, my sister disappeared from the Corlico Plant parking lot."

She didn't have to go further. Suddenly everything came together. Why she asked Herman about the girls, why she would ruin years' worth of work with the Rangers to ask the questions that she wanted to ask instead of letting him and Stevens handle it.

She was searching for her sister.

"Unbelievable," he muttered.

She didn't even have the decency to appear shamed. She shrugged. "Do you how many years I've been waiting to have a case that might connect to Gabby? Do you know how many hours I've spent trying to figure out what happened to her? They never found a body, in all this time. No one ever found a clue that might bring her back to us. I know she's alive. I don't care if anybody believes it or not, I *know* she is."

Her eyes had filled with tears, but they didn't spill onto her cheeks. She looked straight at him, strong and determined, and so *certain* her sister was still alive. He could say a lot of things about Natalie, but she was a strong woman. Obviously stronger than he'd even seen so far.

"Something with that factory is connected. It's too big of a coincidence. She disappeared *there*. Then Herman said he keeps the girls. The human trafficking thing stops there, and that's where she disappeared—before it stopped, I might add. It was late, and she was waiting for my father to get off from his evening shift, and maybe she saw something she wasn't supposed to see, or they saw her and thought she was part of it or…"

"Natalie, that's a lot of maybes. We have to work in fact." He tried to say it gently, but it had been a long time since he'd had to employ gentleness with someone.

"The fact is that this factory has something to do with

this case. It has something to do with The Stallion. Who owns it?"

It hit him almost like a lightning bolt, painful and sharp, and he realized…

He turned to his computer and immediately pulled up the file they had on Victor Callihan. He owned the factory, and Vaughn had done extensive research into his background after the trafficking raid. He'd found nothing that might link the man to any crimes, but maybe it stood to reason to dig again, and deeper.

Callihan was a rich man. A powerful man. He'd have the means to do these things. Including keep his nose clean, even when it wasn't.

It couldn't really be that easy, could it?

Natalie was immediately behind him, looking over his shoulder at the screen. The soft swell of her breasts, accidentally he assumed, brushed his back, and he had to grit his teeth to focus on the task at hand.

"Does the name Victor Callihan mean anything to you?"

"No," she returned. "He's the owner?"

"Of the plant and the corporation that runs the plant. He's a bigwig in Austin. After the raid, we investigated him, but we didn't find anything remotely criminal. But if the plant is the common denominator, we should look into it more."

"But you don't have Wi-Fi."

"That doesn't mean I don't have wired internet." He glanced over his shoulder at her, but only came eye-level to her breasts. He quickly looked back at the computer because the last thing he was going to keep doing was noticing anything remotely sexual about her. He was too professional for that.

"First, I need to send an email to Stevens, so he can look into things from his side. He'll have access to all the Ranger files and faster internet." Vaughn tried to slide out of the chair, but again his shoulder blade kind of drifted across her breasts. Seriously. What the hell was this?

He cleared his throat and walked over to the entertainment center that held the cord he needed to hook the computer up to the internet jack. He didn't look at Natalie, and he felt like a wimpy idiot, but sometimes that was the best alternative. He certainly didn't want her to see the effect she had on him. That could lead nowhere good.

"Okay, so, what could Stevens find that might tip us off? What would we be looking for?"

"First, *you* are not looking for anything. You are an innocent bystander."

She huffed out an irritated breath. Which was better than the worried lip chewing. "I'm the one who brought this connection to your attention."

"You could have brought it to my attention a lot earlier. If you had mentioned your connection to The Stallion or this case, I—"

"I didn't know I had anything to do with The Stallion or this case. I still don't. I mean, I think it's too big of a coincidence, but that doesn't mean he has my sister. It doesn't mean..." She trailed off and looked away, and he knew that she was struggling to control her emotions.

He didn't like how easy it was to put himself in her place. Often, due to his father and sister's fame, his sister had received threatening letters or emails. Paparazzi had gotten too close, and occasionally a fan had gotten too interested. He knew what it was like to have concern for your sister's well-being.

Natalie's situation was so much worse, because for

eight years now she had been in the dark. She was surviving based on faith alone. As much as Vaughn wanted to discount faith, considering you couldn't get much done with it, he couldn't ignore how admirable it was.

It was admirable that she had put herself into a position where she might find some information about her sister's case. It was admirable after all these years she believed, and she hoped. All in all, Natalie was proving to be something of an admirable woman. That was the last thing he needed right now.

"The trafficking incident was three years ago. Something could have come up in the past three years that we haven't thought to put together." She might operate on faith, but he had to operate on fact. "Knowing this little bit means that when we go back through all of that information with a fine-tooth comb. We know a little bit more about what we're looking for. And we can add the details of your sister's case with the other possible Stallion related cases. When you have a man like this, where he has his fingers in so many different things, who runs an organized crime ring, a little connection could be the connection that leads us to him."

Vaughn connected the computer to the wired internet line. She had moved away from the table, so he could sit safely at it without worrying about her body being anywhere near his.

He logged in and typed a quick email to Stevens with all the pertinent information. His instinct was to go ahead and start searching, even though Stevens would have better luck in that department. His partner would have access to all the police files at work, and faster, less frustrating internet. But when Vaughn glanced at Natalie, she was pacing the living room, wringing her hands.

He could read all sorts of emotions in her expression. It wasn't just sadness, it wasn't just fear. There was a myriad of things in there. Anger and uncertainty, hope and helplessness alike. The thing he recognized the most was that antsy kind of energy you got when you desperately wanted to fix a situation, and couldn't.

He could sit here and fool around trying to find the information he wanted, but that probably wasn't the best use of his time right now. Not if he wanted to put Natalie at ease.

Since when is putting Natalie at ease your concern?

He ignored the commentary of his brain and pushed back the chair. "I can do more searching later, but for right now we need to use what little light we have left."

She looked over at him, her eyebrows drawing together. "What do we need light for?"

"I'm going to teach you to shoot."

Natalie blinked at Vaughn. She didn't know what to say to that. It certainly wasn't what she had expected. But she hadn't known what to expect when it came to Vaughn.

She thought he'd be angrier about her not mentioning her sister's case. She thought he'd shut her down and out while he went to work trying to find information out about this Victor Callihan. She kind of wanted him to do *that*, but Vaughn didn't do anything half-assed or foolishly, so she knew there was a rhyme or a reason to him teaching her to shoot.

She couldn't decide if she wanted to know said rhyme or reason. She wasn't sure she wanted to learn to shoot. She wasn't sure what she wanted, except an hour to have a good cry.

"We don't have too much time, so I can only show you the basics, but it wouldn't hurt for you to have an idea."

"Oh. Oh. Okay." What else was there to say?

"I'll get my extra ammunition, and then we'll go outside and get started."

"And you think we'll be safe out there?" They were inside with the windows closed, and so far he'd only let her go outside as a shadow to him. But he frowned at her, as though the question were silly.

For the first time, she wondered how old he was, considering the little lines bracketing his mouth. Actually she was starting to wonder a lot of things about him. Things that she should absolutely not wonder about the man investigating a case that might have to do with her sister. Things she definitely shouldn't be wondering about the man who was keeping her safe.

"I don't suggest things that aren't safe, Ms. Torres. Remember that."

He turned and disappeared down the hallway, presumably to get that extra ammunition he spoke of. She noticed he tended to stick with "Ms. Torres" when he was irritated with her. But when he was a little soft, or a little nice, which apparently he could be—shock of all shocks—he would call her Natalie.

She *definitely* way, way too much liked the way her first name sounded in his rough-and-tumble, no-nonsense drawl.

She really had to get herself together before she learned how to shoot a gun.

There had been a time in her life, directly after Gabby's disappearance, when she had jumped at every little thing and considered getting a gun. Even knowing her sister's disappearance was probably random, she hadn't felt safe.

But in the end, the idea of carrying around a gun hadn't made her feel any safer. In fact, the idea of carrying anything that deadly when she was that jumpy only made her more nervous. So she'd never learned how to shoot and she'd never owned a gun.

But something about Vaughn was…reassuring almost. She trusted him to teach her. And teach her well. Obviously he knew what he was doing with a gun, as frequently as he reached for his.

That didn't even scare her. They were in a dangerous situation, and it had only ever felt comforting that he reached for his weapon when startled. Truth be told, nothing about Vaughn scared her. Except that nothing about him scared her. Yes, that part was a little too scary. How easily it was to trust him and listen to him and follow his orders.

She blew out a breath as he returned. He carried a box and a little black bag, and strode toward the door with his usual laser focus.

"All right. Follow me."

"Do you always express things as an order? You could ask. You could say please."

"I'm doing you a favor. I don't need to say please, and I certainly don't need to ask permission. You can follow me and learn how to shoot a gun. Or you can stay here. I really don't care which one."

She doubted that he didn't care, but she managed not to say that. Instead, she followed him outside and around the back of the house. She couldn't imagine there being much more than twenty or thirty minutes left of light, but Vaughn seemed determined to see this through.

"We're not going to worry about hitting some little

target. We're just going to work with the basics of aiming and shooting."

He set the bag down and opened it, pulling out big glasses she assumed were safety related. He handed her the glasses and two little orange foam things. When she looked at them skeptically, he sighed.

"They're earplugs. You pinch the end, and you put it in your ear. It'll keep the gun noise from bothering you."

"Right."

"Now, I'm going to explain everything before we put in the earplugs, and then I'll position you the way you need to be standing and holding the gun. Understood?"

"Aye, aye, Captain," she said sarcastically, because if she was sarcastic she wouldn't overthink the phrase "position you."

He rolled his eyes, clearly not amused by her. But that was okay, because she was amused enough for both of them.

Vaughn pulled his weapon from the holster at his hip. He began to explain the different components to her, the sights, the trigger. What kind of kick to expect and how to aim. She couldn't begin to understand all the jargon or keep up with the different things. He went too fast.

"Are you following along?"

She hated to admit it to him, and herself, but his speed wasn't the issue. Oral instruction had never been easy for her. She had to do things before she fully understood them.

"It's okay if you don't understand something. You can ask as many questions as you need to."

She hated the gentle way he said that. Hated when he was nice, because it made her feel silly or like a victim, and she didn't want to be either. She wanted to be as strong and brave as him.

"I find it easier to understand something if I'm actually in the process of doing it," she gritted, far more snappish than she needed to be.

He didn't react. He simply gestured in front of him. "All right. Stand in front of me."

She did as she was told, and stiffened perceptibly as his arms came around her sides. She had to swallow against the incomparable wave of... It wasn't just attraction, though that was the most potent thing. He was tall, a hard wall of muscle. He smelled...surprisingly good. He was warm, and she wanted to lean against him. She wanted his arms to hold her.

It's just that you're afraid and in danger. That's all. It doesn't have to mean anything.

So she would keep telling herself.

"Give me your right hand."

With another swallow, she followed his instruction. He took her hand and positioned it over the grips of the gun.

"Put your index finger here, and the rest here. Curl the thumb around." He moved her fingers exactly where he wanted them to go, and the more he did to help her put her hands in the right positions, the closer he got. The hard expanse of his chest brushed against her back.

She tried to suck in her breath and hold really still so he wasn't actually touching her. Not because it was unpleasant, but because it was all too pleasant.

The hand not holding hers on the gun slid to her hip, and she very nearly squeaked when it fastened there. That was not...casual, a hand on her hip. Her *hip*. She could feel the sheer size of his hand, the warmth of his palm. She could feel far too much, sparkling through her.

"You want to plant your feet to maximize the steadiness of your arms. So, take a step forward with your right leg." As she did as she was told, he used the hand on her hip to position her in a slightly different way than she would have on her own.

"There," he said, his voice all too close to her ear, scratchy and, like, holy moly, sexy. Why did she have to find him sexy? Why would she think he was hot right now when he was teaching her how to use a deadly weapon?

She thought she heard him swallow, but she had to convince herself she was crazy. Someone like Vaughn would never be affected by this. He probably touched women all the time, and they didn't have any affect on him whatsoever. He probably thought of her as some kind of criminal, and that perceived swallow was all in her head.

"If you have to shoot, you want to be able to get into this position. Only in the most strident of emergencies should you do anything else."

"What's considered a strident emergency?"

"If a person is in the act of physically harming you, then you have no choice. But if there's any kind of distance between you, you want to try to get in this position. It's going to make your shots straighter and smoother. In a dangerous situation, the last thing you want to do is start shooting willy-nilly. You have to know your target, and you have to be steady."

"What if I'm shaking too hard to be steady?"

"Then you don't shoot."

"But what if someone's in danger?"

"They're going to be in more danger if you shoot when you don't have a good handle on the gun or a good stance."

"Okay. So then how do I shoot?"

He stepped closer, his body pressed to the back of hers. She knew he had to do it in order to show her how to properly shoot the gun, but that didn't mean it was easy to focus on anything but the firm warmth of a wall pressing against her. She wanted to explore it. She wanted to find out what was underneath.

Because she was ridiculous, apparently.

She took a deep breath, trying not to give away how shaky it was. But considering he was pressed against her, he had to know. He had to know that he affected her. That was so hideously embarrassing she almost couldn't concentrate.

"Now, you grip the trigger." His hand tightened on hers, guiding her index finger back to the appropriate spot.

This time when Vaughn swallowed, she had no doubt. He was affected. Granted, he was probably even more horrified by that than she was, but it was still real.

This attraction wasn't a one-sided idiotic thing. It was a two-sided idiotic thing.

"Now you're going to focus on the black spot right there on the hill. Do you see it?"

"Yes," she said, her voice giving away some of her anxiety. She hoped against all hope he thought it was anxiety over shooting a gun, not anxiety about how much her body wanted to rub against his.

"You're going to focus on the black spot. Look through the sight and clear your mind so the only thing you're thinking about is that black spot. There's nothing to be nervous about. There's nothing to be concerned about. All you're trying to do is pull the trigger while focusing on that black spot."

"Oh… Okay." Except focus sounded nearly impossible when he was all but wrapped around her. Sturdy and strong and something she absolutely had to resist.

"You can do this, Natalie," he said in her ear. "I have faith in you."

He couldn't possibly in his wildest dreams understand how much those words meant to her. How big they were even though he was someone she didn't exactly care about. Or shouldn't care about.

Still, his belief, his faith, was more than the people who were supposed to love her gave her. And she understood that. Their lack of faith and belief was mixed up in grief and a terrible tragedy. But that didn't mean she didn't miss it. She understood, but that didn't mean she stopped craving some sort of support.

So when Vaughn said it, even if he was the last person in the world she should want belief from, it mattered.

He steadied her arms, he *had faith in her*. It made her feel like she could do not just *this*, but the whole thing. That together they could find the answers that had eluded her for eight years.

"Pull," he said, and she did. Because he had faith in her. Because he had given her the tools to pull the trigger.

The gun gave a surprisingly harsh kick, but she remained steady and unshaken, even as the breath whooshed out of her.

"You hit it."

She turned to face him, still kind of in the circle of his arms, their hands still on the gun. "Why do you sound surprised? You said you had faith in me."

"Faith in you to shoot the gun, not actually hit the target."

"But you were helping me."

"I didn't pull the trigger. I wasn't looking at the sights. You aimed, you pulled, I just kept your body in position. Hitting the target was all you, Natalie."

She laughed, the surprise of it all bubbling out of her. "You're screwing with me. Trying to build up my confidence."

"Trust me, if I helped, I'd let you know. It's not worth giving you confidence if you don't actually know what you're doing in the process."

She looked at the black spot and the little scarring inside it. She hadn't hit it exactly where she'd been aiming—right in the middle—but she had hit that black spot.

She looked back at Vaughn again, their gazes meeting. Their hands were still on the gun, and she was still pressed up against him. His hand was on her hip, his other arm curled around her other side. It was a very... intimate position—aside from the fact they were both still holding the gun—and yet she couldn't seem to make herself move.

She was pinned by that gray-blue gaze that seemed to have warmed up a little bit in the fading sunlight. Like something about the heavily setting dusk teased out the flashes of darker blue in his eyes.

His gaze dropped to her mouth, and her entire insides shivered and shimmered to life. As though that gaze meant something. As though he had the same thoughts she did—kissing thoughts. Maybe even naked thoughts.

He was so not going to kiss her, what was she even thinking? He didn't like her. He was the consummate professional. Mr. Conventional. Any thoughts about kissing were hers and hers alone, and so out of place it wasn't even funny.

"We should head back in now that it's just about dark."

"Right."

"You can…" He cleared his throat, his eyes *still* on her mouth.

That doesn't mean anything. Maybe you have something on your face. He's not wondering what your lips feel like on his, that's all you, sister.

"You can let go of the gun," he said, that note of gentleness she hated back in his voice as he carefully started to separate their bodies.

"Right." She dropped the weapon all too quickly, but Vaughn managed to catch the gun before it fell to the ground.

They were completely apart now, a few feet between them. Vaughn put the gun in his holster, not even needing to look at the gun to do so. Which, honestly, should ease her embarrassment. He was so in charge and in control and certain, why wouldn't she be attracted to that in a situation like this?

It was just…one of those things. Hero worship or something. Natural to find yourself wondering what a kiss would be like from the man who was dedicated to keeping you safe.

"We'll do more tomorrow. Of the…shooting. We'll shoot more tomorrow. Not… I mean." He cleared his throat. "We'll practice more *shooting* tomorrow."

She stared at him, something in her chest loosening. He had *stuttered.* Ranger Vaughn Cooper had just stuttered at her.

He was walking toward the house now, and she followed, but she couldn't quite stop the smile from spreading across her face.

Maybe just *maybe*, she wasn't as out of her mind as she thought.

Chapter 9

After two days of practice, Natalie had become proficient with his Glock. She had a natural talent, and she impressed him every day.

Vaughn tried not to think too much about that. Because the more he was impressed by her, the more he felt a certain affinity toward her, and that just wouldn't do.

He'd spent half the past two days searching for information on Victor Callihan. He traded emails with Stevens about the man, but so far they were coming up empty. Clean as a whistle, an upstanding member of the community. Vaughn didn't trust it. But he couldn't deny the fact that someone else could be at the center of all this. Just because Callihan was the owner didn't mean he was the perpetrator. There were a lot of people in his corporation who could be The Stallion and thus connecting the Corlico Plant to The Stallion.

Vaughn's frustration with the case was mounting.

Especially after the email from Stevens that informed him Natalie's mother's home had been burglarized while she was at work last night. Vaughn still hadn't decided whether to tell Natalie. Which was why he was currently doing as many sit-ups as he possibly could to take his mind off of the internal debate.

Natalie would be upset. She would be more scared than she already was. He wasn't sure she needed that, but he also didn't like the idea of keeping it from her. Which wasn't personal. It was his code of ethics. He didn't like keeping things from people. That was all.

Sure, that's all.

He continued to do the sit-ups, pushing harder and harder in the hopes of dulling his brain completely. He took off his shirt before switching over to push-ups.

It wasn't just trying to outexercise his thoughts. He needed to stay sharp physically as well, and the more he exerted himself, the better he slept for the short snatches he allowed himself. Which kept him better rested, all in all.

It has nothing to do with the fact that you can't seem to help fantasize about Natalie as you're drifting off.

Yeah, it had nothing to do with that.

The fact of the matter was, they couldn't stay here indefinitely. More important, he didn't *want* to stay here indefinitely. They had to get somewhere in this case so he could go back to his life, and Natalie could go back to hers—what little was left of it. But surely she wanted to rebuild. Surely she wanted to get back to normalcy. God knew he did.

He pushed up and down, and up and down, and up and down, his arms screaming, but his mind still going in circles. How did they prove there was a connection?

How did they get the answers they needed? And how did he take Natalie back to Austin once their time ran out, knowing she would be in imminent danger if they didn't figure it out?

Just another case you can't solve, the obnoxious voice in his head taunted.

Did it ever occur to you that police work might not be your calling, Vaughn? I mean, really. If you need to focus your whole attention on it, and none on me, how can this be what you're good at?

He went down and stayed on the ground, more than a little irritated that Jenny's doubts were creeping into his own mind. They'd ended their marriage because he hadn't been able to give her what she wanted, but it had really ended when he hadn't wanted to fight for someone who refused to believe in his lifework. Because becoming a police officer had never been just a thing to do, or something frivolous or unimportant. It *had* been a calling. It had been something that he excelled at. Her doubts had eaten away at what little was left of the feelings between them.

"Are you asleep?"

Vaughn pushed up into a sitting position and glanced at Natalie, standing there in the opening of the hallway. She was wearing shorts today, which seemed patently unfair. Yesterday she had worn the clothes she'd been wearing the morning they left, but the day before she'd been wearing his sister's clothes again.

On the days she wore his sister's clothes, he pretty much wanted to walk around blindfolded so he didn't have to see the expanse of olive skin, or notice how the casual fabric clung to the soft curves of an all too attractive body.

Most of all, he had to work way too hard to ignore that he couldn't remember the last time he'd been so attracted to someone. And the more time they spent together, the less that was just physical.

"No. Not asleep. Just resting."

"Right. Well. I thought we could practice shooting a little bit more before you go back to sleep."

"You need to eat something. Then I thought maybe we could work on a little bit of hand-to-hand self-defense." Which was the absolute last thing he wanted to do with her—touch her. But he thought it was important. If he had to take her back to Austin without cracking this case, she needed more than a gun to protect herself. She needed every possible tool in his arsenal.

And he wanted to give it to her. He needed to make sure she was going to be safe. No matter what happened here. Even if his superiors ended up calling him back before they could figure this all out, he would consider Natalie under his protection. He wouldn't look too far into why that was. It was just his nature. He was a man of honor, and seeing things through to the end was why he was in unsolved crimes, because he didn't give up on things. He didn't walk away when things got hard.

"Hand-to-hand…self-defense?"

She sounded unsure, so as he grabbed his shirt, he tried to give her a reassuring glance, but he noticed where her eyes had drifted.

Not to his face, not to anything else in the room. She was staring at his chest, sucking her bottom lip between her teeth in a way that made him all too glad he was wearing loose-fitting sweatpants. Because no matter how hard he had to ignore that little dart of arousal that went through him, it was still *there*. Prominently.

"There are a variety ways to protect yourself," he managed to say. "I think you should know them all."

Slowly, way too slowly for his sanity and giving him way too much pleasure, her eyes drifted back up to his face. Her cheeks had tinged a little pink, and she blinked a little excessively.

She was attracted to him. Which he needed to not think about.

"So, there haven't been any breakthroughs in the case, I'm assuming?"

This was his chance to tell her about her mother's burglary. He couldn't do it. Natalie had started to relax, and she didn't seem nervous, most of the time. He didn't want to add to that. He'd tell her before they went back, but not now. Not now when she was on some kind of solid ground.

"Not so far. Callihan continues to come up clean, but we're looking more into your sister's case, and cases similar to it that are unsolved. Herman did say girls, plural."

"So, you're doing exactly what I've already been doing for the past eight years?"

He frowned at that. "You don't have the access to information that we have."

"You'd be surprised at what I found out." She laughed, but it was a kind of bitter, sad sound. And he wanted to comfort her. He could keep ignoring that want, and he would certainly keep not acting on it, but he was having a hard time denying that it existed.

"Maybe we should sit down and talk about it. You can tell me your assumptions, and I can match them with the case details."

She looked perplexed, and she stood there quietly for a few minutes while he pulled his shirt on.

"I thought you'd be angrier that I kept my connection from you."

"Just because I'm willing to help you doesn't mean I'm not angry that you kept something from me. But I also knew you were keeping something from me, so it's not as though it was some betrayal."

"Right. You don't care about me."

It was uncomfortable how badly he wanted to argue about that, but it was best if he didn't. It was best if he pretended like he didn't care about her at all. "I care about your safety."

"Because that's your job."

"Yes." Yes, that was the care. It certainly wasn't something more foolish with some woman he'd known for only a handful of days. He was too rational and practical for all that. Attraction could bloom in an instant, *care* could not.

She didn't say anything to that, but there was something in her expression that ate at him. Something about the unfairness of this whole situation…grating. It was beyond frustrating that he was now part of a case where he was not just failing, but he had to stand in front of someone who was affected by the case, and tell her, every day, that he continued to fail at solving it. That he wasn't doing his job as well as he wanted to.

"I'm not sure what I could tell you about my sister's case that you don't already know if you've seen her file."

"Why don't you tell me about *her.*"

"It wasn't her fault. Believe me, I've been through every police officer who wants to say that Gabby was at fault, that she had to have done something. I have had my fill of people who want to make it into something that couldn't be helped and can't be fixed. I have no interest in doing that with you."

"Look, I can't defend every police officer that ever existed. It's like every other profession—there are good ones, there are bitter ones. Compassionate ones, and ones who've been hardened and emptied or never had any compassion to begin with. But trust me when I say, I don't treat any case as a foregone conclusion. I don't assume things about any case. That's shoddy police work, and I don't engage in it, no matter how tempting a case might make it."

"I keep forgetting you're Mr. Conventional by the Book," she said with the hint of a smile, but her sadness lingered at the edges.

"I have a sister of my own. She's done some really stupid things that I didn't approve of, but blame is different than being stupid."

Natalie looked away, shaking her head. "I don't want to talk about her. I don't..." She cleared her throat as though she was struggling with emotion, and he realized he was probably being an insensitive dick here, pressing her on something that hurt.

"I just miss her. It hurts to miss her, and it hurts to be the only one who believes that she *is* still out there."

"In my professional opinion, after listening to what Herman had to say, you have every reason to believe she's still alive."

"You don't think it's a long shot?"

He sighed, rubbing his hands over his face. He was walking into dangerous territory here. Comforting her when he didn't know anything concrete wasn't just wrong, but it was against his nature. But comforting her was exactly what he wanted to do. "I can't promise that anyone has your sister. I can't promise that she's alive, and I can't promise you anything to do with this case.

But I think you have every reason to hope for all of those things. There's enough evidence to create the possibility."

Natalie visibly swallowed, still looking away from him. She wiped the tears from her cheeks with the backs of her hands, and it was only then that he realized she'd been crying. Again he marveled at her strength, and it took everything in him to fight the impulse to offer her physical comfort.

He got to his feet and crossed to his computer. "Let's make some notes. You and me together. We'll dissect the common denominators between your sister's case and the trafficking case."

"You know, I think I'd rather do the hand-to-hand combat thing," she said, her voice raspy.

"Yeah?"

"I've examined every detail of her case over and over and over. I can't imagine we'd find something that no one else has found. Not when Stevens knows and is looking into it too. Quite frankly, I can't stand sitting around not doing anything anymore. I'm so tired of being shut up in here. The only time I feel like I'm in any kind of control is when you're teaching me how to shoot. So show me some self-defense. Show me something that feels like I'm doing something."

As much as it surprised him to agree with her, he completely understood. There was only so much reading and trying to tie things together you could do before you started feeling useless and worthless and *actionless*.

So, he nodded at the furniture in the way. "Let's clear out the living room."

Natalie felt edgy. It irritated her that part of it had to do with seeing Vaughn do push-ups without a shirt on. She had stood there watching him for way, way too long. Way longer than was even remotely appropriate. She hadn't just watched, she had ogled. But how could she not ogle him when he was *shirtless* doing push-ups in the living room? What was she supposed to do with that?

His arms had been mesmerizing. Just perfectly sculpted muscle vaguely glistening with sweat. She never would've considered a sweaty muscley guy a turn-on before, but holy cow.

Ho-ly. Cow. She felt jittery and off-kilter and kind of achy. Her one and only boyfriend had been so long ago, and she had barely thought about missing out on sex. It hadn't been a big hole in her life not to have it.

But watching Vaughn do push-ups sharply and clearly reminded her what was so great about it, and even though it was stupid, she had a feeling Vaughn would be better at it than Casey had been. Vaughn was so much bigger and stronger and gruffer and…

And then he'd started talking about cases and her sister, and on top of the achy, longing feeling, he brought up all her vulnerabilities. Talking about Gabby's case made her sad and lonely. She was a little too close to suggesting that there were a lot of ways to get rid of sad and lonely, and hand-to-hand combat wasn't one of them.

Instead, she needed to focus on feeling like… Like she had some kind of power. Like she could be strong enough to fight off any threat leveled at her. Because she knew they could only stay here for so long. If no one figured out who The Stallion was, or who'd burned down her house, she'd be in danger when they had to go back.

That scared her, but not as much as it should. She had the sneaking suspicion that even if she had to go back to Austin, Vaughn would keep her safe no matter what.

And you know that is a stupid thought.

"All right." Vaughn looked around the living room that he'd cleared. He did a quick tour of the space as if measuring it. Then he fisted his hands on his hips and looked at her.

His gaze did a cursory up-and-down as though he were measuring her up. It didn't feel sexual in the least, at least until his eyes lingered on her chest. She was wearing one of his sister's shirts, which was unerringly far too tight for her in that area. She didn't think he minded that. If he did mind, it was for a completely different reason than not liking it.

"So." He cleared his throat. "The most dangerous attacks are the ones you don't see coming. There's a certain mindfulness that you have to employ when you know you're walking into a dangerous situation. And—"

"And unfortunately my life is currently a dangerous situation 24/7?"

"Natalie." He crossed to her and rested his hands on her shoulders. "You are safe with me," he said, those gray-blue eyes nearly mesmerizing and the calm certainty in his voice even more reassuring. "Know that. My job is to protect you, and you can ask my ex-wife, I take my job far too seriously."

"You have an ex-wife?"

His gaze left hers and his hands did too. "Yes," he muttered as though he hadn't meant to share that piece of information about himself.

She hated the idea of him being married before, which was stupid, but she liked that he had given her the information against his will. That meant that maybe he had these same feelings irritating the crap out of him. All this conflicted energy. All this longing she knew she couldn't indulge in.

"Come stand in the middle of the room," he ordered.

She'd gotten to the point where she knew that when he was ordering her around, it was because he was a little off-kilter himself.

She definitely liked that too. But she obeyed and came to stand in the center of the room.

"I'm going to come from behind. I'll wrap my arms around your upper body. And then I'll talk you through getting out of the hold."

"All right."

She stood there, bracing herself for his touch. He did just as he said he was going to do, his muscled arm coming around over her shoulders and keeping her arms almost completely immobile. Though his grip was tight, it wasn't at all harsh. It was gentle. And because she was all too antsy, and all too eager to lean into that grip, she sighed.

"You know I don't think a bad guy is going to hold me nicely."

"I'm not going to hurt you while I'm trying to demonstrate how to get out of a hold."

"How can I learn if there isn't some sort of reality to it?"

"First, you're going to learn the strategy. Then, we'll try with a little more reality to it. You need to learn some patience."

"You'll be shocked to know you're not the first person to tell me that."

He chuckled, and his mouth was so close to her ear that his breath tickled over the sides of her neck. They really needed to find out who The Stallion was, because she wasn't sure how much longer she was going to keep herself from throwing herself at Vaughn. She knew she shouldn't, hell, couldn't, and yet it was bubbling inside her like something beyond her ability to control.

"Okay, so the first step when someone has you in a hold like this is to catch them off guard. If they've left your legs mobile, then that's what you use. If you can get your elbow free, that's what you use. You're always going to want to use the sharpest part of your body and hit the most vulnerable part of theirs."

"So what you're saying is, I should kick him in the crotch?"

"Yes, actually, that is exactly what I'm saying."

It was her turn to laugh. "That's not exactly the type of thing I would expect you to suggest I do."

"When it comes to keeping yourself safe, you do whatever it takes. Keep in mind that I have a sister. I've taught her how to do this. I'm taking the same approach as when I taught her."

"You're taking the same approach with me that you took with your sister?"

It was too leading of a question, and she wished it back in her mouth the minute it had come out. But she didn't know how to sidestep the silence that surrounded them. She didn't know how to make it go away. Some silly part of her wanted to know, though. Did he think of her as a sister? As someone he would never think of sexually?

"The same approach…" He seemed to consider this carefully, and she had no business thinking that meant something. Of course it didn't mean anything. She was a lunatic reading into things. Per usual. Wasn't that her pattern?

"I guess not the same approach exactly," he said at last, some odd softness to his voice.

Her breath caught at the admission, and his arm around her loosened, just the tiniest bit. If she hadn't been looking for it, she might've missed it. But he had definitely given her more space.

"Vaughn…" What exactly was she going to say? *Look at me sexually! Please!* She was really losing it.

"If someone is holding you like this," he began, sounding uneven and uncertain. Who knew she could make Vaughn Cooper uncertain? It might be the highlight of her year.

"Let me restate the fact that a bad guy grabbing me by surprise would not be holding me like this."

"Would you like me to hold you rougher? Because I can certainly oblige." There was an edge to his voice, a warning, or maybe it was a promise. She couldn't decide.

Nor could she stop the little shiver that went through her. Because even though he probably didn't mean that sexually, it sure sounded sexual. She shouldn't poke at that. She shouldn't poke at him. But somehow her brain and her mouth couldn't get on the same page.

"I think you have to start over because I lost track of what you were talking about."

This time his grasp tightened instead of loosened, but she didn't think it was because he was trying to be a bad guy. In fact, she hoped for a completely different reason. No matter how much she shouldn't.

Chapter 10

Vaughn was getting in over his head. He had lost track of what the hell he was doing in the first place. But he really lost track of what the hell Natalie was doing, because this was all starting to sound way more flirtatious than it should.

He tried to focus on the task at hand. With his arms around her. Why was he standing here? Because the minute he lost track of *the reason*, was the minute he started making mistakes. And he couldn't afford mistakes. No matter how good they smelled. No matter how they shivered in his arms when he said something far, far, far too suggestive.

"One of the important things to remember is that you want to stay as still as possible if someone grabs you." He forced himself to focus. To concentrate. To lecture.

She was quiet for a long humming second. "So, some

strange man grabs me from behind, and I'm supposed to be calm?"

"You're supposed to try. The more you practice this, the better off you'll be. It becomes habit. When something becomes a habit, then you can deal with things instinctually."

"So we're going to stand here with you holding me all day?"

"Well, if you'd stop talking and questioning everything I do, maybe we could get somewhere, Ms. Torres."

She chuckled at that, and he found that he wanted to laugh too. God knew why.

"You always revert to Ms. Torres when you're irritated with me."

"I'm irritated with you a lot."

"I know." But she said it cheerfully, as though it didn't bother her at all.

He sighed. Not sure why the back-and-forth banter gave him that stupidly light feeling again. The feeling he hadn't had in too many years. It revealed too much about how he'd lost himself, a fact he'd been ignoring for a while. And, more, he hated what it told him about Natalie, the effect she had on him, that it might not be some easily controllable thing.

Ha! He could control whatever he chose to. "So rule number one, what was it?"

She sighed. "Rule number one is try to stay still even though that is the opposite of any normal reaction to someone grabbing me from behind."

"Wonderful. Love the attitude," he muttered, trying to shift behind her without…rubbing. "Rule number two is, you want to analyze the situation as best as your mind allows. You want to try to figure out where the weakness is. You want to know what parts of your body have the freedom to move and inflict the most amount of damage. Obviously, if they've grabbed you from behind, you can't utilize your sight. So, unless they're armed, you want to lean back against them and try to discern the areas that are going to be vulnerable."

"So… You want me to lean back into you?"

Oh, hell. No. "Well, we don't necessarily have to practice that part."

"Shouldn't we practice the whole thing? You know the whole the more you practice, the more instinctual it becomes?"

She sounded far too pleased with herself, and he was quickly realizing how badly he'd lost control of this entire situation. It wasn't the fact that he'd initiated this stupid idea, the fact that however many minutes later he still had his arms around Natalie, it was the fact that she was goading him. She was… Hell, she was instigating.

Do not be charmed by that. Do not give into that.

But he must be going a little cabin crazy, because he wasn't sure how much longer he could listen to the sane, rational voice in his head. At some point, he was going to lose this battle. He was almost sure of it.

"Fine. Lean back into me." Yes, he was definitely losing this battle.

She did as he told her, and he tried to keep himself from softening too much into it. Because he wasn't a soft guy, and he prided himself on his ability to keep things *professional*.

So, he held himself tense and hard against the soft enticing curves of her body now leaning into him.

"How do I know if something is vulnerable?"

Her voice was a little ragged and a little whispery,

and he smiled at that. Because, thank God, she wasn't messing with him without having any sort of reaction of her own.

"What's your first instinct?" he asked, his nose all too close to being buried in her thick curls.

She laughed. "I'm a woman who lives in a not totally nice area, Vaughn. Trust me, my first instinct is to go for the family jewels."

"That is the correct instinct, but you have to make sure you can get a shot. If you panic, you lose the chance of hitting a really nasty blow."

"Are you suggesting I test out a really nasty blow on you?"

"No, not at all. We can practice that move without you doing any damage."

"You trust me to practice without doing any damage? Because not so long ago you didn't trust me at all."

It was said casually, but he had the feeling there was more to it. Much like the discussion about why he was protecting her and it being only because it was his job. There was something more she was looking for, and there was something more he should not in one million years give her.

"I let you fire my gun, Natalie. I trust you."

He could feel her take a deep breath, because her back shifted against his chest. This was the danger. That they affected each other, not just physically, but in the things they talked about. In the faith and the trust that they afforded each other. This was dangerous. They were already in a dangerous situation, though, and they didn't need to add any more danger to it.

"So if someone was holding me like this, I would just reach my leg back between their legs and kick, right?"

Thank God she was focusing on the task at hand. If they could both make each other do that, maybe they'd get through this. "Yes, that's part of it. But you also want to see if you can inflict damage at the same time elsewhere. So you want to get an idea if your elbows are free. The way I've got you held right now, as long as you're not wiggling and struggling, you can get in a good elbow to the gut. If you struggle, they're going to tighten their grasp or they're going to bring their other hand around and hold your arms still, as well."

He demonstrated, which was of course also a mistake, because now both of his arms were around her, and though it was from behind, he was essentially hugging her. No matter how many times he told her what she could do to inflict damage, he was still holding her in a tight embrace.

All this *sensation* waged a war on his sanity that he hadn't faced…maybe ever. It had always been so *easy* to remain in control. Except with Natalie.

"So," he said, his voice sounding rusty and ill used in his own ears. "You want to try to lift up your leg and use your elbow at the same time. I want you to practice it, and I want you to put a little force behind it, but not too much. Especially down low."

She chuckled at that, but it was also a little bit strangled. Yes, they were both affected by this. Yes, they were both stupid. And yes, they were teetering on the edge of even larger stupidity.

Somehow, none of that knowledge made him stop.

Natalie figured she was shaking apart. He had to feel that, and as embarrassing as it was, she couldn't possibly stop. He was essentially holding her. This far too attractive man who seemed to have it all together when she felt as together as a lunatic.

He was *holding* her and talking to her about fighting, but the last thing she wanted to do was fight him. She wanted to turn in the circle of his arms. She wanted to press her mouth to his. The more she thought about how much she wanted that, the harder it was to ignore. The harder it was to stop herself from doing it.

But she had to. She had to stop herself. She couldn't keep doing this either, though. She had to make a choice. Either go for it, or make sure, once and for all, her mind understood that there would be no going for it. There would be no nothing. *That* was the choice she knew she had to make.

"Practice moving your elbow and your leg at the same time," Vaughn encouraged.

She laughed again, that strangled, silly-sounding laugh. How could she get her body to move the way she wanted it to when she could barely get her brain to think the way she wanted it to?

"You know, maybe we should eat something instead of all this. Or talk about—"

"Don't be a coward."

"I'm not a coward," she said through gritted teeth. "I'm trying to make a smart choice."

She felt his exhale against the back of her neck. She didn't think a shudder went through him exactly, not the way it went through her, but there was a change in the way he held himself. She couldn't tell if it was tenser or softer; she could only tell that it was different. That this was all incredibly different. She didn't know what to do about it.

"Well, I don't plan on doing this again, so you better get your practice in."

She whirled to face him, and he either let her go, or he was surprised enough by her movement that he didn't try to stop her. "This was your idea. Why won't we do it again?" Something like panic clawed through her. That he wouldn't help, that he wouldn't give her the skills he *said* he was going to give her.

She was probably never going to *be* safe, but she at least wanted some illusion of it. The belief she could shoot a gun or fight under pressure.

"You really have to ask?" he ground out. Even though she'd whirled around, they were still close. Nearly touching, really. Something glittered in his gaze, and she didn't recognize it or understand it.

"Um, yeah! Why on earth—"

Then his mouth was on hers. Just as she'd imagined far too often. All the swirling, nonsensical thoughts and feelings in her brain stopped. All the panic faded. There was nothing except his mouth on her mouth, and his hands tangled in her hair, keeping her steady under the hot assault of his mouth. All while his hard, lean body pressed against hers.

When his tongue touched her lips, she opened them for him, greedily. She threw everything she had into that kiss. Somehow she felt braver than she had learning hand-to-hand self-defense. She felt stronger than when she was shooting his gun. The kiss was better than everything that had happened to her for far too long in her life.

He was strong, and he was sure, and she wanted all of that. All of him. She wanted the way it curled inside of her, pleasure and light, breathlessness and a kind of steadiness she didn't know existed.

"I can't be doing this." But he said it against her mouth, as though he had no intention of stopping. She didn't want to have any intention of stopping. She didn't want to stop until this aching need inside her was completely and utterly obliterated.

She wrapped her arms around his neck, arching against the hard wall that was him, and somehow *she* felt powerful and in control, even as the need and desire ping-ponged through her completely and utterly *out* of control.

No matter how wrong it was, no matter how little they should do it. It was what she wanted, and didn't she deserve a little bit of what she wanted? What she wanted without worrying about if her choices were furthering her investigations into Gabby's disappearance. Her whole life had come to center around Gabby, and this had nothing to do with it except that she and Vaughn were in the same place at the same time.

Oh, and he's trying to work to help you find your sister and keep you safe.

She wasn't sure who pulled away first. She would've expected it to be Vaughn, but the insidious voice in her head that was telling her this was a betrayal of her sister and her quest to find Gabby made her pause just as much as him coming to his senses probably caused him to pause.

"I apologize. I apologize. This has gotten out of control. It is all my fault. I'm sorry. That was…"

"Really great?" she interjected, pressing her fingers to her kiss-swollen lips. Really, *really* great. Had *anyone* ever kissed her like that? With that searing intensity she didn't think… Even if that was all it ever was, she'd never forget it.

He glanced at her then, and for the first time his eyes were very, very blue. The gray had diminished, and the blue that was left was warm, and she felt like that meant something. That it *could* mean something, anyway.

"I've never..." He cleared his throat and squared his shoulders, slowly coming back to Ranger Cooper. All business, no pleasure. All by the book, conventional, Vaughn Cooper, Texas Ranger.

What a shame.

"This was a mistake. While I freely admit that I am physically attracted to you, any involvement between us could only cause problems with this case. I know how much this case means to you. It means a lot to me as well. This has gone unsolved too long, all of it, and I need to get to a point where I'm solving things. So, this can't happen again."

She chewed on her bottom lip, trying to determine how to change his mind. Except, she knew he was right. Any kind of romantic thing between them could only get in the way of this case that was so important to both of them.

She could keep flirting with him, and pushing his buttons, and wanting more, but the bottom line was everyone involved would be hurt.

There was a selfish part of her that didn't want to care. For the first time in so long, she didn't want to *care*. It had been so long since she'd put her wants or needs ahead of someone else's, except in her want and need to find Gabby.

"Say something," Vaughn said, his voice that rough, ragged thing that shivered across every last nerve ending in her body.

Now she knew what it felt like to have that firm, unrelenting mouth on hers. Surprisingly soft, though unsurprisingly demanding. It felt like a reprieve from the

harsh realities of where they were and what they had to
do. The harsh reality of the possibility of this case re-
maining unsolved, and she could remain in danger, and
her questions about Gabby could never be answered.

It was silly and awful to be concerned about a kiss. To
be wrapped up in it and want more of it. Her whole focus
should be Gabby until she could find her. She was closer
than she'd ever been. To get distracted by Vaughn now...

"I don't know what to say," she finally managed to
get out. Which was the truth. She didn't know what to
say to him when so much of what she wanted was simply to forget, to lose herself in a kiss and more, and not
think or *fear*.

At a time when they probably didn't have the luxury
of forgetting much of anything. At any point someone
could burst into this cabin and take out both of them.
They could pretend that she was learning how to shoot a
gun in self-defense all they wanted, but the bottom line
was those things only worked when you had a warning,
when you knew what was coming.

"You're just a little mixed up because I saved you, so
to speak. It's a little case of rescue wor—"

"No," she snapped, most of the *want* cooling into irritation. No surprise he could flick it off like a switch. "I'm
not stupid, and I'm not mixed up. You are the one who
kissed me. I didn't initiate that. Don't insult me that way.
I know my feelings, and I know why I kissed you back.
It has zero to do with *rescue worship*, you arrogant jerk."

"I only meant..."

"No, I don't want to know what you meant. You kissed
me. Accept that. Or should I worry that you're just mesmerized by my victimhood, and you only kissed me be-

cause you can't keep your brain intact when a victim is around?"

His mouth firmed, grim and angry. Good, because she was angry too. How dare he say that? She wasn't so stupid she thought he was hot just because he'd saved her. That wasn't what was between them at all, and she wouldn't let him get away with that kind of distorted thinking.

"I just think we don't know each other that well."

Again she scoffed. "You know, I'd love an excuse for why this happened, for why I feel the way I do. But the bottom line is, we're attracted to each other. More, whether we want to admit it or not, we like each other. So stop making excuses. Let's deal with the reality of the situation. Isn't that what you told me? That we can't deal with what-ifs and maybes. We have to look at the facts."

"I can't tell you how little I like my own words being used against me," he returned, and though his voice had a cutting edge, there was the smallest hint of a smile on his lips.

"Especially when they're right?"

He smiled, one of those real, rare smiles that made her heart do acrobatics in her chest. He could stand to smile more. He could stand to laugh more.

You don't know him. Maybe he smiles and laughs all the time when you're not around.

But she really felt like she knew him, no matter how often she tried to talk herself out of that.

"Especially when they're right. So…"

"So, you kissed me." She squared her shoulders, determined to be an adult. Determined to take charge of her life in the few places she could. "We're attracted to each other, and as much as it pains me to say it, you're right. We don't have the time or the luxury of pursuing anything. So maybe it's best if we just pretend that it never happened."

"Right. Pretend it never happened. I can do that."

Except his gaze was on her mouth, and she didn't think she could do that if he…looked at her with those heated blue eyes. "Maybe you can tell me all your ex-wife's complaints about you so that I know what annoyances to look for when I'm overcome by attraction."

He smiled wryly. "I think somehow you'll manage, but it's mostly your average 'you care too much about your job and not enough about our marriage.'"

"Do you agree with her assessment?" Which wasn't her business, at all, and she wanted to be appalled at herself for asking personal questions. But she wanted to know, and she'd had to gain a certain comfort in quizzing people in her pursuit of information about Gabby.

He shrugged, finally looking away from her mouth. "Sometimes. I take my job very seriously. There were times I had to miss things. There were times I was in danger and she was scared, and I get why that was hard on her."

"I feel like there's a 'but' coming."

"No but. You can't… You can't have a marriage with someone who doesn't understand your passion. I'm sure it is my failing that my passion wasn't our marriage."

"I guess that's understandable."

"I take it you've never been married."

"No, not even close. The only relationship I've really had ended because he thought I spent too much time obsessing about Gabby."

"So, great, we have more things in common. That's really what we need right now."

She had to laugh at his sarcasm. She had to laugh at the circumstances. At what the hell she thought she was doing.

But she understood what it was like to lose a relationship because you were wrapped up in something else. Something bigger than you. Something that was excessively important to you that you couldn't let go of.

"Do you regret…not changing your dedication level to police work? I mean… Would you go back and do things differently?"

"I've thought about that a lot, actually. It's been three years since she said she wanted to get divorced. The thing is, I didn't… Maybe it shows how far gone I am, but I didn't think that I was that inattentive all the time. Sometimes, certain cases got under my skin a little bit extra, but I stopped going undercover for her. I stopped… Why the hell are we talking about this?"

"I had the crazy idea that it might make me not like you."

"Did it work?" he asked.

"No, I think it might've done the opposite." She wanted to step closer again, but his demeanor kept her where she was. He had made the decision this could only be a negative distraction on a very important case. She had to respect that decision. He deserved that respect.

"I should probably get my sleep in."

She smiled ruefully. "Yeah, you wouldn't want a lack of sleep to affect your decision-making skills."

He laughed at that, a little bitterly. She almost felt bad that she'd pushed him this far. "I'm sorry," she offered to his retreating back.

He stopped and turned, eyebrows drawn together. "What are you sorry for?"

"I know you kissed me and all, but I kept pushing things, and I didn't have to. It had just…been a long time since I'd wanted something solely for myself. You know?"

He swallowed, visibly, audibly. "Yeah, I know," he said, a little too meaningfully, a little too much for her to not feel as though the stopping was the mistake, not doing it in the first place.

But he turned, in that rigid, policeman way of his, and walked down the hallway.

Chapter 11

Vaughn tried to sleep, he really did. He caught bits and pieces of rest, but every time he started to doze, his mind went to that kiss. The way it had rioted through him. The way his completely irrational and stupid body had taken over.

He'd had to kiss her. It had been like there was no choice. Like his life depended on having his mouth on hers. He knew that was stupid now, but in the moment it had seemed imperative.

In the moment, he hadn't been able to think of anything else except her. The easy way she kissed him back, the way everything about her seemed to fit against him in just the right way. He'd been as lost as he'd ever been in his whole entire life.

In the aftermath, he didn't know what to do about it. Apparently run away like some immature teenager was his answer. Cowardly, all in all.

But the more he talked to her, the more he wanted to kiss her again. The more he wanted to ignore everything that his training had taught him about getting mixed up with witnesses or victims or what have you. He wanted to ignore his own personal moral code and have Natalie Torres in his damn bed.

He groaned into his pillow. He felt about as frustrated as a teenager, but with the common sense of a man to make it all that much more irritating. Never in his life had he been tempted away from following his duty to the letter. Not like this. He'd always been able to be calm and rational, even when the stray thought of being the opposite had come up. He'd never gotten overly violent with a witness or perp. He'd always been calm, rational, sensible and, yes, conventional Ranger Cooper.

Why the hell was Natalie the difference maker?

After three hours of more frustrating self talk than actual sleep, Vaughn gave up. There was no use wasting time. He could be researching Callihan. He could be looking at the case. There were a wide variety of ways to employ his mind that wasn't lying there with an ill-timed erection, trying to work out why he was so affected by a woman.

A beautiful, engaging woman who made him have the most foolish thoughts. Like, maybe she…understood. The police work being a bit of an obsession thing. She had her own obsessive situation that had ended a relationship.

He got out of his bed and looked out the window. He needed to get his bearings, and maybe looking at those mountains in the distance and remembering all he'd done to get him here could help him.

God knew he needed help.

The landscape was as barren as it had been since

they'd arrived. Three days now. Three days and no one had found them or come after them. As long as this kept up, Captain Dean was going to call him home sooner rather than later. And they'd found nothing. No connections, no clues, nothing to help.

He glanced at the closet where he kept the corded phone. Since there was no cell service out here, they kept a landline open in case of emergency, but neither he nor his sister cared for people being able to call them, so they didn't keep the phones hooked up.

But sometimes a phone call was necessary.

He grabbed the phone and hooked it up to the jack in the corner of the room.

The emails from Bennet were quick and usually in list form. If he actually talked to him, he might read some frustration level in his partner's tone. And, be able to ask about the time they had left without the chance of Natalie reading the answer.

Making a phone call certainly had nothing to do with having to distract himself from the gorgeous woman in the living room of his secluded cabin. Zero connection to the fact she wanted him seemingly as much as he wanted her.

With irritated jabs, he punched in the number to the office and was patched through to Stevens.

"Still nothing," Bennet greeted him, thankfully not beating around the bush.

"I figured as much," he returned on a sigh. "How much longer are they going to let me keep her out here?"

"It'll depend on the arson inspector's report. We should be getting it today. I can call down and try to speed things up."

"Yeah, I'd like to know what time frame we're working with here."

"That bad?"

Vaughn almost let it slip that it was *terrible*. But not for the reason Bennet would think. He clamped his lips together just in time to rewire his thoughts. "I don't like that we're not getting anywhere, and we might have to bring her back in the middle of it."

"Yeah, this case…" Bennet trailed off. "Without Herman, we're screwed. We've been trying to find someone he works with, someone who'll talk. Nothing."

"Nothing on those guys from the gas station?"

"They had warrants, so they're locked up, but we had nothing on him. Not who they were working for, and not what they were trying to do to you and Ms. Torres."

"I don't like this. It's too quiet, and it's too easy." Which was as true as the fact he wasn't sure how much longer sanity was going to reign in this cabin.

"I'll call Arson, see who I can light a fire under. I'll email you the full report the minute I get it."

"Yeah. Thanks."

"In the meantime, you could relax. Laugh at my hilarious jokes. Unclench."

"When have you never known me to relax?" Vaughn returned gruffly.

"That's kind of the point. There's nothing you can do. There's nothing you can change from where you are. Your only worry right now is keeping the woman safe. Which should be easy enough in the middle of nowhere. You know I'll find any more information before you do out in the desert. So, watch a movie. Make some popcorn. Have some small talk."

"I hate small talk." Especially small talk that had to do with his ex-wife, and any shared sucking at relationships.

"The point is, you can kill yourself over this case, or you can have some sense and save up all your frustrated anger into dedicated business for when it will actually be helpful to us. When you're back in Austin."

"As encouraging as ever, Bennet."

"I'm here for you, buddy."

Even though Bennet was suggesting he relax, when that was the last thing he could do, it was… Well, damn, it was nice to know someone cared enough to suggest it. But that didn't take away his ticking time bomb. "Be straight with me. How much time I got?"

Bennet sighed. "If they get something in the arson investigation, some kind of clue, you might have a few more days. But if there isn't a shred of evidence, and there never has been before, he's going to want you back right away."

Vaughn pinched the bridge of his nose, trying to ward off a headache, and swore.

"Relax. I'll do what I can to get you more time. The arson report comes up empty, I'll make sure it gets lost in red tape for a few days, best I can."

"Thanks."

"You really think The Stallion has something to do with Torres's missing sister?"

Vaughn blew out a breath. "I think it's more than possible. You?" Because he had to know it wasn't just his feelings for Natalie clouding that gut feeling.

"Yeah, man. I do. Herman talking about keeping the girls… I keep going back to that. Gotta be something there. Something that got Herman killed."

"Yeah. Well, I'll be waiting for an email."

"Later. Stay safe."

Vaughn turned to face the door of his room and then paced. He wouldn't tell Natalie anything until he had the arson report. Everything hinged on that, and he hated the idea that there would be nothing in it. Just like there was always nothing in all of these cases.

Maybe it was hopeless. Maybe they *should* head back. He'd find a way to keep an eye on her, but maybe, in the end, this had all been an overreaction. A mistake.

Then he heard the crash.

Natalie was brooding. She tried to talk herself out of the brood, but that never worked. Certainly not when there was emotional brooding, and sexually frustrated brooding, and her-life-was-a-mess-and-she-was-worried-about-sex brooding.

She should be looking at Vaughn's computer, poring over the trafficking case, finding commonalities. Anything but staring at the wall reliving that kiss over and over again. Because it *wasn't* going to happen again.

So, why not relive it if that's all you're going to get?

She pushed off the couch in a fit of annoyance. The few times her personal life interfered with her happiness, she'd been able to throw herself into the minutiae of Gabby's case. Whether it was because Vaughn was now hooked up in Gabby's case, or he was somehow that much more potent than all her other personal problems, nothing about drowning herself in her sister's case was appealing.

But what else was there to do in this godforsaken landscape? She was stuck in this cabin while Vaughn soundly slept in his room. Jerk.

She glared down the hallway as if she glared hard

enough, he might feel her ire. Not that it would matter. He wasn't going to do anything about it, was he? And neither was she, because the sleeping jerk was right. So torturing herself over it was downright—

She heard the distant sound of...something, so incongruous to the quiet she'd been living in for the past days. Though the sound immediately stopped, Natalie knew she'd heard something, and it wasn't coyotes this time. Whatever the sound had been, it was distinctly mechanical. Like a car.

Before she had a chance to even think about what to do, she was already moving toward the hallway, moving toward Vaughn. But a sudden crash caused her to jerk in surprise so violently that she stumbled. She fell to her hands and knees and looked back at the front of the house where the crash had come from.

The sound repeated, and she saw the door shake just as Vaughn entered the hallway.

"Stand up and get behind me. Now."

She scrambled to her feet and did as he ordered, the grim set to his mouth and the icy cold in his gaze crystallizing the fact this wasn't a *mistake* or a random animal this time. Fear jittered through her, much like it had in the gas station when she'd been at the mercy of those strange men, and all she could do was shake and listen to Vaughn.

He had his weapon drawn, and the minute she was close enough, he jerked her behind him.

"No matter what happens, you stay behind me. Got it?"

"But—" She could think of a hundred scenarios where she would have to not stand behind him, but before she could voice any of them, another crash shook the door.

She had a feeling that it would only take one more harsh blow for it to open.

"What are these morons doing?" he muttered. He held his gun at shoulder level, but his other arm was extended behind him, keeping her in the box of his arm and the wall.

With absolutely no warning, he spun and shot his weapon, right over her shoulder. A thud sounded, and then a wounded grunt, and when Natalie caught up enough with the whirlwind of action and looked behind them, she saw a large man's body slumped on the floor.

"Diversion," he muttered, grabbing her arm and pulling her toward the man's body.

Vaughn kept her behind him as he approached the man who was gurgling and thrashing and reaching for a gun he'd apparently dropped. Vaughn kicked it out of his reach easily.

"Pick it up, Natalie. Train it at the front door. Anyone walks in, you shoot."

Natalie tried to agree, to nod, but she stood there shell-shocked and shaking, and—

"Natalie." This time Vaughn spared her a glance. "You can do it. You have to do it. All right?"

It steadied her. Not that she stopped shaking or stopped being afraid, but it gave her something to hold on to, something to focus on, and she managed to grab the man's gun with shaking fingers.

"Put your back to mine."

"I don't—"

"Turn around, look at the door and lean your back against mine. From here on out, you don't move unless I do. We're always touching, unless I say otherwise." He said the command low, and the man flailing about on the floor probably could have heard it, but he seemed pretty preoccupied with the bullet wound in his shoulder.

Natalie blew out a breath and did as Vaughn instructed. She pressed her back to his, absorbing the warmth and the strength, and focused on the door in the front of her. The crashing seemed to have stopped, but she held the gun up, hoping she'd be able to shoot an unfamiliar weapon. Hoping harder she wouldn't have to shoot anyone.

"Who the hell are you?" Vaughn growled.

Since Natalie was watching the door, she couldn't see what the man did in response. But it sounded like the man merely spat in response.

"You'll regret that one later."

Natalie couldn't suppress a shiver at the cold note of fury in Vaughn's voice.

Another crash sounded, and the front door shook again, but Vaughn seemed less than worried about it. She, on the other hand, was *more* than worried about it.

"What are you after?"

The man only groaned, still not saying anything.

"This is your last chance to talk. You don't talk when I ask, I don't ask. And you don't want to find out what happens then."

The man only cursed, and Vaughn remained a still, calm, rock-hard presence behind her. His warmth and his strength soothed a small portion of her concern over her too fast and hard breathing.

"Natalie, link arms with me." He held his arm back, and she did as he ordered. Then he was maneuvering her, always keeping her protected from the man on the floor.

He led her by her linked arm into his room, keeping his gun trained at the wounded man. He'd stopped writhing and was looking increasingly pale, though he kept his hand on the wound on his shoulder.

Natalie looked away.

"I need you to grab the backpack out of my closet. It's black, and it should be very heavy."

Natalie swallowed, and she didn't trust her voice. But she did what he asked. Vaughn's closet was freakishly neat and tidy, so it was easy to find the backpack.

"Is there anything you absolutely without a shadow of a doubt need from your room?"

She had so few belongings left, tears stung her eyes thinking of leaving any of it. But she also didn't want to, oh, die, so she supposed she could do without. "My ID, maybe? Unless you don't think we have—"

His mouth firmed. "I don't want to leave behind anything that might give them more information on you. We're going to link arms again. We're going to get your ID. Do not look at the man on the floor. Keep looking straight ahead until we're inside, and then grab your stuff immediately. Then we'll go out the window. Or at least try."

"And if we can't?" There could be fifty men surrounding the cabin as they spoke. There could be—

"One thing at a time." He maneuvered her across the hall, his grip firm enough to help her push away the thousands of terrible outcomes.

"Go," Vaughn said gently, unlocking their arms. Because she couldn't have come up with a thought on her own to save her life, she went straight for her purse.

It was strange how unmoored and that much shakier she felt without Vaughn's arm connected to hers, but she pressed on. She grabbed her purse, and Vaughn, keeping his gun trained on the door, rummaged around in the closet and pulled out a backpack. It was pink and sparkly and utterly ridiculous.

He gave it a disgusted grunt but held it out to her. "It'll be easier to get through the mountains with your hands free instead of worrying about a purse. Shove it in there and then strap it on your back."

Again, Natalie couldn't trust her voice to actually come out of her throat, so she simply did as she was told. She shoved her purse into the outrageous backpack and then strapped it to her back. Meanwhile, Vaughn pulled on his backpack.

She looked down at her hands, the gun she held, the power she had. This was her protection. This would give her a chance. She hoped.

"You hold on to that. No matter what. If it comes down to it, you'll use it."

"What are they after?" she asked, her voice a shaky, squeak of a thing that would've embarrassed her if she'd had time for it.

He didn't bother to answer. She understood that he didn't have time to stand there and explain things to her. But she couldn't help the fact that she didn't understand anything about this. Not a thing.

"Keep your eye on the door. Keep your gun ready."

It took every ounce of focus and control to do as he said and not watch what he did. She heard the rustle of curtains, and possibly the squeak of the window. Meanwhile, all she could do was watch the door to this room, and fervently pray that no one tried to walk through it.

A shot rang out, and Natalie jerked violently. Through some lucky twist of fate, she didn't pull her own trigger.

"Follow me. Now." Vaughn's voice was terse and urgent as ever, and her feet responded to the order even if her mind whirled.

Though a million questions went through her head, she followed Vaughn out the window. It was only then that she realized there was a sound louder than the harsh flow of her breathing.

Once she was outside, she noticed there was another man slumped on the ground. But he was screaming and grabbing his leg. Vaughn paid him no attention. He was too busy scanning the surroundings.

"Stay at my back."

She was glad he kept saying it, because in her shell-shocked state she would've forgotten. She would've stood there still and silent and barely functioning. This might be the only situation in her entire life where she was *ecstatic* for someone to keep reminding her what she was supposed to do.

She stayed at Vaughn's back, mirroring his movements as he walked toward the screaming man. Vaughn spared him the most disgusted of glances, and then grabbed the large, intimidating looking gun that had fallen out of the man's reach.

"How many more of you are there?"

"Screw off."

Vaughn's mouth was a harsh, grim line. "So none. Perfect. Now, when you crawl your way back to your boss, tell him the next time someone comes after me, it better be the man himself. Because his lackeys are damn bad at this." Vaughn gave the man a swift kick in the chest so the man fell backward, screaming all over again.

Then Vaughn started walking, and Natalie had to remind herself to follow him. It wasn't hard. Not when he exuded calm and confidence and *safety*.

He went to the front of the cabin and there was nothing that she could see, but Vaughn jerked his chin at a vehicle in the distance. "That's where they parked their car. We'll go in the opposite direction in case there are more shooters coming."

Natalie looked in the opposite direction. "But it's just…mountains."

"I hope you're ready to camp, Nat. Because God knows how long we're going to be out there."

Chapter 12

The sun was beginning to set, and Vaughn knew he needed to find a place to camp. But the adrenaline still pumped through him, and the last thing he wanted to do was stop.

He looked back at Natalie, who was…struggling. Struggling to keep up with his pace, and he thought maybe struggling to keep her composure after such a whirlwind of events. He was being an ass for not caring more about what she felt, about the toll this was taking on her.

"It's just a little bit farther. There is a series of caves up here. They'll make good shelter for the night."

"Caves?" she asked, trepidation edging her voice.

"It's perfectly safe if you know what to look for."

"What do you mean, 'if you know what to look for'?"

"Just… Trust me."

"I don't think I have a choice," she said, sounding

exhausted and like she was in a little bit of shock. He couldn't blame her.

Maybe if he distracted her she might make it the last little distance they needed to travel. "You didn't happen to recognize any of those men, did you?" Because interrogating her would be distracting. He made such *excellent* comforting choices.

"No, did you?"

"No. And with no cell service, I can't call in a description to Stevens." He glanced up at the quickly fading light. It was a stunner of a sunset, pinks and oranges, a riot of colors. But how could he care about beauty when he was worried about Natalie?

Which was a problem he didn't have time to consider.

He found the entrance to a cave that looked suitable. Luckily, he'd been exploring the area around the cabin since he was a teenager. He'd been dedicated to making it a safe space for his sister, and he'd spent a considerable amount of time figuring out what that would take. Which meant he had spent some time camping in these very caves, hiking all these mountains.

Unfortunately, he didn't have the equipment he usually had, but he was a Texas Ranger. He knew how to make do.

"So you think more people are after us?"

"Two teams of two so far. I imagine if that piece of trash takes my message back to his boss, we'll see an escalation."

"Do you think he will? Do you think The Stallion would really come after us himself?"

"I don't know, but I'm tired of dealing with his lackeys." Which was an understatement. These weak attacks were practically an insult.

Though the diversion of the man trying to break in the front while another snuck in the back had almost worked. Way too close for comfort.

Natalie inhaled and exhaled, loudly. Fear and exhaustion evident in every breath she took at this point.

"Let me double-check this cave. As long as I don't see evidence of…" Noticing the wariness on her face, he didn't finish his sentence. She didn't need to know what creatures might lurk in the caves. It was best she knew as little as possible.

"Stay put for a few minutes. Keep your eyes on the horizon."

She nodded, and as he ducked into the cave, he couldn't fight the wave of admiration he felt toward her. She didn't argue with him, she didn't get too scared to move. She did what he asked, and he was able to relax enough to trust her to handle some of it.

Not everyone could do that. Hell, there were some kids who couldn't hack it in the police academy with as much poise as Natalie had showed. Even scared as she was.

He did a quick survey of the cave. They wouldn't go very far in. Just enough to have shelter from the elements. There were no signs of predatory wildlife at this particular point, and he'd have to hope that held out for the night.

He returned to Natalie at the opening of the cave, noticing the way she looked around the mountains. Wide-eyed. Awed. Afraid. He wished there was something he could do to keep her mind off of all that was going on around them.

You know what you could do.

He ruthlessly shoved that troublesome voice out of his head and focused on the task at hand.

"I don't have the gear I normally have to camp, but I have this emergency pack, and it'll get us through."

"What if someone finds us?" she asked, those wide brown eyes settling on him. He had to push away the stab of guilt, the harsh desire to comfort her at any cost, with any words, with any touch.

But it wouldn't serve either of them to lie to her. "We have three guns and a tactical advantage, and we'll be watching for them."

She nodded at that and stepped inside the cave with him. He took off his backpack and nodded at her to do the same. He started to rummage for something he could put down so she could try to rest, or maybe some food, but he noted that she was shaking.

He didn't know if it had just started or if she'd been doing it the whole time, but he found a sweatshirt from his pack and handed it to her.

She shook her head. "Unfortunately it's not cold," she said with a self-deprecating laugh. "I just…can't seem to stop."

He swallowed, because his first instinct was to pull her into a hug. Quite honestly, even if he wasn't attracted to her, that would be his instinct. As a police officer, he knew how powerful it could be to simply offer someone a shoulder or a brief, simple embrace. It could give them the courage to make it through a really tragic situation.

Which meant he had to swallow that attraction, and act as though she were anyone else. Anyone else he would offer this to. So he stood and thrust his gun to his hip holster, where it would remain in easy reach. He took the gun she'd been carrying all this time from her shaking fingers and set it behind them. If they showed up, the shooters from the cabin would be unable to sneak around them, and the weapon would be within easy reach.

He steeled himself for what he knew would be a shock of arousal and need, and drew her into the circle of his arms.

She shook there, and he thought she might have cried. Just a little bit of a sob. Against his shoulder. It was strange to feel capable in that moment. To feel like the Ranger he'd been trained to be.

But for the first time in a long time, with Natalie in his arms, he felt in control of the situation. Because he would do anything in his power to protect her.

And that was going to be everything.

Natalie didn't love that she was crying, but it couldn't be helped. It wasn't like she was going to get any privacy to do it any time soon.

Might as well get it out now while there weren't people directly after them. Just indirectly, at some point, in the future. Probably. Did they have another few days? Or were they going have to camp in the mountains for weeks?

She couldn't bring herself to ask Vaughn any of those questions because he always answered them either far too truthfully, or not at all. So she focused on evening her breathing and getting rid of the tears, and finding that inner strength that had gotten her this far.

As she slowly calmed herself, she realized that Vaughn was rubbing his hand up and down her back. It reminded her of the night of the fire, the way he'd put that competent, strong hand on her back and it had been an odd comfort. But it hadn't been personal.

This felt *personal*. Intimate.

She wasn't crying anymore. No, she was absorbing. The strength and warmth of Vaughn, his arms around her, and the gentle, soothing motion of his hand up and down her spine.

It didn't make camping in a cave any more appealing, but it made it a little less daunting. Vaughn would keep her safe. That she knew.

She sighed, and relaxed. Into him, into the embrace. He didn't stiffen against it. Instead, he softened. Vaughn Cooper softening against her. She smiled and burrowed in deeper. Holding him closer.

"I'm going to get you out of this in one piece," he said, his voice a fierce whisper. "One way or another."

"Are you supposed to make impossible promises like that?" she asked, listening to the steady, reassuring beat of his heart.

"I shouldn't," he said, sounding a little disgusted with himself. "But you should know that I'm going to do whatever it takes. I know I can't tell you not to worry, but I can try to give you some comfort."

She looked up at him, still in the warm embrace of his arms. She smiled, and it was odd that she *could* do that in this situation, but something about his fervent need to make her feel safe, made her feel just that. Maybe safe was an exaggeration, but she felt like there was a chance they'd survive this. A good one. Because she trusted Vaughn to do exactly as he said.

"How much distraction would it be if you kissed me?"

Some of that softness left him, a tension creeping into the set of his body. "Natalie…"

She wouldn't be so easily deterred. "I'm just saying that if you want me to feel safe, that would probably do it."

He exhaled something like a laugh.

Then he did the strangest, most unexpected thing. He actually kissed her. Lowering his mouth to hers, something gentle and sweet. The antithesis of the hot and wild thing that had passed between them earlier. This was a comfort, and that made her heart shudder with things she had no business feeling. And yet, she didn't want to stop feeling them.

She wrapped her arms around his neck, deepening the kiss, pressing herself more firmly against him.

His arm pulled her tighter to him, and one hand came up to cup her neck. The warmth of his hand there, the pressure of it, the heat of his mouth and the way his tongue traced her lips and then entered. It was soft and comforting, but it was also more. It was hot and searing. It was a revelation, because she'd never had anything like this. It was fire and sweetness, it was passion and comfort. It was everything she wanted, and all she'd had to do was ask.

She stroked her fingers over his short hair and then down his neck. She wanted to somehow know him. The shape of him. The feel of him. She wanted to understand the texture of his hair, the path of his skin. She wanted more.

That hit her. She wanted more. She wanted it all. She didn't care that they were in a *cave* somewhere. She didn't care that horrible people were after her. Because everything had been going wrong for so long that she just wanted more of this thing that didn't feel wrong.

She wanted good. She wanted Vaughn.

She trailed her hands down his chest. The soft cotton of the T-shirt he wore did nothing to hide what compact, lean muscle he was. Everything about him was hard. Strong. But she thought maybe, just maybe, there was some softness under there. In the way he wanted to protect her, in the way his mouth explored hers.

Even if there was no gentleness in him, he used his strength as a kind of softness. He was a protector, and that was his gentleness. She admired that. Deeply.

"Natalie…"

He didn't have to speak further, she could feel him pulling back, if not physically, mentally.

She clutched him tighter, not willing to let this go. She'd sacrifice her pride for this. "No, don't."

"For every minute we spend doing this, we are putting ourselves in danger. Every minute one of us isn't watching the cave entrance and paying attention to our surroundings, we are increasing the danger that we are in. Exponentially."

"I don't *care*." She knew that was stupid, but she couldn't bring herself to care. Her care was worn out and afraid and *tired*. "We're already in danger, what's a little more?"

She trailed her hand farther down his chest, across the clear indentation of his abs, doing something far bolder and more brazen than she'd ever done. Something she almost couldn't believe she was doing herself.

She placed her palm over the hard length of his erection.

He groaned, sounding tortured and desperate. She smiled, not minding making him tortured or desperate in the least.

"My job is to keep you safe. I can't… Do that…"

"Right now I want your job to be to make me forget. I want to forget I'm scared. I want to forget my life was burned to the ground. I want to forget that I'm on the run and in danger. I want to forget that my sister's missing and there has been nothing I could do about it for years upon years. Vaughn, I want to forget. Let me forget."

She traced the hard length of him, and his grip on her tightened.

"It would be a dereliction of my duty…"

"Derelict with me. Please." She stepped back from the tight embrace of his arms, and he let her. Probably thinking that that was going to be it. That she had come to her senses. But that was the absolute last thing she had come to. She pulled the T-shirt over her head and tossed it toward the backpacks on the ground.

"Natalie." His voice was all gravel, but his eyes were hot and on her.

"I want you, Vaughn. I don't care where we are, what it takes. I want this, and it's been so long since I've had anything I wanted."

She could tell he was fighting a war with his conscience, so she did her best to win it for her side. She shimmied out of the shorts she'd been wearing. Because the ground was rocky, she left her shoes on. It was probably a ridiculous sight, her in her underwear and tennis shoes. Based on Vaughn's tense reaction, she thought she was getting her point across, though.

He took a step toward her, and because she couldn't quite read his expression, whether he was going to insist she put her clothes back on or possibly do it for her, whether he was going to give in to touch her, she held out a hand to stop him.

"No, no, no. Lose your shirt and pants first."

He stood there, a solid wall of granite. The fact he was even standing there, even debating, was a triumph. It was a win.

He clenched his fingers into fists and then relaxed

them, and they went to the hem of his shirt. She exhaled the breath she'd been holding. She was fairly sure that as he lifted his shirt over his head, she whimpered.

He was... Perfection. He had abs and muscles and was just this powerfully broad man whose impressive upper body narrowed to mouthwatering lean hips. She wanted to trace each cut and dip. Possibly with her tongue.

"Pants too," she said, though it was really more of a squeak than her voice.

Again there was a moment of pause. As though he couldn't believe he was doing this. But that didn't stop him. Thank goodness, it didn't stop him. He undid the button of his jeans and then the zipper and pushed them down. Underneath he wore a loose pair of black boxer shorts, but as loose as they were, she could still see the evidence of his arousal. She could see everything. And he was gorgeous and perfect and she wanted nothing more than to be underneath him. Or on top of him. Or both, alternating.

"Am I allowed to approach now?" he asked, the gravel still in his voice, but a hint of humor underneath.

She opened her mouth to say yes. In her mind she said the word regally and coolly. As though she were in control of the situation, as though she were in control of the rioting sparks inside her. In reality, nothing came out of her too-tight throat, and she just had to nod.

When Vaughn grinned at her—at *her*—nothing else mattered. Not the danger they were in, not what might happen afterward. All that mattered was him and now.

He took a step toward her, but his hands didn't reach out to touch. He stood so they were still a couple inches from being toe to toe. He looked at her, right in the eye. It felt more intimate than standing there in her underwear.

The fact that he was looking at her, seemed to look *into* her. That was… Somehow huge and emotional.

"We're going to move a little deeper into the cave. That'll be a safer option. We'll have more of a warning if something happens."

"Remember when I said you were so very conventional?"

"I'm a *man*, Natalie. But I am a man determined to keep you safe, no matter what."

"Are you at least also a man determined to make love to me, not just take off his clothes?"

For the first time since this whole thing had gone wildly out of control, he didn't hesitate. "Yes. More than determined."

It was her turn to grin, and she helped him gather all of their stuff, and even though they were each holding weapons and had backpacks strapped to their bare backs, bundles of clothes in their arms, he held her hand.

He led her farther into the cave, having already pulled the flashlight out of his pack. She tried not to think too deeply about him searching every nook and cranny, and what might be hiding in any of those little places. But he found a little…corner almost, that gave them something like a wall between them and the opening of the cave.

"It'll keep us out of sight, but you're going to have to be quiet."

She giggled at that. How had they gone from running from men with guns to…quietly having sex in a cave?

"What a shame."

"The only shame is that I can't see you."

Those words clutched around her heart and her lungs. She could scarcely suck in the breath to tell him that… She didn't know what she wanted to tell him. She didn't recognize this overfull feeling in her chest. Excitement and lust or something more? She wasn't sure she wanted to delve too far into that possibility.

So she simply held her arms open for him, and he stepped inside. His mouth took hers, his body took hers, and she gave. Everything she had. In a way she never would've imagined. But knowing she had so little, and there was so much against her, it made her open up in a way she's always been scared to.

Because for the first time in her life, she really had nothing to lose. Okay, maybe her life, but she wasn't so sure she was in control of that.

This, she was in control of. Or at least partially in control of.

Vaughn's hands touched her gently and reverently, as though he was trying to find just where she like to be touched. Just where to stroke to make her forget where the hell they were.

In a cave. On the run. Giving themselves to each other. She couldn't think of anyone she'd rather give herself to, and she had the sneaking suspicion that had very little to do with the danger they were in.

Chapter 13

There was the smallest voice in the back of Vaughn's head telling him to stop this madness. But Natalie was nearly naked, all smooth skin and tantalizing curves in the not-at-all-sufficient flashlight beam. Everything about her was like a soft place to land, and the last thing he should be doing right now was landing. He should be leading and fighting and protecting.

But the driving need of his body had taken over. He wanted Natalie as his. No matter how he tried to tell himself that it was wrong, or the wrong time, or some other combination of those things, it got lost somewhere. Usually about the time he had to actually consider taking his mouth from hers, or his hands from her body. He couldn't stand the thought.

Especially when her mouth was so sweet under his, and her hands were so determined to explore him. She seemed to touch every piece of him. A finger traced the

scar on his shoulder from a stab wound he'd gotten undercover. She poked her finger into the dip of his hip. But
the most brain melting was the fact that she kept arching against him, a slow, sensuous rhythm that made him
completely crazy. Incapable of thinking of anything else
but being inside her.

He had no business thinking that or wanting that or
most especially doing that. At this point, he didn't know
how he'd ever stop.

He undid the snap of her bra and slowly drew the fabric down her shoulders and arms. He exhaled, surprised
to find it shaky. Surprised to find how much she affected
him.

"Are you cold?" he murmured as she shivered now
that she was bare from the waist up.

"No," she returned.

"Are you scared?" he asked, rubbing his hands up her
arms, trying to infuse some calm, some surety.

"No." This time she said it on a laugh. "It feels good.
All of it." Those dark, meaningful eyes peered into his.
Her smile was like the gift of sunshine after weeks of
darkness. Perhaps months or years, because he had been
unwittingly, unknowingly in a period of darkness. Something about Natalie lightened him, even in the middle of
all this mess.

"So, I don't know how much you're going to want to
hear this, but I happened to see a packet of condoms in
your sister's backpack when you handed it to me. So...
You know."

He squeezed his eyes shut. "Can you rephrase that in
a way that I don't have to think about the fact my sister
has condoms in her backpack?"

"Why? Do you think she's too young to use them?"

"No, regardless of whether she should or not, the last thing I want to consider right now is my sister having sex. Period. With anyone. Especially in the cabin that we share."

"Okay. New story—I just love carrying condoms around in my purse."

He laughed, and shook his head. "I just haven't..."

She raised her eyebrows, and he realized this was a conversation he did *not* want to get into right now. Right here. It was too close to a truth he was still trying to bottle up. The fact he hadn't slept with anyone since his ex-wife.

The fact he hadn't wanted to, that he'd thrown his life into police work just like Jenny had always accused him of.

That wanting this, Natalie, here, now, it all *meant* something.

But there was too much at stake for that meaning to be dissected in the here and now. "We'll have plenty of time to converse after. Let's not waste our present."

"Take off your underwear, and I might be inclined to agree with you." She grinned, all jokes and fun in the midst of this awful situation for her.

"Grab a condom from *your* purse. I'll lay out some blankets."

She gave a little nod and bent over the pink sparkly backpack. Vaughn focused on the tempting curve of her backside over *where* she was obtaining the condoms from. When she turned back to him, she cocked her head.

"Where are the blankets?"

"Sorry, I was distracted."

She smirked and rolled her eyes. "Then I guess turnabout is fair play. Please bend over and retrieve the blankets," she said with a regal lift of her hand.

He chuckled, but he did exactly as she asked. She made a considering sound, and he didn't waste any time retrieving the blankets. Both pieces of fabric were lightweight backpacking blankets that wouldn't do much to protect Natalie from the harsh, hard ground, but it would keep them from rolling around in rocks and dirt.

Rolling around in rocks and dirt. While armed and dangerous criminals were probably after them. "Are you sure—"

"I simply won't take no for an answer, Vaughn," she said primly. "Don't make me say it again."

He promised himself he wouldn't. He would make sure they both enjoyed this. That they would get everything they needed out of it, and when they had to face whatever they had to face tomorrow morning, they would do it together. Both having had this moment. This coming together.

He crossed to her and took her mouth. No preamble, losing some of the gentleness that had held him back earlier. He wanted. She wanted. It was time to take— and give.

She moaned against him, arching in the way that drove him crazy. He slid his fingers into her underwear, finding the soft, wet heat of her. Stroking and exploring until she wasn't just shaking in his arms, but shuddering. Panting. Desperate.

And he was desperate too.

"The ground is rough. So I'm going to lay on my back, and you're going to get on top."

"You just lay out orders everywhere you go, don't you?"

But she didn't protest when he lay down and pushed his boxers off his legs. Not a complaint, just a steady gaze at the hardest part of him illuminated only by the flashlight he'd rested on the ground. "I believe that means it's your turn to take off your underwear."

She grinned at him and shimmied out of her underwear. She knelt next to him and handed him the condom. He opened the packet and rolled it on himself, watching her as she watched him. She licked her lips and he groaned aloud.

"How on earth are we going to do this?" she asked, and though it seemed like she *attempted* to make eye contact, her gaze never made it very far.

"Just figure out however you feel comfortable."

She straddled him, that intimate place of hers not making contact with his body. She trailed her fingers down his chest and his abdomen. He could only barely make out the tight points of her dark nipples, only barely make out the seductive shape of her body.

But she was here, straddling him, those smooth legs brushing up against his sides, her scent, her warmth permeating the very air.

"Are you sure you're comfortable?" she asked before chewing on her bottom lip in that sexy and distracting way she did whenever she was worried.

"Baby, all I feel is you." Which was true. When it was all said and done, he might notice the way the rocks dug into him, but for right now, all he could see, feel, think, want was her.

She leaned over him, her breasts brushing his chest, her lips brushing his mouth. "Then take me," she murmured.

It was his turn to take the order, and he did, sliding home on a moan, moving deep and steady, paying attention to the way her breath caught and exhaled. The pleasure and excitement coiled so deep and so hard, he wasn't sure he'd ever survive.

His hands dug into the softness of her hips, but he let her set the pace. Slow and tentative at first, and then she moved faster, everything about her softness, her breathy moans, *her* driving him closer and closer to that reckless edge.

She was beautiful, moving against him, sighing, gasping as she chased that rhythm that would lead to her release. It bloomed in him, big and hard, something more than where their bodies met.

She said his name, pulsed around him. He thought he could make out the way the flush in her cheeks had spread across her chest as she sighed out her release.

But it wasn't enough. He pushed himself into a sitting position, pulling her legs around him. Her gaze met his, glazed with pleasure.

"Again," he ordered.

And when she opened her mouth to protest, he covered it with his own.

Again. The harsh, demanding way Vaughn had said those words echoed in her head. Again? She'd just lost herself over some edge she'd never known, how could she possibly do it again?

But he was kissing her, using that harsh, steady, hot grip on her hips to pull her forward. She arched against it, against him. She loved the way her breasts scraped across his chest. She loved the way his hands were commanding and sure. She loved this. Being with him. Being filled by him. Being driven to some sort of climax that was bigger than she'd ever known.

She was starting to think it might be a dream.

But Vaughn kept moving, urging her to take more of him, and then less, over and over again in a steady, unrelenting rhythm. The blooming edge of pleasure began to build again. The heat that should've been unbearable, but she couldn't stand to lose. A fire in her veins that she didn't want to be cooled.

He broke the kiss and his mouth streaked everywhere. Her cheeks, her neck, her chest. He was everywhere, driving her into a faster and faster pace. She could feel his desperation grow, the closeness of his own release, just thinking about that, of being with him, finding that pleasure together, it pushed her over that last humbling, bright edge.

Vaughn held her there, deep and strong, his harsh groan echoing in the expanse of the cave.

She wasn't sure how long they sat there wrapped up in each other, holding on for dear life. She wasn't even sure how long the orgasm pulsed through her. She didn't care. In this dark cave with Vaughn, it didn't matter what time it was. All that mattered was that he was holding her, that he was a part of her.

"You're shaking again, and I think it's cold this time," he murmured into her ear, so gentle and sweet.

It was hard to think she could be cold, but as he grabbed a sweatshirt and pulled it over her head, she realized he was right. She was shivering with cold, *among* other things.

The sweatshirt he put on her was his, oversized and warm, and it smelled like him. Clean and soap and Vaughn. She wanted to snuggle into that smell and him forever.

"We should get dressed."

If he hadn't kissed her forehead and her cheek and

then her neck before moving, she might have been fooled by that tense note in his voice. But he was so gentle, and affectionate, and she realized that his tenseness wasn't about what had passed between them, it was just that he was coming back to the job he had before him.

He was dedicated to her safety. He was dedicated to her. She couldn't help but be warmed by that.

She rolled off him and tried not to watch with too much interest as he got rid of the condom. He handed her a pair of pants that would be too big, but they would keep her warm. The cave was much cooler than the outside air.

"You can change back into your clothes tomorrow when we set out. The sweats will be too big to move in, but the shorts and shirt won't be enough to keep you warm tonight."

"Have you always been such a good caretaker?"

"I guess it depends on who you ask."

"I'm asking you."

Those inscrutable gray-blue eyes met hers in the eerie glow of the flashlight beam. Something in his gaze shuttered, and she realized this was quite the sore spot for him. "You've done nothing but take care of me so far," she said firmly, wishing she could erase those doubts in his eyes.

"That's my job."

"It's more than that."

"Do you want to rest, or do you want to try to eat something first? All I have are some granola bars and some jerky."

"Vaughn, I want to talk."

"We can talk about whatever you want, except about my caregiving tendencies."

She frowned at him as he got dressed. He seemed to

have an endless supply of things in that black backpack of his. She sat on the blankets that he'd stretched out, dressed in his clothes, watching something like irritation make his shoulders hunch.

"So, is this the part where you're just certain that I'm going to look at you like your ex-wife looked at you?" she asked, perhaps too bluntly, but if she was going to have ill-advised sex with the man, she was going to ask him too-blunt questions.

If her life was in danger, she was going to push where she normally wouldn't. She was going to demand what it would never occur to her to demand in her real, unassuming, obsessed-with-Gabby life.

He faced her, and in the light everything about him seemed hard and unreachable. Granite she'd never be able to push through. Except she had. She *had*.

"We had sex once, Natalie. I like you, I do. But you're nothing like a wife."

It was a nasty thing to say, and it hurt even though she knew it shouldn't. She wasn't his wife, she wasn't even close to his wife. She'd be lucky if there was anything they could salvage after this whole ordeal.

But just because words were designed to hurt, no matter the truths or lack of truth behind them, didn't mean that she could let it go.

"I'm not trying to be an ass," he said on a sigh, rubbing his jaw. "But don't make me into something I'm not."

"I'm not making you into anything. I'm reflecting on what I've seen from you, and if you can't accept that part of yourself, that's fine. Don't take it out on me."

"I'm not big on sorry." He said it with such a grave finality she opened her mouth to tell him he was a jerk, but he kept going.

"But I'm sorry. Because I was feeling guilty for letting my personal feelings interfere with this case, and I took it out on you, and that's less than fair."

Her heart ached for him then, because she knew that she'd initiated this. She'd pushed for it. Not that Vaughn hadn't wanted it or hadn't enjoyed it, but it had come at a cost to him. It required him to bend that ironclad moral code he lived by, and that meant something, not easily distilled no matter how great the orgasm might have been.

It was crazy to think she might love him. She barely knew him. And yet everything in her heart said that love was what this feeling was. Love, or the seeds of it. There was so much possibility, and yet so much against them.

"Apology accepted," she said, hoping her voice sounded light rather than as ragged and rocked as she felt.

"Just like that?"

"This wasn't a mistake, but I understand why it might be hard for you to accept. But I'll never regret it. No matter what happens."

"You say that now…"

"And I'll say it always. No matter what." She stood, because she needed to somehow prove to him that she was strong. That she meant it. "That was what I needed, at that exact time I needed it. And you gave it to me. Nothing you could do could take that away. Nothing that happens changes what you gave me."

He stared at her, and she thought she saw some pain there, and she assumed it probably had to do with his marriage that had dissolved. No matter how much or how little he'd given, that relationship had clearly left scars. She wished she could sew them together, kiss them, make everything okay.

But she couldn't. And not just because they had dangerous men after them.

"Let's eat something, and then one of us can try to sleep."

He kept staring at her for a few humming seconds of silence. Then slowly, oh so painfully slowly, he crossed to her. He touched her face, his blunt fingertips tracing the lines of her cheekbones and then her jaw, then her neck. His eyes bore into hers, and her heart hammered against her chest.

She wanted to say silly things like I love you, and she knew she couldn't. She absolutely couldn't.

"For the record, I'll never regret it, either."

When he kissed her, it was gentle, and it was sweet. And Vaughn Cooper gave her something that no one else had for a very long time.

Hope.

Chapter 14

Vaughn managed a few hours of sleep, after he watched Natalie sleep for far too long. It had been tempting to lie next to her, to wake her with a kiss. So, he'd done neither. He'd stood guard the entire time she'd slept, and then he'd woken her by nudging her with his foot.

Because he was a bit of a coward, all in all.

Though his brain and body were nothing but a swirling mass of confusion he didn't have time for, exhaustion won out and he slept quick and hard.

Natalie woke him at the first sign of dawn, just as he'd instructed, and then he began to pack everything.

"Are we going back to the cabin?" she asked him, trepidation coloring her every movement.

"No. We're hiking farther."

"Until what?"

"I know the area well enough to lead us toward civilization. Somewhere our phones work and we can call for help. It's too dangerous to go back to the cabin."

"But what about your truck?"

"They slashed the tires," he returned. He hadn't wanted to tell her all the things he'd noticed as they'd escaped from the cabin. That they took care to not shoot anyone, that they'd snuck their way into a position to *take* not murder.

He supposed murder would be scarier, but the idea of Natalie being held by those men… He wasn't going to let that happen.

"When did you notice that?" she asked incredulously.

"When I kicked Worthless Number Two over, I saw the tires were flat." And that the man had been carrying handcuffs and rope. Duct tape. Vaughn swallowed at the uncomfortable ball of rage and fear in his gut.

Natalie blew out a breath. "How long will it take to get us back to civilization?"

Vaughn pulled out the map of the Guadalupe Mountains that he kept in his emergency pack. He'd studied it last night while Natalie was sleeping, but he was worried and thorough enough to look at it again.

He inclined the map so she could see too. "This is the path we're going to follow." He showed her with his finger the mountains they would have to cross to get inside the national park and finally find service or a ranger station to assist them. "I don't know exactly where we'll get cell service, so we just have to keep going until we get it. Or find someone who can help us. My hope is that they don't expect us to keep moving forward this way, and it'll give us enough of a head start that by the time they realize it, we'll be close enough to call for help."

Natalie chewed her bottom lip and studied the map. "Do you have enough supplies to get us through all of this?"

"It'll be tight and we'll be hungry, but we'll survive."

"You don't know the meaning of sugarcoating, do you?"

"Do you want me to sugarcoat it?" Because he would, if that's what she wanted. He wasn't sure who else he'd afford that to.

She sighed again, pulling her hair back in a ponytail. It stretched the tight T-shirt across her breasts, and he had to stop himself from wondering how much he'd be able to see if they indulged in each other right now. In the pearly light of dawn easing its way into the cave. Her skin would glow, she would—

They didn't have time for that, and even if he'd lost his mind once, he couldn't do it again. At least not if it meant wasting daylight. Maybe tonight…

He shook his head and told himself to focus. "First things first, we're going to start moving toward higher ground. Hopefully that gives us a tactical advantage, and we can see if anyone's following us before they catch up."

"What do we do if they are?"

"Well, that depends on how close they are. We'll either book it, or we'll pick them off. But that's a lot of what-if, Natalie."

"You shot those other men. Do you think…" She swallowed, and he didn't know if it was her conscience or something else bothering her, but either way that was something that she was going to have to work out on her own.

Every officer who vowed to protect the innocent and took up a weapon had to come to terms with what that meant and the power it offered. They had to come to grips with what they were willing to do. He couldn't convince her of his morality or his lack of guilt, and, in the next few days should she have to use her weapon, only she could deal with the aftermath of that. He couldn't do it for her, no matter how much he'd like to.

Because if he had the choice, he would save her from every hard decision. Which was another thing in a long line of things he didn't have the time or energy to think about right now.

"It was my intention to give them non-life-threatening wounds, but without medical attention, it's hard to know if they survived, and quite frankly I can't concern myself with it. The only thing I can concern myself with right now is keeping you and me safe."

She didn't say anything for a long while, and he let her be quiet as they walked out of the cave. They would need to make it to another shelter by nightfall, and though he could read the map and do some general calculations, he couldn't be sure where they'd end up when the sun set.

So, they needed to head out and get as far as they could. He didn't think they could make it to cell service today, but if they got good enough mileage behind them, they could hopefully get there tomorrow.

They hiked in silence for most of the morning, and though Vaughn was sorry that she was obviously brooding about a difficult situation, he couldn't feel bad that there wasn't any conversation to distract him from his task at hand.

Occasionally they stopped and ate a snack and drank some water. Vaughn would consult the map, but mostly they walked. He knew she was exhausted, and probably on her last legs, but he also knew that she was strong and resilient, and that he could push her and she would survive. That was one of the things he most admired about her.

"You're holding up remarkably well, you know," he said as they sat on rocks and Natalie devoured a granola bar.

She glanced at him, the granola bar halfway to her mouth. Her gaze didn't bother to hide her surprise. "I haven't really had a choice, have I?"

"We always have a choice. One of the choices is to lie down and die, to give up. One of the choices is to think that you can't, and so then it's a self-fulfilling prophecy. You could be so busy complaining about the lot you've been given that we never got anywhere. But you've chosen to move forward. To keep fighting. Not everyone could have done that, not everyone has that kind of wherewithal. I'm not sure anyone should *have* to have that kind of wherewithal, but it's special. And you deserve to know that."

She smiled a little and looked down at her granola bar for a second before leaning over and giving him a long, gentle kiss. Her arm wound around his neck, and it took all the willpower he had not to lean into that, not to pull her into his lap. He couldn't let her distract him, but...

She pulled away, that sweet smile playing on her lips. "You know Vaughn, I like you a lot. That's not something I would have said about five days ago."

He chuckled a little at that. "Well, that's very mutual."

It was her turn to laugh, but she sobered quickly. "When we get back..." she began, emphasizing the *when* meaningfully. But her seriousness morphed into a grin. "You're going to have to let me hypnotize you."

He narrowed his eyes at her, but he couldn't help from smiling in return. "Like hell, Natalie."

"Why not? Are you afraid?"

"No. You told me that the person has to be willing. I'm never going to be willingly *relaxed*. Unless it's by things other than hypnotism."

She snorted at his joke. "Do you have secrets to hide that you're not willing to share, Ranger Cooper?"

"I don't have any secrets." Which had become true the minute they'd discussed his marriage. There was nothing about himself kept under wraps, because there wasn't much there. Work.

She might not know he was related to a few celebrities, but that wasn't *his* secret in the least.

Natalie looked down at the last bite of granola bar, something in her gaze going serious. "I guess I don't really have any more secrets from you, either." Her eyebrows had drawn together, and she didn't look at him. "Everything in my life has been Gabby for so long…"

She swallowed, and Vaughn could tell she was dealing with some big emotion, so instead of pressing or changing the subject, he gave her time to work through it.

"I want her back so much, and I just *have* to believe she's alive… But…" She shoved the granola wrapper into her backpack forcefully, irritated. "I feel terrible saying this, it feels like a betrayal, but when we make it out of here, I want a life that isn't solely focused on her." Her brown gaze met his, and he had a bad feeling he knew where this was going.

And where it couldn't *possibly* go. Because his feelings for Natalie ran very deep, but he'd been here before—loving someone and knowing that her views on the world would never allow them to make something permanent, to make something real.

"One step at a time. Remember?"

She frowned at him as though she could read his

thoughts, as though she could read everything. He didn't like that sensation at all. But in the end, he didn't have to bother figuring it out because a shot rang out in the quiet, sunny afternoon.

Immediately Vaughn had Natalie under him, protecting her body with his, scanning the horizon for where the shot might have come from.

"Wh-where?" Natalie asked in a shaky voice.

"I don't know." Based on the sound, he didn't think it had come from behind them. It seemed more likely it came from higher ground. From someone who'd presumably assumed his plan all too easily. He swore viciously and tried to reach for his pack without leaving Natalie vulnerable.

Another shot sounded, a loud crack against the quiet desert, this one getting closer. It had to be coming from the other side of the mountain they were climbing. They couldn't stay put, they were too vulnerable, too exposed. And he had no idea where to shoot toward.

"We're going to have to run from it," he said flatly, his eyes never stopping their survey of their surroundings.

"Run for it? Run where?"

He pointed to a craggy outcropping a little ways behind them. "You run there. No matter what happens to me, you run there and get behind those rocks."

She tried to twist under him, but he wouldn't let her. "What do you mean no matter what happens? You can't honestly expect me to—"

"The most important thing is that you stay safe. Out of the way of a bullet. If I—"

"What about you? What about your safety?" she demanded, a slight note of hysteria in her voice.

"Natalie, listen to me," he said, his voice calm, his

demeanor sure. Because not only was it his *job* to take a bullet for her if the circumstances necessitated that, but he wanted to. He'd never be able to live with himself if she ended up hurt because of an error in his judgement.

"My job is to keep you safe."

"Well, Vaughn, I want *you* to be safe too, regardless of what your job is."

He'd analyze the way those words sliced a little later. "I'll be safe. If you listen to me, we'll both be safe. We're going to make a run for it. You first. I'll follow."

"I don't like this."

"Unfortunately, Nat, it doesn't matter what you like, this is what we have to do."

She exhaled shakily, and it wasn't until she spoke that he realized it was anger not fear. "If you get shot," she said, her voice trembling with rage, "I will finish off the job myself. Do you understand me? You will not get hurt saving me."

Everything inside him vibrated with a kind of gratitude and hurt and all number of things he couldn't work out at the moment. He kissed her temple, which was the only place on her head he could reach.

"You just listen to me, and everything will be fine. I've gotten you this far, haven't I?"

"Yes, and I know you'll get me the rest of the way. We'll get each other the rest of the way."

He hated that she was worried about his safety. Her safety was of the most importance, not his. He was a man who could be replaced easily enough, but there was no one like Natalie.

But if she cared about him, and her safety depended on his, then he would keep himself safe. He would keep them both safe.

"On the count of three, we run. That's our destination. If I happen to get hit, you keep going. You can't save me if you're dead."

"And you can't save me if *you're* dead," she argued.

Another shot rang out, and Vaughn knew that one was way too close for comfort. The next one would hit, and if they weren't trying to kill them, all the more danger.

"One, two, three, go." He launched to his feet, pulling her with him, and then they ran.

Natalie ran, just as Vaughn instructed. There was a certain hysteria bubbling through her, but with a specific destination—behind that rock—she managed to focus enough to get her feet to move, as fast as they possibly could.

Another shot rang out, and Natalie jerked in fear and surprise and almost tripped at the sound, but Vaughn's steady grip on her arm propelled her forward. She tumbled behind the rock, and Vaughn was right behind her, covering her with his body again.

As glad as she was to have someone protecting her, someone like Vaughn, so sure, so capable, worried about her safety, she had fallen in love with the man, and she hated the thought that he was ready to give his life for hers.

She knew this was his job, but that didn't make it easier. Certainly not easier to know he was risking his neck for her. She didn't feel worthy of it. She didn't feel worthy of any of this.

Why were these men after *her*? All she'd done was pathetically fail at trying to find her sister for *eight* years. Failure after failure. Why on earth did they think her worthy of this kind of manhunt?

Now was not the time to worry about those questions, about her failures, but every insecurity, every pain, every hurt seemed to center inside her along with this bone-deep panic.

Vaughn made an odd grunting sound as he rolled off her. She glanced over at him, and he was trying to pull off his jacket. She didn't quite know why he was bother-ing with that when—

"I'm going to need your help," he said, his voice strangely strained.

"What's wrong?" she asked, despite the way her throat tightened. Something was off, something—

Then she saw it, the angry streak of red in the middle of a rip on the T-shirt fabric across his shoulder. She felt like *she'd* been shot, seeing that horrible gash and the way the blood trickled down his beautiful, strong arm. For her.

He spared her a glance. "Not going to pass out, are you?"

"No," she said firmly, though she did feel a little woozy and light-headed at the sight of him bleeding so profusely, but she wasn't going to be so weak she couldn't help him. She would find a way to push through her physical reac-tion and give him everything he needed.

"Tell me what you need me to do."

"Grab something out of the backpack that you can wrap tight around the wound." He had his gun pulled and was holding it with his good arm. Ready to take a shot. Ready to protect her in the middle of this barren moun-tainous desert. "I can do it myself if you want me to—"

"I can do it." Natalie would do whatever he asked, whatever he needed. Over and over again.

He kept his gaze trained on the area around the rock

that protected them. Natalie did her best to hurry to find something she could wrap his arm with. She hoped this was at least a little bit like in the movies, because then she would at least know a little bit of what to do.

There was a T-shirt at the very bottom of his pack, and she pulled it out. Without thinking too much about it, she pulled and pulled until she ripped a good strip. She repeated the process over and over until she had several strips. While Vaughn remained the lookout, she folded the strips over the worst part of the wound and then tied the longest one around his upper arm as tight as she could manage.

He hissed out a breath, but that was the only outward sign that he hurt.

"That should hold for little bit," she said, scared and worried that she'd screwed it all up. But what could she do? All she could really do was everything he asked, hoping for the best. She had no other options here, so there wasn't even a point in worrying about what else there was. Like Vaughn kept saying, there was only now. No time to worry about later.

"On the slim chance that we have a signal, check your phone and mine."

Natalie scrambled for both, powering them on and checking their screens. But there was no service. She wanted to cry, but she blinked back the tears. Tears would get them nowhere.

A shot hadn't rung out in a while, and the longer the silence lasted, the more both their nerves seemed to stretch thin and taut.

"Pull up the texting on both phones. I want you to put in a message to this number, and hopefully if we try to send it now, it'll send the first second we have service without us having to keep checking."

Natalie furiously typed the information Vaughn gave her. She kept glancing at the T-shirt bandage, and because it was a white T-shirt, she could see the blood already seeping through. She tried not to panic at that.

"Get out the map." Though he still sounded like cool and collected Vaughn, that strain never left his voice.

He'd been shot. *Shot.* It took everything she had to pull out the map and spread it out for him. Her hands shook, but he still handed her the gun she'd dropped while trying to bandage him up, trusting her. Believing in her. She held on to that fiercely.

"Shoot at anything that moves."

She swallowed and nodded, watching the harsh surroundings and fervently hoping nothing moved.

"We don't want to retrace our steps," he muttered. "We need to keep moving forward. We've got to keep searching for cell service. We don't get out of this without help."

She wanted to make another joke about him not sugarcoating anything, but her voice didn't work anymore. Whether it was panic or fear or some combination of all of the emotions rioting through her, she couldn't push out joking words. Only desperate ones.

"Are they going to come after us?"

"They might. I didn't get a glimpse of where they were coming from. I still have no idea what the hell they're trying to prove. If they want us dead, they could have had us dead on the road before the gas station. I don't get this at all, unless they want us. Alive. Or…"

He didn't have to finish that sentence, and she knew, sugarcoating or no, he wouldn't. Because he meant *or they want you.* She could tell that bothered him more than anything. That he didn't know what they were trying to do, that she might be the target.

Natalie didn't really care what they were trying to do. As long as they were shooting at them, she wasn't a fan.

"To keep cover we're going to have to backtrack a little bit, but then we'll circle around, really try to get higher ground on the off chance there's a tower around here somewhere. If you hear the message sent notification from either phone, tell me. Otherwise we need to stay completely silent, just in case. They don't want us dead. Or at least they don't want you dead, and that's pretty damn frightening."

"But…"

For the first time his glare turned to her, rather than their surroundings or the map. "What the hell do you mean, but…"

"If they have Gabby…" She swallowed at the lump in her throat. Maybe they wanted her too. If they did…

"No. No way in hell. You're not sacrificing yourself for her right now. First of all, not on my watch. Second of all, because you just told me you want a life beyond all that."

"I didn't know how close I was."

"I'm sorry. I know she's your sister, and I know you'd do anything to find her, but it's been eight years. If she survived that, a few more days won't hurt her. You don't know what they're trying to do to you, so we're not taking that chance. Not even for your sister, Nat."

"You'd do it for your sister," she returned, quiet and sure. He'd sacrifice himself for less, she was certain.

"It would depend on the situation, and not in this one. If they had my sister, I'd do exactly what I'm doing now. Which is trying to get them. Because if we don't have them, everyone under their control is in danger."

She saw a point to that, but the idea that if they took her she might be reunited with Gabby. If they took her... Vaughn might be safe.

"Natalie, you have to trust me on this. I need you to promise me."

Natalie swallowed. She hated lying to him, but she also knew they wouldn't get anywhere if she didn't make that promise. She forced herself to look him in the eye—those gorgeous blue eyes she thought she'd never be able to read—and now she knew she'd never not be able to see what was in those depths.

He was strong and he was brave, and he knew that he could get them out of here. But he was also afraid, because whether he was going to admit it, whether he would admit it, he cared about her too. He wouldn't have slept with her in the middle of all this if care wasn't part of that. That she knew.

"All right. I promise," she said, holding on to the thought of care, of love.

Vaughn swore harshly. "Don't lie to me." He grabbed her arm and winced a little, since he'd used his bad arm. But he didn't back down. "I don't have time to argue with you on this, but if you put yourself in danger you will answer to me. Now, let's go."

He didn't give her a chance to argue; he pushed and pulled her in the direction he wanted to go. And Natalie let him lead, let him order her around.

But she had no doubt if the situation presented itself, she'd sacrifice herself for both the people she loved.

Chapter 15

Vaughn didn't know what to do with the searing rage inside him. She was lying. How dare she lie about something so important? How could she be willing to sacrifice herself with so many unknowns and so much at stake? She didn't even know for sure if her sister was alive or with The Stallion. All they had were hunches and possibilities, and Vaughn was beyond livid that she would take such a chance with her life.

It didn't matter that he would do everything in his power to make that impossible for her, because it wasn't about him. It wasn't about what he could do. It wasn't about how well he could keep her safe. It was about the fact that she was *willing*. It was about the fact that...

She should've cared more about herself. She should've cared more about her future.

Which does not include you, so maybe calm down.

Frustrated with himself, more than frustrated with the

situation, he pushed them forward at a punishing pace, doing his best to keep them behind things that would keep them out of sight and safe from bullets.

But even as they hurried and zigzagged and did their best to stay low, Vaughn could hear the sound of an engine getting closer and closer. He swore, because no matter how good he was, no matter how strong he was, no matter how smart he was, he could not outrun a vehicle. He couldn't outrun whatever was coming after them.

They'd made it around one of the craggy desert mountains, and whatever was coming for them would have to come around one of the sides. Vaughn kept his weapon drawn and his eyes alert. "We're going to find somewhere to hide you."

"But—"

"No but. You will listen to me. You will follow my directions. If I tell you to hide, you will damn well hide." He didn't have time to see how she was taking that harsh order. He didn't have time to look at her and make sure she was okay. He was a little afraid if he did take that time, he'd fall apart.

He'd been in some dangerous, uncomfortable, scary situations, and he'd never been scared that he might fall apart. It poked and ate at him. Hell, it just about killed him that she'd become that important. Which meant the only choice was to keep going.

He found a very small opening, more crevice than cave, in the base of the mountain. With less finesse than he might have had otherwise, he gave her a little push into the crevice. She fit, though barely. But it would keep her out of sight.

He looked around to make sure he couldn't see a car

anywhere. He could hear that engine, so they were close, but not close enough to see him just yet.

"Stay here. No matter what. You do not come out of here until I come to get you. Someone tries to get you out, you shoot him wherever will do the most damage." He didn't even have time to ask if she understood. He gave her one meaningful look and tried not to let those big, soulful brown eyes undo him.

He didn't have time for that, or to ascertain whether she would listen to his order. He could only keep moving. Because if he stayed there and the vehicle came around one of those bends, they would know exactly where to find Natalie.

Vaughn took off running as fast as he could, ignoring the screaming pain in his shoulder. His heart was pounding and his breath was scorching his lungs, and he had the sinking suspicion it had more to do with the fact that he'd left Natalie alone than with the fact that he was running.

He slowed his pace, took a quick look at his surroundings. He could still see the crevice where he'd pushed Natalie, but he couldn't see her. He was far enough away that it would take a lot of searching for anyone to find her.

Now he had to figure out which direction he wanted to go to, and—

The sound of a gunshot made Vaughn skid to a halt. He glanced around, trying to ascertain where the sound had come from. There were little craggy outcrops all over the desert. There were cacti and other plants that a stealthy person might be able to hide behind. Vaughn searched and searched, but he didn't see anyone, or anything.

The sound of the engine had stopped, and he did his best to keep his gaze everywhere rather than always on where Natalie was. He didn't want to give it away, because who knew what these men had. They could be watching him with binoculars, they could have an army of cars. They could have anything, and he didn't know.

He couldn't think about the what-if. He had to think about the right now.

"Ranger Cooper."

Vaughn whirled to see a man walk out from behind the opposite curve of the little mountain. He appeared to be alone, but Vaughn wasn't stupid enough to think that was true. Any number of people could come pouring from the other side of the mountain. There could be an *army* of men behind the curve, and that was daunting, but it couldn't stop what Vaughn had to do.

"Mr. Callihan, I assume?"

The man laughed and spread his hands wide, though Vaughn noticed that the gun he carried was pointed directly at Vaughn's chest regardless of the gesture.

"It took you only how many years to figure that out?"

"A lot fewer years than it will take me to kill you."

The man kept walking closer and closer, and Vaughn's hands tensed on his gun. He could shoot the man and be done with it, and there was a very large part of him that wanted to. But he resisted, because his mission wasn't to kill every bad guy who roamed the earth; it was to bring them to justice.

He believed in justice, and while he believed in using his weapon with deadly force if necessary, as long as this man wasn't actively trying to kill him, or take or harm Natalie, Vaughn was having a hard time rationalizing shooting first.

Maybe some of it had to do with the fact this could potentially be the only man on earth who knew where

Natalie's sister was. If Vaughn killed him without trying to retrieve more information, what might Natalie think of him? What might she lose?

It was the absolute last thing he should be concerned with, but, still, he didn't shoot.

"But you see, Ranger Cooper, I know you, and I know your type. It's why I've managed to do as much damage as I have. Because you're all so honorable, or easy to buy off."

"Try to buy me off and see what happens."

The man chuckled, all ease and...something like charm, though Vaughn wasn't at all charmed by it. Still, these were the most dangerous criminals to deal with, the ones without much at stake, except their own pride, or whatever was going on in their warped heads.

Of course he'd be charming and smooth, men like him were always charming and smooth. That was why people didn't suspect them. That was why he'd gotten this far. But also because reason and rational thinking wouldn't change their course. Nothing would. The man standing before him could do anything with zero remorse.

"But I'm not here for you," Callihan said with an elegant flick of the wrist. "I'm here for the woman. I have plans for the woman who thinks she can get her sister away from me."

Vaughn's entire body turned to ice. Even in the quiet desert, he didn't know if they were close enough for Natalie to hear that, but it was an admission. It was a certainty that Natalie's sister was with this man, and that he was after Natalie. For very specific reasons.

His finger itched to pull that trigger, to end this, now. Though they were still yards apart, Vaughn thought he saw Callihan's gaze drop to his gun.

"Lucky for me, Ranger Cooper, I don't need you. Quite frankly, wherever that woman is, I'll find her, but you'll be de—"

Vaughn pulled the trigger. The whistle of the shot, followed by the man's piercing scream, were barely heard over the beating of his heart.

He'd purposefully shot for the man's weapon-wielding arm, and as Vaughn raced toward the dropped gun, Callihan started screaming for someone in Spanish.

Even though he knew Callihan was yelling for backup, which likely meant people with even larger weapons would be coming around that bend, he raced for the gun. Even though he knew he might have signed his death warrant, there was always a chance Callihan had only a few men with him, a chance Vaughn would be able to pick them off before...

But there was *no* chance if he didn't get to Callihan's weapon first.

Vaughn was so intent on reaching the weapon, and reaching Callihan that he didn't realize there were footsteps behind him.

"If you so much as touch that gun with a fingertip, I will shoot you, and I'm not a very good shot, so if I aim for your heart, I might just hit your head."

Vaughn skidded to a stop and looked back at Natalie, who was walking steadily toward them. She had the gun he'd taken from one of the men in the cabin trained on Callihan's writhing form.

The man merely smirked, his hand still reaching for the weapon, before Vaughn could pull his weapon, Natalie shot.

"That's the problem with women," Callihan all but spat.

"They can never shoot on tar—" She shot again, and this time Callihan howled.

Red bloomed at his stomach, and Natalie kept calmly walking forward, though now that she was close enough, Vaughn could see the way her arms were shaking. Callihan was screaming for someone named Rodriguez while he thrashed and moaned on the ground.

Right before Natalie and Vaughn reached Callihan's weapon, a large man stepped out from behind the curve of mountain. He was dressed all in black, had black sunglasses and black hair, with multiple guns strapped to him—all black. Everything about him was large and muscular and ominous.

"Shoot them!" Callihan screamed. "Kill them both. What are you doing?"

Vaughn didn't pull his trigger, and not just because the man didn't pull out a gun. The man was shockingly familiar. Not because he'd arrested him before, not because of anything criminal. He'd *trained* him a few years ago on undercover practices, though Vaughn couldn't come up with his name.

Callihan kept screaming at him to shoot, but the man didn't make a move to reach for a weapon. He walked calmly toward the three of them.

"Tell your woman to put down the gun," he said in Spanish, nodding toward Natalie, who was holding the gun trained on the man.

Vaughn glanced at her then, noting that everything about her was shaking and pale and scared. But she was ready to take the shot.

"Put it down, Nat," he murmured.

"I won't let anyone kill us. Not now. Not when that man has my sister."

Callihan made a grab for his supposed henchman's leg piece, but the man easily kicked him away.

"Ma'am, I need you to put your weapon down," he said, steady and sure, making eye contact with Natalie. "I'm with the FBI. I've been working undercover for Callihan. I know where your sister is. She's…safe."

Natalie didn't just lower the gun, she dropped it. Then she sank to her knees, so Vaughn sank with her.

"Does this mean it's over?" she asked in a shaking, ragged voice.

"I think so," he said, stroking her hair. "I think so."

Natalie sat in a truck squished between Vaughn and this… FBI agent. Vaughn and the man discussed the case, the particulars of the FBI's involvement and what the agent was allowed to disclose.

Natalie knew she should be listening, but everything was just a faded buzz. She couldn't seem to stop shaking, and all she could concentrate on was the fact the man in the back had become completely silent.

She'd shot him. Right in the stomach. He hadn't shut up though, he'd gone on and on as Vaughn and the agent, Jaime Alessandro, or so he said, had done the best to bandage Callihan, while also keeping him tied up.

Callihan had shouted terrible things about what he'd done to Gabby, but before he'd really gotten going, Agent Alessandro had knocked him out. Just a quick blow to the head. Then, they'd taped his mouth shut and thrown him into the truck he'd brought out to the desert.

All Natalie could concentrate on was how she'd tried to kill a man, and failed. She should be glad that she had failed, she should be glad that she hadn't apparently hit any internal organs, and that he would probably survive. She should be glad that he would stand trial.

All she felt was regret. She wished she would've killed him. For Gabby, for Vaughn, for herself. She wished he was dead, and she didn't know how to reconcile that with who she'd thought she was.

Despite being sandwiched between these two, strong, powerful men who were fighting for what was right and good, Natalie felt alone and vulnerable and scared. Which was something she didn't understand, either. Because it was over. This hell was over and they had survived, and with very little hurt.

But Gabby had been hurt. Gabby had survived eight years of that horrible man, and Natalie didn't know how... Now that it was over, *over*, she didn't know what on earth would possibly come next.

Jaime pulled into what appeared to be the national park's ranger station. "If you stay put, I'll have them call for an ambulance, as well as call your precinct. We'll see if there's any word on the raid on Callihan's house, where your sister was."

Vaughn nodded stoically and Natalie just...stared. Word on the raid where her sister was. How was she supposed to respond to that? What was left? What was she supposed to do?

"Do you have questions about Gabby?"

She didn't glance at Vaughn, because she didn't know how to look at him. She didn't know how to look at the future. It was like dealing with all the fear and the threat had completely eradicated her ability to look beyond... anything. And now...it was all gone.

What did she do? "I don't know what to ask," she managed to say. Because she was numb and somehow still scared, and she didn't know why.

Vaughn didn't move or say anything for a long time, but eventually his hand rested on her clutched ones. He rubbed his warm strong palm over her tight, shaking hands.

It was warm, it was comfort. But when she looked up at him, his gaze was blank and straight ahead. Though he was offering her comfort, it was much more like the comfort he'd offered her that first night after the fire. There was something separate about it. Something stoic.

This wasn't the hug he'd offered her at the cabin, and that lack of…personal warmth made the frozen confusion inside her even worse. So she mimicked him. She didn't look at him anymore, she didn't move, she stared straight ahead.

When Agent Alessandro came back out, he explained that an ambulance would be waiting for them at the exit of the park, and he would have agents there who would confiscate Callihan's car. He would accompany Callihan to the hospital and keep him in FBI custody. Someone from the local police department would be there to escort Natalie and Vaughn to the airport, where the FBI would fly them back to Austin, after a medic checked Vaughn's wound.

He began to drive, explaining all sorts of things Natalie knew where important. What would be expected of her, what she would need to do and what questions she would need to answer before she was released.

But she couldn't concentrate. All she could think about was… "What about…"

"Your sister?" Agent Alessandro supplied for her.

"Yes."

"As I mentioned, the FBI is conducting raids on all

of Callihan's properties while I had him...distracted, so to speak. The property your sister has been at is on that list. As I've been working my way up in his organization, I've released some of the women, but—"

She whipped her head to face him, this stranger who'd helped them. "But not my sister?"

Something in his face hardened. "She wouldn't go."

"Wouldn't go? What does that mean?"

"I'm afraid that's all I'm at liberty to say." His hands tensed and then released on the steering wheel. "But now that we have Callihan in custody, and with all of the information that I've gathered over my two years, there should be no doubt that the trafficking ring, and his entire business, will be gutted. You have my word on that Ms. Torres."

She didn't care about trafficking rings or business or anything like that, though she supposed she should. All she cared about was her sister, and why her sister could have been saved and wasn't.

Natalie pushed out a breath, doing her level best not to cry. Not yet. Not in front of Alessandro and Vaughn.

Only then did Natalie realize that Vaughn had released her hands. No comfort. No connection. Just an officer and a victim.

If she had any energy left, she might've felt bereft. She might've cried. And now... Now, all she wanted to do was go home. To be alone. To deal with the last week in the privacy of her own house...

Except she didn't have one, just a burned-out shell. She had so very little. She'd come out of this ordeal with her life, and she knew that was important.

Maybe in a few days, when the shock wore off and

she saw Gabby again and held her and understood what had happened, she'd know how to feel.

Maybe it would take a few days for all the dust to settle, to hurt and grieve and *feel*. But for the time being, all she could do was feel numb.

Chapter 16

Vaughn wasn't sure he'd ever felt so numb. Not even after his undercover mission years ago. He had never in his entire career left a case feeling so completely screwed up inside.

He'd stayed with Natalie through the debriefing. They'd been with each other through their medical evaluations. And yet, they'd said almost nothing to each other. They'd offered no reassuring glances, no comforting touches. The last time he'd touched her in any sort of personal capacity had been to put his hand on hers in the car.

He'd made sure to stop in that moment, because he'd realized he couldn't do this anymore. He couldn't possibly pretend that what they'd had in the cabin was real, and he couldn't give her false hope that he could be anything other than the man that he was. His job would always come first, someone else's safety would always come before his own.

How could he possibly tie another woman to him knowing where that ended?

It took days to get everything situated, questioned, figured out. When Natalie finally got to go home, or at least to her mother's home, he hadn't gone with her. She hadn't asked him to, and he hadn't offered. They had turned into strangers, and he felt like a part of him had simply…died.

It was so melodramatic he was concerned about his mental state, but he couldn't eradicate that feeling. He felt a darkness worse than after the failure of his marriage, more than his most difficult undercover missions. He'd lost some piece of himself, and he didn't know where to go to find it.

That's a lie, you know exactly what's missing.

He ruthlessly pushed that thought away as he talked to Agent Alessandro about the release of Natalie's sister. They would be reunited today. There was no reason Vaughn should be there. At this point, the case been taken over by the FBI, he'd released all files potentially related to The Stallion over to Alessandro and he'd…been expected to move on.

So, he had no reason, no right to be there when Natalie saw her sister again. In fact, even if they hadn't left things so oddly, it wouldn't be his place to be there. She deserved a private homecoming with her sister.

"You know, if you'd like to be there, I can see if I can make arrangements."

Vaughn ignored the tightness in his throat as he responded to Jaime. "I'm not sure that would be…what they wanted."

"I can check, though, is what I'm offering."

"You'd been under for a long time, hadn't you?"

Vaughn asked, changing the subject, turning it away from the numbness in his own chest.

The man on the other end of the line was silent for a while. "Yes, I had."

Jaime had been in the academy right after Vaughn had left undercover work, before he'd gotten on with the Rangers, and before Jaime would have gotten on with the FBI. Vaughn had taught a class on undercover work.

He didn't remember all the recruits, but he remembered the best ones. The ones with promise. Jaime had been one.

"Well, in all the tying up of loose ends, I don't think I thanked you. You sure made getting out of that situation a lot easier."

"I was just doing my job. You know how it goes."

"Yeah, I do." Too well. How often had he been doing his job and giving nothing else?

"I can ask if they want you to be there. Clearly..." Jaime trailed off, and Vaughn was glad for it. He wasn't looking for a heart-to-heart.

"I'm glad the case has been resolved. If there's anything else you need from me or the Rangers, you know where to—"

"You know, that class you taught back at the police academy...it stuck with me. In fact, there was something you said that I'd always repeat to myself, when I needed to remember what I was doing this all for."

Something trickled through the numbness. Not a warmth exactly, some...sense of purpose. Some sense of accomplishment.

"You gave a big lecture about not losing your humanity, and being willing to bend your rigid moral obligations, without losing that human part of yourself. That was…by far the hardest part. Because I only had myself. At first."

"At first?"

"I guess it changes you, or should. Shifts your priorities."

"What does?"

Jaime was quiet again, a long humming stretch of seconds. "You know, finding…someone." He cleared his throat. "I just assumed you and Ms. Torres…"

He let that linger there. *You and Ms. Torres.*

"Well, anyway, I've got plenty to do. But, if you want me to pave the way for you, I can try."

"No. It's not my place."

"If you say so. I'll be in touch."

Vaughn hung up and scowled at the phone. Him and Natalie. Yeah, there'd been a thing, but it had been a thing born of fear and proximity. He'd known Jenny since he was fourteen. They'd dated for six years before they'd gotten married.

What disaster would he cause if he tried to build something on a few days of being in the same cabin? No matter what pieces of themselves they'd shared, it was based on a foundation that hadn't just crumbled, but no longer existed.

I guess it changes you, or should. Shifts your priorities.

It had. Profoundly. Not Jenny or his love for her, but police work. It had altered him, and Jenny had never been satisfied with those changes.

He thought about that time, about how it had been easier, for both of them, to blame the job rather than admit there was a problem deep within themselves. How it had been far easier to blame some failing inside him than change it. Easier for her to blame his failings too.

He thought about those moments in the desert when he hadn't cared about all the moral choices he'd made as a police officer. When he hadn't cared about anything but Natalie's safety.

He pushed away from his desk. This was insanity. He scrubbed his hands over his hair, ready to throw himself into another case, into anything that wouldn't involve thinking about *him*. Or most especially *her*.

A knock sounded on his office door and Captain Dean stepped in. "Cooper," he greeted with a nod.

"Captain."

"I've just talked to a supervisor from the FBI, along with the officers from the gas station incident, and the other agencies involved in The Stallion case."

"Sir?"

"Everyone has what they need from you, so you're free to go."

"Go?"

"Vaughn, don't be dense. You've been working round-the-clock for nearly a week, you have an injury."

"Doctors and psych cleared me to do desk work."

"Go home. Sleep. Recharge. That's not a suggestion, Cooper. It's common sense."

Vaughn could have argued, he could have even pushed, but for what? In one FBI raid, half his cases had been wiped out. Families were being reunited, people were getting answers.

The crimes that had been committed would leave a mark, there were still people to find, but Vaughn had what he'd been on the brink of losing his mind over. Case closure.

He still felt dark and empty.

Because things *had* shifted. Natalie had given him light for the first time in a long time. A priority that existed beyond cases and police work. Someone who understood what it was to put someone else first, and the complexity of dealing with the unsolved.

Natalie *understood*, in ways most people probably couldn't. The unknowns, the toll it took, the complex emotions.

And that…that was a foundation that existed. A foundation that was stronger than any he could build with his own two hands. Possibly…possibly even a foundation that no one else could touch.

Natalie was nothing but a bundle of nerves. Her mother sat stoically next to her in the hospital waiting room, and her grandmother was saying fervent prayers over her rosary.

The relationship between all three of them had been strained for so long, Natalie didn't know how to breach it now. For eight years she'd been certain her mother and grandmother's irritation and frustration with her obsession with Gabby's case had been a weakness.

It had been a betrayal. How dare they give up on Gabby?

But now…she realized they had all dealt with tragedy in the ways they could. They were all strong, independent women who had endured too much loss and hurt, and had dealt with it in the differing ways that suited them.

A nurse came through the door first, holding it open for a woman. Though she was nearly unrecognizable from the young woman Natalie remembered, it was too easy to see Dad's nose and Mom's pointed chin, and Natalie's own big eyes staring right back at her.

Natalie didn't remember getting to her feet, and she barely registered Grandma's loud weeping. Everything was centered in on…something indescribable. This woman who was her sister, and yet…not.

Her skin prickled with goose bumps, and she could scarcely catch a breath. Was she moving? She wasn't sure, but somehow she was suddenly in the middle of the room with…her sister.

Taller, older, *different*. And yet *hers*. She was flesh and blood and *here*. Natalie reached out, but she wasn't sure where to touch, or how.

"Nattie."

Even Gabby's voice was different, the light in her eyes, the way her mouth moved. Natalie was rendered immobile by all of it, crushed under the reality of eight years lost. Of the grief that swelled through her over losing the sister she'd known, that nickname, and all it would take to…

Her outstretched hand finally found purchase…because Gabby had grabbed it. Squeezed it in her own. It didn't matter that she wasn't the same person she'd been all those years ago, because Natalie wasn't the same person, either.

But they were still sisters. Blood. Connected.

"Say something," Gabby whispered, barely audible over the way Mom and Grandma were openly sobbing.

"I don't know…" What to say. What to do. Even as she'd thought about this moment for *years*, actually being here… "I'm so sorr—"

But Gabby shook her head and cupped Natalie's face with her hands. "No, none of that."

Which broke Natalie's thin grip on composure, and

soon she was sobbing as well, but also holding on to Gabby, tight, desperate. Gabby held back, and though she didn't make a sound, Natalie could feel tears that weren't her own soak her shoulder.

"Mama, *Abuela*," Gabby's raspy voice ordered. "Come here."

Then all four of them were standing in the middle of a hospital waiting room, holding on too tightly, struggling to breathe through tears and hugs.

Gabby shook, something echoing all the way through her body so violently, Natalie could feel it herself.

"Are you all right? Do you need a doctor? I'll go get the nu—"

But Gabby held her close. "I'm all right, baby sister. I just can't believe it's real. You're all here."

"They...told you about... Daddy?"

Gabby swallowed, her chin coming up, everything about her hardening all over again. "The Stallion made sure I knew."

"But..."

Gabby shook her head. "No. Not today. Maybe not ever."

Natalie had to swallow down the questions, the need to pressure. The need to understand. She could want all she wanted, but Gabby would have to make the choices of what she told them herself. That was her right as survivor.

"One of us needs to get it together so we can drive home," their mother said, her hand shaking as she mopped up tears. Her other hand was a death grip around Gabby's elbow.

"I'm all right," Natalie assured them. "I'll drive. Right

now. We're free to go. We're... Let's get out of here. And go home."

"Home," Gabby echoed, and Natalie couldn't begin to imagine what those words elicited for her sister. She couldn't begin to imagine...

Well, there'd be therapy for all of them, there'd be healing. One step at a time. The first step was getting out of this hospital.

But as they turned to leave the waiting room, someone entered, blocking the way.

It took Natalie a moment to place him, because the last time she'd seen Agent Alessandro he'd had much longer hair, a beard. He'd looked as menacing as The Stallion, if not more so.

He'd had a haircut and a shave and today looked every inch the FBI agent in his suit and sunglasses.

Gabby stopped and everything about her stiffened. "Agent Alessandro," Gabby greeted him coolly, and despite the tear tracks on her cheeks, she was shoulders-back strong, and Natalie couldn't begin to imagine what Gabby had endured to come out of this so...self-possessed, so strong.

"Ms. Torres." There was an odd twist to the FBI agent's mouth, but his gaze moved from Gabby to her. "Ms.... Well, Natalie, I've got a message for you."

Gabby's grip tightened on her arm, but when she glanced at her sister, all Natalie saw was a blank stoicism.

"It's from the Texas Rangers Office."

It was Natalie's turn to grip, to stiffen. Because she heard "Texas Rangers" and she thought of Vaughn, she wanted to cry all over again for different reasons.

Anger. Regret. Loss. Confusion.

Mostly anger. She didn't have *time* for anger, all she had the time and energy for was Gabby.

Agent Alessandro held out a piece of paper and Natalie frowned at it. "They couldn't have called me? Sent an email?" she muttered, and though it was more rhetorical than an actual question, she glanced up at the agent.

His gaze was on Gabby again, and she was looking firmly away. They'd obviously had some interaction when Alessandro had been undercover, and Natalie could only assume it hadn't been a positive interaction.

She glanced at the piece of paper, a handwritten note of all things. She opened it and scowled at the scrawl.

Once you've settled in with your sister, there are a
few pressing questions I'll need to ask you in person for full closure in the case.
Vaughn

Everything about it made her violently angry. That he'd written a *note*. That he couldn't have called and been a man about it. That he'd dared sign his name *Vaughn* instead of Ranger Cooper when that was *clearly* all he wanted to be.

She didn't want to get settled with her sister first. She wanted all of this to be over. Now.

"Agent Alessandro, would you be able to escort Gabby and my family home while I see to this?"

His eyebrows raised. "I'd love to be of service, but I doubt your sister…"

"Oh, no, please escort us, Mr. Alessandro. *I* don't have a problem with it in the least," Gabby replied, linking arms with Mama and Grandma. There was a battle light in Gabby's eyes that Natalie didn't recognize at all.

She almost stepped in, ready to put her own battle on the back burner. But Gabby's intense gaze turned to her. "Tie up loose ends, sissy. I want this over, once and for all."

"It will be," Natalie promised. It damn well would be.

Chapter 17

Vaughn paced. He hadn't expected Natalie to come right away. He figured she'd want time with Gabby, and it would give him time to set up everything. But Jaime's clipped message had said that she was on her way. And it would probably be quick, despite the fact the hospital was on the other side of Austin.

"Can't lie that I don't mind seeing you like this," Bennet said companionably as Vaughn stalked his office.

"Thanks for your support," Vaughn muttered trying to figure out what the hell was trying to claw out of his chest. He'd expected time...possibly to talk himself out of the whole thing.

"You have all my support. In fact, I'm going to be the nice guy here and tell you that a simple apology probably won't cut it."

"You don't even know what the hell is going on." But

apparently he was transparent because everyone seemed to know.

"You're right, I don't. But I know you're all tied up in knots, and I'd put money on the hot little hypnotist—"

At Vaughn's death glare, Bennet didn't even have the decency to shut up. The jackass laughed.

"Yeah, you're hooked."

"Define hooked," Vaughn growled.

"Going feral any time anyone even begins to mention her was the first hint."

Vaughn wanted to argue with him just for the sake of arguing with him, but Natalie was on her way over here, and he didn't have time. "So maybe something happened," he admitted through gritted teeth.

"And you screwed it up, of course. I'm not one to tell you what to do, Vaughn," Bennet began, all ease and comfortable cheerfulness.

When Vaughn snarled, Bennet laughed.

"Okay, maybe I don't mind telling you what to do all that much, but point of fact is, if you're trying to woo a woman, especially this particular woman, you're going to have to do something that I'm not sure you have in your arsenal."

"What's that?"

"Anything remotely romantic that includes putting your heart on the line. I think you're incapable of that."

"I'm not...incapable," Vaughn grumbled, but he was a little afraid that he was. Afraid that no matter what he decided about trying to start something with Natalie, something real, something that might turn into something long-term—a *chance*. All he wanted was a damn chance.

But Bennet was still yammering on. "Since you don't have flowers, I'd figure out a romantic gesture or two."

Vaughn might have physically recoiled at the phrase *romantic gesture*.

"Probably something she'd never expect you to do, but you do because you want her."

Damn it. He *hated* that Bennet was right. Because he'd screwed this up, worse than he'd screwed up his marriage. Because the past few days of treating Natalie like a stranger at best… He'd known it was wrong. He'd felt it, in his bones, and the only thing he'd had to do to fix it was *speak*. Reach out. Put a little bit of pride on the line.

But he hadn't. So now that he was doing it, now that he was done being a little wimp, he had to not just put it all on the line, but offer it up wrapped in a damn bow.

"I need an interrogation room, and no interruptions. Can you make that happen?"

Bennet grinned, but he didn't give Vaughn any more crap. "On it. Good luck, buddy."

Yeah, luck. Strange all Vaughn could feel was an impending sense of dread.

But no matter how much dread he felt, no matter how little he knew about putting his pride or his shoddy heart on the line, he knew that the minute he saw her, that's exactly what he had to do.

Natalie burst into the Texas Rangers offices, and after jumping through all the hoops she had to jump through to get to the floor with Vaughn's office, Ranger Stevens was there to greet her. "Ms. Torres. It's good to see you under better circumstances."

"*Are* they better circumstances?" Which was flippant, because of course they were better. Her house hadn't burned down today, and she'd been reunited with her sister.

But she was angry, and she wanted to fling her anger at everyone who got in her way. Every second she was away from Gabby, she was going to be angry.

"Follow me," Ranger Stevens offered, sounding far too amused.

She followed him, pausing at the door to an interrogation room. It was the interrogation room where she'd all but signed Herman's death warrant. Where she'd set everything into motion, because she hadn't been able to keep her mouth shut.

She wasn't foolish enough to think that had put *everything* into motion. Obviously the FBI had had its own thing going on. It was happenstance she had gotten mixed up in it.

It was all *too* much, and Vaughn—the man who'd been *silent* for *days*—had the gall to send her a note—a *note!*—to answer more questions.

She ignored the part where she'd been silent too. Because she was afraid if she let go of any of her rage, she'd simply fall apart.

"He's waiting."

She scowled at Stevens, but then she entered the room on that last wave of fury.

Vaughn stood with his back to her, his palms pressed to the interrogation table. It hurt to look at him. To look at him and not touch him. It seemed that seeing Gabby this morning had broken that dam of feeling that she'd been hiding behind since she'd shot the man who'd kidnapped Gabby.

She'd been numb for days, but now, all she could do was *feel*. All she could seem to do was hurt. She was afraid she was going to cry, but she swallowed it down as best she could.

"You summoned."

Vaughn turned, and she wasn't prepared for those gray-blue eyes, the way the sight of his body and mouth trying to curve in a smile slammed through her.

She wanted to hug him and to cry into his shoulder. She wanted *him*.

But despite that a world of emotion *seemed* to glitter blue in those smoky eyes, he merely gestured to a seat at the table. "Have a seat, Ms. Torres."

"I think you're damn lucky I've taken a vow of anti-violence, because I'd as soon shove that seat up *your* seat as sit in it."

She had clearly caught him off guard with that, and she felt a surge of victory with all that anger. Let him take a step back. She wanted him to react.

"Natalie, just sit down and—"

"Go to hell." Which was probably cruel, but she wanted to be cruel, because maybe if she was, this could be over, and she could move on. She whirled toward the door.

"I was going to let you hypnotize me."

She whirled back, somehow every sentence he uttered making the violent thing inside of her larger. "What?"

"It's supposed to be romantic," he returned, clearly irritated she wasn't falling into line.

"What the hell is romantic about me hypnotizing you? You can't tell me how you feel unless I put you under?"

"You gave me a whole lecture about people being unable to give information under hypnotism unless they want to, and I'm trying to show you how *willing* I am to—"

"Then just *say* it!"

"I love you."

They both stood in stunned silence for Natalie wasn't

sure how long. She clutched her hands at her chest and tried to…process that. Meanwhile Vaughn stood stock-still, his eyes a little wide as if he was shocked by his own words.

"I don't…believe in a lot of…" Vaughn rubbed his palm across his jaw and then took a step toward her. "Natalie, I fell in love with you. Your strength, your dedication." He swore. "And I thought that'd go away, or dull, or… I don't want to *fail* someone else. I'm so sick of feeling like I failed, and I just wanted to show you that I'd do it anyway."

"Fail?" she asked incredulously.

"Try!"

"Oh." He loved her, and he wanted to try. He was try-ing to be…*romantic*. Vaughn Cooper. For her.

"Will you sit now?"

"No."

His eyebrows drew together, but before he could be too confused over her refusal, she found the courage to do what she'd wanted to do the moment she'd stepped in the room.

She moved into him, wrapping her arms around him, holding him through the ragged exhale he let out. "Nat—"

"I love you too," she whispered fiercely. Because that was such a better emotion to focus on than anger. *That* was what she should have taken away from this morning and being reunited with Gabby, not feeling *anything*… Love. Hope. Faith.

"I wasn't sure… I'm not sure I know how to go from the most important thing to me being your safety—and me *keeping* you safe, to you just…being safe. How does… any of this work?"

She pulled back a little and tried to smile, but a few

tears slipped out instead. She could tell it bothered him, but he didn't rush to stop her. No, for all Vaughn's gruff, by-the-book protector conventions, he always seemed to give her the space she needed to work it out.

And hold her through it if she needed.

"My life is literally burned to the ground, and I have a sister who's been held prisoner for eight years finally back in it. I don't know how *any* of this works, but I just guess you…figure it out."

"Together?"

"We make a pretty good team."

He wiped away one of her tears, his rough thumb a welcome texture against her cheek, his mouth gently curved, that *love* shining so clearly in his eyes. "We do," he agreed, his voice rough and…true.

Because Vaughn didn't lie, and he didn't sugarcoat. This man, who understood obsessions and failures, violence and the absence of it. How to keep her safe, how to give her space.

They made a *wonderful* team, and Natalie was certain that's exactly what they'd continue to be.

* * * * *